# *Facing Facts*

Cornelia sat trembling, anxious before Dane—the child psychiatrist trying to help her daughter, Livvie. She was drawn to this strong but gentle man, enjoying the time they spent together. But now Cornelia couldn't believe what he was telling her.

"Nothing is wrong with Livvie. But she *is* slower than the children she's with."

"But that's horrible."

"No. Unless you've decided she has to be an academic whiz. This may not be the right school for her."

"But The Boston School is the best."

"Maybe not for Livvie. You know you've got to show her you love her the way she is . . . even if she never learns to read. If you keep pushing, it's going to hurt more."

"It *couldn't* hurt more," Cornelia said, thinking he had just destroyed every dream she'd had of loving him. . . .

*Private*
# SCORES

# Private
# SCORES

BY
## ANNE
## TOLSTOI
## WALLACH

A SIGNET BOOK

**NEW AMERICAN LIBRARY**

PUBLISHED BY
THE NEW AMERICAN LIBRARY
OF CANADA LIMITED

NAL BOOKS ARE AVAILABLE AT QUANTITY DISCOUNTS WHEN USED TO PROMOTE PRODUCTS OR SERVICES. FOR INFORMATION PLEASE WRITE TO PREMIUM MARKETING DIVISION, NEW AMERICAN LIBRARY, 1633 BROADWAY, NEW YORK, NEW YORK 10019.

First Signet Printing, September, 1987

2  3  4  5  6  7  8  9

SIGNET TRADEMARK REG U.S PAT OFF AND FOREIGN COUNTRIES
REGISTERED TRADEMARK — MARCA REGISTRADA
HECHO EN WINNIPEG, CANADA

SIGNET, SIGNET CLASSIC, MENTOR, ONYX, PLUME, MERIDIAN AND NAL BOOKS are published in Canada by The New American Library of Canada, Limited, 81 Mack Avenue, Scarborough, Ontario, Canada M1L 1M8

PRINTED IN CANADA
COVER PRINTED IN U.S.A.

*For Justin, of course*

Private scores make public scandals.

The Boston School
70 East End Avenue,
New York, N.Y. 10028
Second Grade Report
Olivia Fuller

Livvie participates in class activities to a far greater degree than last year. Her work is careful and painstaking, and she is starting to speak up in our group discussions. Much of her shyness is leaving her, and we are helping her communicate her ideas more successfully.

Arithmetic skills are surprisingly easy for Livvie. She grasps number concepts and has made great strides in basic problem-solving. We wish her reading were progressing as well. We endorse the recommendation of the remedial teacher for daily practice at home in a supportive setting.

We are also encouraging Livvie in her relationships with her classmates, which are still not as mature as we would wish.

*Kit Montgomery*

October


THE THUNDERCLAP WAS sudden. It crashed into Cornelia's sleep, shocking her awake.

Breathless, she sat straight, feeling as if she were hearing a drumroll heralding some terrible event, a hanging, a burial, the end of the world.

Then, as the heavy rumble died away and rain began spattering the window, she realized what *was* about to happen.

Reading practice.

Reading with Livvie, first thing in the morning, today, tomorrow, maybe forever.

Cornelia bent, rested her forehead on her knees till her heart stopped pounding.

It's *not* frightening, she told herself. Just something to get through, that's all. Like those mornings when I was pregnant with Livvie, knowing I'd wake with a thick head and a cotton tongue, a stomach that had to erupt before the day could really begin.

She lifted her head, opened her eyes wide. Everywhere she looked, something wrong.

Not the cozy, crowded room she loved, books stacked in corners, bright beads draped over the long pier glass, theater posters covering the walls, pillows piled on the Turkey carpet, Livvie's Halloween costume half-finished at the foot of her bed, the old trunk crammed with letters and photographs next to it.

More like an attic, Cornelia decided. A prop house. Livvie's doll there, on the floor, looking dead. Those jars and bottles of makeup I never touch now. All the silver picture frames tarnished. And my lace curtains limp, one of the ribbon tiebacks missing because we used it for Livvie's hair and never put it back.

A good mother would have a neat, restful place to welcome her child mornings. A good mother would *want* to read with her little girl, be delighted to help if the teacher asked.

Cornelia lay back, thinking of all the marvelous mornings before there were any teachers. Lazy, quiet mornings, with Livvie warm against her side under the old quilt, choking her with hugs, telling outlandish stories, singing funny little songs.

Just the two of them, together.

Raindrops were starting to drum on the flat top of the window air conditioner. Cornelia knew that the dreary sound made the rain seem worse than it really was.

What if Livvie couldn't catch up with her class? What if she never learned to read? And what if her mother's worrying was making her problem worse, too?

But it *is* worse, Cornelia thought. Livvie's been getting more stubborn about that stupid book every morning. Yesterday it took forever before she'd try a word, a one-syllable word.

Cornelia felt her insides churning. She closed her eyes, hoping the pain would stop if she really relaxed.

She remembered when Miss Montgomery had first suggested reading with Livvie. A picture had formed immediately in Cornelia's mind. The two of them nestled together in bed. Livvie sounding out words in a story. Cornelia smiling, helping a bit with the hardest ones. Another wonderful way to enjoy each other, feel good together.

Who'd have guessed that Livvie couldn't sound out even easy words? Or that every time, her reading would be more tentative, every morning worse than the last?

Feeling shaken, Cornelia had tried a change of scene, a different time for reading, before supper, before bed. But she couldn't count on any other time. She didn't get home till six-thirty or seven, even on ordinary nights when there wasn't a play, a nightclub act, an Off-Off Broadway show in some out-of-the-way theater. Anyway, evenings Livvie was tired from her own long day, school, park, bath, supper. On weekends, there were better chances. But weekends weren't enough. Miss Montgomery had said *every* day. That was the only way Livvie could hope to catch up.

Cornelia clutched at her middle, imagining a race, hundreds of little girls running swiftly on smooth green grass, with Livvie stumbling in sand, far behind.

Oh, Liv, she thought, I'd love you no matter what. But how can *you* ever be happy if you can't keep up?

Then the image vanished as she saw the bedroom door move slowly, heard a soft brushing sound along the carpet, felt a cold little breeze. And there was Livvie, head just level with the doorknob, padding in on bare feet, a small, pale ghost in a long white nightgown. In front of her, held tightly in both arms, was the large, flat first-grade reader.

As the child came closer, the book seemed to grow larger.

Poor Livvie, Cornelia thought, making herself smile. You used to rip in here, hair flying, jump in this bed so hard we'd both bounce. And you'd giggle, tell me stories, give me lots of kisses. I *loved* waking up to you.

She reached for Livvie's shoulder, pulled her close. The child's slight body felt cold, stiff, as if it were hard plastic, like one of her dolls. Cornelia's heart went heavy. She began rocking Livvie as if she were still a little baby.

I made you, she thought. Tim didn't want a child, but I wasn't going to stop you from being born. All the time you were coming, he grumbled, said you'd ruin my career, but I knew I could work and have you too. I made you, and you're perfect, far and away the most wonderful thing I've ever done.

Burying her nose in Livvie's soft hair, Cornelia felt a rush of hope. Maybe today she'll catch on. It has to happen sometime. Please, let it be today.

"Hello, hello, hello," she said softly.

Once she'd known exactly how to rock peace and contentment into this child. Now everything she did seemed somehow wrong.

Livvie's face was blank, eyes down, mouth tight.

And if *I* feel everything's wrong, what about *her*? She's the one who'll have to stand up in class with all those other little girls giggling.

"No good-morning?" Cornelia asked.

Livvie's chin remained on the book's edge. Her eyelids looked violet, as if she'd just put on eye shadow. Her pale hair gleamed in the soft light from the window.

Cornelia loved the way Livvie looked. Silver hair, where her own was ordinary brown. Violet eyes so different from her dark ones. Slenderness, everywhere Cornelia was thin, angular. And lately, this grave, dreamy expression, as if she were listening to music nobody else could hear.

" 'Morning," Livvie said.

A statement, not a greeting. Resigned, weary, not the way for a seven-year-old to sound.

Suddenly Cornelia wanted to tear the book from Livvie's arms and sling it straight through the window, so the glass could shred it, the rain drench it into pulp.

Controlling herself, she pulled Livvie gently into the bed, straightened the covers, balanced the book across both their laps. Livvie's foot, touching her thigh, felt cold, lifeless.

Cornelia reached down to take the little toes in her hand, warm them.

God knows I hate doing this work as much as, *more* than Livvie, she thought. But I'm the grown-up. It's got to be done for her sake. So let's go. And in half an hour we'll jump out of bed, go cook something good. I'll think of a special treat while she's reading. Hot orange juice. Bacon. Pancakes with lemon marmalade.

She looked down at Livvie's fine hair parted on her neck

as she bent over the book, showing creamy skin over the ruffled collar. Livvie smelled like baby powder and peaches, fresh, new, beautiful.

Down in the street a horn blared, a car probably blocked by someone who'd double-parked. Someone bursting with rage, taking it out in blasts of punishing noise.

Cornelia wanted to make noise too, slam at the cover of the book, hard. Childish. She'd better take it easy, or Livvie would tense up too, catch her anger as if it were some infectious disease. Could that have happened already?

I'm not angry *at* you, she wanted to tell Livvie. It's the whole stupid system, tests, grades, scores.

Livvie wasn't moving. Her head was too close to the page. Cornelia reached to smooth back a lock of Livvie's hair, tuck it behind the small ear. She must smooth away everything, even the lightest wisp of hair, that could distract the child. The other children at school could read. Damn them, Livvie would read too.

Then the horn outside stopped and the room seemed ominously quiet. Cornelia grew aware of the soft hum of her bedside clock, the scratching of a pigeon out on the windowsill, the faint rumbling of the elevator far off in the hall. Every sound except the one she wanted. Words, the words in the book, from Livvie.

"Let's go," she said briskly. "Remember, yesterday we got up to here."

Yesterday. Why had she brought that up? Yesterday had been horrible. Livvie had decided to be silly, pretend to read, holding the book high up in front of her, rattling off a nonsense story, almost a parody of the reader. At first, Cornelia had thought it funny. But when she'd said to stop, get serious, Livvie only giggled and kept on. Suddenly Cornelia had grown angry. She'd snatched away the book, closed it, startling Livvie so much she'd quieted down, actually managed to sound out some of the words. But Cornelia had felt shaken by the force of her own emotion.

It wasn't Livvie's rebellion, she realized quickly. It was rage at herself, for agreeing to be part of the system.

But what can I do? she thought. I'm wrong for this, I'm

no teacher. If I get upset, she'll end up hating books. She'll end up hating *me*.

She closed her eyes, feeling sick, dizzy.

All her life, Livvie had been so gentle, so compliant. She hadn't needed teaching. Somehow, all by herself, she'd begun to sit, crawl, pull herself up by the crib railing, to pick up a spoon and pop it in her tiny mouth.

It's so different now, Cornelia thought. And reading is just the beginning. Soon there'll be French, math. What if some teacher wants me to help her with her algebra?

If only Livvie would say something, make a start.

Cornelia knew, of course, that she mustn't hurry the child. Impatience made things worse. The teacher hurried Livvie, so the other children wouldn't get jumpy, and then she froze. She looked frozen now, head down, her tiny body so still she didn't seem to be breathing.

Cornelia clenched her fingers on the book, tried to stare at the page and think about nothing.

After a moment she decided to read the page to herself as slowly as possible. When she finished that, she tried reading it still more slowly backwards, from bottom to top.

Not a sound from Livvie.

Then Cornelia felt her annoyance fade, disappear, revealing something worse.

Terror.

She felt weak with terror for Livvie.

"Come on, Liv," she said as brightly as she could. "This page won't take long. Anyway, I'm hungry for breakfast, aren't you?"

Christ, she thought, hearing herself. That's *wrong*. As if I only care about getting this over with, like taking nasty medicine. Only, doesn't she want to finish too? And how the hell can we finish, if we don't get started?

She looked past Livvie's head to the clock, clicking its way toward seven. Today they'd *have* to finish by seven. Usually they could go on till seven-thirty, still have time to eat, dress, get to school, to work. But today she had a special reason to be at the office early.

Livvie, for God's sake, she thought, make a sound. Read a word. Shall I tell you one? Will that start you?

The first word was "horse," easy, with a picture to help. A stupid picture, amateurishly drawn, gaudily colored, unlike any real horse Livvie could have seen. The whole book was dumb, really. About farm friends, stories of cows and sheep and pigs. What city child had farm friends? Livvie thought animals belonged in the zoo, that milk and eggs came from the supermarket.

Suddenly Cornelia couldn't stand the silence. She longed to clutch Livvie's shoulders, shake her, force the words out of her mouth. Years ago a mother would do that, shout, spank, even, anything to make a child learn.

But who could think of hurting Livvie? She was fragile, defenseless. Her manner was so gentle, her voice so shy. In nursery school she'd hidden for days behind a rubber plant at the window, watching the other children play. Only a *monster* could harm her.

Cornelia wanted to take the book out of Livvie's hand and put it away, far out of sight.

Why am I doing this? she wondered. I'm impatient, scared, the world's worst reading teacher. Why can't they help her in school, where they're supposed to? They can't even decide what the problem is: did I read to Livvie too much so she's gotten lazy, or didn't I read often enough? And school costs so much money, money that's damned hard to make, more than six thousand dollars for one little girl.

Because I'm her mother, she answered herself. Because I desperately want her to have what she'll need to survive in this world. Because I know a little about how tough life can be, how much it takes to survive.

"Livvie," she said, feeling despair. "Sound it out. Tell me the first sound in that word."

She felt the little body stiffen, saw Livvie's fingers curl, her small thumb grip the page. Slowly the thumb turned pink. She's trying, Cornelia thought, fear filling her throat, choking her.

"Huh," Livvie said.

It sounded like a cry for help. But Cornelia was so relieved to hear even a tiny sound that she relaxed, felt the thickness in her throat subside.

"*Good*," she said. "And what's the sound after that?"

"Oh."

"Terrific. Now put both those sounds together and you'll guess the rest, the whole word."

Just a word, she prayed, a little victory. We both need it so.

"Huh. Oh," Livvie stammered.

The two small sounds shot panic into Cornelia again.

Jesus, she thought, the one person in the world I care about, and I can't help her. What's the matter with me? With *her*?

The panic grew. She knew she mustn't ask that. Nothing was wrong with Livvie. Nothing.

Cornelia shivered.

Was this what terrified her at night, made her feel sick as she woke mornings? *Was* something wrong with Livvie?

"Horse," Cornelia said, bursting, as if she could block out the hideous thought, cover it over with sound. "Look. It's the same word we had over here on this page yesterday. Horse."

I sound like a shrew, she thought. And my whole body is pulled tight.

Wretched, she looked down, saw Livvie's fingers joining her thumb, forming a rosy fist. She saw the fist lift, rise, smash down hard on the book.

The child turned her head, lifted her chin, opened her violet eyes wide.

"Fuck," Livvie said, more distinctly than any word she'd ever pronounced in any reading session.

Then she seemed to crumple. Head bent low, arms wrapped around her knees, Livvie became a limp little bundle, holding herself together.

Cornelia felt misery wash against her like an ocean wave, crash on her head. She shut her eyes against the salt sting, held her breath to keep her lungs clear.

By the time she'd exhaled, Livvie was gone in a flurry of sheets, a slam of the door. Cornelia heard her stamping into the kitchen, scraping a chair across the linoleum toward the chain for the ceiling light. She was still too small to pull it without climbing onto something.

I made that happen, Cornelia thought. And she probably learned that word from me. That's my fault too.

She got up, stood still for a moment, to clear her head. Then she went to the window.

Cold autumn rain streamed over the panes. Mist hung

in the air, smudging the harsh outlines of the city's rooftop water towers, the apartment windows across the dark street.

Cornelia saw herself in the streaked gray glass.

When did I start looking like a Victorian heroine? she wondered. Was it six months ago, when Tim finally left? I could play Jane Eyre. Elizabeth Barrett Browning. A girl out of Trollope. Thin, pale, intense. Such a mass of hair. All I need is a poke bonnet, a reticule, a fan. And a hero, dark and dashing, to rescue me.

Looking closer, she saw a rip in her nightgown.

What's the difference? she thought. Now only Livvie sees my nightgowns. The best ones are in that bottom drawer, anyway, with an empty perfume bottle. Maybe I'll never open it.

She frowned at herself in the dark pane.

Stop dramatizing yourself, she could almost hear her father saying when she was little, when she'd first wanted to be an actress, examining herself in a mirror. Poor Father. He'd had enough acting from his wife, whom he'd rescued from the musty barns of summer theater and the ramshackle dressing rooms of amateur playacting. And then only to have her spend half her life in mental hospitals, in for a year, out for two, and back in again. Poor Mother.

But I'm *not* "poor Cornelia," she thought. I've got Livvie. And if I didn't manage to be a great actress, at least I'm on my way to being a hell of a good casting director.

She picked up Livvie's book, set it on the bedside table, and went slowly out to the kitchen.

Under the fluorescent glare Livvie sat, a jelly glass full of milk in front of her. She was staring down into it like an old woman hunched over a drink in a neon-lit bar.

Cornelia forgot her mother, her problems, everything, in a rush of misery that *anything* could do such damage to Livvie, make her look so defeated.

Quickly she moved to wrap her arms around the sad little figure. As they touched, Livvie began to cry, gasping in huge, gulping breaths that sent shock waves through Cornelia's heart. The sounds were terrible.

"Don't," Cornelia said. "It's only reading. You'll get it soon. Everybody learns to read. Don't, Livvie."

The child's body seemed breakable as crystal, as if the sobs could splinter, shatter it. Finally Livvie grew quiet.

Cornelia leaned Livvie back, reached for a paper napkin to dry her tears.

Then she stood up, found the cocoa powder, dug in a drawer for a spoon, and stirred the sweet, crumbling stuff into Livvie's milk. The cocoa was meant for Sundays. But if she couldn't make Livvie happier right this minute, Cornelia knew she'd dissolve into tears herself.

It seemed to help.

Livvie dried her eyes with the back of her hand and picked up the glass.

Cornelia felt better as she set out cold cereal for Livvie, ran water for coffee. While it boiled, she watched Livvie eat a spoonful or two, sitting beautifully straight, holding her spoon like an adult, neatly, precisely.

Perfect manners, she thought, there's something to feel proud about. Most kids her age grab the whole handle. Those smartass kids, who know how to read.

Drinking her coffee, Cornelia remembered.

"Livvie. Don't say 'fuck,' all right?"

"You do."

"Yes, well, I drink coffee and you drink milk. Later when you're old, you can say anything you want."

Livvie seemed to consider that gravely. Her eyes still glinted with leftover tears. Her long lashes were spiked together, mouth still compressed, lips faintly blue. But there was a chocolate mustache under her tiny nose. The tip of her tongue was edging toward it.

Cornelia put her arms around the child, hugged her, hard.

Mine, all mine, she thought. Not Tim's. He'd have no time for her problems, never had. His own were far too fascinating to him.

Watching the chocolate disappear from the child's face, Cornelia felt easier, happier. Anyway, soon they'd go to school and everything would be better.

At least, she thought, I've got school, my own old school. Whatever I can't do for her, school will do. And whatever I've done wrong, school will fix. Thank God. Livvie loves it, the way I did, even with reading trouble. Never hangs back in the morning, or says she doesn't want to go. When she finally came out from behind that plant, she adored the place. Even at three, tiny, she was so busy, so self-contained, heading for the sandbox, plumping down with a pail, working till she filled it. Funny, looking back in time, when Livvie's only in second grade.

Her school, special, so different from all other schools, a home, a family, a life. She'd started there as a baby, like Livvie, grown part of it more every year.

The Boston School brought a million pictures into Cornelia's mind. An expansive red brick building, with enormous windows. Classrooms like welcoming living rooms, never a desk or a dull color, just shabby, comfortable chairs and tables, bright tile floors. A stately library, a cathedral of books, where everyone whispered, tiptoed. A cozy lunchroom, filled with clatter and laughter, smelling of steam and oranges. The theater, vast, rows of splendid red plush seats, the huge ebony piano, the metal spotlights. The bronze plaque in the front hall engraved with the school motto, that everyone touched for wishing, for luck.

And Cornelia's pictures were crowded with people too. Teachers like Miss Vollmer, a thousand years old, with skirts that grazed her puffy ankles, reading aloud, sitting on one of the broad window seats cushioned in red, books she simply assumed they'd enjoy, never pausing to explain, never simplifying anything because they were children. Sometimes she'd even read in her beloved Latin, so that the girls learned early to think about words and sounds, to distinguish the lilt of Virgil from the trumpet notes of Cicero. Cornelia remembered how the books had looked, big, brown, thick, the pages rounded at their edges from thumbing. Sometimes those pages were torn, where Miss Vollmer had turned them too fast. But she'd done that to keep the story exciting, *never* to hurry the reading along. And then, fatherly Mr. Chasen, bow-tied, shabby, pacing while he coached the Shakespeare plays, insisting on perfect pronunciation of every word. All of them wise, inspiring, individual, like ladylike Miss Lynch, who at least once a year would stand on her head to shock a rowdy class into silence. And the girls, her friends, wearing the same uniform Livvie wore now, navy jumpers for small girls, skirts for the older ones, everyone in white blouses, knee socks. How those knee socks had pinched, left marks that didn't fade until bedtime, even though she always stripped them off the moment she got home.

Nobody ever really leaves the Boston School, Cornelia thought. They come back to teach, or just to sit in on classes, they crowd every reunion, every alumnae event. The Christmas pageant was our religion. The poetry reading, plays, music, the painting and sculpture classes, were beauty to us. The manners and honor of those teachers set lifelong standards for everyone. No wonder we all want our children there, so we'll have an excuse, a reason for coming back, year after year. No wonder no other school seems right to any of us, no wonder we all think we're depriving them of an Eden if they're not in our school, when we all were made to feel so good, so clever and beloved there.

Looking up, she saw the clock. Seven-fifteen.

Feeling at peace, she hugged Livvie, told her to run and dress.

That school was my refuge, my saving grace, she thought. And it's going to be Livvie's. Why, she belongs already, even in second grade. She can button her jumper, tie her navy oxfords, pack her blue knapsack all by herself. Even now, they've made her a model Boston School girl. Soon she'll be a model reader too.

Feeling comforted, she went back to the bedroom, reached for clothes in her jumbled closet, the first pair of pants she touched, a silk shirt, wide belt, one of the scarves she'd been twisting at her neck lately to hide her collarbones. A touch of Vaseline on lids, mouth, and she was ready.

How she'd fussed about clothes, Cornelia thought, when she'd been looking for acting jobs, making rounds of the casting offices every day. Now that she was choosing actors, her looks didn't matter. Who cared what the casting director wore?

Sometimes, though, a girl would come in to read for a part. She'd look the way Cornelia had seven, eight years ago, slim, quick, wide-eyed, with a mass of chestnut hair. And talk as Cornelia had talked, breathlessly, as actresses talk, of all the wonderful things that were bound to happen soon.

What's bound to happen, Cornelia thought, is that soon

I'll turn thirty-five. Still, I've got Livvie. And my work. And freedom, freedom to choose for myself.

Then, feeling a pang, she remembered why she wanted to be at work early.

Freedom cost money. Freedom meant bills with her name on them. She'd been piling up bills for several months now, crushing them down into a desk drawer. This was the day she'd sworn she'd deal with them.

Cornelia sighed, reached for the briefcase Tim had given her when she started working in an office. She hated the thing, boxy, leather, with brass corners that always needed polishing. It looked corny, a piece of wardrobe for a career woman. Usually she grabbed up a paper shopping bag for the theater programs, photographs, newspapers, scripts, the stacks of papers she carted back and forth. She saved bags from the good stores, and then, somehow, wound up carrying hideous ones from the supermarket. Today, though, in the rain, she'd better take the briefcase.

She carried it to the hall desk, reached for the big drawer and pulled, looked inside.

Immediately her heartbeat doubled. So many bills.

Fear flooded back, seemed to circulate rapidly through her body. She knew she couldn't pay them all. Somewhere in the pile was one from the dentist, more than two hundred dollars. If she took care of only that, a lot of others would have to wait. And some had waited awhile already. She'd juggled bills before, knew how to juggle them. But never so many.

A wastebasket stood next to the desk. Cornelia looked at it longingly. How great, she thought, to turn the whole drawer over, spill all the envelopes into it. Then she could waltz Livvie to school in the rain, clown around. They could tilt their faces up to catch raindrops on their tongues.

But then the phone would ring, she'd hear from department stores, collection agencies, even lawyers. She'd *have* to face the bills, pay some, anyway, promise to pay others. If she reached the office by eight-thirty, she'd have a good two hours alone. Actors all hated early mornings. They were either in shows or working nights, as bartenders, baby-sitters, waiters.

Livvie appeared, looking perfect. Even her socks were pulled up straight. Over their tops her knees showed rosy, the only spots of color on her creamy skin. She could have posed for the cover of the Boston School catalog.

Together they turned off the lights, and Livvie pushed the bell for the elevator while Cornelia double-locked the front door. The elevator wheezed slowly up. The building was old. Nothing worked quickly. But the rent was stabilized.

Thank God, she thought, for *something* stabilized. Anyway, maybe soon they'll make it a co-op, and I can buy it somehow and sell it right away for lots more. Thank God, too, that Livvie looks brighter.

They did dance to the crosstown bus stop, enjoying the rain on their upturned faces. Chilly, delicious, it trickled into Cornelia's mouth, tasted so good, made her so lighthearted she did a wild hoedown for Livvie at the bus stop. Waving the briefcase, she danced, while Livvie laughed in delight, and the waiting people stared. When she finished, though, one man applauded. Cornelia, out of breath, laughing, curtsied to him like a prima ballerina.

The bus came, splashing, and everyone leapt back to avoid the spray, then surged forward to climb on. Cornelia kept a hand on Livvie's back, steered her up the high step. While she paid, Livvie maneuvered between people to get to the back, just the way Cornelia had taught her. There was one seat in the last row, and Livvie stood firmly in front of it, waiting for her mother to sit down. Then she climbed into Cornelia's lap.

Cornelia put her arms around the child's sticky yellow slicker and decided she felt terrific, even though the bus was suffocating, its floor flooded with water from dripping umbrellas and raincoats. Next to them a fat man held his damp newspaper wide open, commenting on the news aloud. Cornelia shifted Livvie away from him so she wouldn't be tempted to ask embarrassing questions about whom he was talking to.

Then she realized that Livvie's attention was already focused somewhere else.

Across the aisle another mother sat holding a child on her lap, a black woman with a very small boy. He looked three or four, half Livvie's size, with a red slicker just like her yellow one. His tiny feet bobbing, his head tilted against his mother's large bosom, he was reclining happily, jabbering away. Cornelia leaned past Livvie for a moment, admiring his bright eyes, the alert look of his coffee-colored face under the red fisherman's hat.

All of a sudden Livvie's weight seemed to change, increase. She seemed to become limp, boneless, heavy.

Cornelia felt surprise, wondered if she were slumping back, simply imitating the other child.

She looked again. Suddenly she understood why the boy's head was tilted so far back.

He was reading.

He was staring at the ads mounted on the walls of the bus, sounding out every word, even the ones in the tiniest print. She strained to hear.

" 'Keep your milk from getting . . .' What, Mama? What's that word after, Mama?"

Cornelia couldn't hear a reply. The child waited a moment and began again.

Above the whine of the motor, through the noise of people getting on and off, even over the sound of the door buzzer, Cornelia heard the small, high voice.

She began feeling assaulted, as if the child's voice could pierce her eardrums, as if it were a burglar alarm shrilling in a closed car, past endurance.

" 'Lone-ly,' " the bright, clear voice was saying. "How can milk be lonely? 'End child abuse. Telephone 555-6800 to report . . .' What's 's-i-g-n-s,' Mama? How can you put 'g-n-s' all together like that? What's 'abuse' anyway, Mama?"

Jesus, Cornelia thought, he can't be five years old. And he's really reading. He's fascinated by all those words. Does Livvie have to listen to people her size and smaller, day after day in school, reading like that?

Cornelia's pleasure vanished, leaving a vast emptiness.

Livvie's head was drooping. Her hat dripped onto Cornelia's raincoat. Her feet hung, bumped against Cornelia's legs.

Cornelia felt the empty space inside her filling with heat. Her blood seemed to pump faster, a red film to cover her eyes.

She knew she had to stop the sound, stop listening to a child reading as Livvie couldn't. She had to get away from it before she began shouting at the little boy, telling him to be quiet.

She stood up, tipping Livvie abruptly to her feet, grabbing for her hand, pulling her toward the door. She banged at the buzzer, raging, longing for the bus to stop, so they could escape.

After what felt like hours, they thumped down into the wet street.

Cornelia felt overheated. Her collar seemed too tight, and its button dug into her neck. She breathed the cool air, trying to calm down, stood still, holding Livvie's hand.

When she could, she looked at her child, expecting tears, maybe the same kind of rage she'd felt herself. She began marshaling words to reassure, comfort, cheer Livvie up again.

But Livvie didn't look sad, or angry. She looked just the way she had in the kitchen. Resigned. Blank. Her face was a doll's face, waxen, with glassy eyes that seemed to see nothing.

No, Cornelia wanted to shout. I will *not* have my child look like that. I'll wake her, get life into her, warm her, if I have to dance a fandango in this filthy street.

She stooped down, put her face level with Livvie's. Setting the briefcase down in the wet, she took the child by the shoulders, shook.

"Listen to me, Olivia Fuller. Forget that boy. Just forget him. You're you, and he's somebody else different from you. You can't read yet and he can. But it doesn't mean anything. You'll learn soon, maybe you'll read better than he does. So fuck him, Livvie. Say it with me, go on. Fuck him."

Livvie's eyes widened. She stared at Cornelia, her face suddenly becoming a little girl's face, not a doll's. She didn't make a sound, but the corners of her mouth began turning up.

Cornelia reached for the dripping briefcase and stood up. She took Livvie's hand firmly, started to walk. Worry grew with every step.

Should she have ignored the other child? Pretended she hadn't heard? Had she been wrong to sweep Livvie off the bus? Made things worse?

After a block of steady trudging Cornelia finally heard Livvie make a tiny sound.

A minute later the sound grew clearer: a soft giggle.

And then Cornelia could smile, quicken her pace, move in a straight line toward school, where Livvie would be protected and nurtured, where they would know how to fix whatever was wrong.


In the later afternoon, Livvie followed Margaret Rose down the front steps of the school. The sun, shining on the red of her nanny's sweater, surprised Livvie's eyes, so she had to squeeze them tight shut.

Sun was nice, she thought. Now they could go to the playground. She could jump on the leaves, all the different colors, red, yellow, crackly brown. The others could line up for the swings, crawl on the jungle gym. She would play by herself till the windows of the buildings around the park turned shiny gold.

Feeling light, bouncy, she opened her eyes so she could jump down the last step.

Then she saw him.

Right away, Livvie felt herself get small, the size of a tiny little baby.

The bad man was right where they had to walk.

Her skin felt too tight. She could almost feel him reaching for her, sniff his garbage smell.

And Margaret Rose was pulling her hand, hurting.

Livvie shook her head so her hair would come over her eyes. Then she peeked through. The bad man wasn't looking at her. He was busy doing something to the handle of the gate with a hammer.

Hearing the awful banging noises, she began feeling the way she always did when bloody pictures and gun sounds came on TV. But she could turn those off, or go somewhere else if Margaret Rose wanted to watch.

And she could *say* she hated those pictures.

She couldn't say *anything* about him. Never.

Maybe he won't see me, she thought, her tummy starting to ache. Maybe he'll think I'm some other girl. Not *his* girl, the way he said.

She bent her head down till she could see the cracks in

the sidewalk, put her face against Margaret Rose's tough skirt.

"Don't drag, Livvie," she heard from high up. "Walk like a little lady."

Livvie's tummy twisted up.

Oh, Margaret Rose, she wanted to yell, *why* did you say my name? Now I can't hide. He'll know it's me.

She lifted her head. At least she'd know what he was doing.

He was turning around. Standing up.

*He was looking right at her.*

Livvie felt her skin get pinched and creepy, as if bugs were crawling on her. He could do terrible things with his eyes, she knew it. Gross eyes, black as patent-leather shoes, different from anyone else's. Those eyes could shine through the walls and see her *anywhere* in school.

"Good afternoon," she heard Margaret Rose say. "Livvie? Can't you say good afternoon?"

Now her middle hurt as much as the time she'd eaten baby apples in the country. Was Margaret Rose going to stop till she said it?

No, she was walking. And pulling, so Livvie's shoulder cracked.

Livvie didn't mind *that*. They were going away from him, and the corner was coming close.

Anyway, she thought, his eyes don't work when I'm with Margaret Rose. She's not afraid of anybody.

Livvie remembered Margaret Rose shouting at the money lady in the supermarket till she changed the green numbers on the machine. And even scolding the *policeman* for not stopping the turning cars.

Margaret Rose was probably the bravest person in the world. Still, she wasn't always right. Livvie knew that from her birthday.

Over and over, Margaret Rose had said that when Livvie was seven she'd know how to read. So on the morning of her birthday, while it was still dark out, she jumped out of bed and grabbed for her schoolbook, sure she'd know the words, like everybody else.

And she didn't. She saw just the same old letters in bunches. The same fuck book.

But she *is* brave and fierce, Livvie thought. If only she

could stay all day with me in school. Some of the little kids' mommies and nurses stay. Sitting crunched up on those benches in the rooms.

But Livvie knew she wasn't little anymore. Nobody ever stayed with second-graders.

Now they were crossing the big street into the park. She could feel Margaret Rose's safe black hand squeeze, the way it always did near cars.

No, nobody could help.

She'd just have to try to keep far away from him by herself.

But how *could* she? When he could go anywhere?

He could open the classroom door and walk right in, even when everyone was working quietly. Or into the gym, the music room, even the bathroom, where the toilets and sinks were little, and even teachers never came unless someone was throwing up.

*The bathroom was the most awful.*

"What's is the *matter* with you today?" Margaret Rose said.

"Nothing," Livvie said.

To make it true, she opened her eyes wide and looked at the park. Anyway it was nice to be here in the park, in the sun. To see all the people. Men reading books. Nurses pushing baby carriages. The old raggedy lady who always brought bread in a paper bag for the birds. The man who slept on a whole bench, with newspaper on top of him.

The sounds from the playground were nice too. And now she could see kids high up at the top of the jungle gym.

Anyway, Livvie thought, today wasn't bad. Betsy was home sick. Lunch was mashed potatoes with gravy. And I could read a whole lot of the horse story to Miss Montgomery, because I remembered it from Mommy.

She pushed back her hair, wriggled her knapsack into a nicer place on her back.

Maybe it was dumb to be so scared of the bad man. But then, she *was* dumb. The kids all knew that. Seeing her sitting alone with Miss Montgomery. They laughed. Even today.

Would they laugh if she told them about the bad man?

But he'd said: Don't tell *anybody*. She shivered, remembering the mean sound in his voice.

In the playground, Margaret Rose sat down on a bench and took her newspaper out of her big bag. She pulled off Livvie's knapsack and put it right next to her so nobody would take it.

Livvie walked to the fence and kicked at the pile of leaves.

It was so hard not to tell.

She remembered once almost telling Margaret Rose. After that first time. When he'd found her in the bathroom with wet pants and promised to help her. But Margaret Rose had been scolding mad for Livvie's coming home in pants with someone else's name tape on them. When Margaret Rose was mad, you couldn't talk to her.

Livvie kicked at the leaves to make them pop. But today it wasn't fun.

Daddy didn't listen either. He took her to plays and lots of restaurants, but he always said that if things went wrong she should just be a good, brave girl.

*And that's what the bad man said too.*

Mommy listened the best. She was always interested in the things Livvie told her. But most of all, she couldn't tell Mommy. The bad man had said what he'd do to Mommy if Livvie told her.

Livvie could almost see his big knife, red, like blood, with so many sharp things sticking out of it, even a scissors.

She kicked her shoe on a big stone to stop thinking about it. The kick came up her leg into her stomach so it ached more. She felt her eyes getting wet, so the leaves looked smeary. She rubbed the tears away with her hands before anyone could see.

Then, like a surprise, she had an idea.

Maybe there *was* something.

She could run.

Get fast enough to run away from the man whenever he came to get her.

She could practice, run all the way around the playground, learning to go faster and faster.

Livvie got ready, got set, and ran, ran till her hair blew back, till she saw the fence race by, the colors of people's clothes smudge like finger paint.

She got hot all over, puffed, with a big pain in her chest, and finally stopped.

Then she curled her fingers through the wire fence and held on tight, looking out at the park, wondering how far she'd have to run to get away.

## THE BOSTON SCHOOL

The Boston School is a day school for girls from Nursery through Grade Twelve, divided into Lower, Middle, and Upper schools, each under the guidance of a head teacher.

Founded in New York in 1920 by Margaret Sills Creighton as Miss Creighton's School for Girls, the school was incorporated in 1927, and moved to its present modern building on East End Avenue. At the same time its name was changed to honor the city of the founder's birth and background.

Miss Creighton, the product of a regimented education, deeply believed in the uniqueness of the individual. Thus, the school's aim is to develop the mind and character of each girl to their greatest potential, so she can meet the demands of a changing world.

The school takes its motto, "*Respiciens Discipulam*," from Boston's own philosopher, Ralph Waldo Emerson:

*The secret of education lies in respecting the pupil.*

NANNY KNOWLTON STEPPED quickly into her cubbyhole office and closed the flimsy door.

All the long morning she had kept herself perfectly controlled. She had checked supplies, greeted the children by name, ticked off the sick list, as always. Now, at last, she could take a deep breath and let the unusual excitement inside her take over.

Nanny shivered with delicious fear, like someone enjoying a horror movie. If only there were a lock on her door. With a key. It was hard for any teacher to get away alone during school hours, almost impossible for a head teacher. Everyone with a problem came straight to her. Ordinarily, that was how she liked it. But now she longed to be alone.

She stood still, listening. Now that the children were behind closed classroom doors, voices blended into a low buzz, like the sound of a radio turned far down. Surely nobody would need her.

Nanny felt a vein in her temple throb, knew that her breath was coming in little bursts. Feeling warm, she undid the top button of her navy smock. Then, her excitement building, she put her hand in her pocket. The coarse fabric brushed against little cuts on her skin, a hangnail.

The irritation didn't matter.

What mattered was the bra deep in her pocket, rolled into a soft little ball.

Trembling, Nanny looked again at the door. Did she dare take the thing out? She'd waited so long. But suppose somebody came in? How could she explain? Why, she could scarcely understand it herself.

She considered the small room. Nowhere to hide. Only bookcases, file cabinet, desk, a pair of battered chairs. Nothing to slip behind, nothing to protect her if the door suddenly were to open.

Then Nanny noticed the big wooden box in the corner. A rough cube, knocked together in the school shop, crudely painted bright red, "Lost and Found" stenciled in white on the top.

Her breath came still faster. Perfect, she thought.

The box would be filled with little clothes, everyone's stray sweaters, socks, shirts, sneakers, even books and toys. If she took everything out and heaped it on her desk, made a little wall, then she could put the bra just behind it. And if anyone came, well, they'd think she was sorting the clothes. Excellent.

Nanny's vein pulsed harder.

She lifted the heavy lid, hands unsteady. Quickly piled everything on her desk in a raggedy heap.

So much, she thought, amazed. A small mountain. And it's only fall. Imagine what there'll be by May, June. Those mothers. So careless. So extravagant. They don't even notice when a child comes home with one sneaker. No sweater. Or worse, no underwear. But now, how useful.

Nanny smiled.

How appalled those mothers would be to see her brushing her fingertips against another woman's bra.

She began shaping the clothes into a heap, mounding

the sweaters and hats as high as they would go without
tumbling back.

Touching a knitted vest with a price tag still on it, she
winced.

Incredible, she thought. So many wealthy parents here
now. Not like my day, when they made an effort to balance
the student body, searched for good families down on their
luck, gave scholarships to artists' children, teachers' children. Manners are different now, anyway. In the forties,
mothers made us hunt for a lost scarf, let alone a sweater.
And we didn't care about fancy labels.

The bra had a fancy label. Bergdorf's. Nanny had seen
it when she'd whisked the little scrap of fabric down from
the shower rod. She'd had just time enough to glimpse it,
to sense the tremendous difference between the tiny thing
and her own sturdy white cotton one.

Angry as she'd been at Kit, she'd hesitated a moment
in admiration. Who would ever imagine a bra could be so
beautiful?

Now Nanny couldn't wait. She wanted the pretty thing
out in the open, to look at, to hold.

She glanced once more at the door. Then she curled her
fingers around the bra and brought it out to the light. How
different from the children's clothes. All blue and white,
like a wisp of cloud in a summer sky. The fabric almost
seemed to shimmer, a soft iridescence against the hard,
bright colors of the other clothing.

She touched it gently, felt longing come over her. Oh,
Kit, she thought. You're gone. This is all I have left of
you.

Slowly Nanny moved her hand, ran her fingertips along
the sleekness of the satin, the crispness of the lace edging,
the surprising chill of the little silvery hook.

Then, breath coming in little gasps, she moved her fingers toward the rounded cup. She put a finger just at the
center, where Kit's small coral nipple would be if she were
wearing the bra.

Kit. How I longed for you to be the one, the right one.

And you're gone.

But at least I have this.

Nanny's fingers moved, circling and circling the beautiful softness.

If Kit had only understood. If she had only come closer, instead of taking flight.

Nanny closed her fingers on the satin, lifted the bra close to her face. It seemed to hold Kit's fragrance, light, spring-flower fresh, a girl's fragrance. Breathing it sent a burst of delight into Nanny's head, a tingle down her spine.

A door banged out in the hall. Nanny froze. Somebody small scampered by. Her heart chilled to ice.

She thought: If anyone saw me. . . Sitting here holding a bra. Disgusting. Something I stole. *Stole.*

No. Kit left it behind. Forgot it. Exactly the way she'll forget me.

Nanny crushed the bra into a pale blue flower in her fist, and remembered Kit.

Kit, slight, slim, willowy, dark hair swirling as she turned from the hall into this very office last spring to ask about a teaching job. Kit, standing in a crowd of children like a queen among her subjects. Kit, like all young teachers, unable to find an apartment she could afford, clapping her hands with delight on seeing Nanny's huge spare room, so thrilled, so grateful. How she had filled that room, throwing the window wide to the air, spreading a bright cover on the bed, playing sprightly music on her little cassette machine. And how Nanny had cared for her, choosing plump oranges from the fruit stand for Kit's breakfast, walking with her to school mornings, lending her a clock, a raincoat, bus tokens. She had even telephoned Mr. Watts at Neville Rodie and asked for extra money from the small trust that allowed her to get by on her school salary. How Kit had filled her senses, sometimes singing to herself, brushing past Nanny like a caress, bringing high spirits into the dark apartment. She'd hung on Nanny's stories about school, and marveled at Nanny's ideas for teaching the children.

Kit had been like the children. So open, so eager for new experience. Different from the upper-school girls, all whispers and silly giggles, thinking only about boys. The little ones were beautiful, their skin fresh, their eyes innocent, their hair springing with soap-and-water cleanliness. And Nanny knew all about them, understood how to challenge the quick ones, coax the shy ones, work patiently with the slow ones. Nobody was more expert with little children.

But children grew and changed. And so had Kit. In two brief months she'd become different. She'd withdrawn, grown secretive. First, telephone calls, then evenings away, finally a weekend spent somewhere.

Nanny had ached to command, forbid, put Kit in a corner, lock the door. But a teacher of small children understands patience. She had waited quietly for Kit to return to her.

And then last night, "Nanny, guess what? I've found this fabulous apartment. Only a studio, but mine, all mine!"

Nanny had felt the words pierce like tiny poison darts, turn her hands and feet numb.

As Kit spoke of her plans, Nanny had felt the numbness reach her heart.

She had achieved nothing, built nothing. She had wanted to clutch, kiss, hold, to own every inch and ounce of Kit.

All night Nanny had shifted about in bed listening for sounds on the other side of the wall. She had *ached* to get up, go to Kit's bed, kiss the fresh mouth, put her hand on the flat belly, move her fingers to the soft, moist place between Kit's slim thighs. She had longed to hold Kit's wrists in one of her own strong hands, while her other hand moved slowly to show Kit why she should stay, how wonderful it could be, dear God, if she would stay.

And then, this morning, when she had gone into the bathroom with swollen eyes and a thumping headache, there the bra had been, nestled behind the shower curtain, forgotten. She had been startled by the gleam of blue satin, so surprising in the dull bathroom.

At first she thought about putting the bra into Kit's suitcase, perhaps leaving it folded on top. The tiny thing was costly, anyone could see that.

Once she touched it, though, Nanny had known she could not let it go. It felt small, soft, beautiful, like Kit. Trembling with longing and misery, she had thrust the little bra into her bureau under Mother's old quilt, as if she were shutting Kit safely away.

Then, dressing for school, Nanny realized with a shock that Kit might search for the bra, find it among Nanny's things. So she'd gone back, reached again under the puffy folds, curled her fingers around the bra. It could comfort her during the long day, keep her from feeling so desolate, so bereft.

She had nothing to look forward to, nothing. Eight-thirty, school. Ten, milk and cookies. Noon, lunch. Three, greeting mothers and nurses, an idle father or two. Four, tidy up. Six-thirty, supper. Seven-thirty, papers, budgets, lists, reports. Nine, a volume of Trollope, brandy, with ice to make it last a little longer. June, Newport with her sister. September, school again.

So she *needed* the bra. A tiny scrap of joy, a little token of promise. Even if the promise had never come true.

Nanny put her head down and closed her eyes.

She pictured Carola as she always did, trim in tennis whites, lithe, smooth arms tanned, flame hair streaming down her slender back. Carola, sixteen then, to Nanny's twelve, a radiant girl, all smooth grace. She'd been kind when the other girls had giggled at tall, lanky Nanny, who could never run fast or stroke a ball properly. Carola practiced with her, taught her to serve. Nanny had been over-come at the attention, and from a girl so magnificent. She'd loved Carola's coaching, the warm hand on her wrist, the brown arm against her shoulder, the light chuckle when Nanny's steel-rimmed glasses slipped down on her nose. The lessons had kept on, grown longer. All through that spring Nanny's head had whirled. Daydreaming, she'd seen only Carola, heard the laughing voice in her mind, lived for afternoons on the green lawn near the courts. When her friend allowed Nanny to take her slim hand, carry her gym bag and books home from school, Nanny knew pure joy. Such a small step, so natural, to obey Carola, touch where she told Nanny, be touched in return. Afternoons in Carola's bedroom were all discovery, excitement, de-light. They'd promised to be best friends forever. But then, one day, Carola graduated in a white dress, went off to Holyoke. Nanny wrote, each day a letter, for over a month, with never an answer. At Thanksgiving, trembling, she'd phoned. A maid told her Miss Carola couldn't come to the telephone.

She'd been desolate, brooding, all through Christmas and into the new year. Her mother had puzzled, despaired, sent her off to the pediatrician. By spring Nanny had resigned herself to loneliness. Never would anyone mean so much, bring her such magic. Certainly not any of the stupid boys her mother pushed at her, down from St. Paul's and Exeter and Groton to the junior dances, pawing her with their huge, moist hands, pressing their hot bodies against her on the dance floor.

So Carola had gone. And now Kit.

Someone was knocking. The sound seemed to rap on Nanny's heart. She jumped, thrust the bra deep into the pile, sat straight. A blush warmed her neck. She could feel her skin prickling.

"Yes," she managed to say.

"Miss Knowlton? Can I come in?"

*May* I come in, Nanny thought automatically. And then: Dear God, I'm sitting here like a madwoman with another teacher's bra in my hand, and correcting someone's speech.

"Of course," she said.

Acknowledging her own foolishness soothed her, somehow made her feel less wicked.

The door opened. A senior girl, silky brown hair folding over the shoulders of her white blouse, knees just peeping out under the blue serge skirt. Elinor Something, Nanny recalled, new, here just a year or two. Must have money. The school didn't add girls in the higher grades unless they were somehow special. No room in those classes, with college just around the corner. But this child looked only pretty, not special.

"I'm on school service," the girl said nervously. "There's this note for you? From the headmaster's office?"

Note. Why would the man be sending her a note? Why hadn't he simply used the phone?

"Thank you, dear," Nanny said. "And, Elinor. Remember to look at people when you speak to them."

Saying that made Nanny feel quite herself again. It would *help* the child to know. She was a *good* teacher.

Anyway, the bra was deep in the pile of clothes. The girl couldn't possibly have seen it. She was only anxious to get on with her job. All the older girls were required to give an hour or two a week to this sort of thing, licking envelopes, running messages, helping with office work.

Nanny waited until the door had closed. Then she felt for the bra, moved it swiftly to her pocket. Good. If an

adult had come in, she would have handled things just as
well. But this girl had rather lifted her spirits. Reminded
her there were other girls with slim bodies, glowing hair,
obedient ways.

To the devil with Kit, she thought. Someone new will
come. Someone gentle, lonely, eager to be taught. To be
loved in secret.

The note, now.

Nancy unfolded it. A few typed lines: "The captain's
compliments, and will Miss Knowlton please join him at
one o'clock, when the children will be resting? Thanks,
see you then, Dr. Connor."

The man did have odd ways of expressing himself. Still,
the note was jaunty. And fancy his remembering when her
children would be silent on their cots. A good sign. It
showed interest in her lower school. The upper school,
with the girls headed for college, was usually the admin-
istration's first concern. Which was stupid. After all, what
got them ready for good colleges?

Nanny had been pleased to learn that a man was taking
over. Miss Creighton had grown so ancient. And she sometimes reminded Nanny of her girlhood, made her feel a
naughty twelve-year-old again, caught slipping out of gym
class, copying someone's homework. And lately there had
been times when Miss Creighton had looked sharply at
Nanny. She had felt so frightened. Some people today
could be open about their sexual preferences. But not
teachers. At least, not in this school. Nanny knew now
that the school had always had plenty of teachers who'd
loved women, but all of them had covered up, spoken of
lovers lost in wars, tragic disappointments. Miss Creighton
probably believed them.

So it was a relief, good for the school, good for her,
that Miss Creighton had finally gone, retired.

The new man looked interesting, totally different from
anyone in the school, ever.

Well, she would know more at one o'clock. She'd never
been alone with him, only seen him in large gatherings.

Good thing she'd worn her nice brown skirt, a fresh
white cotton blouse, polished her beautiful Belgian oxfords. And her hair, too, was newly washed, falling naturally into its soft pepper-and-salt waves. She would re-

move her glasses, add a touch of lipstick before she went down. Her fine skin needed no other makeup, even though little lines had begun fanning out from the corners of her eyes. But then, only fools thought makeup concealed anything.

Dr. Billy Connor. Why on earth not "William," she'd wondered when she'd first heard his name. "Bill," even. "Billy" had put her off. But then she'd remembered that the search committee had worked for months to find just the right person. And all the gossip so far had been favorable. Dr. Connor had come in every single day over the summer, one of the secretaries had told Nanny. He'd gone through records, histories of the school, budgets, reports, even the textbooks assigned to each grade. The librarian said that Dr. Connor had meticulously gone through all the stacks. Others chimed in. The man had visited every corner of the building, basement storage rooms, gym, science labs, the theater, supervised the building of the new observation room with its one-way mirror. After Miss Creighton, it would be fine to have so energetic a person in command. If only he were truly forward-looking, if only now Nanny could at last get the support she wanted.

Especially the one thing she wanted most.

The Saturday school.

Almost since Nanny had started to teach, she had been thinking about it. Here sat this beautiful building on weekends, classrooms silent, gym empty, theater dark. Pianos were closed, educational games packed away, books untouched in the libraries. And away went the children to mothers who wanted to sleep late, had errands to do, who sent the children off to silly play groups.

But if Nanny could start her own Saturday school, just for the smaller children? Wonderful.

She'd been planning it for years, first in her mind, then on paper.

The purpose would be individual help. So important to make everything clear. Once, a teacher of Nanny's had been cross when the children wouldn't join a line, until one little girl had asked, "What's a line?" So Nanny's plan was for each child to work alone with a teacher. A gifted girl like Michele Norton could do foreign-language work, write for a newspaper, have music lessons. A slow reader, like Cornelia Fuller's child, could use a comic book, a brightly illustrated magazine, something different from the reading texts.

Poor, darling Livvie. Nanny's heart hurt for her, and for the other problem children. So often, the problems had nothing to do with capacity. The brightest child could have private visions that made class teaching difficult. Trouble at home, like divorce, could paralyze any child, especially a small one. Perhaps that was Livvie's trouble now. She seemed so tense, so unhappy. Nanny couldn't bear seeing any of her children miserable. Yes, *her* children, even if they only belonged to her part of their day. How she longed to make each one happy, successful. With the school dossiers to guide her, Nanny could tailor each lesson plan. And do it better than those psychologists, with their silly remediation work. Ridiculous word, "remediation." How could anyone teach who couldn't speak proper English to begin with? Nanny only needed student teachers, the girls with special zeal for early-childhood education. Hadn't some philosopher said that the best school was a log with a teacher at one end, a pupil at the other?

With Miss Creighton there had been no point whatever in proposing new ideas. But now? Perhaps even today she could hint at her plan. If she felt the slightest encouragement from Dr. Connor, she would put her papers in better form, show him how essential it was to give special attention to the children who needed it.

She would have to see. She knew so little about the man. When the faculty had gathered in the theater to meet him, Nanny had been held up, arrived in the middle of a speech by the head of the search committee, a lawyer, who had been eloquent about Dr. Connor's background and accomplishments.

When the new headmaster had finally risen to speak, Nanny had been fascinated by his elegance. Tall, dapper, he'd worn tweeds that fitted perfectly, even at the knee, a white handkerchief squared off in his breast pocket that seemed to glow in the light from the lectern.

When the first polite applause had stilled, Dr. Billy Connor had surprised them all. He had walked off the podium, stepped forward, and in one smooth move had sat down— *sat down*—on the steps that led up to the stage. With his forearms on his knees, hands clasped gracefully between his legs, Dr. Connor had smiled beguilingly. Nanny had thought suddenly that he looked as if he *practiced* relaxing before audiences.

Dr. Connor had talked, in a voice at once lilting and slightly nasal, of his pleasure in being chosen, his respect for the tradition of the school, his wish to meet each of them personally. Nanny, though she could not see his eyes, watched him turn his head smoothly, so that he seemed to reach out to each of them. Afterward, she had realized that she had been so interested in the way he spoke, the odd way he mixed the newest slang with polysyllables and psychological jargon, that she could remember little of what he actually had said.

But when he had answered questions, one of his phrases had stuck in her mind. That they were the leaders, the ones who would bring new teachers with them as they contributed new ideas and changes to the growth of the school. And Nanny's mind had quickly shot to her own dream. How much she wanted to send each child from her lower school on to the fourth grade solidly grounded, eager to learn more, free from problems and fears. And how her Saturday school could help.

Nanny snapped back to the problem of Kit's bra.

What on earth was she to do with it? She wouldn't wear her smock to Dr. Connor's office. It had a spot of milk, a crayon smear on its front. Would the bra fit in her purse? It could *not* remain in her desk drawer, and there wasn't really anywhere to hide anything in the office. Teachers popped in all the time, wanting an aspirin, a pencil, a stamp. Suppose, for once, someone actually went through the clothes in the lost-and-found box?

Noise was starting out in the hall. Children out of the rooms, pattering to the bathrooms, banging their locker doors. Soon the carts with the lunch leftovers would rumble back to the kitchens. Not much time.

Ridiculous worry. When she needed to marshal her ideas for the headmaster.

And dangerous. There must be no shadow over her now.

Wait. There's a fresh smock in my closet, nicely pressed. I'll go down in that. My badge of office, really. And I look well in it.

Relieved, she pushed her hands into the mass of clothing. When she pulled, one hook grabbed at a small shirt. She freed the bra carefully, rolled it up, and went over for the other smock, thrusting the bra deep down in its pocket. On top, she added her handkerchief. Her hands were always in her pockets anyway. She could feel safe knowing exactly where the bra was.

Ready, Nanny felt excited again, charged up. Perhaps the little bra would even bring her luck.

Her hopes churning, Nanny walked toward the big twin elevators at the end of the hall. *Her* hall. She glanced automatically into the classrooms along the way through the glass-paned doors strengthened with chicken wire. For safety, of course. A detail. But details were vital in a school. And details had been ignored so often in the past. Perhaps now all that would be different. Nanny's step quickened.

She reached the stainless-steel carts, sticky with spilled food, the maids waiting to push them into the elevators, back to the kitchens downstairs. They smelled now of overcooked meat. The school tradition was for everyone to have a **hot** lunch. But most of the food was scraped back into the garbage. The girls gobbled only bread, crackers, a little fruit. They even turned their noses up at desserts: tapioca, bread pudding, prune whip, lemon snow. Not that Nanny blamed them. She'd loathed the school food as a child. Perhaps that was the sort of thing she could change, if Connor would give her authority over the senile nutritionist. Crunchy sandwiches, firm bananas, sweet brownies, bright red circles of sliced tomato. Far better. Oh, she had so many ideas to take to this man.

In the close air of the elevator the greasy smells seemed overpowering. Nanny, to fight a little wave of nausea, tried to recapture the clean, grassy fragrance of Kit. Nausea receded, but she felt worse, so empty, thinking of Kit back upstairs somewhere, reading a book while her second-graders squirmed on their blankets. Does she feel relieved to have left me? Did she guess my feelings? Will she talk? Not likely. She'll be too busy now, caught up with new people. With a man.

Nanny got off at the second floor. The handsomest floor in the building. Deep carpeting in a soft rust, to match the papered walls. A background for the antique cabinets and benches, the magnificent Chinese paintings and ceramics that Miss Creighton had brought from the Orient after teaching there years before. Even the wealthiest parents had no finer furniture, no lovelier art. Museum pieces really. And Nanny's favorite, everyone's, was the school symbol, the Kwan Yin statue in its niche at the far end of the hall, soft, female, ageless with its carved stone draperies and enigmatic smile. No child was allowed alone on this floor. Even the upper-school girls came only for special meetings, college interviews, school-government reports.

Nanny walked silently along the thick carpet. The headmistress's office—headmaster's now—was at the far end. First, there was a little anteroom. She knew all about this set of offices. Some of her most important moments had been spent here. Her college conference, with her mother, homeroom teacher, and Miss Creighton. They had quickly agreed on Smith, and Smith it had been. Things seemed so simple then. A recommendation from the Boston School meant everything. And then, in the same room, Nanny had been hired. She had returned after graduation, neat in low heels and a navy linen suit, her thesis on Montessori educational materials rolled in her gloved hand. Miss Creighton had hardly looked up at her. She'd announced the infinitesimal salary and the date in September when Nanny was to appear. She was always pleased to get her girls back. They understood things, needed no tiresome explanations. And they *all*, Miss Creighton used to say often, spoke *beautifully*, had good manners.

Nanny entered the anteroom, and felt odd, disoriented. The inner paneled door was shut. Miss Creighton had never, never closed it.

Nanny greeted the secretary, who was new, had come with Dr. Connor. She'd seen the woman in the lunchroom, thought she looked efficient, polite. The secretary asked Nanny to wait just a moment while the doctor finished a call. The word seemed odd, "doctor." It belonged to white offices, hospitals, disinfectant smells, not this beautiful, beloved place.

A buzzer sounded. Nanny felt amused. Everything now was so crisp and perfect, like a proper business office.

The secretary motioned Nanny from her chair. She

knocked at the heavy door, pushed it in, and announced to the large, echoing room that Miss Knowlton was here.

Nanny moved past her. Immediately she felt disoriented again, jolted even, as if someone had invaded her apartment and moved everything in it to a different place.

Miss Creighton's desk, which always faced the windows, had been turned clear around. Four men must have been needed to move it, a great Chinese partner's desk, scrolled, intricately carved. Now the light from the big windows shone directly onto the empty chair for visitors.

"Super of you to come down on such short notice," Dr. Connor said in that curious voice. The N's were sounded through his high-bridged nose like a Connecticut Yankee. But the ups and downs were soft Irish, the lilt of the voices of maids in Nanny's house when she'd been small. Super? Had he really said that?

Nanny looked directly at the man. She'd not noticed his eyes before this. He'd been too far off, even when she'd shaken his hand at the big cocktail party for teachers, he'd glanced away, distracted by all the women fluttering about. Now he looked straight at her, bright blue eyes unwavering, unblinking. Somehow, she thought, the eyes didn't match the mouth, move when his mouth moved. What they matched was a small blue cornflower, brilliant, small, perky, in the buttonhole of his neat gray suit.

"I've looked forward to talking with you, Dr. Connor," Nanny said.

"Pity we won't have much time today," Dr. Connor said, keeping his eyes on her face as he seated himself, waving a hand to indicate that she should sit too.

Behind the massive desk he still looked tall, slim. He leaned back, and to her enormous astonishment, hitched once in the big chair and swung his feet to the desktop. His soles faced her, only barely scratched. The heels were perfect, she couldn't help noticing. She remembered how he had *acted* relaxed in the school theater. Was this acting too, a sort of technique? Should she be wary, careful not to seem too stiff? And with what was in her pocket! She felt goose bumps start on her arms.

"I need something from you, Miss Knowlton, and urgently," Dr. Connor said, staring.

Better. Nanny felt reassured. He needed her help. He

didn't suspect. Perhaps he wouldn't even care if he knew. He was young, a man who had been around.

"What I need are ideas," he said.

Nanny felt a little rush of pleasure.

Connor watched the large woman across from him relax, and felt his muscles relax, leaving him loose, easy. She was clay, putty. He could pinch here, squeeze there, and she'd shape up. The formidable Miss Knowlton, they'd all told him. Christ, he'd dealt with old biddies like her almost from the day he'd started teaching. Years ago, anyway, so many were like her, straight-backed, plain, old maids through and through. A little flattery, a little respect, and they were yours. This woman probably gave her whole heart to the school, with no feeling left over for a living soul. A cat, perhaps, or a little dog?

"There are problems in this school, Miss Knowlton, formidable problems. So much of this place is absolutely nifty. The rest is like a wonderful old grandfather clock that doesn't run. My job is to decide which is which."

Nifty, Nanny thought. Not a Boston School word, and from the headmaster. It made her uncomfortable.

"The biggest problem, as I see it, is the tremendous amount of what I can only call dead wood. Something to clear away so we can begin moving ahead."

Nanny felt a touch of sadness. But she understood. Old Mr. Radley, forty years in the chemistry lab. Probably totally out-of-date now. And Miss Bevin, the school nurse. She'd seemed ancient when Nanny was a girl. Sad, thinking of them as dead wood. But true, of course.

"What I need from you, from all the head teachers, is help in pinpointing this dead wood."

Pinpointing? Of the old teachers? Could he be talking to other teachers about her? My God, what if any of them said something about her and Kit?

"I've made my own assessments," Dr. Connor was saying.

Nanny shifted in her chair. She felt horribly conscious of the little bra in her pocket. She was starting to feel frightened.

"I've checked all the test scores, reports, class records," Dr. Connor said crisply.

Nanny felt utter confusion. Why couldn't she follow this man? Was *she* a grandfather clock?

"Some of the names are obvious, at least they seem so to me. The low-IQ students in the high school—the upper school, that is. One or two that stick out visibly in the middle school. But you see, your bunch is much tougher."

My bunch?

"It's well known that choosing beginners for a private school is like choosing potatoes in the dark," Dr. Connor said with a brilliant smile. "Problems surface only when you start to work with the kids, to teach, sometimes not until second, third grade. Of course you know what I'm talking about. You deal with it all the time."

Nanny felt a great burst of relief. She understood. He meant the children, thank the Lord.

But dead wood? Certainly difficulties surfaced at six or seven, when the pressure to learn was on. And Nanny knew perfectly well where the problems were. But the children had all been tested, enrolled in the school. The Boston School did not dismiss any child without the most diligent soul-searching, without trying and trying again to help, without careful consideration of the next step for that child. Nanny could hardly remember the last time it had happened.

Dr. Connor seemed to read her thoughts. He smiled reassuringly. But his eyes remained fixed, even as his mouth turned attractively up.

"Progress brings problems, Miss Knowlton," he said. "We must know what we're dealing with, know precisely. The most promising thing about any school is its children. That's really all we have, kids who go on to top colleges, make records for the ones who follow them. People flock to schools with kids like that: Dalton, Trinity, Collegiate, Brearley. That's why the ones who aren't smart need noting. The ones who *are* need an extra push. You know, one of the things that fascinated me most about this job, being at an elite private school, was the chance to know the individual students, concentrate on the right ones. You have no idea, in public schools, how difficult that is. Here we have a unique opportunity."

But exactly, Nanny thought, excitement stirring in her.

"Dr. Connor," she said, sitting straighter, "I do so agree.

And this school has always been dedicated to the individual child, to bringing out and developing each one."

Her words seemed to hang in the air.

Billy Connor looked away. Then he swung his feet off the desk. He stood up in one swift, graceful motion and began to pace between the two windows.

"Miss Knowlton," he said. "Tell me. How much of your time now is devoted to doing that? To developing each child?"

Excellent. Nanny leaned toward him. Now she could try to aim this talk where she wanted.

"Don't you have too much to do for all that?" he continued. "Isn't your day full of getting the kid who's screaming out of the classroom? Mopping up after the one who spills everything? Working with the kids who can't read? What about all the chitchat, reports, conferences with complaining mothers, the stuff you have to do when a kid can't cut it?"

Of course, Nanny thought, excitement blossoming. That's just what I want to work on.

"You're a splendid teacher, Miss Knowlton, everyone agrees. Why should your valuable time be used so disproportionately? Calming crazy kids, spoon-feeding slow ones? Why not put your talents to use where they'll count most?"

A splendid teacher. Nanny flushed with warmth, saw stars, bright ones, before her eyes. Miss Creighton had never said that.

"I've been through your lower-school reports," Dr. Connor said. "And I have a pretty good idea of the kids who take up most of your time. What I'd like to do now is put my ideas together with yours. As I said, to pinpoint. You're the one who deals with these kids. So I'd like a special report on them from you."

Nanny watched him, but in her mind she saw the children.

Rachel, whose family was so orthodox, and who needed time off for Hebrew school, odd holidays.

Tucker, with her unusual hearing disability, diagnosed only recently, after everyone had been baffled by her lack of attention.

Fat little Joanne Strauss with a punctured eardrum. It had happened right in class, the child had actually stuck a pencil in her ear. Joanne simply couldn't stop fidgeting. But when her parents had talked about suing the school, Nanny had calmed them, assuring them she would give Joanne all the special help she needed, even if it were after school. Nanny was happy to give up her time for something so important. And she'd felt such joy each time she managed to conquer a child's problem, get past some terrible barrier.

"I'll need your ideas quite soon, Miss Knowlton," Dr. Connor was saying, sitting down as smoothly as he had risen. "End of the week, actually. Like to make some calculations over the weekend. Put your information together with other things, financial things. Do you know, there's not one computer here? Amazing. Top priority, that's for sure."

Wait, Nanny thought. Too fast. You haven't asked for my ideas.

"Thanks for coming down," Dr. Connor was saying firmly.

Nanny got to her feet feeling confused. She wanted to explain at least the essence of her plan. Was he that busy? Couldn't he give her ten minutes?

To help herself think, she slid her hands back in her pockets, where, immediately, her fingers met satin smoothness.

Doubt attacked her.

Maybe Kit's bra is a reminder not to push, press him, the way I may have pressed her.

"We'll rap again, Miss Knowlton," Dr. Connor said. "This is just a beginning. Quality among teachers, frankly, especially lower-school teachers, is rare. You are particularly rare."

And then she was past the door, still smiling, still with her hands in her pockets. The secretary nodded. Nanny moved along, a little dazed.

While she waited for the elevator, she realized that he would have to consult her again about ways to handle these special children. And *then* she could propose her plan. She was wrong to feel slighted. The man had a hundred other problems. He might be delighted to leave the little children all to her.

Nanny hugged herself a little, alone in the elevator. She saw herself on a lecture platform, showing slides of happy children, explaining her Saturday school to an audience of teachers. She saw a half-page in the second section of *The New York Times*, perhaps with her picture, an article about her program. The real joy, of course, would be the children saved. But how lovely, as well, to have her own efforts recognized, after so many years.

Back on her floor, all was quiet. The children were in darkened rooms, still resting.

Nanny suddenly felt tired, drained too. But she couldn't rest. Not quite yet.

Kit's bra.

It had helped her with the pain of Kit's leaving. Maybe brought her luck, too, in her first meeting with Dr. Connor, a high compliment.

But now she had a job to do. The bra would only distract her, remind her of a bitter disappointment.

Besides, she felt ashamed of it, and herself, as well.

And she'd finished with Kit, hadn't she?

Nanny reached for the big scissors tucked safely away in the back of a drawer. They felt heavy in her fingers.

First, decisively, she cut the bra in two, just where the cups met.

Then she snipped each piece into strips, as if she were preparing fabric for a braided rug. It took no time. Snip, and she cut away Kit. Snip, and she sliced away the memory of her terrible lapse in taking it. Snip, and the tiny thing was a pile of shredded satin.

Nanny touched the pile with her fingertips. A jolt of pain shot through her. She had hoped so much, offered so much. Now nothing would ever bring back her feeling for Kit. All that beauty gone, ruined.

She made herself put back the scissors, reach for an envelope. She swept all the strips into it, brushed away the tiny blue flecks.

Let it go, she thought, forget.

Now maybe there is something more promising for me. This new headmaster. To give me my Saturday school, so young teachers will flock to me, look up to me. Everyone will know I've given something back to the Boston School, something new to my beloved children.

And perhaps, among those teachers, just perhaps, there will be someone else for me. Someone to bring me a cup of tea in bed on a cold Sunday morning, to listen when I read a noble book aloud, applaud with me at the ballet matinees, laugh with me in the kitchen while I fix supper. Someone to love, who will love me in return.

Nanny sighed as she buried the envelope deep among the papers in the wastebasket, hoping that her pain would be buried along with it.

## THE BOSTON SCHOOL

Tuition Fees:

| | | | |
|---|---|---|---|
| Years Three Through Five | $5900 | Grades Eight Through Twelve | 7800 |
| First Grade | 6000 | *Additional Charges:* | |
| Second Grade | 6100 | Application Fee | $ 75 |
| Third Grade | 6200 | Registration Fee | 100 |
| Fourth Grade | 6400 | Testing Fee | 100 |
| | | Athletics | 200 |
| Fifth Grade | 6600 | Lunches | 600 |
| Sixth Grade | 6800 | Midmorning Snack | 50 |
| Seventh Grade | 7000 | | |

Books, school supplies, transportation service, trip expenses, testing fees, tuition-refund insurance, and accident-insurance plan are extra. School bills will be rendered in August, December, and June. A tuition-installment plan is available on inquiry. The prompt payment of all charges will be appreciated.

CONNOR MADE HIMSELF smile pleasantly at the fire inspector as they walked together across the school lobby.

Pity he couldn't shove the man right out the front door.

Bad enough, he thought, this mick dropping in without warning. Worse that he's energetic, ballsy, that he comes on like God's gift to the school. He acts as if he's swung off a hook-and-ladder just in time to save the kids from an inferno.

The last thing Connor needed this morning.

Come on, inspector, he begged silently. You're looking for fire hazards and my school is blazing. And today's my meeting with the one man who can help me. So come on, move your emerald ass.

They were nearly done, thank Christ, heading for the big theater. Connor had kept it for last, hoping the inspector might get tired, might have another appointment somewhere.

No such luck.

He's caught all the petty violations I knew about, Connor thought, even found some on his own. Wait till he sees that balcony. He could even padlock the school. Thank God, at least, he's an Irishman.

They reached the theater doors, heavy, carved mahogany. Connor forced himself to concentrate. He'd need all his wits here.

"Sound, these doors," the inspector said approvingly.

Wait, inspector. Wait till you walk through those sound doors, climb up to that balcony. See the wiring up there, black and frizzled, like burned bacon.

He led the man briskly toward the stage, away from the balcony stairs. The place was warm, stuffy. He had to strain to breathe.

Only two hours now till his meeting with Harvey Bache, and he'd planned for them. Just enough time to reread all the stuff in his briefcase, his notes on enrollments, test scores, financial projections. And to go once more through his presentation. It *had* to persuade Bache.

And here was this Captain Spaight screwing up everything.

The man was a rock. They'd been through the whole building, roof to basement, crisscrossing every floor, using the concrete stairs at both ends. The stairs were broad, good and clean, thanks to that redskin superintendent, but Connor hadn't expected to walk all of them this morning. He'd dressed for downtown, good tweeds, Turnbull shirt, carnation in his buttonhole. Now there was dust graying his shoes, a paint streak on his sleeve. No wonder fire inspectors wore navy blue.

At least the super had done his bit, gotten the inspector through the basement without a complaint. Connor remembered feeling uneasy when he'd first met the man. Good Christ, a Navajo, born and raised on a reservation, and with a twisted leg, too, so he drank a drop or so to ease the pain. Not everyone knew that, but Connor had sniffed it out right off. Johnny, though, was a genius at patching up the old building, keeping things running. Connor didn't know how he'd have gotten this far without him. Though there was something ugly in the man, something that showed in his eyes, especially when he bitched about the old hag who used to run the school.

Now Spaight knelt to check electric sockets, opened fuse boxes, lifted the lids of the big backstage garbage cans. He peered into cupboards and under worktables in the scenery shop. For dark corners he produced a flashlight from an inner pocket, followed its beam with a narrowed eye.

A few violation orders, Connor knew he could swallow. The minor kind, thirty days' notice to cure. But on anything threatening, like the balcony wiring, he'd be in deep shit.

He saw it in his mind, as he'd discovered it going through the empty school last summer. Frayed cords splaying out from overloaded outlets, the kind firemen called octopus plugs. A lot of the wiring was buried, plastered over in the balcony walls, for looks. Whatever was wrong made the lights overheat, start pouring out smoke within minutes. Proper repairs would mean tearing up half the theater. He'd put the balcony off limits. What the fuck else could he do? He didn't have two cents for any major repairs.

At least, not until the tuition raises go through. *If* they go through. If *anything* I've planned goes through Bache today.

Could he somehow, some way, get the inspector past the balcony stairs?

He'd already managed to walk the man by one or two bad spots by carrying on about his last school, in Santa Barbara. Connor did miss the physical plant of that place, so much space and greenery, such laid-back comfort. California schools weren't like ten years back, before Proposition 13, but they were still damned safe. This place, smack in the middle of Manhattan, had been carelessly cleaned, sloppily patched up for years. They'd handed him Violation City.

This captain had probably ordered some of the patchwork. He knew the building too well. Connor had only come along in the hope of heading off trouble. And to size up the man.

There might be a way to put a lid on *all* the fire inspections.

Spaight seemed pleased to be dealing with a man. That old headmistress, fine lady, of course, had refused to see him personally, imagine. She never recognized the problems, usually ignored his warnings. Made it tough, since he hated slapping summonses on a school, but what was there to do? One time the woman even went over his head, if you please, appealed to some parents with City Hall connections about one of Spaight's orders. In fact, just before Connor took over, the captain had himself been thinking of talking to the chairman of the board. After all, Spaight knew fire hazards. Hadn't he been on the trucks? Worked them for years? Wasn't he ready to go out anytime again, for a real cooker?

"Understand," he'd said pompously, breathlessly, as he hauled his bulk up the second set of stairs. "I only see to the major locations myself. Schools, hospitals, nursing homes and that. Places the commissioner himself keeps an eye on. I like to head off trouble, whatever it takes."

So do I, inspector, Connor thought.

His first idea, of course, when the inspector barged in, was a bribe. New York officials, everyone said, were all on the take.

But watching Spaight at work, earnest, careful, had changed his mind. The man, with his map-of-Ireland face, looked honest.

Playing for time, Connor had trotted out his own Irish: Would you believe it now, that the both of them had mothers from County Limerick.

And if my mother had come from Galway or Clare, from Minsk, for that matter, today she'd have been born in Limerick.

Meanwhile, a spark of an idea kindled in his mind, maybe a way around. Man-to-man joking had helped. But the balcony wiring was no joke. It would save endless grief if he could just steer the man past those balcony stairs.

Connor realized he was now uncomfortably warm, wanted to loosen his tie, run a finger around his collar. Bad. He

was proud that he almost never sweated, proud of his cool.
But they had finished backstage, were heading up the aisle
toward the front of the theater.

Go, bog-trotter. One step past that staircase and I won't
have to kiss your ass. *Keep going*.

The inspector paused at the foot of the stairs and turned.
Too bad.

Well now, he'd have to do it carefully, sit the man down,
give him a whiskey. Get the talk around to Spaight's family, his children. He *had* to have children, probably a pack
of them. At the very least, some nieces. And he, inspector
of this fine school, one of the city's best, the country's.
Would he never have thought, now, of sending a girl of
his to a terrific school like this one?

Connor felt himself cooling down, relaxing. Waiting for
someone else's verdict always got to him. Making something happen, even planning it, calmed him.

Of course, there was still the slight hope that Spaight
might aim his flashlight in the wrong direction. But the
captain was dead-on.

"Now, here's trouble, Mr. . . . Dr. Connor," Spaight
said, his tone heavy, pompous. "See these wires? Insula-
tion is the old kind, we've got rid of it most places now.
Those big lights would spark, smoke. Maybe even flame
up."

Would they now, Connor thought. Fancy that.

Michael Spaight kept his head down, eyes on the slim,
dapper shoes of the man with him. Cool customer, he
thought. Jim-dandy for looks. What we used to call a mick
on the make. Still, better than that old bitch, who acted
the Dowager Queen of England to any workingman who
put foot in this building.

This Connor had gone to work on him straightaway, he
was well aware. Good. Let the schoolmaster worry about
him, not the other way round from now on. Connor plainly
had gone over the school, looked in places where few
teachers set foot. But he was no electrician. These spotlights, now, were far less dangerous than he'd know. Smoke
didn't always mean fire. These lights, Spaight knew, would
smoke for hours, die out and away, never set off any other
thing. Nothing else *to* set off. Plaster doesn't burn. At
worst, choke a few silly throats. The wiring was no bless-

ing, of course, but no great threat, either. Why else would the department have passed it for years on end?

Still, useful. Help him stay on top of things here.

"No good at all, this," Spaight said. "Wires are half-buried. Big job. All needs to be broken out, torn up, replaced. And I'd like to know which of my men checked this out the last time."

So would I, Connor thought. And why didn't that same lad come around today?

He frowned. But the problem was out in the open now, and he felt cooler, easier.

He stared at the wires, a nasty spiderweb of rotting black. Of course, he wanted the place perfect. Nobody knew better how a school should be. Holy Christ, hadn't he published papers on optimum room arrangements, traffic patterns, the response of schoolchildren to color, all that stuff?

"This balcony should be off limits now," Spaight was saying.

Right. Fine. He thinks I'm losing sleep over this balcony, he's shitting peaches and cream, Connor thought. I'll lock the whole fucking theater.

He took a big, calming breath.

"Inspector," he said. "I read you. Now I have to be getting back. Take your time. When you've seen all you need, there's a grand bottle of Black Bush from Antrim upstairs in my office. Before you go, come up and share a glass with me. Drink me luck. I don't meet many people here who even know where Antrim is."

Spaight looked up. "Used to be a pack of us here in this neighborhood. All the bars on Third filled with the Irish. Rents too high now. Go in a church once, you'll see. Nothing but old women."

"There's enough on my spade right here," Connor told him dryly, truthfully. "This theater, now. I'll have to lock it up awhile, I can see. Once I have the school on its feet, *then* I'll look around the neighborhood. Go in a church and thank God."

Not bad, he thought. Like one of my own uncles. The old profs at B.C.

Spaight was turning, moving toward the stairs.

Good. Connor began to feel himself straighten, his chin go up. It might all work out.

Spaight came with him, walked up to the second floor at his side. When they reached the deep carpeting, Connor asked the man if he wanted a wash.

"And me black with soot from those burned-out spotlights? Right, Dr. Connor. And you'd better see to that balcony."

Shit. Spaight hadn't even appeared to *look* at the lights. Smart. But a good thing, maybe. A smart man would care about his children.

Connor smiled, took the inspector to the tiny men's room off the hall. It always made him think of the private bathroom he wanted for himself, next to his office. Though this place was almost his own. So few men in the school, and those, queer as the pixies. Well, what would you expect in a low-paying private school?

"You know the way," he said to Spaight. "I'll just go and pour out."

He walked lightly, quickly, back to his office, excitement tingling in him.

Connor unlocked a cabinet, took out a bottle and two squat glasses. Then he reached for his briefcase to set it ready. He looked in at the neatly ranged folders, different colors, blue for the most urgent matters. Nothing about fire hazards in there. Other things were more vital. *Somebody* had to prioritize. He had. And with luck, he'd keep to his priorities.

A light touch, now, with the captain. Harvey Bache would have no use for a headmaster who couldn't handle a fireman.

Jesus. What if it didn't work?

Connor arranged himself in his throne of a chair, took a couple of good deep breaths.

A far move from his cubicle in Dorchester. He remembered the triumph of it, the expansive feeling of bringing his mother in to see that tiny office after hours. Paradise, compared to a desk in a classroom. Bliss, watching all the lines in her face turn up with pride and pleasure. He'd felt himself such a boyo seeing that look, he'd pledged himself to keep it on her all her days.

In that cubicle, taking over for a principal who'd had a

stroke, he'd begun to plan. A doctorate, the license he'd
need, however long it took. His mother would help surely,
use her own bit of savings, thrilled that one of her boys
had ambition, wanted to be more than a barkeep, a city
clerk on the Boston tit. Then he'd get out of Massachu-
setts, where his accent held him down at the bottom of
the heap, move out West. And then on, to bigger schools
in bigger towns. He'd groom himself to act down-to-earth
with scholars, scholarly with administrators. He'd be decisive with anxious parents, above it all among the money
men.

That evening, sitting on at the old desk after his mother
had gone home blessing him, he'd foreseen a whole life.
How one day he'd come back East, where everything important happened, to a private school, maybe one a bit
down on its luck, but with a solid tradition. He'd make it
a brain-trust school, good as any the Harvard boys in the
Square had come from, fill it with brilliant children.

And here he sat at a desk so fine, he'd never have
believed back then that such a piece of furniture could be
in *any* school. Pity his mother was too frail now to come
down and see *this* office. Connor's heart twisted with the
regret of it. She'd always been so good to him, keeping
those dumb-sod older brothers from beating on him too
badly, saving the pick of the food for her baby.

But she'd caused him pain, too. At times, he'd all but
hated her.

Those damned clothes.

Working as a Harvard biddy, picking up after the rich
college boys, cleaning their messes, straightening up their
lavish rooms, and what was worse, proud of the job. And
thinking always of him, she'd pinched stuff in those rooms.
A silk tie here, a shirt there, a pair of fine cotton drawers
with buttons to them. Only for him, never his brothers.
Of course, she'd *said* the rich boys gave her things. But
he'd always known she took them, risked her employment,
had to confess the sin of it, all for him, and his heart had
gone out to her. But those clothes, fitted to brawny, well-
fed college boys, were too big. And since she'd slipped
them into her bosom one at a time, they never matched
anything, never belonged together. And he, a scrawny

six-, eight-, twelve-year-old, having to wear a flapping shirt,
a crested tie to school. Of course the bully boys laughed.

Connor saw himself again, shrinking from the worst of
them, a ring of beefy hoods, dummies kept back in their
grades year after year, slow, stupid. He'd been terrified
over those boys, ganging up on him, punching, even kicking him. He could feel them still, yanking at his Porcellian
tie, tossing away his crimson crew cap. They hadn't belonged in a good Catholic school. They'd belonged on the
docks, in factories, behind bars, with turnkeys watching
them. Not even the nuns could have pounded sense into
their thick, ugly heads.

Watching his mother frowning over his bruises, over the
holes and rips in the handsome clothes she'd whistled away
for him so deftly, how he'd hated them.

Dumb kids, jealous of smart ones. Making trouble. They'd
make trouble for him here at this school, too. Make it
harder for him to fulfill his dream, his promise to his mother.
He'd vowed to make it up to her, her work and worry,
her abiding love. At least he'd guaranteed her comfort. If
only there were more she wanted, more to give her now.

But now, he told himself, worry about your own next
years.

Where the hell is that fireman?

Ah, Spaight was standing in the door, smiling.

Connor poured liberally, the good, amber Irish whiskey.
They drank, and Spaight exhaled with pleasure. It was
time.

"You've a family, Captain?"

"Certainly. My boys are fourteen and thirteen, good
kids. Not into all that dope, smash-and-grab, and that."

Yes, and your girls, Connor thought. This is a school
for girls.

"And my daughter's just eight. Audrey. For Audrey
Hepburn, my wife's favorite."

Eight, Connor thought. Perfect. Bache would have to
back him, understand the spot they were in. Jews always
thought of the Irish with packs of kids. He'd go along with
just one little girl, surely.

But would the inspector?

"Where is she at school?" Connor asked.

The New York question, the eastern-seaboard question.

Important, more so than college for upper-class people. School set their course for life. Their schools were their religion, stayed with them for life. They hadn't a clue about climbing out, scrabbling upward.

"She's with the sisters at Holy Name," Spaight said. "Bright little girl, mind. We're even thinking Bronx Science, Music and Art, Hunter, for high school. My boys aren't students, but Audrey has a brain in her head."

Connor looked at the man, wanting to laugh. My God, it's ordained, it's a setup.

"You have any interest in a school like this?" he asked, looking away from Spaight, concentrating on his drink, feeling his stomach knot up.

Silence. Well, he'd known the man was clever.

"You're taking them free this year, then I'd be interested," Spaight said, smiling. "Not many like my girl in this place. Catholics, to be blunt."

It was time to give Spaight a taste of something more heady than whiskey.

"What I want to do in this school," Connor said, "is to broaden things. Enlarge the experience of the children, the parents. One kind in one place isn't always good, you know. Especially in this city, where the mix is the richest in the world."

Spaight shifted in his chair, the noon light full in his eyes. "Is that right? Well, good luck to you," he said, setting down his glass.

Connor tossed off caution. He leaned forward, looking straight at the inspector.

"Come on, Captain. You know what goes on in this kind of school. See our black kids? Black faces in every class, as if a computer counted them out, so many to each group. For display. Us, now, we're different. We don't show. There's an ambassador's girl, Italian. And a few too wild for Marymount, Sacred Heart, girls like that. A good, solid neighborhood Irish girl? That would be something else for this school."

The captain laughed, a big laugh, encouraged by the confidence, the drink.

"You're thinking I've saved up my pay all these years? Or maybe I got a pile I took under the table, for looking the wrong way? No, man. Poor but honest, that's me. The sisters cost money, of course, but a tenth what this place gets, that's sure."

Connor sipped, watched the captain. Now, he decided.

"If you quoted me, I'd deny it like an Englishman," he said. "But where do you think the spooks here get the money? Sure, some are show-biz kids, UN. But not all, not *half*. You don't imagine they pay what the rest do?"

"Never thought about it," Spaight said.

And that's a lie, Connor knew. What man with a daughter, a man smart enough to work up from hook-and-ladder to shield, wouldn't have compared this school to the parochial ones, with their old-biddy nuns?

"Maybe you should," Connor said shortly. "I'm after making some changes around here. I want the dummies out. I don't want one of everything, including Zulus. I want merit. Smarts. Wherever they come from, whoever has them. That's what a good school means. Is your Audrey smart?"

Spaight stared at him, focused now.

"Straight A's, a Blessed Medal," he said.

Connor could almost *see* Spaight's eyes blur over, sense the dizzy whirl in the man's mind.

"Then she'd probably test well. Think about it, talk to your wife. You'll be back here, when, next month? Not tomorrow man, for God's sake. Take my word. I'll close off that balcony, shut the whole bloody theater till I can get it right. We don't want another patch job around here. And I'll get onto the minor violations today. But the theater, you have my promise. No one in or out."

Connor felt Spaight staring at him. Fine. Let him think it over, think of the possibilities. Connor had said nothing, not even about the nigs, that Spaight could report. Maybe to his wife. But if she didn't feel the same, Connor would be damned to eternity.

Go, inspector, he urged silently. Now. For Christ's sweet sake, don't write out an order for my theater. Go home, talk to your wife. Be a hero.

He held his hand out to Spaight, looked him in the eye. Spaight didn't move.

A heat wave came over Connor suddenly, made his palms damp, his neck prickly. He'd gone too far.

"I'm late, Captain. It's been a grand chat," he said, burning with fear now.

Spaight put down his glass, stood up.

Slowly he reached for Connor's hand, took it.

Connor felt as if he'd run off the burning grit of the sand at Revere Beach into the cool, bracing Atlantic.

"Well," Spaight said. "Next month, then. Same date, probably. You'll get a call, I'll see you're notified."

Connor smiled, feeling ocean spray, soothing waves.

"And if there's not a gate, a barbed-wire fence, so to speak, skull and crossbones on that balcony," Spaight was saying, "I'll personally tear out those wires. Get me?"

Connor hardly heard him. The man's strength had been pierced. His power deflated. A good morning's work. And a story he *could* tell Bache.

He said a curt good-bye to the captain, feeling more and more braced.

The briefcase made an armrest as the cab sped down the East Side Drive, lurching, changing lanes to make time. Wonderful fall day. Sunlight sparkling a million diamonds on the river. Sightseeing boat, last of the season, probably, gliding past. Beautiful bridge, probably built mostly by Irishmen. Thank Christ, Spaight hadn't asked his mother's maiden name. Connor couldn't for the life of him remember the family names in Limerick. He'd never bothered with that rot, anyway. The Emerald Isle had been more handicap than help till this morning.

He was meeting Bache in a restaurant, the Antica Roma. A lawyers' place, a short block from the courts, Bache had said. The driver crawled through crowded Chinatown, found the street, pulled up in front of a low building next to a small playground. Most of the kids on the swings and slides were Oriental, Connor noticed as he paid the fare. Swell kids, bright, teachable. Disciplined at home. Not like the brats at the Boston School.

The place was ordinary to look at, small, noisy. Connor was disappointed. He ate out so seldom at noon, usually stuck to the teachers' lunchroom, where they kept a special table for him. He'd hoped Bache would have him to one of the clubs, those wood-paneled places that smelled of old money, or to a man's sort of restaurant, big tables, quiet, steaks that overlapped the plates.

He told the stout man at the door that he was meeting Mr. Bache, Harvey Bache. As they walked farther in, he realized this *was* a man's restaurant. Jammed, lawyers in dark suits and scruffy shoes, overstuffed briefcases near every chair, heads together in talk, big gestures, at all the red-checked tables. The men were piling in food. Connor's mouth went wet, and he realized the smells were wonderful, sharp cheeses, roast meats, spicy salads. Bache liked good food, he remembered with enjoyment. Some of their planning together over meals had treated Connor to the best food he'd had since he'd left the East. In Santa Barbara, nobody knew food. In the whole of California, for that matter, they knew how to charge in restaurants, but not how to cook.

"Mr. Bache's assistant called. He's on his way now," the host was saying. "You come downstairs, his table, okay? Have a glass of wine, he'll be right along."

Wine, Connor worried, on top of that whiskey? Better not.

He sat facing the stairs, to see Bache before Bache saw him, and tried to relax.

Well, he'd made a big score with the fire captain. And little ones so far in the school. The teachers were a walkover. Mr. Cross, from the upper school, positively fulsome, offering his list of low-end students within twenty-four hours. He'd grasped the situation right away. Mrs. Knott, though, silliest of the lot, hadn't understood him at all. Wouldn't, either, until all the dolts were gone. And that Knowlton woman was touchy, as well. Sentimental. Not that the dolts weren't entitled to an education. But in their own schools, where the work would be easier, where they'd make friends with their own kind. And not be holding back able kids.

Luckily, he did understand teachers. Knew all their pressure points.

But Harvey Bache?

An elite school, he began, as a final run-through of his pitch. Erudite courses, Chinese, Russian, computer sciences, astronomy, philosophy, God knew what-all. And kids who could handle them. Any school can do English, history, math, French. It's expected. We'll have the unexpected. And by eliminating the idiots and the cripples, we'll produce a group who'll look great to the colleges. Lift the level in one quick move.

Bache *has* to see it.

It's the only way I can make a mark in the two years they're giving me.

Connor heard a patter of steps, a rising tide of loud talk and laughter, and then saw Harvey Bache bringing his own tumult with him, causing heads to turn as he passed the tables, leaving a word here, a joke there, a quick burst of conversation over his shoulder. A real politician, Connor saw, as if he were barreling through a crowd of voters.

"Told you how to handle that, Seymour," Bache was saying, his head turned back even while his large moist hand stretched toward Connor. "You go over that story with him, do it one more time. Tell him he's got to remember better, a lot better, remember details. If that fall of his turned out to be five yards closer to the building line, just five yards, Seymour, the whole case could change. I told you already. Get him to explore his memory. Explore it hard. Get a Polaroid of the curb, the doorway, a fireplug, anything to jog his memory. Could change everything. It'll be fine, you'll see."

By the last words he was facing Connor, smiling widely.

"Billy. Good of you to come all the way down here. I've got a dame in that courtroom driving me nuts. A bleeder, cries all the time. Make it up to you with a great lunch. Terrific food here."

Connor gathered his strength. Bache had to approve that list. Now. Today.

"Harvey, good to see you," he said. His own voice sounded high, deferential. Bache's voice had boomed. The man was pitched to boardrooms, courtrooms, auditoriums.

The heads of the other diners turned back to their food as Bache settled, shaking the table. Immediately the host was there, leaning his hand on Connor's chair.

"Emilio," Bache said heartily, turning his full attention on the man. "Special today, what?"

"Today, manicotti, just made, fresh, very nice."

Connor saw the heavy lids flicker for an instant.

"Too much," he said. "Just give us a veal piccata, plenty of extra lemon. And tell Roberto a bottle of that Soave he gave me yesterday. Cold. And salads."

He turned to Connor before the sentence ended, business accomplished. His posture was exaggeratedly good, almost military, even over a lunch table. Connor guessed that it was to make up for a lack of height. Bache was five, six inches shorter than he, but the effect of mass was always there. Broad shoulders, well-tailored suit, powerful muscles under the sleeves all combined to give an impression of drive, command. The man made Connor feel reedy, storklike. After a board meeting at school once, someone had said that Harvey Bache looked like a butcher, but a very smart butcher.

"Let's go," Bache said.

Connor bent to his briefcase. Then, feeling as if he had bowed down, he straightened up quickly. Stacking the folders, he handed them over. If Bache was going to go this quickly, he too would skip the preliminaries. Let the work speak for itself.

The wine came, was offered to Bache for tasting. He waved the bottle on without bothering, or even raising his eyes from the typed pages.

Connor watched Bache read, drumming his fingers, fidgeting, jiggling the wooden table against the wall with a knee that wouldn't keep still. Energy sizzled out of him. One of his boasts was that he hardly ever slept, never more than two or three hours a night. He was always in the midst of tremendous cases, sensational divorces Connor saw covered in the papers, one a landmark decision with some whole new ideas about alimony, child support, custody. Bache was president of the Matrimonial Bar this year, head of the board at his Park Avenue co-op, director of perhaps twenty corporations, members of all kinds of clubs and committees. He'd written a book about palimony and the new divorce laws, was the kind of lawyer they called a bomber, got huge settlements for his clients. His two daughters were in the middle school, plump, bright girls with strident voices, no manners. Bache obviously was buying gloss for them, the right kind of friends. The rest, money, clothes, dancing lessons, riding, sailing, tennis lessons, he could provide.

A little amused, a little disturbed by the man's intense concentration, Connor reassured himself that Bache always tackled one thing at a time. Obviously, he could walk out of a tense courtroom, command a lunch, absorb Connor's plans for an hour, and go back to the legal battle without an intruding thought.

Fine. Good partner for me. Until I get my long-term contract. Then, by Christ, it will all be my way.

Bache skimmed the papers quickly, a part of his attention flicking across the table to Connor for an instant now and then.

Tough face to read, Bache thought. Poker. Make a good lawyer. That suit. London? Savile Row? It's like having lunch with Mr. Chips. A character from Masterpiece Theater. But he looks right, just what I wanted. Parents like a little British rub-off. Wonder why he never married? Is he another fucking Mary? God knows, my mother would have called him *very neat*. At least if he's a fag, he won't bring along any kids, thank God. We can't handle any more freeloaders. We could even cut some. And he's hit it right: the tuition hike is the first big thing.

He watched Connor sip some water, carefully wipe his mouth. He'll be easy, he'll do the job. Likes this work, I can see it. Likes what goes with it, too. The expense account, country place, nice roomy co-op apartment. Well, what's not to like? Where else would he come to a Park Avenue apartment?

The silence seemed long to Connor, discomfiting. He cleared his throat, feeling his nerves jangle.

It was such a perfect plan. For an ideal school.

"It's all there," he said. "A full précis. You know most of it. One big worry is that damned building. Eighty or ninety thousand, just to patch. I had a fire captain in this morning. All kinds of violations. But I handled him. Still, we can't afford any real negligence."

There. Later he could slip in a word about the man's daughter.

Bache smiled without looking up from the folder in his meaty hand. "Just behind me, best negligence man in this county. Owes me a few, too. Don't you worry about negligence, Billy. We'll get to it in good time."

Connor wanted to keep him talking now, not sit silent and wait.

"There's a lot on the head teachers. They were no trouble at all. They know the difficult kids, they're with me.

That Knowlton woman was bursting to talk about more staff. Hadn't occurred to her that the best way to free up teachers is to weed out kids."

"Right," Bache said as the salads were crashed down on the table.

"House dressing, Roberto," he said, with a broad smile for the waiter.

The smile stretched the enlarged pores on his tanned face, showed his strong, yellow teeth. Bache seemed to have a year-round tan, played tennis four or five times a week. Probably hadn't played games till he'd grown rich. Connor knew plenty of tennis-lesson machos. But they didn't look as formidable as Bache.

Did the man have to do *all* the ordering? Connor would have preferred oil and vinegar. But what was the difference? He'd eat the damned tablecloth, if only the man would buy the plans in those folders.

Connor felt on edge suddenly, and put a hand to his tie, loosening it.

There was a piece of his life in those folders. A whole long summer in a muggy, dusty, empty, echoing building, while everyone else was out in the sun having a good time. The stuff was right, he knew it. But if Bache chose to nitpick, there would be more work, nights, weekends. Anxiety heated in him, took away his hunger. When the food came, his veal seemed greasy, unappetizing, floating in pale yellow sauce.

Bache lifted his fork and tore into the meat, as he tore into everything he did.

"I've pinpointed the unsuccessful kids," Connor said, no longer able to contain his own uneasiness. "The learning disabilities, dyslexics, that spastic kid, the one they think is brain-damaged. All the Educational Records Bureau low-end scorers, Harvey. They're a nonresult group. We'll never get where we want with them. I've cross-checked with the financial reports, too. Some are slow payers. One setback would blow them out of the school anyhow. And the tuition raise has to come first, that's vital. So we'll be killing two birds with this list."

"Right," Bache said. His plate was already clean, wiped shining with chunks of the delicious, chewy bread. It could have been put back on a shelf without benefit of dish-washer. The man's table manners were primitive.

"So. . . ," Connor pointed. "First, there's this list to be notified. There'll be objections, but isolated. No mother or father wants to tell the world a kid is being kicked out of school. We'll have quiet. At least until the big parents' meeting in late May, the one they tell me is a tradition. And by then I'll have hot news to distract our good parents. New advanced placement courses for next year, museum loan exhibits, hands-on computer instruction, some daz-zlers. I'm planning two tracks, matched. Journalism for the slows, poetry for the bright ones, the start of a total tracking system. Not slow and fast tracks. Good and better. I've even talked to Tiffany's, would you believe, they do a book on teen manners, come in, teach a course for the girls."

A course *you* could use, he thought, watching Bache still stuffing his mouth with bread, tearing huge chunks for those yellow teeth to grind at.

Connor poured some wine into his water glass. The stuff soothed his nerves, warmed his stomach.

Bache will say yes, he told himself. Most of this stems from him, anyway, so he's *got* to.

But Bache was busy snapping his fingers at the waiter, ordering two coffees.

"Hold up," said Connor, sitting straighter. He turned to the waiter. "Espresso for me, lemon peel."

He felt better when he saw a twitch of annoyance on Bache's face.

Just to let you know, Connor thought, I'm not your toady, even if you did get me the job.

"This list," Bache said, smile suddenly gone, all busi-ness. "I'll take it, check it out. Meanwhile, there's some-thing important I want to discuss."

Connor felt irritation stir in him.

"Actually, someone important," Harvey went on. "You've met Mrs. Irving, Alison Irving."

For Christ's sweet sake, Connor thought, stick to the point. I know all about Mrs. Irving.

Rich, he recalled, was the main thing. A family foun-dation, huge anonymous contributions that everyone seemed to know all about, still bigger gifts with names attached, the Irving Wing at the Public Library, the Irving Center at New York Hospital. The Arts Council met in her Park Avenue triplex. There were other homes, too, East Hampton, Santa Fe, Palm Beach. She had the title of secretary to the school's board of trustees. And the child's name was, wait a minute, Kilty.

"Wealthiest family we have, no question," Bache said. "Major asset. Potential, anyway. That's it. Like to see you get close to her, Billy. I've spoken often with her about a gift, something substantial, endowment, a bunch of scholarships. Softened her up. Now I'd like to see a room, a wing, with her name on it. Something visible."

Connor felt angry at the distraction. Still, he could see the possibilities. For himself.

"Invite her to lunch at school, walk her up and down, tell her what we need," Harvey said. "Work on her, Billy. You know how. It's one of the reasons I boosted you. You want to impress the board, the parents? No better way. By the time that May meeting rolls around, you'll be solid. Miss Creighton didn't see that Alison Irving means real job security. Too much of a great lady to ask for money. You ask, Billy."

I'll ask, Connor thought. And I'll get, if I can. But I came here with my own bright ideas. And you haven't given me the answer I want yet.

"Not to worry," he said. "Just up my alley. Now, about that folder. The list has been checked. Rechecked. The names are the right ones, the teachers have vetted it. It names every kid who doesn't belong, should never have been admitted. Not one name on it will ever do us credit, Harvey."

"I'll take care of it," Bache said heavily.

Connor felt suddenly hot. In his mind a match struck, flared.

Damn. He *had* taken care of the list. And with a hell of a lot of effort.

"Harvey," he said slowly, "every name is there for a reason. Documented. A score, a report, a test measure, usually all of them *together* somewhere behind it. I've seen the paperwork."

But Bache was folding the list, tamping down the creases, tucking it in his coat pocket.

The son of a bitch was going to take it away with him.

Connor felt as if an oven had opened nearby, inundating him with hot, heavy air.

"Billy," Harvey said, "let it wait a little. Most of your stuff looks great. In fact, all of it. It's great thinking. But you don't have the whole story, you couldn't, yet."

Rage was smoldering in Connor, about to ignite. Like the time he'd seen a Sierra brushfire, first a spark, a flare, suddenly a noisy wall of flames.

"Harvey," he said, hating his own light voice, prim, boyish, "I've spent my life thinking about a school like the one in these plans. It's a miracle of a school. But there can't be exceptions, or nothing will work. Everything depends on a bold move like this."

Christ, he thought. *I've* got the work, managing the teachers, the parents, stroking that Mrs. Irving. All *he* has to do is back me on what we both know is right.

Bache was scraping his chair back from the table, turning to see where the waiter was. Bastard.

"Billy," he said offhandedly, "there's a kid on this list whose grandpa owns half the office buildings in midtown. And most of SoHo. Probably good for a start at the best fund-raising drive we ever had. I don't care if the girl is the village idiot. She stays. Now, leave it to me."

Connor felt real fire, blurring his vision, heat burning his face.

"Harvey," he said, "fuck that check a minute. This is *crucial*. I want a student body second to nobody's. The brightest, most teachable minds one school ever gathered, all kinds, all colors, but smart, Harvey, *brilliant*. There's nothing you can't do with a group like that. They'll attract the money, Harvey, it'll come rolling. Let a rich idiot give way to a rich girl who's smart. There are plenty of them around. Let's do it that way."

Through the stinging in his eyes, Connor watched Bache turn to him.

"Listen, Dr. Connor," he said heavily, "let's get something straight."

Connor felt the menace blazing close to him, searing, terrifying. Bache leaned into his words, so near that Connor felt his warm breath, smelled garlic and alcohol.

"I wouldn't want to spell it out for a doctor, a doctor

of education," Bache said, almost spitting out the words. "I'm not in this because I need the work, more meetings to keep me busy, more papers to push. Not at all. I run that school for a reason, doctor. And you better understand that reason."

Connor drew back from the words, the strong smell, the animal teeth.

"There are times when a place in a good school is very, very important, doctor," Bache said. "Back there in the dark by the stairs there's a judge, man with gray hair. He's eating the special, cheapest thing on the menu, that's what he can afford in this place. And he's got a daughter, doctor. Just like everybody else, he wants the best for that daughter. If a place in the finest school in New York makes him happier about a case of mine, a case I haven't seen much happiness in, I want that place, doctor. I want it for him, whether that girl is smart, dumb, whatever. Makes no difference. Do you understand what I'm saying?"

Connor was burning, as if flames were licking at his flesh.

"You see, doctor, it won't be often, but it'll always be important," Bache was going on. "I'm a matrimonial lawyer. I've seen how rotten people can be, so I've learned not to let anyone snow me if I can help it. Hell, I get new clients to hand over their papers, jewelry, supposedly to keep safe from their spouses, but actually so I've got a hold on them, in case they decide to chintz my fees. I live on bargains, trade-offs, compromises. Right now I'm going back to a courtroom to fight a woman who'll give up anything, money, Park Avenue apartment, East Hampton house, an art collection, anything, if she can get custody of her kids. Suppose I could offer her attorney something big, promise that woman her girls will go to the best school around, the Boston School, provided their father gets them. Don't you think that could be a big help to me, doctor?"

Connor kept terribly still, waiting for the fire to let up. He felt turned to ash, burned out, used up.

Bache reached for the check and the pencil stub on top of it, scrawled his name.

"Don't let it worry you, Billy," he said, a new man, a new voice, friendly, soothing. He pushed back his chair, rose to his feet. "You're doing just fine. Your dream is just swell. It'll come, little by little. We want some protection, that's all. I can bring a ton of pressure in that school if things get rough. You've got two years to make a mark, a nice, pleasant two years. You couldn't do worse than that old woman, whatever you do. Relax. I've handled divorces for half the parents there, they trust me. Some of those fathers are lawyers. Never know when they might need me, want me on a file for them. There's a broad over there now, a mother, who's running for a judgeship, needs my help. Don't let any of it worry you. Just keep managing the school, handling the firemen, fixing things up. You want the kids smart, make them smart. Get rid of anybody you want. Provided you check with me before you do it."

Bache turned, kicked aside the napkin that had fallen from his lap when he rose, moved rapidly toward the stairway.

Connor stood at the table absolutely still, unbearable heat all around him. For a horrifying instant he felt as if he were bound to a stake, flames rising around him. He could almost smell the bitter smoke. Mom had told him again and again of the blessed martyrs who burned for their belief, their insistence on the true faith.

By the time he could force himself to move, Bache was out of sight at the top of the stairs.

## THE NEW YORK TIMES
## CLASSIFIED ADVERTISING

### Household Help Wanted

NURSEMAID-HOUSEKEEPER for 7-year-old girl, working mother, East Side, 4-room apt. Excellent salary, benefits, weekdays only. Must be responsible, warm companion for child, all else secondary. Recent references. Write Box 3097, N.Y. TIMES.

MARGARET ROSE WALKED as fast as she could along the crowded street. She felt as if she were hurrying in powder sand, sinking, wearing herself out, getting almost nowhere.

Dear God, she thought, everything goes against me.

The pavement was disgusting. Dangerously cracked concrete, dog mess, fruit peelings, sour-smelling garbage bags oozing slime. And people forever in her way, standing about, leaning against parked cars. Their faces were dark, but not true black like her own.

A man in a filthy shirt emptied a Bacardi rum bottle and tossed it past her head into the gutter. It shattered, sending a piece of glass to sting her ankle.

Women with fleshy arms and big breasts leaned from windows, sprawled on the stoops. They screamed like beach birds at the children darting back and forth through the traffic.

Scum, Margaret Rose thought. Filthy Spanish. The lowest Jamaicans are better.

Rounding a corner, she almost crashed into an orange crate and rickety chairs where two old men were playing backgammon. She had to pull up, lose important time. She wanted to swing at them both, scatter them out of her way.

Every day my girls walk here alone on this terrible street while I am with Livvie downtown where it is clean and she would be safe even without me. It is wrong. Wrong. In a proper world it would not be allowed.

Margaret Rose wanted to weep.

Her face, she realized, was hot and wet now, her blouse pasted to her back. With every step, her handbag banged at her thin hip painfully. Now noises were startling her—the sudden blare of a radio, a car horn, an ambulance shrieking past. And the smells were sickening—rotting fruit, a backed-up sewer, marijuana.

I knew this street was bad. But inside the school? Should they not be safe inside their own school?

She ached to rest, catch her breath, fix the stocking spiraling around her ankle.

Not now, not yet.

At last, down the block, she could see the squat five-story building.

Margaret Rose had hated the school, all caged windows and chipped bricks, from the day she had brought the girls to register. Then it had seemed like a prison. Today she suddenly imagined a hospital crammed with children, crying, blood seeping through their bandages.

Far off as she was, she could hear shrieks and screams from the playground. Were more children being hurt?

Dear God, do this one thing for me? Let my Samantha be all right. Let her be safe. Please.

When the voice had come over the telephone, Margaret Rose had been too shocked to ask how, why, what had happened. She had flown. Left Mrs. Fuller's kitchen floor half-waxed. Forgot about having to fetch Livvie. Grabbed her purse, raced to the subway.

The questions had come while she stood on the train, her thin body trembling, the strap biting into her fingers. A fight, the voice had said. An older boy. Out in the playground.

Hurt, but how badly? Why was such roughness allowed? Where were the teachers? How could I be so stupid, to bring Samantha and Lucy to this dreadful, cruel city?

There at last, the wide wooden center door. Shut, of course, with chains across it. On each side were smaller doors, carved letters over their arches, one entrance for boys, the other for girls. But the letters were from long ago. Now boys and girls mixed, to fight and hit each other in their play time.

In the concrete yard the children swarmed, playing on

the cracked concrete, running crazily over broken glass, chasing each other. The noise they made hurt her ears.

Hurrying past a huddle of boys, Margaret Rose caught the glint of metal. A knife? Shocked, she looked back. A handful of wristwatches. Stolen, of course. Traded in this playground, the way decent children trade cards.

Little beasts. And some not so little.

The dark foyer smelled of urine and cheap pine disinfectant. Dirt-colored walls were overlaid with small handprints, the lumpy linoleum floor curled at every corner. A bell clanged, metal hammering on metal. She wanted to cover her ears. With a rush, children began shoving past her, jostling, shouting.

Ready to slap the nearest ones, Margaret Rose looked frantically around for the principal's office.

There. A half-open door with a makeshift cardboard sign. She pushed toward it through the crowd and almost stumbled into the room.

She saw a colored woman wearing white, sitting. Nurse. And on her lap, limp, Samantha.

Margaret Rose felt as if the ceiling had crashed on top of her. Her eyes blurred with tears. Blind, breathless, she moved forward and reached out.

Dear God, how wonderful to hold Samantha. She felt the skinny little body shaking with sobs. But the child was warm, alive.

Cradling Samantha, Margaret Rose rocked back and forth, feeling tremendous relief.

A picture came into her head of Samantha at home with her doll. Always so gentle. Lucy bossed her doll, scolded it, spanked the thing so often its bottom had cracked. Samantha, never. She held her blond baby as tenderly as Margaret Rose held her now.

But Samantha is still a baby, Margaret Rose thought in a great rush of love for her child. She remembered how when she came up the stairs at night, Lucy would run to tell her what had happened, see what she had brought for supper. But Samantha would always press her toward the kitchen chair, climb into her lap.

And when I close my eyes and rock her, I am at my own home again, young, smelling cool mountain air, rocking with my first baby pulling at my breast.

Margaret Rose abruptly remembered where she was, what she had to do.

Stop, baby, poppet, stop crying. I am here. It is all right now. All right. Still rocking, she freed a hand to stroke the soft head. Gradually Samantha grew quiet.

Margaret Rose got her breath and blinked away her tears. She held the child a little away, looked her over carefully. No blood, bandages, broken limbs. And yet they wouldn't summon her rushing to school just because Samantha was crying.

She lifted her head and looked past Samantha at black shoes and a dark skirt.

A tall woman. White. The principal?

Margaret Rose put the back of her hand to her wet forehead and looked around the room. She saw paint peeling from the drab walls, ragged scratches on the dark finish of the desk. Light from the barred window cast a pattern of stripes across the floor.

But that was all. No bad boy. No one here to blame, scold, slap. Only the principal and that colored nurse standing by the window, wearing a soiled white tunic, pants, sandals.

And smiling. Silly woman. What was there to smile about?

She looked back at the white lady. Her hands were clutching each other. She, at least, was not grinning like a fool.

"Mrs. Trevor? We spoke on the telephone. I'm the principal. Leona Marks. This is Mrs. Howard, the school nurse."

Is this woman crazy, then? Does she think this is a tea party?

"Nobody saw exactly what happened. The child kept saying a boy pushed her down. That's all she would say, over and over. I almost never call a mother. But the poor thing was just beside herself. Mrs. Howard tried hard, but she couldn't stop the crying."

Mrs. Howard plainly could not stop a nose from running. Or set a dress to rights. Fine school nurse.

"Nothing to fret about, honey. Samantha's just shook up, that's all. Wanted her mom. We thought you better come, get her on home for today."

The nurse's voice was as fake sugar as her smile. Sweet talk, these American blacks called it.

No. This could not be allowed. Margaret Rose loosened her hold on Samantha and got to her feet. They must understand whom they were dealing with.

She lifted her chin, determined to speak out as if she were back in sixth standard, on the platform, declaiming to the whole form.

"You said a boy hurt her. You have found him, then? Punished him?"

"You better believe we're looking," the nurse said. "See, they've got cops in the high schools now. So troublemakers have started coming where the little kids are. Don't you worry. We'll handle it. Just take Samantha on home."

Margaret Rose looked sharply at the woman. Anger flooded her mouth like strong rum, burning her tongue, trickling fire down her throat.

These bitches. They didn't call because Samantha needed me. *They* needed me. To take away a child who was becoming a nuisance.

Anger made her feel reckless, wanting to burst out.

You dare tell me not to worry? When you scare the heart out of me, make me run all the way up here? Make me leave my work?

Fools. She would show them. Margaret Rose Trevor was no spic, no welfare good-for-nothing sprawled all day watching the television. She was cut from a different cloth. She would not let these fools be till they found that boy. Brought him in. Till she could slap him silly, smash her handbag on his head. She would make sure he never touched Samantha again, or any baby girl.

Margaret Rose reached in her handbag for a clean handkerchief and wiped Samantha's nose.

Then she took stock. Samantha's dress was ripped from hem to waist, an ugly tear that left a strip of skirt hanging, showing the white petticoat underneath. There was grit all down her back. It prickled against Margaret Rose's palms.

She ran her hands up the little legs, down the silky arms. No cuts or bruises, small thanks to these fools. She touched Samantha's head, smoothing the rows of narrow braiding, straightening the tiny golden earrings.

A baby. Only a beast would hurt her.

"Samantha," she said, crisply. "You are safe. Now, you must tell me what happened, which boy hurt you."

Samantha closed her eyes, crinkled her face.

"Samantha. Can you show him to me? You know his name?" She put her hand to the child's chin, lifted it. "Say it in my ear. Whisper."

Samantha made a little tunnel with her hands, leaned close. Margaret Rose could feel warm breath blow at her ear. Words came, muffled, soft. Not her usual clear chirping.

Big boy. Pushed me down. Pulled my dress up.

"Yes," Margaret Rose said patiently. "That is terrible. But you must tell me his name."

Samantha's head was going down. She was perfectly still. Margaret Rose shook her just a little. The boy must be found, no matter how long it took. She could wait.

Then Margaret Rose remembered, with a terrible pang in her stomach. She could not wait. Not another minute.

Livvie. Margaret Rose must be at the Boston School by three. It was terribly important. Livvie would probably be good, wait patiently. But she might grow restless and slip out when no one was watching. Bad enough if the child walked home alone, for the doorman to see and report to Mrs. Fuller. But if she wandered about the streets, lost? If she never came home?

Margaret Rose felt herself ripping in two.

If I go now, she thought, who will find that devil and punish him? No, it isn't right to let him go. Livvie must wait.

Samantha was pulling at her dress. Whispering. Something about her drawers. Had the child wet herself? Was that why she was fussing so? Ashamed? Margaret Rose reached under the filthy petticoat, the way years before she'd felt for a wet diaper. Her fingertips touched a break in the soft skin, a long scratch against the satin of Samantha's thigh.

She *was* hurt.

Down there.

Startled, Margaret Rose put both hands under the petticoat.

The child's drawers were gone.

Margaret Rose felt as if someone had boxed her ears. She almost felt the thud of the blow, the ringing in her head as the pain began.

She tried to keep her voice from shaking, took Samantha's face in both hands. "Look at me," she said. "Where are your drawers? What happened to them?"

Samantha's eyes filled with tears, but she said nothing.

Margaret Rose suddenly wanted to slap the child. How could the boy be punished if Samantha was silent as a baby?

"Do you hear me? Did someone take them? Tell me this minute," she commanded.

Silence. But perhaps the child had no words for what had happened. If the boy had torn off her drawers, what else had he done?

Head spinning, Margaret Rose closed her eyes.

If only she could be gone from this room, this city, somehow be back in her mother's house, with her auntie to make a poultice, her big brothers to hunt for the boy.

Margaret Rose made herself open her eyes, look at the principal.

"The child is hurt. A doctor. She must get to a doctor. The boy took her drawers. She is wearing nothing. Who knows what else he did?"

The principal moved back. Her mouth opened a little. Red came up on her neck, washed over her pale face.

"Oh, no," she said, her hand up, palm out. "You're imagining things."

Margaret Rose felt her hand tighten into a fist. She heard her voice grow strong. "How do you know? You do not watch. There could be murder out there. You would see nothing. She was attacked in your yard, this baby. Pushed down, her clothes pulled off. How dare you say I imagine?"

The nurse took her arm. "Cool it, honey," she said. "Don't get crazy. Think of your little girl."

Margaret Rose turned to stare at the brown face. It seemed to float in a watery haze.

"I *am* thinking of her. I am the only one who does. You must find that boy. Question him. Take him to the police."

The nurse pressed her shoulder, urging her toward the door. "Okay," she said. "Let me clean the kid up, take a good look at her."

The principal, her hands together again, was nodding

eagerly. "Yes, do. Of course, if there's the slightest question of real harm, we'll certainly take action."

The noise in the schoolyard seemed to mix with the noise buzzing in Margaret Rose's head. She heard voices shouting out a skipping rhyme, the slap of a jump rope against the concrete.

> Johnny over the ocean
> Johnny over the sea
> Johnny took a milk bottle
> Put the blame on me.
> I told Ma
> Ma told Pa
> Johnny got a licking
> Ha ha ha.

Margaret Rose had skipped over thirty-five years ago to that same rhyme and could still almost hear her friends in their school middies laughing as they waited their turns, smell the warm grass on the village green in Mandeville, see the old church steeple bob up and down as she jumped.

The floor seemed to be tipping up, as if someone were lifting one end.

The nurse's hand felt heavy on her shoulder.

"You all come on," she was saying. "You look a little rocky."

Margaret Rose tried to move, but her legs had turned to Jell-O. She turned her head to the principal.

"Please. If that boy has hurt her like a man, you must find him. You cannot leave him to do it again."

The white woman was walking toward the door. Samantha and the nurse were already out in the hall.

"Do go along with Mrs. Howard," the principal said. "We'll handle everything. Take Samantha home. If she's still upset tomorrow, we'll have her see our psychologist. But we don't want to put ideas in her head. I'm sure she'll be fine."

The principal had reached the door. Above it was a clock.

Twenty minutes past three.

Livvie.

Margaret Rose could almost see the clock on the receptionist's desk at the Boston School. A silly woman, that receptionist. Angry at latecomers. She could not go home until all the small children were picked up. She wouldn't dare scold the mothers, so she enjoyed being cross with nurses and maids. She might even complain to Mrs. Fuller.

Margaret Rose felt as if the clock were tilting from the wall, crashing down on her.

The whole world was against her. There was no time to do right. She had to go. Now. She must take Samantha with her. Find a taxi, if any ever came up here. Go downtown. Fetch Livvie, put her in the taxi too. Go to Mrs. Fuller's. And then bathe, soothe, examine Samantha correctly.

Should she try to reach Mrs. Fuller? She'd help, Margaret Rose was certain of it.

She remembered the first days of her job, when Samantha was just five. So many new things to deal with, and the child screaming two whole nights with pain in her ear. The clinic had given her antibiotics, drops. Nothing helped. The third day, Margaret Rose had telephoned to say she couldn't come to work. And Mrs. Fuller had come swooping uptown in a taxi, flown up all the flights of stairs, kissed Samantha, peeked into her ear. She'd called her own doctor and coaxed the child to open her mouth wide, finding just what he'd said to look for, what those clinic doctors had missed—a huge abscess in a back tooth. What was more, she'd whisked them straight to her own dentist and announced an emergency. He'd put the child peacefully to sleep with gas and pulled out the tooth. Samantha had forgotten it all in a day. Margaret Rose hadn't forgotten. She'd love Mrs. Fuller all her days.

She drew a deep breath. "Hear me. Someone must see my Lucy home. A teacher, you, even. She is not to walk alone on that street."

"Oh, yes," the white woman said. "Of course. Lucy. Lucy Trevor. Which class? Four B, isn't it? I'll make sure someone walks her home today."

She looked as if she would gladly hire a big black car to take Lucy home if only Margaret Rose would get out.

I know, Margaret Rose silently raged at her, you think you have seen the last of me.

"Count yourself lucky," she said. "I must go or lose my

job. Otherwise you would not see my back so fast. But if something is wrong, I will be back here. I am not a fool. Do not think to be rid of me so easily."

Think about that, you bleached bitch.

Margaret Rose collected Samantha, took her hand firmly, and hurried to the street. For a wonder, there was a passing taxi. The driver had to unlock the doors before she could push Samantha in. Taxi men hated these neighborhoods. They were afraid. With reason.

The cab swooped east, sped downtown. Samantha's eyes had opened wide when her mother stopped the taxi. She seldom rode in an automobile, knelt on the seat to see out the window. Margaret Rose put a stop to that. But she was relieved that Samantha seemed herself again.

Dear God, if only I didn't have to do every single thing, clean two houses, cook for two families, punish evil boys, make sure about Samantha, get to Livvie on time. No one can do all that. God, I *need* my William. And I have let him go far away, clear across the ocean.

She had been so sure she could manage by herself. Just three years.

Now she knew it was impossible. And there was another year still to get through.

She thought of William standing beside her at home in Jamaica, dependable, strong, skillful. He could fix any car in Kingston, make the oldest wreck run again. He'd brought home more money than they needed to spend. She'd been so proud. For years, they'd been respectable, well-off. And then, gradually, there was less and less work. Hundreds of boys coming out of basic school with technical training were willing to work for next to nothing. And then, as if that wasn't bad enough, the bad politics kept the tourists away.

After the worst, the tourists came again, but not as many as before. And they had learned to fly straight in to Mo' Bay, staying behind gates in the beach resorts, Montego, Runaway, Negril, Ocho Rios. By the time Samantha was born, William was always out of work, always home. But never idle. He would rock the baby, sing to the rest, stay up with them when they were sick. The children loved William's meat patties better than her own. And he was

such good company. Even when she felt cross and overworked, William could make her laugh.

Finally he got a job carrying suitcases at the Inter-Con-
tinental. Margaret Rose worried for him, bowing his head,
holding his hand for tips, while everyone they knew talked
freedom, blacks as good as anyone, drive out the whites.
When they walked out together, William would stop to
stare at a handsome car, and Margaret Rose would feel
sick.

And then the letter from Glasgow, from William's brother.
Ten years he had been there, working in a garage next
door to Radio Clyde, saving every pound and penny. Now
the owner was retiring, and the brother was putting all his
money down on the place, paying off the rest month by
month. He had the radio men's trade, brisk, steady. And
he offered William mechanic's work and a bed in his own
house. Not much, for an experienced man. And no room
for Margaret Rose, the children. They would have to wait
until William could put by money too, and then send for
them.

Margaret Rose remembered the smile on William's face,
the light in his eyes. She told herself that plenty of Ja-
maican women waited for husbands to make places for
themselves in England, America, Canada. She kissed William and said yes, go, she would wait. But how? Move
back with her mother in Mandeville, try for part-time at
one of the guesthouses, the big hotel? There were ten girls
for every job in Manchester parish, the pay a pittance.

She asked around the city. And one hot, sticky day, she
climbed the stairs to a tiny office on King Street where a
fat woman was in charge of arranging overseas sponsors
for maids. Margaret Rose had heard the woman could get
her to England, but she said not. However, there was
plenty of work in the States. Especially New York. That
was where more ladies went to work in offices and needed
nannies. Island women were in demand. Hadn't Trujillo,
when he'd run the Dominican Republic, sent maids to his
American mistresses, keeping their families hostage for
their good service? Margaret Rose, mature, well-spoken,
could command high wages. And she would be paid in
cash, keep every penny from the tax collectors.

She told William. She would take the girls to New York,

and save money. Soon they could all be together in Glasgow.

Margaret Rose read through a sheaf of letters and chose the Fullers. One child, mother away all day, small apartment. And the father an actor, no doubt famous. He would make plenty of money, never forget to pay her or question what she spent for the house, for food.

Margaret Rose rushed through the journey, flew with the excited little girls to Kennedy Airport. She approved of Livvie the moment she saw her, fair and dainty as a proper English child.

The pay was a fortune, three hundred dollars for Monday to Friday. She could get her girls to school, do her own cleaning in the small uptown flat Mrs. Fuller had somehow found for her, reach work by eleven. Then she would shop, straighten, fetch Livvie at three, take her playing in the park, bathe and feed her, stay till Mrs. Fuller came from her office. Margaret Rose had been pleased she'd planned so well.

She gave good measure, ran the house right, trained Livvie properly: please, thank you, curtsy, look people in the eye. And comforted the child when Mr. Fuller packed and left home.

She had expected to *work*, be weary at night, doing everything for two families.

She had expected to be lonely, to miss William. But to be afraid, to watch always for danger—that she had not expected. And danger was everywhere.

Her own street was as ugly as the worst of the Kingston slums, boys with knives, girls just as bad; dope sellers, using children to distribute their snorts, their ganja; men sleeping on gratings for the warmth from basements below; old women wrapped in rags, carrying all their belongings in torn paper shopping bags. When Mrs. Fuller paid her, Margaret Rose put half the money deep inside her brassiere and half in the heel of her shoe. Still she feared to have it grabbed away.

Even inside her own building she never felt safe, with Puerto Ricans, Cubans, ignorant blacks from Haiti for neighbors. Every night there were fights, screams, shouts, even gunshots. Margaret Rose had spent good money for two big locks on the door, nails for the windows. Still, the

thought of someone breaking in at night nagged at her.
She kept the big frying pan right at the side of the bed.

And now she had to fear danger in the school too.

The children knew her rules and obeyed them. Never,
never go out alone. Walk together, hand in hand. Bar the
door and turn all the locks. Let nobody in, even a neighbor.
Be careful of the stove, windows, heater, television wires.

But they were little girls. Who would ever think to warn
them about rape?

Margaret Rose saw herself reflected in the taxi's glass
divider. It was there, she knew, to block off criminals who
hit drivers from behind, stole their money, shot them. In
the smudged glass her face glistened, her hair frizzled out
of its pins, gray coming in it. She looked tired, old. Used
up.

Another year? How could she manage another day?

She closed her eyes. Way back in time, in Port Royal
harbor, there had been a terrible earthquake. The whole
city had crumbled and slid under the sea. People said that
sometimes, from deep down in the water, the clang of the
church bells could be heard. Now, forced to be idle for a
little while, Margaret Rose felt a pain she'd buried deep
inside her, something she'd feared to stir because it hurt
so much.

Willie.

Her oldest. Seventeen. Not in New York, not in England. At home still, with her mother. She had not seen
him for two years. Photos came, showing a tall, reedy
young man, not the grinning, skinny boy in a khaki school
uniform she remembered. If Willie were here, he would
go in that schoolyard and avenge his sister. But then, that
was why she had left him at home. She somehow had
known she could never watch over a grown boy in New
York.

Hurry, William, she thought. I need you. I am afraid.
For our girls. For myself. If something happens to me,
what will become of our children? And I am so lonely. I
wake in the morning with my hand between my legs, against
all decency. If you do not write for me soon, I will sicken
and die.

The taxi stopped in front of Livvie's school, blocked by
a line of black cars with chauffeurs waiting to pick up

children, and a large motorcycle, with a father waiting, plastic helmet on his head, a smaller one in his hand, to drive his daughter home. A movie star, Margaret Rose had heard someone say. Well, she knew about actors now, from watching Mr. Fuller before Mrs. Fuller pushed him out. He had talked a good game, but the money came home with his wife.

She paid the shocking cab fare and helped Samantha to the pavement, feeling ashamed that the child looked like a ragamuffin.

But if she worried about Samantha now, she would go mad waiting here for Livvie. Later, at Mrs. Fuller's, she would consider what to do. The child was all right for now. And all the girls in this rich school came out dressed like beggars, carrying on as they pleased. Samantha, at least, knew how to behave properly.

Afternoons, the school lobby was always like a marketplace, noisy, bustling. Today, girls in uniform burst from the elevators, raced to the doors. Some of the older ones held cigarettes ready to light the moment they got past the school windows. One wearing roller skates sailed silently by on the marble floor. Margaret Rose always longed to reprimand the naughty ones. But nobody else cared. Certainly not the silly mothers in their expensive jeans and English tweed jackets with gold bracelets and chains, gaudy stuff the English would never wear. One today was carrying a horse's saddle, probably for her daughter to take to a riding lesson. All the mothers were dressed too young for their ages, chattering, rude like their children.

The nurses weren't much, either. The Europeans wanted nothing to do with Margaret Rose. They collected their charges and scuttled out the door like so many sea crabs. The American colored girls kept off too. Not that she wanted to talk with any of *them*.

Some of the adults waiting were looking at Samantha. It made Margaret Rose uneasy.

She stooped down. "You must be very good and quiet here," she said.

Samantha clung to her skirt and stared. She seemed fascinated by all the girls chattering, running about.

"Mama," she said, softly. "Mama, come down."

Margaret Rose leaned toward her.

"Who are they?"

What could the child mean?

"Where is this?" Samantha whispered. "And why do they all wear the same dress?"

Samantha didn't understand that this was a school.

"It is Livvie's school," Margaret Rose said, feeling annoyed that the beautiful lobby was so different from what Samantha was used to. "The girls wear uniforms. If we were at home, so would you."

"Why?" said Samantha.

But the small children were coming now, shouting to their mothers and nurses, running back and forth. They were harder to round up than the older ones. Some ran back for toys and books they'd left behind; they had to be herded into the lobby.

Margaret Rose hushed Samantha and watched for Livvie.

Not her class. These children were bigger, nine or ten. They carried books, tennis rackets, hockey sticks. One little girl had a violin in a black case.

They had so much, these children. Margaret Rose once had seen the big library here, hundreds of shelves, thousands of books. She'd heard, waiting in the lobby, music from the theater, where the older girls had orchestra practice. Livvie would learn French, paint pictures. Already she had been on trips to ballets and museums. And in this school, Margaret Rose had seen more than once a proper nurse, with a starched uniform, a cap, a gold pin.

Not all the girls here were white, either. Margaret Rose had watched the rock singer's cocoa-skinned daughter going home each day in a long, shining limousine. A diplomat's child was collected by a nurse in a long African dress to the floor, a cloth on her head. But none were as neat as Lucy and Samantha. Her girls went to school starched and pretty, with tidy hair, no dirty blue jeans. And they knew how to behave.

Margaret Rose had taught Livvie manners, too. Mrs. Fuller was no help there. She acted a lot like a child herself, running and skipping in the streets, dressing up in silly costumes with Livvie, and dancing around so the lamps fell over on the floor, her bedroom a crazy junk shop, her handbag stuffed with so many pictures of Livvie, so many bits and pieces of sewing and knitting she couldn't find her keys or her wallet half the time. Why, if Mrs. Fuller had to work several nights in a row, she'd come home late at night and wake Livvie up to talk and play. And she often took Livvie to unsuitable films and theaters where street language was spoken right out.

Mrs. Fuller couldn't keep her dignity any more than a child, either. Like the tantrum she'd had about the trip to California.

A talent search, she called it. Mr. Fuller had put his foot down, said she could search for talent right in her own house. Mrs. Fuller said she could hardly put him in every commercial on the air, especially now he was smashed half the time. Margaret Rose heard the whole row, heard Mrs. Fuller shouting that it wasn't a ball, it was a job, Mr. Fuller slamming out the door in a fury. She'd closed Livvie's door and sung to her, top of her lungs, so *she* wouldn't hear too. And then, later, she'd offered to ask a neighbor to help with her own girls and stay evenings the whole week, if Mrs. Fuller wanted. But Mrs. Fuller, pale, still, had said never mind, she'd swallow this one, but it was the last time.

Then Margaret Rose had been truly shocked. She'd told Mrs. Fuller sternly that if only she could be with *her* husband, she'd give him every last thing he wanted. Mrs. Fuller smiled then, hugged her just as Livvie would have, and said that Steven Spielberg couldn't give her husband everything *he* wanted, whatever that meant. Mrs. Fuller couldn't see that someone had to be boss. In a proper family, the man bossed his wife. The mother bossed her children. Then everyone knew where they were.

Margaret Rose shifted on the bench.

Still, she thought, Mrs. Fuller would do anything for the people she loved, certainly anything at all for Livvie. She'd jump on that dangerous motorcycle parked outside to get to Livvie, if she had to. Probably she would *like* booming around on that motorcycle. But she was foolhardy. Thinking she would be able to do without a husband. Manage all alone with a child.

Margaret Rose sat up straight. Miss Knowlton, finally, with Livvie's group. The woman reminded her of the tomboy girls in her own form at school, always wanting to put an arm around her, take her hand.

Four little girls, thought Margaret Rose. With Mr. Fuller gone, I am in charge of Samantha and Lucy and Livvie and Mrs. Fuller.

Livvie's class came on the run, laughing like wild things, stamping on the marble to make a big noise. Betsy Halliday the loudest, as always, even though she was far in the back near Livvie, whose sweater was tied round her waist. Margaret Rose, in spite of everything on her mind, felt annoyed. She hated seeing a good sweater stretched out to fit a monkey.

She stood up. Livvie saw her and waved. Margaret Rose sighed. At last she could get moving.

Because she was standing, looking down into the crowd of children, Margaret Rose saw the trouble begin. Fat Betsy was making a face, sticking out her tongue, saying something Margaret Rose couldn't hear, and Livvie was turning to face her. The way Livvie's head was going down, her back stiffening, made Margaret Rose step forward, but the big room was crowded. In another moment she saw Livvie's face go red, her eyes narrow.

Pushing through the crowd, Margaret Rose watched Livvie's hand going up, back.

She swung hard, a clumsy motion, but with her shoulder in it. Her hand caught Betsy on the ear with a smack. Betsy began to howl, holding her head with her pudgy hand. Livvie pushed in at her. Margaret Rose knew she was going to hit again.

Someone shouted, "Livvie's freaking out!" A child near Betsy began to cry. Another called to Miss Montgomery, come, quick. In no time, Margaret Rose found herself in a mess of children, pushing, excited, all of them shouting. Their noise echoed from the marble walls. And then the elevator door banged open to spill more people into the crowd.

Margaret Rose reached past a squealing child to grab Livvie's hand. She squeezed hard and twisted the child around, her face stern.

Close up, Betsy's wailing rang out, louder than all the other noises.

As if things weren't embarrassing enough, the other el-

evator door opened and a tall man came into the lobby.
The headmaster, Margaret Rose realized, horrified. She
had seen him before, heard the mothers talk about him.
And to come now, just when Livvie had hit another child.

Suddenly Miss Knowlton was by her side. She was looking at the headmaster too. Margaret Rose felt her heart
flutter as she saw him turn his head sharply, then change
course and come closer.

"Trouble, Miss Knowlton?" he said, frowning.

But he wasn't looking at Miss Knowlton. His cold gaze
was moving over the group of children. They were coming
to rest on Livvie.

For a moment the room seemed terribly still.

Then Margaret Rose saw that Miss Knowlton's face was
reddening, her chin going up. She was moving forward
quickly now, as if to block Livvie from his sight.

"No, no," she was saying. "All's well."

Feeling frozen, Margaret Rose watched the headmaster
take a step back to keep his eyes on Livvie.

"Who's this?" he said.

"It's just Miss Montgomery's class, Dr. Connor," Miss
Knowlton said. "High spirits, you know."

Margaret Rose held her breath, seeing his head lift, his
eyes examine Miss Knowlton's face. Finally he nodded,
then turned and walked quickly toward the far end of the
lobby. In an instant he had disappeared.

Margaret Rose wished she could disappear too. But Livvie was rigid at her side, the other children still pushing
and fussing. Miss Knowlton was still leaning over Betsy,
Miss Montgomery looking helpless. As usual, nobody
managing anything.

Margaret Rose decided enough was enough.

She stood straight, spoke out over the children's heads.
"Miss Knowlton, Miss Montgomery. I am sorry for Livvie's hitting," she began.

Miss Knowlton raised her head, keeping her plump arm
around Betsy.

"She was wrong to fight back," Margaret Rose went on
resolutely. "Is Betsy all right now?"

Betsy was wiping her runny nose with her hand. Hideous
child.

Miss Knowlton was taking a handkerchief from her smock pocket.

"I think you should take Livvie home now," she said, voice raised over the children's noise. "We'll talk about it with her tomorrow."

Margaret Rose felt stunned. She couldn't believe what she was hearing. Tomorrow? Something should be done now. She felt grateful to Miss Knowlton for standing between that chilly man and Livvie. But still, Livvie must apologize for hitting. And Betsy for starting the fight.

"Quiet, now," she commanded the group of children around her. Nobody else was saying it.

Then she looked back at Miss Knowlton. "But we cannot go now," Margaret Rose said. "Not until Livvie says she is sorry."

The crowd shuffled as one mother moved in to take her child's hand. Then a nurse. The big room settled down as the children scattered.

Miss Knowlton stayed put. She was shaking her head.

"No, no," she said. "I'll speak to Mrs. Fuller. Please don't feel responsible. It's hard for Livvie not to get angry. We're all aware of that."

How ridiculous. Hard for anyone not to be angry when someone teases. Especially a fathead like that Betsy.

Miss Knowlton was going on. "What is your name? I'm so sorry not to remember."

"I am Mrs. Trevor," she said, chin high.

"Yes, but what does Livvie call you?"

"Margaret Rose."

Miss Knowlton blinked. "Oh. Like the English princess. I see. Well, Margaret Rose, we must think *why* Livvie hits, what makes her want to hurt another child. Saying she's sorry won't help, if it's not so."

Margaret Rose felt her chest get heavy with rage. Were all the teachers in this country crazy? Children fought. Here, they hit. In Samantha's school, they did worse. But in both, nobody was boss. Nobody punished the children to make them stop.

"Please," she began.

But Miss Knowlton was smiling politely now, and turning away.

Get home, Margaret Rose thought. Before you truly

lose your temper. She gave Livvie a push toward the door, walked back for Samantha. She, at least, had stayed on the bench like a little lady. Margaret Rose took each girl firmly by the hand.

Once out of sight of the building, she stopped, looked sternly down.

"Livvie. How could you behave so? Is that how I have taught you? Aren't you ashamed?"

Livvie looked at her shoes.

Samantha stared up at her mother, then back at Livvie.

Both children were a sight. Samantha's petticoat was showing, her dress filthy. Livvie's shoulder button was gone, her jumper hanging unevenly. Margaret Rose knew she too looked like a shopping-bag lady. Mrs. Fuller's haughty doorman was sure to say something.

She marched the children down the street. And with every step her rage grew hotter.

So much extra still to do. See to Samantha. Scrub and wax the floor she had left half-done. Even Livvie's jumper button would take time. And it must be fixed before school tomorrow. Mrs. Fuller sewed fancy things, needlepoint, embroidery, but never a button. And she too had attended Livvie's school, where girls hit and grown-ups did nothing. Where nobody knew how to apologize, mend, do anything womanly. Where nobody ever heard of a good spank on the bottom.

Livvie and Samantha were hanging on her hands, twisting around her to look at each other. Margaret Rose shook them. Children forgot their troubles. But she couldn't. She had asked for this life. No help from William. Far from her Willie.

"Mama," Samantha said, pulling at her skirt.

The child was standing still. She looked puzzled, frightened. Worse than frightened—crazed.

Margaret Rose dropped to one knee to get close. She felt the rough pavement scrape her stocking.

"What, Samantha? What is it?"

The child's face seemed to be melting into tears. "It hurts," she said. "Between my legs. When you walk so fast, it hurts."

Margaret Rose felt her insides explode. Hot red rage flowed all through her.

She slammed her fist on the concrete, hurting her hand, sending a shock up her arm.

I will call Mrs. Fuller.

Even if I interrupt her work, I will call. Last time, she asked her own doctor what to do for Samantha. Surely she'll help me, make that doctor *see* the child. After all, Samantha is as good as anyone. Yes, as good as Livvie. She deserves a true doctor, not just some lowlife nurse in dirty pants.

She swung Samantha into her arms like a baby and walked fast, for once leaving Livvie to trot breathlessly at her heels.

Dear Mrs. Fuller:

Cricket's birthday is on Saturday, the fifth, and she has expressed a wish to have the whole class at her party.

We have chartered the *World* yacht for an afternoon of fun and learning experiences. The skipper thinks we can manage the trip around Manhattan if the weather is good to us. Certainly we want Livvie to join the other girls. I will simply assume she can come unless I hear from you to the contrary.

Best,

*Alicia Miller Marden*

(Mrs. William C. Marden)

THE TELEPHONE BUZZED, startling Cornelia so her hand shook, jostling the video camera. Annoyed at being interrupted, she stopped rolling tape.

Who on earth would Stella put through to her now? She had to know Cornelia was in a crunch. Their first assignment from Procter & Gamble. Casting a spokeswoman for a new detergent with a multimillion-dollar budget. The actress who got the job would be set for years, like Mrs. Olson, like Madge the Manicurist. She could afford to do Shakespeare in the park, Beckett, feminist one-acters, for rave reviews and no money at all.

Cornelia, thrilled to have the assignment, had called every talent agency in New York, gone back over every résumé in her files, scouted the theater, even the acting schools. She'd been auditioning over a hundred possibles, coaching the best of them, for days now. Four finalists were down on tape. The last three were in the waiting room, with the Procter people due in two hours. If Cornelia found someone they loved, the news would spread, reach the trade magazines, every commercial producer in

New York and Hollywood. If she'd blown it, Procter would find another casting office, another casting director, and someone else would get rich and famous.

How could *any* phone call be more important?

She picked up the phone, shrugging an apology at the model who stood holding two pillowcases toward the camera, one filthy, the other brand-new, dazzling white.

"Stella," Cornelia said into the mouthpiece. "Out of your mind?"

"It's your husband. *Has* to talk to you right away."

Panic froze Cornelia.

Full force, the terrible time came back, Tim relaying an emergency call from a strange nurse, reaching her in a studio. Livvie, struck by a swing in the playground, rushed to the nearest doctor's office by Margaret Rose. Shaking, Cornelia had flown uptown, found Livvie with a jagged gash in her forehead, the doctor struggling to hold her for stitches, Margaret Rose hysterical, screaming. Cornelia, swooping Livvie up, had moved to the operating table, folded her arms and legs around the child, whispered that they'd count off the stitches together and rent a video movie for every one. Not till they climbed into a cab, Margaret Rose fanning herself with her handkerchief and Livvie proudly eyeing her bandage in the car mirror, had Cornelia leaned back and allowed herself to feel limp, faint.

Now she shook off the memory. There had been other calls since, with problems and questions—annoying, but not frightening. What now? Had some second-notice bill reached him by mistake? Had she given one of his friends a part he'd coveted? Or was it money again, another small loan to tide him over till he landed his next part? Such a boy, Tim, so irresponsible. And yet he insisted on acting as if he could run her life, when he couldn't even run his own. Why hadn't she seen that before she married him?

Cornelia sighed. All right, I'm sorry for him. I'll find a hundred dollars somewhere, if he needs it.

"He's holding," Stella whispered.

It's the dress, Cornelia remembered then. The one he was so furious about. Not her own. She'd bought nothing for herself since he'd gone. But she'd coveted a tiny, elegant Japanese designer dress for Livvie, mauve, like her eyes. When the round of class birthday parties had begun, Cornelia had splurged. One hundred and twenty-eight ninety-five. Last weekend, Livvie had shyly showed it to her daddy. Tim, seeing the price tag on the sleeve of the plain little dress, had shouted for Cornelia. When she'd come into the hall and seen Livvie's scared, pinched face, Cornelia had longed to push him out the front door and slam it, hard. But later, when she'd calmed down, she realized Tim was jealous. He'd remembered the surprises, silk ties, cashmere sweaters, she used to buy for him. He'd always wanted all her attention, and still did. The anger had left her then, and she'd felt sorry for him.

Only where was he? She hunched her shoulder to hold the phone to her ear and waved to the actress to relax, sit down.

Only a few years ago her heart had expanded with warm pleasure whenever Tim called. It was always up news—a lead part in the offing, a repertory invitation, once the promise of a trip to Amsterdam, the English theater there, for them both. When they'd met, Tim had called five, six times a day.

She'd loved Tim with all her romantic heart, adored his fantastic looks, his beautiful voice, his consuming presence. Nights with him were heady, exhausting her last reserves of passion, and yet, mornings, waking with his blond head in the curve of her arm, her whole body would quicken again. When other women eyed him at a party, when he commanded a stage, she'd felt overcome with her own fortune, her happiness. Poor Tim. Still waiting for the big break, still all for himself. Still amazed, resentful that she'd stopped worshiping, grown up. At a distance, she could feel sorry for him. But seeing him, hearing him on the phone, could strike sparks of rage in her faster than she'd have believed possible.

Cornelia realized, feeling edgy, that she'd better get into her own office. If she wound up furious it would be better not to have a gossipy actress in the room.

"Stella? Hang on, would you, till I get to my desk? Then come in here and keep things moving. It's so late. Just put the rest of the talent on tape, mark the takes. I'll rush it."

She straightened the camera and began rewinding the backup audio player, a precaution in case the video broke down. Sounds echoing in reverse filled the room, barnyard squawking that hurt her ears. Reaching quickly for the controls, she banged it to a stop.

"Sorry," she said to the actress, who was looking pained. "Back in a minute. Think about the demo. Maybe try something crazy, a different approach?"

"Well," the actress said. "There's lots better props than tacky pillowcases. Want one each on my boobs?"

Cornelia made herself smile, pushed open the heavy soundproof door, and raced down the hall. All three lights on her phone were blinking. She jabbed at a button.

Only Stella, saying to hold, Tim would be back in a minute.

Mr. Star, Cornelia thought. He *has* to play stupid games, *has* to make me wait. It's pathetic.

To keep from getting angry, she tried to think about something pleasant.

Stella Waldman. Thank God, one beginner who *could* manage a session alone. Cornelia remembered her coming for an interview, straight down from Bennington, frizzy hair framing her mobile face, eyes fierce with intelligence, her plump little body straining the seams of her jeans.

Hands waving, big mouth wide, Stella had said she'd loved backstage work, painting flats, hanging lights, making Xerox copies of scripts, prompting, soothing actors when they quailed. After all the actressy applicants who obviously wanted to use casting as a stepping-stone to the stage, Cornelia welcomed this mix of brains and bounce. She'd thought Stella's giggle might be fun to have around.

It had been. Stella had fitted immediately into the crazy hours and crazier people, never tried to straighten up Cornelia's desk, a jumble of files, photographs, postcards, sweaters, aspirin, cookies, sewing kits, speed pills, Kleenex, Valium, Visine, Band-Aids, nail polish, breath spray, foot powder, joints, makeup—everything an actor might possibly need. She'd just plopped her motorcycle helmet upside down on a shelf, filled it with sourballs and sugarless gum for clients, picked up the telephone, and started working. Somehow, Cornelia's files were soon in a state of perfection, alphabetized and cross-indexed in clean manila folders. Every reel in the office acquired a listing, a case, a label of its own.

Stella was born for casting. If she saw a face once, she knew it again even in different makeup and lighting or under a wig. She thought free theater tickets and screenings were manna from the skies, not onerous extra work, and she loved Cornelia for passing them along.

After a month, Cornelia realized they'd completed casting for twelve commercials, an industrial film, and the pilot of a new soap opera, and she'd gotten the owner of the agency to give Stella a raise. After a big hug, the girl had disappeared and returned with daisies for Cornelia and a glittering robot toy for Livvie, announcing that if, in ten years, she could handle the job like Cornelia, she'd die happy.

Suddenly Tim's deep, theatrical voice startled her.

"Hello? Hello? Nell?"

Imagine, *he* was acting impatient. And using that dumb nickname, as if he still had a special call on her.

"I hope this is important," she said reproachfully, trying not to feel guilty because she'd stopped listening to that call. His voice reminded her so of other commands and demands. Nell, my coat needs cleaning. Who's mixed up the Shakespeare volumes? Where's my shoe, my evening scarf?

"You can bet it's important. More important than what you're doing. I just got a call from Margaret Rose."

Cornelia felt the impact just below her heart, a hurtful pressure, as if someone had thrown a stone and hit her there, hard.

"Now, don't get excited, it's not Liv. At least, not exactly."

She hurt so she had to hunch over.

"The woman was hysterical. Kept saying Liv was terribly upset over something that happened in school. When I got her calmed down, which took a lot of effort, I might add, it turned out the real trouble was her own kid. Some boy pushed her around up in Harlem. Margaret Rose thinks she was raped."

Cornelia felt the hurt ebb away. Not Livvie. Livvie was fine. But my God, Margaret Rose's little girl?

"What she wanted, when she finally made herself clear, was for me to come right up and take over so she could get to a doctor. Had the nerve to say *you* were busy. Nell. Are you listening to me?"

"Raped," Cornelia found herself saying politely, as if she needed to prove she'd heard properly. Almost immediately, shock, fear for Margaret Rose, for the child, welled up inside her.

"I doubt it," Tim went on. "But she's all wrought up, not responsible. She took her little girl along when she went to pick up Liv. Walked in on some squabble and saw Liv hit another child. That put her over the top, so she thinks I should drop everything and get over there."

A different feeling started up in Cornelia.

She knew what was coming next.

Tim hadn't called to give her this news. No. He was not going to leave the big armchair, the television set where he was probably watching the soaps, bad-mouthing the working actors. He'd want her to go. The great Ferris Timothy Fuller, actor and director, was busy. His mind was too filled with creative thoughts for him to remember the names of Margaret Rose's girls, get straight which one needed help. Especially when Cornelia was grubbing around in a lowly casting office. So, in a moment, he would ask her to drop everything and go home. Ask, hell. He'd tell her.

"I have an audition," Tim said. "But I took the time to call you. Better get a cab, go see what's what."

Cornelia discovered she'd made a fist with her free hand. Her nails were slicing into her palm. She always forgot Tim could make her so angry, so fast. Each time he did it, the shock seemed new.

"It's an emergency," Tim said, as if it were a line from some bad play.

Cornelia felt herself growing hot. Dear God, she thought, don't I make my living on emergencies? Isn't every casting session a zoo, every production a roulette game? Don't I manage when actors oversleep? Overdose? Have temper fits? Get picked up for sexual approaches to little kids? But none of that would mean anything to Tim. She'd wanted to be a mother, and mothers were supposed to handle things like this, no matter how busy.

Tim's voice kept on, rich, stentorian. "You'll have to see when you get there. Maybe call Rosenzweig. Send her to the New York Hospital emergency room. Maybe you better plan to take the day."

Cornelia felt fury flowing out into her fingers, toes.

Bastard. You probably haven't had a part in weeks. Even a reading. You're too bloody good to do extra work. And *I* have to plan to take the day?

"Why me?" she said, trying hard to keep her voice easy, knowing perfectly well he wanted her angry, as if his ability to irritate her would prove she still loved, wanted him.

"You're not going to start that, are you?" Tim said wearily. "I told you, I've got an audition. Important. For God's sake, I haven't even time for this conversation."

"Or for your daughter, right? Well, I'm earning a living, remember? They're waiting for me to get off the phone, too. And this one's a million-dollar deadline."

"You never change, do you, Nell? You never stop competing. You'd leave Liv in the hands of some hysterical nursemaid until you're good and ready to go home."

Damn him, Cornelia thought, he's turning it back on me, making it my fault.

"Listen, Tim. I'm not your dresser. At least, not anymore."

Harvey had figured him, she thought. Typical actor, self-involved, arrogant, a God complex. She almost said so. Just in time she remembered that with Tim, just as with Livvie, *she* was the grown-up. And that she hadn't time for this, what with actresses in the waiting room, Procter men landing at La Guardia, outrunning the other passengers for the first cab on the line. She couldn't change Tim. There was no point in playing this scene.

"Don't worry, I'll handle it," she said wearily. "Good luck with your audition."

"No problem," he said. "Wait till they hear me read."

She heard him take a breath.

"Cornelia," he said then, in a quieter tone. "Sorry if I came on too strong. But I'm concerned, I don't want my daughter upset, hearing things she can't understand from some ignorant black woman. You should be concerned too."

It was as if he'd put a cold compress on her forehead. He had a point. Margaret Rose wasn't ignorant, far from it. But she could be in a terrible state. And she *could* upset Livvie.

What was more, he was saying he *did* care about Livvie.

Relaxing her grip on the receiver, she decided to say she'd call home right away, get there as soon as she could.

"What's happening to you?" she heard, then, from the phone. "When did you turn into such a rotten mother?"

Pain hit her, jagged and sharp, like another stone flung straight at her heart.

She banged the phone down, shaking.

A good mother, she thought. What does he know? He lets Livvie watch him shave and thinks he's spending time with her. Takes her to Sardi's and doesn't notice when she falls asleep in the booth while he's running on and on. When she was little he bitched about the noise she made, the mess she got his precious things into. Anyway, does *he* get up mornings to read with her? Brush her hair, play with her toys, dance with her? Listen carefully to every word she says, take her in bed and hug her?

A check once a month, that's all. That is, when there's no actors' strike, no lost part, no brilliant, imaginative excuse.

She leaned back, ran her hands through her hair.

Imagine, once she'd admired him so, been proud of his charm, courtliness, good looks, yes, and grown hot just at the sound of his beautiful voice, the lightest touch of his fingers. If she'd stayed on the fringes of the theater, buried herself in him, he might have mesmerized her forever.

But she'd wanted work of her own, even if Tim despised the money part of the theater. She'd longed for a child, in spite of his lack of interest in any life but his own. While he'd been in good parts, making a name, he'd tolerated a baby, a busy wife. But when he'd started to flop, when the telephone grew silent, he'd lashed out at both of them.

And then, finally, in desperation, Cornelia had grown up.

Poor Tim. Marrying an ingenue. Who'd started, she could see now, by acting a part. Who'd crossed him up by changing because she'd had to change for Livvie and refused to act that part forever.

Cornelia jabbed at the telephone buttons and got Margaret Rose on one ring.

"Margaret Rose? Are you okay? You called Tim?"

"Mrs. Fuller, I thought a father should take charge." The words came quickly. "Livvie had a fight at school, only imagine. With Miss Knowlton there, angry. And I was distraught already, you see, because of my Samantha. She was truly *hurt* today, I had to fetch her from school, bring her here. I thought if Mr. Fuller called the doctor, he would come faster than for me. See to Livvie. And perhaps Samantha as well."

"What's happened to Samantha, Margaret Rose? How'd she get hurt?" Cornelia couldn't repeat what Tim had said, rape. It was hideous even to think about.

"It is terrible, Mrs. Fuller. The teachers said only that a big boy pushed her. But his hands were on her. And what is worse, he pulled off her drawers. Now she is saying it hurts her to walk. She *must* see a doctor."

"But what *is* it?" Cornelia said, shaken. "Is she cut, bruised, what?"

"She is hurt, Mrs. Fuller," Margaret Rose said mysteriously.

"But, Margaret Rose, I'll call Dr. Rosenzweig myself, this minute. Ask him if he can come, say it's an emergency. You know how nice he is. And if he can't, you take both the kids to his office. I'll ask his nurse to call you right back. I'd give anything if I could leave this minute, but I'm stuck. Probably till six, six-thirty. Then I'll be home like a shot. Don't even think about coming in tomorrow, I'll figure out something. Just try not to be too upset, all right?"

"But, Mrs. Fuller," Margaret Rose said, almost in a whisper, "what if inside Samantha is bleeding? And my Lucy, alone in our flat, waiting?"

Jesus, Cornelia thought, bleeding. Samantha's a baby.

Margaret Rose continued. "At least Mr. Fuller could stay here while I went home."

Yes, Cornelia thought. He could. But he won't.

"Tell you what," she said. "Look in my book for the taxi number and send a cab up for Lucy. Call her, tell her to get in it and come to you. You'll all be together till I get there. And listen, what happened with Livvie? She was in a fight? Who with?"

She heard a long breath.

"That Betsy," Margaret Rose said. "The fat one."

"Is Livvie upset?"

"Not now. She is helping me calm Samantha."

Poor Margaret Rose. Cornelia could almost hear the anguish behind that no-nonsense voice. "Well, I'll call the doctor, fast. Don't worry about the money, either, I'll take care of it. And I'll be there soon."

"Thank you, Mrs. Fuller." The voice came flat, resigned. "Please, as soon as you can."

Something in her tone worried Cornelia.

Was Margaret Rose feeling slighted? Angry? Would she maybe start thinking of leaving?

Cornelia dialed Phil Rosenzweig's number, feeling panic. If she ever had to find a new nursemaid, she'd be in a real mess. Who could ever be as bright as Margaret Rose, as competent, as loving to Livvie? She was a friend. Livvie adored her.

Tough, Cornelia thought, to do everything right, with your mind on five things at once. Or anything right. Ten past four. I'll never finish the casting in time. I've screwed up both jobs. Bad mother. Rotten casting director.

Phil's nurse came through for her, promising to take care of things. Thank God, someone was on her side.

Feeling slightly less depressed, Cornelia dashed back to the studio, pushed through the heavy soundproof door.

My God, the lights were out. Stella and the production guy were standing slumped, staring at the monitor screen.

"Hey, we finished," Stella said, turning. "It's only just past four, there's even time to review. I'll write down the takes. Anyone you don't like, I'll skip by hand when the client comes. Some of them are dynamite, Cornelia. Procter will *know* we're good."

Cornelia felt another chunk of the heaviness inside her dissolve. Thank God for Stella.

They ran the reel through. It *was* good, Cornelia thought. Nobody with marbles in her mouth. Nobody too classically beautiful to play a housewife. And most important, nobody with looks clients always called "ethnic," which meant Jewish. The actresses all looked nice, sounded enthusiastic, sincere. Only a casting tape. But when the talent looked wonderful without makeup or wardrobe, with one camera and flat lighting, chances were the real shoot would be terrific.

Just before five there was a knock. Joan, who ran the front office, peered into the studio, making an exasperated face.

"They just called. The Cincinnati plane was late into La Guardia. They haven't even got their bags yet."

"Wouldn't you *know*?" Stella said. "If we hadn't finished, they'd be early. Cornelia? You look funny."

"Something in the air today," Cornelia said.

"Trouble?"

"Tim. Margaret Rose called him. He was sore, ended up telling me I'm a bad mother."

Stella's huge eyes grew even bigger.

"You? You're a fantastic mother," she said fervently. "The best. I mean, all you really care about is Livvie."

It helped. Stella always helped. Cornelia felt as if she'd been handed a cup of soothing tea. Stella knew Livvie was all Cornelia cared about. Tim knew too, really.

"Thanks," she said. "It helps to hear. Hey. I've got something in my office that's a perfect counterirritant. My bills. If you want to go write up those specs for the Chrysler job, I'll go start on them. They've been hanging over me like bats."

She turned, feeling upset about Livvie, Margaret Rose, Tim, the bills, the hurry-up-and-wait of her work. Depression seemed to slow her steps as she walked down the hall.

In her office, she wished for the hundredth time that she had a couch. Who had room? Two television screens, two video recorders, a radio, three buzzing phones with four buttons each. Papers, files, bulletin boards flapping with pictures, cans of film, big boxes of videotape, small boxes of audiotape, cardboard cases of slides, stuff everywhere, the tools of her trade. Boxes with costume props, scarves, veils, handbags, product props, towels, sheets, pots, pans, pitchers, cups and saucers. A feather boa, white, glamorous, dusty, lying on the windowsill, left over from some commercial or other. Usually Cornelia loved the jumble. Now it seemed to increase her uneasiness.

The bills would settle her, she thought. Like a mustard plaster, a new kind of pain.

She swept the desk clear, took the stack from the big briefcase, began piling them up neatly. Then she counted.

Thirty, she thought. Thirty bills hath October. Thirty envelopes with my name on them, typed, computer-printed, handwritten, rolled off an addressing machine. Mrs. Timothy Fuller. Ms. Cornelia Fuller. One says Mrs. Simothy Puller. Do I have to pay that one? Sorry, yes. It's from my corner drugstore. They know bloody well who I really am.

She found her bank statement, slipped the canceled checks into numerical order, wondering why, with all those computers, the bank couldn't at least do that. She ticked off the stubs, using the calculator to add the missing ones.

All right, she thought. The bank believes I have twenty-four hundred dollars. But it's actually more like eighteen hundred. Why do I feel guilty? As if I'm deceiving them? God, once upon a time eighteen hundred dollars would have seemed like enough for anything. Now it's zip.

Tim's check, assuming it came, would get her back up to twenty-three hundred. She had such mixed feelings about that check, needing it, hating to see his florid handwriting, his expansive signature.

At least she felt good about her own paycheck, more than a thousand dollars after taxes. She'd have over three thousand dollars.

Sounds good, Cornelia told herself. Thirty bills divided equally, a hundred apiece. Each of these people can have a hundred dollars and my compliments. Only then how do we get through the month?

She knew she was getting silly. Still, better silly than sunk.

She dug into the pile.

Rent. Thank God she had a rent-stabilized apartment. Small, sunless, cramped, but close to Livvie's school. One day maybe they'd be able to move to a big West Side place, huge rooms, fireplace, blazing sunlight.

Cornelia wrote the check, realizing that next month's rent was almost upon her.

Then she made a neat list of the cash she'd need. Cash for Margaret Rose, the supermarket, the bus, all the every-day quarters and dollar bills. It was hard to figure. One chipped tooth, one high fever, even a good sweater left at school could turn her estimates upside down.

In with the bills she found a tiny envelope that had to be a child's party invitation.

Extortion, she thought. Last month, five separate parties. The school encourages everyone to ask the whole class, so nobody feels left out.

The parties were fantastic, sailing parties, magicians, fancy restaurants, video-game arcades with piles of quarters for everyone. Cornelia knew she couldn't spend less than ten dollars on each present. Even ten was chintzy. Last month, when the fourth invitation had come, she'd had to borrow from Margaret Rose and felt ashamed of herself.

She'd squeeze by, Cornelia figured, on eight hundred. That left seventeen hundred for the bills.

And there she was, with the old problem. Which ones to pay? And which to keep waiting?

The Boston School, thank God, had a tuition payment plan. The six thousand dollars plus could be paid out monthly. That made the total larger, of course, because interest was added. Six hundred and eighty-three dollars. Cornelia found the envelope, put it aside without bothering to open it. That figure was engraved on her brain.

Funny, she thought. One thing I never thought about, when I sent Livvie to school, was money. When I was little, we didn't know which girls had it, which didn't. Nice people, they told us, never discussed money.

She wrote the checks. Phone, Con Ed, newspaper delivery, drugstore, cable TV, people who'd cut off service if she failed to pay. While she worked, she thought how much she'd learned about money since school. Putting checks in the wrong envelopes so they'd come back and provide a breather, mailing letters without stamps, writing checks incorrectly, even sending them off without a signature.

I hated doing those things, she thought. Better to be honestly late on everything, even if they do make those embarrassing phone calls, write those stuffy letters.

After the basic checks, she figured out she had eight hundred dollars left for the rest. Nowhere near enough.

That dentist's bill. She'd put off making the follow-up appointment, but soon she'd have to go.

Eight hundred dollars. Suppose she gambled it all on lottery tickets and made it into eight million? Or bought a fabulous dress and went out and vamped a millionaire?

Cornelia closed her eyes. She'd thought paying the bills would make her feel better. But every envelope was a reproach, a printed certificate of failure. How had she *ever* thought she could take care of Livvie all by herself?

Wait, she told herself. There's *one* bill you like paying, one that makes up for all the rest.

She thumbed the pile, found the big envelope from the Bank of Phillipsburg, embossed, all curlicues and flourishes, as if it came straight from the nineteenth century.

Just holding it seemed to make her see the house in the country.

Cornelia always pictured it from a little way off, at the turn in the dirt road. A square jigsaw puzzle of a stone house, crowning a hill. Looking slightly out of plumb, as if a giant hand had gently pushed against one side.

Everyone had told her to sell it. They'd started the day her grandmother's will was opened and the family learned she'd left it to Cornelia. Her brother talked endlessly about the cost of fuel oil, of replacing the ancient plumbing, of a new roof, spraying the trees, taxes. Tim carried on about the crumbling mortar in every outside wall, the pointing so urgently needed to keep out wind and rain. Pointing cost a fortune. And Tim hated the place anyway, hated New Jersey, and said the trip was too far. That was before he'd gotten hot for the Hamptons, half again as far, five times as expensive. Every time they'd needed money, he'd been after her to get rid of the place. Even her lawyer, Harvey Bache, said she couldn't possibly hold on to that house.

Cornelia had told her brother she'd think it over, and refused even to discuss it with Tim. It was hers. And Livvie's.

To Cornelia, the rough gray stones jigsawed together into a magic place that held pleasures from her past and hopes for her future. When she looked at the apple trees she almost tasted the sweet richness of her grandmother's jelly, saw the pink and white of Livvie's wedding bouquet.

In the russet barn, with its smells of a hundred years of cared-for horses and polished leather, she was both a child in the hayloft and a mother welcoming Livvie's college friends for a visit.

At the house, Livvie was always brilliant, asking questions about animals, trees, birds, knowing the quickest way to climb the apple tree, helping Cornelia cook at the stone hearth.

In the city, Cornelia never had time to dream about her future. But on the country porch, she would rock in her grandmother's chair with Livvie in her lap. In some of the dreams, a man would be with them in the house. She could never quite see his face. But she knew he was good and kind, chopping firewood, picking pears and cherries, carrying Livvie on his shoulders into the orchard. Once, after she'd been up in the attic and seen the old cradle there, she'd dreamed of Livvie rocking a baby in the parlor.

I will keep that house, Cornelia thought, if I juggle bills till I'm as old as Grandmother.

Because she'd been so stubborn, Harvey had in the end arranged a second mortgage. Amazingly, it produced money for the leaking roof, the tumbledown barn, for propping up the fruit trees and fixing fences. Cornelia thought second mortgages were wonderful, Harvey a genius.

She wrote the Phillipsburg check, trying to ignore the overdue stamp on the bill. And that the amount would have covered almost all the remaining bills. American Express, MasterCard, Bloomingdale's. Window cleaner. Exterminator.

I don't care, she thought. Ten years from now I'll still have bills, but the house will be there for us.

She hesitated over the two square envelopes from doctors, the kind she hated most, with a side that zipped off so you could tuck a check inside and reseal it. For Livvie. The remedial teacher had told her to check Livvie's eyes and ears. Cornelia had felt stupid for not thinking of it herself. And then, hopeful. Just suppose a pair of eyeglasses or a little lump of wax removed could make all the difference? Cornelia had almost wished the doctors would find some tiny ailment or other. And then felt rotten wishing it.

She dropped those envelopes in the wastebasket, then ripped open the school bill.

Last one, she thought, her spirits rising. At least I've done it. And fast. Stupid to wait so long. I could have spared myself a whole bunch of guilt.

The paper in her hand, though, wasn't a bill but a large sheet of the school's heavy, creamy stationery, folded. An announcement, she wondered, a fair, a book party, a meeting of the PTA?

She unfolded it and began reading.

> We are sorry to tell you that your daughter, Olivia, has been judged to fall short of the academic standards of this school.

There was more. But something was happening inside Cornelia's head, hurting her. A hideous electronic sound, high and whining, was piercing her eardrums and entering her brain—like a tape played in reverse, turned to top volume.

Cornelia put her hands to her ears. The crisp paper crunched sharply against her cheek.

She took her hand down and looked again at the paper.

> It will be impossible for her to continue her education with us. Before the April contract renewals we advise you to make plans for Olivia elsewhere.

The noise rose, reaching a terrifying pitch. The lights in the room seemed to flicker crazily. Now Cornelia's ears ached unbearably, and her eyes began to pool tears.

> This school maintains the highest standards of intelligence and achievement. We feel certain that your daughter will succeed in a less-demanding environment, and that a change is in her best interests. Our new policies and practices make this decision imperative and irrevocable.
>
> Dr. Billy Connor
> Headmaster

I have to get out of this room, Cornelia thought. It's dangerous here.

But she knew, really, that the menace, the screaming noise and frightening lights, came from the letter.

Her mind began to race.

Academic standards? Livvie was in second grade. What academic standards in second grade?

Impossible to continue? She's a baby. She's only just begun. She hasn't even started to read.

Cornelia felt the anguishing pain in her head swell, radiate down into her neck and shoulders.

Jesus. Did they want Livvie to leave because she was slow at reading? But they were helping her. Anyway, Livvie's last report had been fine.

Now the pain seemed like the worst migraine, blinding, pounding, filling her head with garbled sound.

She looked again at the paper.

Elsewhere? There isn't any elsewhere. Of course, there are other schools, good ones. But they won't want Livvie now, after this. And the public schools, a million kids to each teacher, and rough, some of them. Look what's happened to Samantha. Anyway, I'd be depriving Livvie of something wonderful I was given. I'd be cheating her. Irrevocable, imperative. Latin. A command from the emperor. Dr. Billy Connor is an emperor?

Suddenly the rushing pain stopped. The room turned silent, as if someone had pulled the plugs on all the out-of-control electronic devices.

She felt a sickening emptiness. Tim was right. She was a terrible mother. Somehow she'd known it the moment he'd said the words, guessed it this morning, reading with Livvie.

The letter was her fault.

There *had* been warnings, plenty of them. Remedial teachers. Eye doctors. Ear specialists. Reading practice. Those all were warnings, and she'd refused to take them seriously or acknowledge how far behind Livvie really was. They'd told her. But no, she hadn't listened.

Cornelia snapped back in time, to her geometry class, her uniform skirt heavy on her knees, the back of Molly Cummings' curly head filling her eyes. Everyone understanding the weird problem on the blackboard except Cornelia. And the girls all waiting, wriggling, drumming fingers, tapping feet, while Miss Kroner explained it again, slowly, just for her. And then, when she still didn't see, Molly turning around, hissing, "For Pete's sake, you're holding us all back." And Cornelia had gone hot with embarrassment, felt herself swelling up to a hideous giant size.

Was *that* how Livvie felt? That she was in the way, the others hating her for making them wait while the teacher explained again and again?

But Livvie was too small for such misery.

Cornelia's hand moved to the telephone. She'd call Miss Montgomery. No, Nanny Knowlton.

Nanny remembers me from school, even though I was younger, Cornelia thought. In those days nobody would write a letter like this. It wouldn't have been possible. If they had wanted someone to leave, they'd have handled it gently, helped make other plans, nursed the child over the break. I can talk to Nanny. Say it's not Livvie's fault, it's mine, and that we'll practice harder, really work at it so Livvie won't hold up the others anymore.

She was just touching the phone when it buzzed, sending a tiny shock into her hand.

"Cornelia. Were you sleeping?"

Stella? Why was Stella on the line?

She came to, remembered. The office. The casting session.

"Are you all right? Cornelia. They're here."

The Procter people. They'll have to wait. I *must* call the school.

"Are you listening? They're in the screening room. I've given them all a drink, left the bottle there. But you better come, they're waiting. Cornelia? Is something wrong with this phone?"

Cornelia looked at her watch. Quarter to six. Nobody would be at school now. The windows would be shut, blinds down, doors closed, locked, to her, to Livvie.

"I'll be right along," she said.

Carefully, slowly, her ears still echoing with strange sounds, Cornelia got to her feet, started for the screening room.

Men in white shirts, polyester suits, laughing, talking,

glasses in their hands. Two stood when she came in; another, older, sprawling across two chairs with his feet up, didn't. Tape rolling. Stella smiling at the sprawler, the boss, the important one. Cornelia had known his name, long ago. Now she couldn't recall it.

"Here she is," Stella said brightly as Cornelia came in, turning, sending her a warning look. "Now, tell her yourself."

Trouble?

Cornelia felt removed, uninterested, as if it had nothing to do with her, as if she were viewing them all from behind the glass of the engineer's booth.

"Congratulations," the man said, extending his hand.

Not trouble, Cornelia realized, wondering why he sounded so far away, why when his hand touched hers she felt no warmth, no pressure.

"Some job," she could hear him saying as from a distance. "Really *thoughtful* casting. There has to be a winner on that tape. If headquarters isn't happy, I'll be mighty surprised."

Cornelia heard the words, absorbing them. She even understood that they would have delighted her only an hour earlier.

Now they seemed to bounce off her as if somehow she'd turned to stone.

Biographical Directory
of the American Psychiatric Association:

**NILSSEN, KURT KNUD** b Odense, Denmark, Feb 19,
39. *Educ:* Columbia Col, BA 60; Cornell Univ, MD 64.
*Int:* Michael Reese Hosp, Chicago, 64–65. *Psychiat Res:*
Arizona State Univ Hosp, 65–67. *PG Training:* PsAn
med, PsAn Clin, Columbia Univ, 67–72. *Past Prof Exp:*
Ass Att, NY Hos, Clin Assoc Prof, Cornell Univ, member Acad Med, AGA, Am Psychiat Ass. Private practice NYC.

THE TELEPHONE RANG. Dane was across his consulting
room in two strides.

"Dr. Nilssen," he said, feeling as if someone had finally
handed him a tall drink after a long, burning thirst.

"Hold for Dr. Rosenzweig, please," said a woman's
voice.

Dane's mouth went dry again. What a time for Phil to
tie up his line.

Holding the receiver, he stretched both arms toward the
ceiling. Straining, he could just touch it. Usually the pull
relaxed him, eased the tension in his neck and shoulders.
Tonight it was nowhere near enough. He felt like punching
right through the plaster.

"Dane? Dane?" Phil Rosenzweig's rasping voice buzzed
from the phone in his hand.

Where the hell was the Arizona call? Was everyone in
the Indian Health Service out basket-weaving?

"Phil," he said. "Working late?"

"I always work late. Pediatricians don't keep nice regular hours like shrinks."

We get a few midnight calls too, Dane thought. Suicide
threats. Nightmares. DT's.

"Listen," Phil said urgently, as if Dane might somehow
hang up. "Business. Someone I want you to see. Lady
who's a special favorite of mine. She needs bolstering up."

Dane smiled in spite of his irritation. Bolstering up. As if he were a gardening stake to prop up a drooping plant.

"Phil," he said evenly, glad he was trained to keep his feelings out of his voice. "One hundred and thirty-five thousand Navajos need bolstering up. I'm waiting now for a call from out there."

"So what's keeping them? They have enough medicine men already? Don't need you?"

"Maybe they have better things to worry about than a new medical director. Like forty-percent unemployment among their patients. Federal cutbacks. Forgetting their language. People out to grab their land, for everything that's on and in it. Hey, the antique dealers are even looting their ancestral burying places."

"How are you supposed to help? Isn't the director usually an internist? Why all of a sudden do they want a sophisticated psychiatrist?"

Dane smiled. "Maybe because you medical men don't trust each other. You all get together against a shrink."

"Sounds risky," Phil said. "Plus it's a long way from a loaf of New York rye. And I have a beautiful squaw for you right here."

Dane wanted to open his hand, drop the phone on the floor.

"Phil, I can't take on anyone new. I'm practically gone."

"You're here now, aren't you? Dane, this girl needs help."

Christ, Dane thought. All Phil's Upper East Side mothers need help, desperately, immediately.

Still. Phil. No better friend. The only time he'd left Grete's hospital bed that endless day she died was to keep step with Dane for an odd moment up and down the corridor.

But a new patient? Now? He'd find out something about her, suggest someone else.

"What's the problem?" he said, forcing himself to sit down.

"A little girl I've taken care of since she was born. Seven now. Just been kicked out of school."

"Seven? What did she do, go berserk? Attack the teacher?"

"It's not funny," Phil said sternly. "It's really thrown

the mother, she's in the middle of a divorce. She could go right out a window."

"Literally?"

"Well of course not," Phil said impatiently. "Do I have to watch everything I say with you people? She's all worked up. I want you to calm her down."

"What's the specific problem?" Dane couldn't help feeling irritated at the prospect of one more rich divorced woman. "Is the child disruptive? Learning-disabled? Hyperactive?"

"Spare me your fancy terms. They didn't give a reason. As far as I can see, she's just a pretty little girl. Shy. Quiet. A relief in this office, let me tell you. I blame myself for not paying attention. The school had me recommend an eye man, then an ENT. That usually means they're getting ready to make a case. I'd have been more alert if she were older. Seven, for God's sake."

You're not up on things, Dane thought. Second grade. Valley of Decision. Teachers overlook kindergarten and first grade and pass the child along hoping it will straighten out. At seven the real work starts, and that's when they clamp down.

"Actually," Phil went on, "another of my patients got almost the same notice. A lady lawyer looking to be a judge. Different kind of dame, older, tougher. And the child is wonderful. Wonderful. The mother's wild. Even talking about suing the school."

Great, Dane thought. Forget the child, charge into court.

"Phil. Listen, please. I just can't handle anything new."

"That's dreck. We better talk. Joe tells me you've quit Monday tennis. You never come around for bridge. What's the matter with you?"

Dane stood up, began to pace as far as the telephone cord would let him.

"Try to see it, Phil. I'm dead tired. And not sleeping."

"I do see. And still drinking, I suppose?"

Phil got high on a glass of beer and never understood how Scandinavians could drink.

"Phil," Dane said. "Don't push it."

"Come on, man. Grete's been dead for half a year. You're a doctor, you know fifty ways to get hold of yourself. You know more about alcohol than I do. Anyway, it'll do you good to get your mind on something new. I'm really concerned about this lady. She's stubborn. Impetuous. She wanted the divorce, no one could talk her out of it. Now she's ready to blow up the school. It's bad, for her and for the child."

"Call Jerry Fowler or Bill Gates. I'm turning patients over already. Longtime people, people I really care about."

"I called you. You're not in Indian Territory yet. You can still handle a consultation. Besides, you've met her. You were sort of interested, in your slow Swedish way, as I remember."

What in hell was he talking about?

"Phil," he said, straining the phone cord to its limit. "Danish. That's how I got my nickname, remember? Swedes and Danes are different. And I can't remember any woman I ever met, with or without you, who'd interest me now."

"Well, try Cornelia Fuller."

The name meant nothing. Dane said so.

Phil coughed. That meant he was coming to something he found difficult, Dane knew. The little sound took him back to the battle with the young resident who'd insisted on an autopsy for Grete. Dane had been adamant. Grete was dead, wasn't she? What difference why? They'd had no children who would need a medical history. But Phil had coughed and then bullied him into it, citing commitment to the hospital, medical knowledge, psychological completion. That last phrase had sounded so ridiculous coming from Phil that Dane had given in.

"I'm talking about Mrs. Fuller. The electrician."

A picture formed in Dane's mind through the headache that always came with memories of Grete's last day.

He saw Mrs. Fuller. In close-up. More exactly, he saw Mrs. Fuller's ass.

Last spring. A backers' audition Phil and Shulamith were giving for a patient who produced musicals. The big living room was jammed with doctors and their wives, women with chic clothes covering ugly bodies, strident voices, showy jewelry. All of them were saying "we" as only doctors' wives can, we diagnosed a case, we have a patient. Dane had downed vodka after vodka, angry that these creatures were alive when Grete was not.

Finally everyone was sitting, facing singers, speakers,

tape recorders. Phil, speaking enthusiastically, turned on
the equipment with a flourish. Spark, flash, and a whip-
crack of sound, followed by a burst of laughter, groans
from the crowd. Two men knelt under the table, but soon
got up shaking their heads. The producer sulked. Per-
formers chattered nervously.

Dane had felt relieved. He could get out, go home,
where there was aquavit—better, stronger than vodka.
He'd stood up and seen, under the table that held the
speakers, a flash of white. Focusing on it, he'd realized he
was looking at a small, shapely, round rear end. It was
perched on two narrow shoe soles, black and highly polished, like a white pear set on two black leaves. Its owner,
down among the maze of wires, was tinkering with something.

Dane had paused to watch. Technician? Women today,
you never knew.

The little bottom had wriggled itself backward toward
him, become part of a girl rising, brushing dust from the
knees of her white pants. Skinny, a lot of loose dark hair,
long, slender flanks like a boy. He looked for her breasts.
Small, like Grete's, not even rounding out that clinging
jacket. She lifted her head and he saw that, white as the
suit was, her skin was whiter, stretched over the bones in
her face to make a background for enormous dark eyes.

An arresting face. The first that had caught his imagination since Grete's death.

And then Dane had felt a stirring in his crotch, the first
in months. Astonishing. His clinical observation sent the
feeling away almost instantly.

People had begun moving around, and he'd lost sight
of the girl. When he shifted to see her again, she was
perched like an Oriental, feet on the ground, little ass just
off the floor, arms wrapped around long legs, as if waiting
for something. It hurt Dane's own knees to watch her like
that. But she seemed quite comfortable, as if she could
have held the position forever. Finally Phil had come struggling through the crowd, holding a screwdriver.

The girl took it, slipped under the table like a cat. Did
she know the dangers of metal tools and electricity?

But no more sparks. She turned something, rocked
smoothly back on her heels, stood up and stepped towards

the speakers, touching her hand to a switch. A burst of sound blasted the room, turning all heads. Then she'd reached quickly for a knob on one of the machines, brought the sound down, nodded to Phil, and walked away. The audition began and seemed to last for hours. After it, not seeing her anywhere, Dane had asked Phil what had happened to the electrician. He remembered her, and what she'd made him feel.

Dane realized Phil was talking.

"Cornelia's living in the past when it comes to schools. No idea what goes on in them now. They don't want problems. Just potential Ivy Leaguers. One flop and out the door. The minute a kid's in nursery school the mother is after me for hormones, vitamins, nutrition experts."

Dane's headache throbbed.

"Phil," he said, "I can't talk anymore. It's seven here, still only four out West. Inmed could still be trying to reach me."

"Who's Inmed?"

"My new bosses, I hope."

He thought about the clinic, paint peeling in strips from the walls, screams, babies crying. The ER more hellish than Bellevue or St. Luke's, throngs of broad-cheeked men and women, the Diné, they called themselves, looking strangely like the Lapps of his childhood, doctors running, helicopters taking off for faraway trouble, paramedics tipping stretchers askew, nurses with blood on their sleeves. He'd seen cardboard boxes on a high shelf crammed with knives, hammers, axes, even guns. Rows of ancient-looking women in bright, cheap dresses, with babies at their breasts. Numberless drunks, men who got out of fast cars with liquor bottles in their big hands, dried vomit down their shirt fronts, faces seamed and blotched from gallons of cheap wine.

"I've told you. They fascinate me, Phil. Danes drink because it's dark half the year. Out there they drink in the hot sun. You know I toured duty stations, Rapid City, South Dakota, among small tribes, Mandan, Hidatsa, Pawnee, Oklahoma, the big Navajo reservation in Phoenix, a mental-health center in Farmington, New Mexico. It's different. Important. Those people are appreciative, they turn out in bunches for talks from doctors. I can concentrate, forget Grete. Not like New York mothers whining about their kids."

"Cornelia Fuller doesn't whine. She's crazy about her kid. So crazy that now she's making herself a lot of trouble. Anyone less obstinate might give up, stick their kid in some second-rate school. But she went to this place herself, has a lot of sentimental feeling about it."

Explanations didn't get rid of Phil. Maybe a gentle joke would. In any case, thirty seconds more and he'd hang up.

"I remember Mrs. Fuller. I liked the way she saved your party. She's damned attractive, but I can't take patients I find attractive. It's against the rules. Leads to malpractice suits."

"I'm talking about a little guidance, Dane." Phil's voice rose. "Not *National Enquirer* love therapy. You're getting as nuts as the old-time Freudians. She's attractive. Is that supposed to mean she can't see a doctor?"

Dane couldn't argue anymore. If he gave in, at least he'd clear the phone line.

"All right, Phil. I'll do what I can in one session, point her in the right direction. But then she goes to Bill or someone."

"Okay, okay. Just sit back and let her distract you."

What in hell was Phil really up to? Doctoring him?

"Phil," Dane said. "Is she in your office? Now?"

"Well of course," Phil said. "Why else would I be pressuring you? What are you rushing off to? Dinner in some greasy spoon? A few more shots of that Scandinavian poison? She'll be right over."

The thought of greeting someone new, listening patiently, taking notes, hearing another set of woes, made Dane want to throw on his coat, double-lock the door, and stride out into the cold. Even with nowhere to go.

"All right," he made himself say. "Send her around." At least, if the call came, he'd be in the office to take it.

"You've got it," Phil said. And hung up.

Dane realized he was rubbing his bad finger, and stopped. Since Grete had died the habits of his childhood were returning. And the memories.

His mind always shot to the blackest one. The dank underground room, every shadow frightening, every creak terrifying. His mother, tall, blond hair strained back in a braided bun, working over the mimeograph machine, her hands glistening with dark purple ink, like blood. And Dane, a small, thin boy crouched halfway up the stairs. He'd been too young to be able to read what she was printing, but old enough to be choked with terror at the grim look on his mother's face and the dreadful machine spitting out pages. Before he'd ever heard the word "Resistance," he'd had nightmares about a day the enormous German soldiers would stamp down from the street to take her. He knew he could never stop them, that she could never save herself or him from their boots and rifle butts.

Once he had burst with anguish into that room, pulled at her apron, and shouted at her to stop, they were coming.

His mother had turned, raised her arm high, and slapped him. "You," she had whispered. "If only I didn't have you."

But he'd been right. The soldiers did come.

Thank God, the two of them had just enough time to get everything into the hiding place under the outhouse.

The Germans hadn't found anything, even after shouting at them over and over and twisting his mother's arm, even after taking the butt of a handgun and smashing it down on his finger.

How old had he been when he'd learned that over twenty-four million copies of illegal pamphlets had circulated in Denmark during the Occupation? And that his mother was a heroine?

But in another country, after so much time, after years of analysis, he could still feel his head snap back, his ear ring, the smack of his mother's fingers wet with the terrible ink. Worse than his smashed finger, worse than the dreaded Germans, worse than the fierce pain in his hand.

And here was Phil's Mrs. Fuller, probably working some ugly machine of her own, too self-involved to hear her child calling for help.

Grete had kept him from remembering. In America, living on his small grant, struggling with textbooks beyond his knowledge of English, patients whose problems seemed foolish and alien, Grete's letters from Denmark had sustained him. When he'd finished at Cornell, got his citizenship, saved money for a fairytale wedding in Copen-

hagen, a rowdy Danish farewell at Kastrup Airport, he'd
felt invulnerable, open to happiness forever.

Everything from Grete's hand, the intricate, delicious
food, the handsome sweaters and scarves and socks she
knitted, the pretty illustrations she sold for children's books,
dimmed the memories of his childhood. So had his joy in
bringing her a cup of tea the way she liked it, cooled down,
a flower in midwinter, surprising her with a plump, soft
feather quilt like the one she'd left in Denmark. How he'd
loved her in all that softness, burying his face in her pale
hair, stroking her silken shoulder, taking one of her smooth,
small breasts in his hungry mouth till she arched her back
with delight. Even in the endless hours of her pneumonia,
nails ice-blue, mouth wide and gasping under the plastic
oxygen hood, she'd seemed to him a little girl about to
cross a dangerous street.

The buzzer sounded.

Phil's patient.

Mrs. Fuller was as beautiful as he remembered, but
changed. Dane thought of a forest creature, frightened,
thin, every movement angular and quick. Her huge eyes
were like a fawn's eyes, wide, strained. Not a trace of the
triumphant look, the confident posture he remembered
from the party.

Phil was right. She did need to talk to someone.

Mrs. Fuller's hand felt warm, soft. Surprise. He'd almost
expected the touch of a tiny cleft hoof and a sudden scamper
out the door, down the hall.

"Thank you for seeing me so quickly," she said.

Another jolt. Her voice. It didn't match her looks. She
seemed wind-tossed, casual, her clothes thrown together.
But her voice was poised, her tone formal. A stage voice?

Taking her coat, Dane found himself noticing that Mrs.
Fuller's neck was slender as a child's, that her heavy hair
smelled like soap, fresh, unperfumed.

He led her into his consulting room, pulled out a chair.
She folded herself into it smoothly, reminding him of the
way she'd moved at Phil's. Was she an actress?

"I seem to have stage fright," she said, as if answering
his unspoken question. "I've never been in a psychiatrist's
office before. Funny. With everyone I've ever known in
some kind of therapy."

Dane waited. Everyone said that. She meant, of course, please be gentle.

"Dr. Rosenzweig told you? That I'm terribly worried about my little girl?"

He told me; now you tell me. Is it really your little girl that worries you?

"They want her to leave school. Maybe it's easiest for you just to read this letter."

Dane watched her reach for it, quickly, no fumbling. Even in that enormous handbag, the largest he'd ever seen a woman carry, she seemed to know precisely where it was. She held the letter as if it burned, handed it over fast. Plainly she hoped he'd cool it for her. He didn't often read letters, preferring to hear a patient's impression of anything written, but somehow found himself taking this one.

Cornelia felt uneasy watching him unfold the letter, hearing the crackle of the stiff paper. She'd read it so often, by now it seemed a vital document like a birth certificate or college diploma—a piece of paper that changed her life, divided time into before its existence and after, into innocence and experience. Dr. Rosenzweig, reading it, had coughed, frowned, looked oddly stricken. What would Dr. Nilssen do? She kept her eyes on his face.

Interesting face. Unusual. He looked like Olivier playing Hamlet, beautiful bones, deep-set eyes, silver hair, the color only a towheaded child turns later on. How much later? she wondered. He looked ten, fifteen years older than she. Perhaps it was because of his formal manners, that serious expression. Unusual man. The faint singsong accent seemed right for a prince of Denmark. And she guessed at something of Hamlet's dark passion behind his polite manner, something to discover. But then, *he* was supposed to do the discovering. Phil Rosenzweig, she suspected, didn't think much of shrinks. But he'd warned her to have one in her corner before she saw anyone at school. This man looked like perfect casting.

Christ, if only he could *do* something, not just act in some drama she'd have to stage. If only he could make them see they were wrong.

Dane saw Mrs. Fuller's hands twisting, fingers knotting, and realized he wanted to reach over and touch them, get her to relax.

"You see," Mrs. Fuller said, "they say take her some-where else. And it's terrible. The most terrible thing that's ever happened to me."

To you. Yes. And it *is* you who's in pain.

"I'm sure it was a shock," he said quietly. "How do you explain it?"

She moved to the extreme edge of her leather chair, looking more like a skittish fawn than ever.

"I can't. They say she falls short academically. That has to mean reading."

She stressed the word as if it were a synonym for leprosy, AIDS, bubonic plague. "Everything else is fine. She's even good at arithmetic. That's harder, isn't it? And she's a great little girl, alert, sweet. It's *only* reading."

She put her hands up to cover her face. Her knuckles turned to pearls.

Dane waited, making a deliberate effort now to keep his hands relaxed. Better for her to get it all out.

He let his mind drift till it wandered to his own school. A single room in a timbered farmhouse. Why had that small place seemed so peaceful? Because he'd been safe there, away from his mother and danger.

Mrs. Fuller abruptly put her hands down. Her face was flushed.

"I did everything they said," she began again. "I had her ears examined, and her eyes. I checked things with the remedial teacher who worked with her in school and did what she told me, practiced reading every morning. I mean, I did *everything*."

Would his mother have said that?

"I can't bear it," Mrs. Fuller said suddenly in her clear voice.

"Well. Tell me your situation," he said gently. "Do you take care of your little girl yourself?"

Her chin went up.

"I'm separated," she said. "My divorce will be final next year. Of course I know that has to be upsetting for a child. But I can't believe the school—this school—won't wait through the adjustment with me, help me."

"And your husband? What's his feeling?"

"I only got this letter day before yesterday. I haven't

told him yet. I don't know *how* to tell him. He'll blame me. He's angry about the divorce, so he'll say it's that."

No father, Dane thought. Like me. But this woman is brittle, more vulnerable than my mother.

"So you called Phil Rosenzweig?"

"That night. I had to know if there could be brain damage, something like that."

"Why brain damage?"

"Actually, I was worrying about mental illness," she said, her voice suddenly flat, toneless. "My mother is sick that way. Schizophrenic. She was gone often when I was a child, in hospitals. She's in one now, has been for a long, long time. Actually, that's why I've never been to a psychiatrist. My father said my mother had seen dozens, and none of them could help her. He's dead now, and my brother doesn't live in New York, so I'm legally responsible for my mother. I never worried about anything like this before, my little girl seemed so perfect. But of course, Dr. Rosenzweig knows, and yesterday he said there's nothing, not the smallest thing, wrong with her. And he's been her doctor since she was born."

Her beautiful voice seemed to go up at the end of her sentence, questioning. Phil assured her, but she hadn't quite believed it.

"Then I tried to reach an old friend. A head teacher at the school now. I couldn't. So when I saw Dr. Rosenzweig, I asked him to speak to the school for me. And he said I'd do better asking you, that you're the best psychiatrist he knows." She paused, looked straight at him. "Actually, he says you're the *only* one who's any good."

Dane smiled. "Did he tell you I'm not taking on anyone? That I'm leaving New York? I'm going out to work with people who mostly earn less than five thousand dollars a year. They need a lot of help. What I *can* do for you is help you find some ways to handle this, steer you to someone else."

The fawn took a deep breath.

"Dr. Nilssen, I hoped you'd come to school with me, help me talk to them. I didn't plan on a lot of time. I can't afford it. I shouldn't even be here now, two hundred dollars, Phil Rosenzweig said."

"Well," Dane said. "What if I send you to someone who

charges a little less? Or you talk it over with your husband. Wouldn't he want to help? You've had a shock. He'll know it would be better for the child if you were calmer."

Suddenly, dazzlingly, Mrs. Fuller smiled. The smile transformed her, turned her back into the girl with the screwdriver, stunning, totally sure of herself.

"My husband is an actor, down on his luck. That gives him a lot of free time to talk to people at his clubs, to be an authority on everything. He says any actor who goes to a psychiatrist is paying for what he should be paid *for*. In fact, just thinking about his reaction made me want to come to see you."

Dane felt the change in his crotch as it happened, the same sensation he'd felt at the party. Again, it was gone in a moment. But if her smile could stir him so, what would happen if he could take her hand, pull her close?

He cleared his throat. "Was this a complete surprise? No clues in your daughter's report card? What's her name, by the way?"

"Livvie. Olivia, really, but that's too long for her, she's so small."

Saying the name, her face bloomed, her voice lingered over the soft syllables. Livvie, Olivia. No doubt how she felt about the child. And that was half the battle. If only he could make her aware of her own feelings, get her to see they were the answer to everything.

"They don't have report cards," she said. "Just comments. Livvie's weren't alarming. The school does a lot of testing. But the results are private. They don't tell them to the parents of little children. Too much comparing, they say."

But the teachers compare, Dane thought.

"Then I think an independent testing situation, so we can measure Livvie against other children her age," Dane said.

For the first time, Mrs. Fuller sat back in her chair, crossed her long, slim legs.

"And you ought to talk to the people who do the testing, find out what *they* think is the trouble."

"But wait," she said, leaning forward, a flush starting on her pale face. "This morning I got hold of Miss Knowlton, that head teacher. At first she said she couldn't discuss school business. But I started to cry. That got to her, she's older, and she remembers me from school. She said it wasn't only Livvie. There were three children in the lower school whose parents got letters like mine. And more in the upper school, she thinks. Nanny didn't sound too happy about all this. But she isn't responsible, of course."

"I see," Dane said. "Who is?"

"Well, there's a new headmaster. Supposed to be quite good. She thought I should talk to him. That's what I wanted you to help me do. She says he's brilliant, really interested in the small children. She thinks he's going to make it a whole new school."

Impatiently Dane found himself wishing he could go with her, kill the dragon for her. Or better still, take her in his arms and tell her not to worry, he'd manage the whole thing. Almost immediately, he felt disturbed. No woman had stirred him like this since Grete. He'd even felt relieved about that, till now.

"That's probably a visit you'll have to make yourself," he said carefully. "Though we can talk about what to ask, what to listen for. Tell me. If this school were to turn out to be changing into a whole new place, would you mind Livvie's leaving?"

Mrs. Fuller opened her wide eyes wider.

"Fucking A, I'd mind. Excuse me. That means yes."

"How come?" Dane was amused. Not so vulnerable, after all. "Perhaps there's a better school for Livvie."

"I can't *imagine* a better school." Mrs. Fuller seemed shocked at the thought. "I loved it there. I'm the person I am because of that school. We all felt that way, my friends and I. We thought college was easy, flat, afterward. In fact, I was bored at mine, didn't last more than a year. Well, I *couldn't* give Livvie less than I had, some school she'd just tolerate. I couldn't stand to see her miss the kind of teachers, the art and music, the standards they gave us. I'd always feel I'd let her down. And there's something else. Nanny Knowlton warned me. Those schools share records. The next place will *know* Livvie got kicked out."

"It may be good for them to know," Dane said. "Help them help her. Anyway, everything changes. Maybe this new headmaster means bad changes."

Mrs. Fuller put her hands out, as if to push him away. "But I'm her mother. I'm supposed to protect her."

"How?"

She curled her hands into fists. "Fight for her. I thought you'd give me some ideas. Weapons."

Weapons, Dane thought, his gut twisting painfully. She should know what happens to children whose mothers take arms.

"Let's stick to Livvie," he said.

She was frowning.

"That's what I thought we were doing. I need statistics. Case histories. I've heard things about how awful Churchill was in school. That Einstein was slow, didn't even talk till he was four. And Truffaut, Edison, Jack Kennedy, kidding around, getting bad grades. Lots of famous people weren't great in school. I want to tell them it's crazy to predict what's going to happen to a seven-year-old."

"If they're crazy, why bother with them?"

Mrs. Fuller stood up in a move so swift her purse slid off her lap to the floor with a thud.

"But you don't understand. *I want to talk them into keeping her.*"

Dane no longer saw a fawn, skittish, delicate. Now she had the look of his mother, a Valkyrie riding the skies above Asgard. In a rush of heat he found himself wanting to reach out, pull at her arm. He wanted to break his most important rule, never to talk about his own experiences, as so many foolish therapists did.

"Mrs. Fuller," he said, careful to remain still, to speak quietly. "Do you *believe* what you just said, that lots of people were slow in school and turned out right? If you do, why worry so about your little girl? Wouldn't it be better to focus on the school? Are you saying that no matter what's happening there, you want your child to stay?"

"But it was the central experience, the best thing I've ever had. Anyway, it's supposed to be one of the best schools in New York, maybe the country. People kill to get their children in. She's *there.* I just want her to stay."

Dane realized he was rolling his pen between his hands, not the greatest way to keep his rising anger from showing.

"It's a big job. And there may not be much point in it."

"Not much point? It's the whole point."

Was she blind? Obsessed? Terrified to dig for problems in case they turned out to be too difficult even for her precious school to fix?

Now Dane's blood seemed to be heating.

"Look," she drove on. "If I can convince them they've made the wrong decision about Livvie, they might change it."

Christ, if she *did* succeed, how terrible that might be for the child. Didn't she know how teachers can give up on children? How strong kids prey on weak ones? If her Livvie was in trouble now, what disasters would come in a few years? How many high-school kids did he hear about with ulcers? Drug problems? Suicide attempts? Why the hell did therapy have to be so damned slow? If only he could just shake her, explain, argue.

Knock it off, he told himself. Get to work.

"There are fights you can't win," he said. "Look. Livvie should be tested by a psychologist, immediately. I'll give you a name, someone who'll fit her in quickly. That way we'll have an independent evaluation. Then we can decide what's best for her. Not for the school. Not even for you. For the child and her future. That's what's important, right?"

"Of course," Mrs. Fuller said crossly, as if she meant quite the opposite.

"Meanwhile, why not go and observe Livvie in her class. Watch. Hear her read in school and see how she interacts with the teacher, the other children. Hold off talking to that headmaster until then. You may see things that'll make you want to get her out. Or maybe she'll be so terrific you can tell them they're idiots. Don't decide this minute. See for yourself."

Mrs. Fuller sat down, back straight, eyes wide, mouth set firmly in a beautiful line.

"I can't remember when I didn't love the Boston School. My feelings couldn't possibly change. I want my daughter to stay there. Please, can't you help me make that happen?"

Poor, smashing, impatient, beautiful, beleaguered Mrs. Fuller. What the devil was her first name? He glanced down at her card.

Cornelia. Latin. Wasn't Cornelia the mother of the

Gracchi, the one who'd sent for her twin sons, when other women were displaying their necklaces and rings, and had blasted them all by saying, "These are my jewels"?

This Cornelia wanted to blast a whole school.

"Look," he said. "It's a terrible hurt—fresh and still bleeding. Give it a little time. And talk to your husband."

"That's no good. He'd like Livvie to be a little doll and end up in one of the free public schools for the arts. Or if he hit a big part, go to Nightingale, Spence, Hewitt's, one of those curtsying places. If he thinks about it at all. When he hears this, he'll *know* he was right."

You, of course, are wide open to suggestion and change, Dane thought, wryly.

"Would you like to schedule another meeting, say at the end of the week?"

As he spoke, Dane couldn't believe he'd said the words. What, after all, could he accomplish in one more session?

Cornelia stood up again, began to pace restlessly. "Dr. Nilssen. The woods are burning. And you want me to start being analyzed?"

"I can't think of a better time," he said gravely.

Obviously she was angry, impatient, unsatisfied. Christ, had he gotten through at all?

He was reaching for his index file, almost ready to give her a referral number, someone else to call. But a glance at her stopped him.

Her words were angry, impatient. But her face was the face of a frightened child.

I know about fear, he thought. God knows I've seen plenty of it. Something bewildering, devastating, is happening to someone she loves, someone she's responsible for. She's asking a question I can almost hear. If she doesn't know why the child can't read, *what else* is going on inside that child's mind that her mother doesn't know?

Fighting that sort of fear, he thought, made her anger brave, admirable. She *was* taking arms, refusing to give in.

He'd better switch subjects, end on something less intense.

"What work do you do? You speak like an actress. But I've seen you handle electrical equipment."

She stopped still, stared at him.

"At the Rosenzweigs. Their backers' audition, last spring. You saved the day. I remember it very well. You looked competent, happy, totally sure of yourself. I'd like to see you looking like that again."

She smiled. She *had* to be an actress. He'd rarely seen such changes of mood, so quick, so complete. Again, the smile dazzled him, felt as if someone had flung open a curtain to let in glinting sun.

"I wanted to act. I wasn't good. But I *was* a decent dancer. When I quit Cambridge, I danced professionally for a while. Actually, I backed up Diane Keaton in the company of *Hair*. My finest hour. Now I'm a casting director. And I'm terrific. We use all that electronic equipment. It breaks down every five minutes. So I learned to fix it."

"I see," Dane said. Then she does have some sense of what she can and can't do. Build on that.

"Look, Mrs. Fuller. At that party you gave a star performance. You fixed something, made something happen. That probably gave you a wonderful feeling. But work problems and home problems can be quite different. What's right in one place rarely is right in the other. Children don't fix fast."

The smile vanished faster than it had appeared.

"That's sanctimonious shit," she said, without taking a breath. "I'm the only one who can fight for Livvie. And that's what I'm going to do."

"Be my guest," said Dane before he could stop himself.

"It was dumb to come here." Her eyes were wide. "Dr. Rosenzweig's idea. He's old-fashioned and thinks a woman needs a man to help her fight. Well, not me. Everyone tells me how helpless I am. You can't leave your husband, they said, and I did. You can't keep your house in the country, and I did. Now they say I can't keep Livvie in school, but I will."

Dane felt like shaking her. For God's sake, he wanted to say. It's all right to be frightened, all right to worry about your child. But it's not all right to blame the school. It's nobody's fault she can't read, not hers, not theirs, not even yours.

Carefully, quietly, he said, "Help, yes. Hired gun, no. Being determined for yourself is fine. But being determined about what someone else will have to live with, especially when that someone is a very small child, that's rotten."

He heard her breath catch, saw her eyes grow moist.

For an instant he felt great.

And then, quickly, he was ashamed of himself—so ashamed, so sorry for her he actually felt his heart shrink and constrict painfully.

"You're wrong," she said, more softly. "Even about that party. That wasn't a performance, I wasn't impressing anybody. I was working, checking out the lead singer for use in a commercial. I wanted the equipment fixed so I could get the hell out. I hate parties."

"I could explore that with you," Dane said. "Only I hate parties too."

He waited for the tightness in his chest to ease. And Mrs. Fuller helped. Suddenly she seemed to become the fawn again, posture relaxing, the corners of her mouth softening.

"I thought you weren't supposed to tell me things. Just listen. While I lie gracefully on a couch. Isn't that what goes on in psychiatrists' offices?"

"Used to. Not much anymore. Some people find it easier to talk about their problems when there's no eye contact. But that's not you. You're very articulate."

Wrong, he thought. But very articulate.

"Dr. Nilssen, Phil Rosenzweig told me your wife died last year."

Another switch. By now, he should have known she was good at changes, but this one caught him off guard. Even with her anguish about the child, she'd seen right through Phil.

He nodded.

"Somehow I get the feeling that Phil Rosenzweig is putting two lonely hearts together. Trying to fix two birds with one consultation. He's not much for divorces or single mothers."

"He's down on death, too, as it happens." Dane smiled. "And single men."

"Well, I should warn you. I'm nobody's fix. I have Livvie, and a house in the country. And that's all I want. All."

She'd said it so fiercely, he felt she'd almost convinced herself.

"That's good," Dane said. "Because anything else, as it happens, is highly unethical. It's a pity. You have something that makes you absolutely irresistible for an analyst. Wrongheadedness."

"You aren't *my* analyst," Cornelia Fuller said with a tiny smile. "I can't afford you. If your medical sense, or whatever it is, makes you think I'm really wrongheaded, I'll try to listen. Visiting school is a good idea. Honestly, I only want to save Livvie misery. I can't *stand* it when she's sad. She's so small, so breakable. The thought that somebody doesn't want her . . . Well, I'd like to throw a bomb at that headmaster."

You're small too. And fragile. And if you'd only hear me, I'd help you not to break, not to feel this misery.

"Of course," Dane said. "But you can't. Parents can't save children from all trouble and pain. Someday you won't be there to help Livvie, and she'll have to do it by herself. Why don't we get you in shape to help her?"

Sanctimonious shit, all right, he thought. Concentrate, for God's sake.

The telephone startled him. He picked it up.

Buzzes, hums.

"Is this Dr. Nilssen?" asked a male operator in a deep nasal tone. "Shiprock, Arizona, calling."

Now? But he needed time, wanted to finish his thought, make himself clear to her.

"This is Dr. Nilssen," he said, swiveling his chair so he wasn't facing her.

"Dr. Nilssen? Dane? Charlie Whiteriver," the cheerful voice boomed across the map of the United States. Whiteriver was a reservation Navajo who'd somehow made it through Harvard and Harvard Med. Dane was fascinated by his theory that Indians were unfairly called alcoholics. They couldn't get liquor on the reservation, he said, had to drive to buy bottles, so the drinking was all out in the open.

"Right, Charlie," Dane said. "I've been waiting for you. What's happening?"

"Everything's moving, but a little slower than we expected. The ORD guys have been over from Tucson, into everything in the Service Unit this month."

Office of Research and Development, Dane reminded himself. With the government, everything's initials.

"That kept Bill Kornhauser tied up here awhile longer, accounts, personnel reports, that stuff. Plus we had a great case, a paranoid Ute woman who shot everyone driving down her road, convinced they'd wear it out. We got the highway guys to dig a second road, so hers could be left in peace. You'd have enjoyed the fuss. Anyway, Dane, Bill's had to extend. Couple of months, that's all. Shouldn't change anything."

Dane felt relieved. He wouldn't have to leave right away.

And then he was furious at himself. Was he so easily distracted now? Could one new person who needed help make him so unsure? Had he become Jesus Christ, out to save anyone who walked in his door?

No, not anyone. This woman: beautiful, terrified, stubborn, intriguing. Who made him *feel* something, after so much emptiness.

"All right," he said. "Just so you're not having a council of war. Second thoughts."

"Ordinary delay. You'll get used to it. The med-school grads working out here to pay back their government loans get used to it first thing. Inmed will send formal notice, of course. But I knew you were impatient."

Earlier, he'd been impatient.

Now?

He thanked Charlie, said something about a clean slate, asked after the new wing at the hospital, and turned his chair a little to watch Cornelia Fuller's small foot fretfully tapping the air.

## Judicial Candidate's Night

Come meet Park River's dynamic Democratic candidate for Civil Court Judge, Rhea Rosenzweig Cantor!

Ms. Cantor has been found qualified by the Combined Bar Association Judicial Screening Committee. She is widely known as a fighter for tenants' rights in the battleground of West Side urban renewal. She has compiled an enviable record in the areas of discrimination against women, minorities, and the aged. She holds academic distinction as an assistant adjunct professor at New York Law School, and has lectured at the New School for Social Research.

A partner with her husband in the firm of Cantor, Cantor, Harrison and Tripoli, she is a member of the New York City Bar, the County Lawyers Association, and the Metropolitan Women's Bar. Working lawyer, wife, mother, Ms. Cantor is committed to the concept of equal justice for all.

RHEA CANTOR BURST out of the elevator, marched down the hall, and rounded the corner into the headmaster's anteroom. Her whizbang entrance, she was pleased to see, startled the secretary who guarded his inner door.

Good. Come on strong. Try to *feel* strong.

The door was heavily carved mahogany, and knocking stung her knuckles. She ignored that, turned the handle, pushed.

You've got a right, she told herself. You're a paying parent here. With a gorgeous little girl. Where is it written he can throw her out without warning or even discussion? If this yuld won't come to the phone, he should be expecting a visit.

Squaring her shoulders, she stepped into the huge room.

And stopped cold, feeling as if she'd walked into a battery of spotlights: sunlight, blazing from the high uncurtained windows.

She heard the scrape of the secretary's chair. The woman was getting up, coming after her.

Rhea turned and shut the door.

Good. She'd managed to get in. The worst worry.

The rest should be simpler. It was her profession, after all, to build arguments, cajole, persuade. And what was she asking for? Just time, breathing space. Right now she couldn't *begin* to think about a new school for Rachel. Later, God willing, when she'd finally put on a black silk robe and been sworn in as a judge, *then* she'd handle it.

Hadn't she postponed everything else? Her cases, *pro bono* work, teaching, the house? And when had she and Saul last gone to bed at the same time? Who could even remember?

Running for judge took twenty-seven hours a day.

Another school year, she needed. Then she'd have trained a law secretary, settled into the Civil Court, published a solid opinion or two in the *Law Journal*. Maybe even have been named an acting Supreme Court justice. Then she could concentrate on Rachel, on interviews, tests, reference letters. After all, they weren't married to the Boston School. Dalton, Ethical, Walden, Columbia Grammar, plenty of choices. And Ramaz, of course, where Saul really wanted the child.

But to switch now? Not even a supermother could handle that.

Pity that Saul had a court appearance today and couldn't come too. But he'd helped her plan, item by item, methodically, the way they always planned an important case.

She'd begin reasonably, pleasantly. If persuasion didn't work, she'd get tough. Threaten bad press for the school, an injunction, even. And if *that* didn't do it, she'd bring in her heavy artillery.

Harvey Bache was not exactly her favorite person. But last year Rhea had let up in a custody battle against him after he'd convinced her in the corridor that her client drank, that the kids would suffer if Rhea's client got them. So Harvey owed her. And he ran that board.

She blinked to get her eyes adjusted to the light and took another step forward.

The room was empty.

Rhea wanted to burst into tears. Her brave march past that secretary, for nothing?

Then, peering into the room, she felt a sudden shock.

Connor *was* there, hidden by the high back of the desk chair, turned completely around to face the windows. And silent, because he was on the phone.

Got him, Rhea thought, feeling steadier.

Connor was steady. The man had to know someone was standing over him. But his hand wasn't tightening on the receiver or his head turning even slightly.

So what else did she expect? Nobody human could have signed that letter.

Two-thirty this morning she'd opened it, trying to get through the mail, eyes gritty, calves aching, after a candidate's evening at her political club. Hundreds of questions from the audience, some provocative, some hostile. She'd thought she'd never be able to stop smiling.

Holding the letter, Rhea had burst into the bedroom and shaken Saul awake. While he read it, then reached to hug her, rage burgeoned inside her like a terrible menstrual cramp.

Now she tried to recapture that feeling, so she could channel its force, use it.

But what if Connor ignored her to take the wind out of her sails?

Not my sails, she thought, feeling staunch. I've been kept waiting in a hundred courthouses. Biding time is part of my work, my success.

She'd act like any parent with an appointment. He had to get off the phone sometime. Better yet, she'd use the time to her advantage. She'd move his visitor's chair. Why sit facing the sun, leaving him in shadows, where she couldn't read his face?

It took all her hundred and fifty-one pounds, more strength than she would have imagined, but she did manage to shift the massive Chinese chair. She put her hands on its back and leaned, waiting.

Keep hiding, Dr. Connor, she thought. You'll learn. Like old Judge Patrick, who likes to pretend he can't hear women lawyers, says they don't speak up. Last month he was stunned at how clearly that jury heard me.

Connor moved suddenly. "Right, Mrs. Irving," he said into the phone. Then he hung up, swiveled around to face her.

Rhea stared.

In the enormous chair the headmaster of the Boston School sat cross-legged, feet tucked up under him. A kelly-green vest and the white chrysanthemum in his buttonhole made him seem jolly and harmless, some overgrown pixie on a toadstool.

"Hi there," he said pleasantly.

An elf? Rhea felt disarmed.

Then she caught herself. His letter hadn't been jolly and harmless.

She began feeling the quickened pulse and shortness of breath that always preceded an encounter.

She made herself relax. Then she marshaled her best voice, strong, for a jury of twelve, clear for a court stenotypist.

"Good morning," she said. "I'm Rhea Cantor, Rachel's mother. You couldn't take my calls this morning. Your secretary wouldn't make an appointment. So I came."

"Right on," Dr. Connor said.

Launched, Rhea felt easier. She moved around the huge chair and sat down.

"I got your letter. Last night, late, when I finished working. Naturally, a shock."

"We haven't met, have we, Mrs. Cantor?" Connor said brightly, chin in his hands, elbows on the knees of his crossed legs. "You weren't at the monster rally when I dished with the parents."

Rhea was catching on. Connor used words to confuse, get people off kilter.

Why bring up *that* meeting? Is he suggesting that Rachel ought to leave because we weren't there?

"Dr. Connor, I'm a candidate for a Civil Court judgeship. The night of your meeting I could have been ten different places, political clubs, churches, shaking hands at subway stations, running my campaign."

"Very impressive," Connor said, his tone conveying a weary lack of interest. "Still. This school has a lot of jazzy parents, you know. Famous. Actors. Artists. Musicians. Heads of corporations. Busy people. Quite a crew made it that night."

He *was* miffed. These private schools wanted blood. As well as a fortune in tuition.

Rhea couldn't help thinking of her own PS 93 on Amsterdam Avenue. Had her mother ever set foot in the place? Still, the Boston School had so much Rhea had missed. Art, music, dancing. Imaginative teachers, nice children from educated homes. When she'd gotten Rachel into a top school that went from first grade straight to college, she'd felt sure she'd done right.

Certainly she'd felt no need to watch or question anything, any more than she would question Park Avenue Synagogue about the way they ran their Hebrew school. She and Saul gladly paid the fourteen hundred a year, and didn't mix in.

"I suppose that was one meeting we just couldn't make," she said calmly. "Was it important?"

"Depends what you consider important."

"My daughter's place in school, I consider important. Believe me, after election day, when I'm on the bench, I'll come to all your meetings."

"Election day? I thought you people were appointed these days, by political leaders, the governor."

"I've got the Democratic nomination. And I'm pretty sure of the Liberal line, as well." Superstition forced her on. "Of course, nothing's final till the voters confirm it."

"You women get a lot of help these days, don't you? A lot of push into high places."

From your mouth to God's ear, Rhea thought. Only you're wrong by a few years. The day is gone when just being a woman with ten years at the bar is enough. Plenty of qualified women now who'd love to be judges.

Only not many as set on it as I am.

She could hardly wait to get free of the firm, desks in the hallways, lines at the Xerox machines and at the Lexis computer, phones ringing off the desks. They were making fantastic money, true, and God knew, *that* was for Rachel. But going in earlier, staying later, working lots of Sundays. She and Saul would be hammering out an argument and realize it was midnight. There had been no evening at home, no Rachel. Last spring, an upstate case had kept them in a motel for a solid week. The work came home, too, cases argued through dinner and the dictating machine next to their bed. So that always in the back of her mind was the nagging sorrow, the guilt: when will there be time for my little girl, lazy time, playing time, teaching time?

With judges, things were different. Judges kept regular hours. They could adjourn a case for a pediatrician's appointment, a school play, even a PTA meeting. Plan their lives, know where they'd be any day of the year. Best of all, there were long vacations—five summer weeks, two more at Christmas. The same as school vacations. And never broken by calls from the office: come in right away, we can't find the file, nobody can handle this nudnick but you. If she were a judge, Rachel's life would be so much better. Worth all the scrounging for campaign funds, the indigestible dinners, the endless handshaking, even worth hardly seeing Rachel at all these last weeks.

Certainly worth missing one meeting at school.

"I'm not unopposed. But I have a fine record, a lot of support. And friends all over town, not just in my district."

One in particular, by the way. "The chairman of your board is on my side. Harvey usually picks winners."

Dr. Connor looked down at his desk for a moment, as if guarding his expression. Then he unwound his long legs, set his feet neatly under his desk. His athletic spring made Rhea feel heavy, stiff.

In the last weeks, she'd put on at least ten pounds. And she couldn't afford even one. Not that she'd eaten a whole meal anywhere. A knish here, a sticky bite of baked Alaska there, a few Mallomars in the kitchen at midnight.

All right, so she wasn't one of the chic mothers Connor was used to. So her suit needed a pressing, and her thick curls certainly could use a trim.

Rhea remembered her glasses and put a hand up to the earpiece. Oh, boy. Broken yesterday, fixed temporarily with a bent paperclip. Connor wasn't the type to miss noticing it, either.

Okay, you didn't make it on your looks, anyway. You've got brains, remember? Later, you'll diet. Get yourself all fixed up. Buy a sensational dress for your induction party.

As if he'd heard her, Connor looked stern.

"Mrs. Cantor, some things won't wait. Like a child's problems. They get worse. Is your daughter supposed to mark time until you become a judge?"

Bastard. Paskudnyak.

"Dr. Connor, what's this about?" she said, making her

voice stronger. "Your letter was our first indication that anything was wrong."

"If you'd come and rapped, you'd understand. That's why I asked. At that meeting, I stated my purpose. You see, Mrs. Cantor, I have a mission here."

He paused dramatically.

"This school has been failing. Failing its students. Its parent group. Its community. And I do not preside over failure."

Well, well, Rhea thought. Where's the pixie now?

"I was chosen to change that," he went on. "To bring the school back to its original eminence. It's rotting, from the inside out. Pipes. Wiring. Risers. Teachers. Students. Greatness could happen here. But first, something has to give."

Again, the pregnant pause. Yes, doctor, and will you tell the jury what that is?

"I'm an elitist, Mrs. Cantor. I believe in operating like the Greeks, the British schools in their glory days. The best minds, the best teaching. And good hard work."

So no argument. Rhea *wanted* Rachel to learn the value of work.

Dr. Connor was sitting straight now. "American education is in crisis," he proclaimed. "In New Jersey colleges last fall, one-third of the freshmen couldn't speak English correctly. Let alone write the language. Half the students entering Ohio State last year took remedial math. Twenty percent of our schoolchildren can't find the United States on the map. Seventy percent of our sixth-graders never heard of reading for pleasure. The public schools *have* to take what they get. We don't. We're interested in brains. So we can teach at top speed, maintain the highest standards. Not everyone can handle excellence. Some children won't be able to keep up."

He leaned back, looked into her eyes.

"One of them happens to be your daughter."

Rhea felt as if he'd punched her in the heart.

Listen, gonif, she wanted to shout, Rachel talked on her first birthday and read when she was four. When I go in to kiss her good night, her bed is full of books. She concentrates so hard, sometimes she doesn't even lift her head.

"Dr. Connor," she said, forcing herself to keep to the

plan. "I happen to agree with you. I even applaud your ideas. But Rachel is only eight. What makes you so sure she won't be able to keep up?"

He looked away, kept still.

Rhea grew aware of a slow ticking sound. A clock, tall, old, stood in the corner of the enormous room. Its pendulum swung back and forth several times before he opened his mouth again.

"Have you been so busy you haven't bothered to read Rachel's reports, Mrs. Cantor?" Dr. Connor spoke, finally.

Reports. A thick envelope stuffed with little oblongs of paper, each signed by a different teacher, homeroom, phys ed, music, art, plus Miss Knowlton's overall assessment. There was always something in them to depress a mother. Yes. Last month the head teacher had written that Rachel seemed distracted, inattentive, sometimes got up and walked around during class. Rhea had assumed someone would make Rachel sit down and study.

"Perhaps you'd explain," she said. "My husband and I have a reputation for fixing problems. Something's so wrong, we'll go to work."

Dr. Connor got up, began pacing.

"Mrs. Cantor, in our letter we said 'irrevocable.' And that's what we meant. We worked on these decisions. They're final. 'Case closed,' I think you lawyers say."

Irrevocable. The familiar word was soothing. Rhea knew all about irrevocable. That cunt doesn't get one cent of alimony. Positively my last offer. Or, no way the kids can visit while that whore, that kurveh, is in his house. Definite, final, absolutely, I'll never change my mind. But sooner or later, all negotiable.

These decisions, he'd said. A number of cases, then. Not just Rachel.

Trained cross-examiner that she was, Rhea went for her answer.

"But why single out my little girl, Dr. Connor?"

"Nobody's singled out your little girl. She's one of several who'll be better off in easier, more supportive schools."

Schmendrick. He'd stepped right into it.

"I see," Rhea said, her brain filing a reminder to check out the others.

Connor stopped just behind her chair, put his hand lightly on her shoulder. "Look, I know this is unpleasant, a shock. That it hurts. To be frank, it hurt us to decide about these children."

Rhea ignored the hand, starting to feel the excitement of dealing with a hostile witness.

"These children," she said slowly, emphasizing the phrase, as she would for a jury. "What exactly do you mean by 'these children'?"

He took his hand away. "The ones who can't cope."

"I see," Rhea said briskly. "Can't cope. Now, that can mean a couple of things."

She spoke slowly, clearly. "Are we talking about kids who can't cope with the work? The ones who need extra tutoring, remedial help? Children with blocks of some kind, who can't handle things now, but who could with some psychiatric help? Or children who are disturbed, who need heavy therapy?"

There, she thought. Boxed you in. We'll get Rachel a tutor. Or a psychiatrist. Or any other thing you want.

Dr. Connor walked back to his chair. Once there, he seemed to fold himself up. He wrapped his arms protectively across his vest, tucked his fingers out of sight.

"I mean children who can't be helped. At least, not fast enough for this school. Problem children. Like yours, Mrs. Cantor, I'm sorry to say. Like Rachel."

"Dr. Connor," she said, breathing deeply to keep her anger under control. "What exactly do you say is wrong with Rachel?"

"Oh, it's not what *I* say. It's the whole picture. Rachel's teachers find her unfocused. The music teacher says she doesn't pay attention. There's a general feeling among the lower-school faculty that she can't retain what we teach her. We don't share our scores with parents. They're a private assessment. But I can tell you that her intelligence seems normal. And her written work isn't bad. Still, the psychological testing reveals listlessness, a lack of connection."

Rhea's antennae caught something. An echo. Someone else, recently, had said Rachel didn't listen. Who?

"Mrs. Cantor," Dr. Connor sighed. "Let me be honest."

Rhea was searching her memory. But Connor's sigh made

her still more alert. Liars often mentioned honesty just
before they lied.

"We find Rachel disturbed. And disturbing. She's slow,
and she slows the others. Something is wrong with her
entire mental process. Maybe mild retardation. Brain damage. Or an emotional condition a psychiatrist might be
able to work with. Over time. But we don't have that
time."

Dr. Connor shook his head, a look of sorrow on his
long, handsome face.

"I'm afraid you're in for a rough deal. You see, in a
blue-collar family, this wouldn't matter. Rachel would fit.
But a Harvard couple, intellectuals, achievers, both hotshot
lawyers? She's bound to have trouble relating. I'm really
sorry."

Rhea had a vision of Saul, descendant of learned rabbis
and scholars, playing a noisy Atari space game with Rachel,
chasing her wildly around the living room after she'd won.
He thought Rachel was a gift from heaven. He'd adore
her all his days, even if she grew up to be some dumb
dancer.

Don't get sore, she told herself. Think. Is there anything
in what he says? Does Rachel listen? When did I last have
a real talk with her? Not just a kiss good night or a cab
to school with her when Dahlia came late. I've been grateful Dahlia's kept her busy, with the house so crazy now,
with phones, meetings, volunteers checking petitions, doing
their two-fingered typing, stuffing envelopes. How long
since I sat down and ate with Rachel?

Suppose Rachel *is* reacting to the campaign mishegoss?
Wouldn't that prove she's smart, sensitive?

And it's *temporary*. Once I'm inducted, everything will
settle down and be better than ever before.

"Dr. Connor, I've been swamped by this campaign. It
would be odd if Rachel didn't react. But we're aware of
her needs. My husband and I have discussed them, thought
about a trip, a vacation with Rachel. Maybe Jamaica. Sailing, fishing, sun, time to be together as a family. Why not
hold your decision till after that? See if things don't straighten
out?"

Dr. Connor waved his hand quickly, as if he were telling

her to scat. The gesture was annoying, but she held on to her smile.

"Besides," she said. "Change takes time. Classes are full already in most schools."

Connor put his hands on the desk, as if to show he was concealing no weapon. Beautiful WASP hands, long, straight fingers, fine blond hair on the wrists, snowy shirt cuffs.

"First-rate ones are full, I suppose," he said. "But Rachel is not a first-rate child. The local public school will, of course, have to accept her."

Rhea felt last night's cramp return, swell up to a hard knot.

No need now to search her memory. She remembered when she'd first heard *that* phrase.

It was when she called Phil's office to tell him she had big news, a new patient for him, thrilled that she was pregnant after years of trying and failing. Wasn't it a miracle, a baby at forty? Wasn't she a real Sarah, conceiving in her old age?

And then her brilliant brother had hesitated and asked her to come straight over. In his office, he'd put an arm around her gently and begged her not to have the baby, to let him arrange a speedy abortion. "We don't want anything to happen to you," he'd said earnestly. "And Saul's too great a guy to be stuck with a baby that's not erstklassig, first-rate. Statistics are against you, Rhea. There's eight, ten times as much danger of a damaged baby than if you were in your twenties. God made women to have babies in their teens, never mind Sarah."

Rhea, frightened, hurt, had managed to scoff, tell him no chance she wouldn't have her baby.

But she'd gone home feeling sick with fear.

Because Phil insisted, she'd had genetic counseling and the fuss and misery of amniocentesis. She'd held her breath when they showed her the sonogram, reached out a finger to trace the image of her unborn baby's fragile spine, the precious, tiny head. And she'd swallowed her mother's nagging "Quit going to business, stop starving yourself, enough with the pills, the drinks, the staying up late."

Shopping at Bloomingdale's for a layette, she'd be overcome with terror. Tiny sweaters required two arms, rompers two legs, little caps a face with perfect eyes, ears. What if something inside her was old, dried up, hurting her baby, causing something horrible that wouldn't show on a blurry sonogram?

In Rhea's eighth month, her ankles, then her legs swelled up so, she had to stay in bed, not on her back, but her side, to drain her kidneys, rid her body of toxins. For hours Saul read to her while she tossed, arms aching and elbows tender, sweating with desperate worry.

Her delivery, even with Saul holding her hand, looking so doctorish and strong in green pajamas with trailing strings, was a confused, hideous dream.

The baby was facing the ceiling, in the position they called sunny-side-up. Phil said that meant a long, hard labor. The pain was worse than any friend had warned her, worse than anything she'd read about in books. And each wave sharpened her panic over the baby's life and health.

Finally they showed her Rachel. Rhea had reached for the bloody, beautiful infant and silently said a bruchele to God for this miraculous child.

Now, staring at Connor, the terror came back, almost choking her. Was he right? Was it becoming clear only now that Rachel—beautiful, grave, dark-eyed Rachel— was not first-rate?

Rhea shut her eyes.

If it *was* true, it would be on her own head. She'd refused to listen to Phil, who loved her. She'd continued going to business straight into her ninth month. Once, even after Saul objected, she'd interviewed a witness at Riker's Island in the filth of the visiting room. She'd fasted on Yom Kippur and stuck with her committee work for the Women's Bar, determined to keep up with pregnant girls ten years younger, not let any of her clients down just because she was carrying a baby.

Stop it, Rhea told herself.

It's not so. Phil spends lots of time with Rachel, he's a distinguished pediatrician, and he thinks she's fine. And if anything *is* wrong, Saul and I will make it better. And I'll be a judge, full of patience, kindness, wisdom, the best possible mother for Rachel.

"I'm sorry," Connor was saying, dismissal in his tone,

his nostrils pinched, as if he smelled something bad. "In your case, particularly. After all, I'm committed to a broad ethnic sweep in the school."

Rhea's mind seemed to snap to attention.

A cross-examiner treasured the odd phrase, the remark out of context. A broad ethnic sweep?

They were far from the only Jewish family in the school. There were all kinds, German, Russian, Conservative, Reconstructionist, Reform, even the would-be goys only other Jews could recognize for sure. But Rhea had wondered more than once, where were the Jewish teachers, or better still, the blacks? The school's liberal policies died when it came to hiring and paying minority members.

True, the Cantors were more observant than most. Keeping kosher was something Rhea could have lived without. But Saul was something else. He'd been raised Orthodox. And when he became a partner, when money was no object, they'd bought two adjoining apartments, broken through the walls, so they'd have, not just two sets of dishes, but two whole separate kitchens for milk and meat.

When Saul, second in his class at Harvard Law, had actually asked to marry her, Rhea would have put on a sheitel if he'd insisted. But Saul was no zealot—just patiently, firmly committed to his God. It hadn't been easy, either, never eating meat in a restaurant, turning down Friday-night invitations, getting up early Saturdays. She remembered an Irish judge blowing up when Saul requested a postponement for Shevuoth, a holiday the man had never heard of.

But Rachel? Was it too hard on her, leaving early on Wednesdays for Hebrew school, kosher lunches, being different from her classmates?

"Perhaps we've loaded Rachel down," Rhea said briskly. "She handles a lot for a third-grader. Suppose we cut out extras, like piano lessons and Hebrew school? Will *that* make it easier to keep her?"

Looking away so he could absorb the implications of her statement, she noticed on his desk an open box of the school's stationery.

A look at the creamy paper helped her. It brought back the thing she had been straining to remember.

Last month. The living room. Rhea, with a speech to give, typing on a rickety bridge table. And her mother waving a piece of that stationery at her. A letter from the nurse at the Boston School.

"Head lice. In that fancy school. I haven't heard head lice since Warsaw, when my mother washed my hair in kerosene, since the concentration camps."

Rhea had thought, here it comes, the Jewish Sonata.

"When you went to school for nothing, children were clean. Now, thousands of dollars, and a disgusting thing like this. I'd like to know what head lice are doing in that school?"

"So would I," Rhea had said wearily.

When her mother started on the war it took hours, as if she'd actually been in it instead of having reached New York in the 1920's as a child. Her whole life she'd been proud her family had left in time.

When the parks in Warsaw first had signs, "No Jews," she would tell Phil and Rhea. "When the first laws were published, no Jews in the public schools, no bank accounts, that's when my father, may he rest in peace, sold what he could and came here."

And ever since, after what had happened to the Jews, her mother had pounced fiercely on any sign of impending trouble.

"We're handling it," Rhea had said. "Phil gave us a prescription, and Dahlia's washing her hairbrush every five minutes, and what do you want from me? Half the schools in this city have lice, even expensive ones."

"You leave too much to Dahlia," her mother told her, unmoved. "Good girl, you're lucky to have her. But a maid, not a mother. Don't let this judgeship go to your head. Rachel is your responsibility. She's going through something, too. Doesn't listen when I talk to her."

"Maybe she's thinking about something else," Rhea had said, looking pointedly down at the typewriter.

"In this family, the lesson we had in Europe, we should know to head off trouble before it starts."

"Mother, for heaven's sake," Rhea had exploded. "Who doesn't turn off when you talk? You go on till people's ears close up. Rachel's a little girl. Maybe her mind wanders when you go on and on."

"Rhea, I taught you and Phil to listen. That's how you learned, became something in life. Children can't learn if they don't listen."

Rhea, in Connor's office, felt ice water in her veins. Rachel didn't listen. Or couldn't. Her own grandmother said so.

"I can never understand why you people are so stubborn," Connor was saying angrily.

Ah. Now the poison was coming out in the open.

"You people. What people?" she asked gently.

"Mothers, of course. Well, there it is."

Connor, retreating. He wasn't dumb.

"Mothers?" Rhea pressed him. "Or Jews, you mean?"

"Don't put words in my mouth," he said carefully. "I have nothing against Jews. But, Mrs. Cantor, I must tell you, unlike a great many people, I have nothing in particular *for* them, either."

He paused, looked solemn. "My single standard here is intelligence. Being Jewish, I'm afraid, doesn't guarantee you're bright. We have some brilliant children here from Jewish families. But there *are* stupid Jews."

All right, she'd made him say it. What she'd give for a tape recorder.

"Mrs. Cantor," Connor said in a softer voice, obviously thinking he'd finished her off. "I don't understand you. If you think we're so wrong, why trust us with your child? I should think you'd *want* her in a different school."

"Not right now," Rhea said. "I'd prefer to straighten this one out and not have to tell her she's going somewhere else after the summer."

How awful to break this news to Rachel. Tell all your friends good-bye, empty out your cubby, bring home your school sweater, your paintings, your stories. There's no room for them anymore. No room for you.

Terrible. Rachel would think it was her own fault, that she was being punished.

Could Rhea lie? Say that she and Daddy thought Rachel would be happier in a different school? But Rachel *was* happy. And anyway, they'd *never* lied to her, not once. Something precious would vanish the day Rhea stopped being straight with her child.

It took so little to upset Rachel, send tears to her eyes,

turn her mouth down. How would she ever cope with a new class where friendships among the kids had already been formed, circles closed up?

Maybe Saul was right and she should get Rachel away from these cold goyim and into Ramaz, where she'd feel safe and comfortable with her own kind.

Wait. Not so fast. Remember the plan. Who says Ramaz can take her next year? They pick and choose, just like all the schools. Besides, Rachel's all right just now, she's happy at this school. Two years. That's time enough, even to prepare her for a change. Two years.

"Dr. Connor, you say you're sorry. Let's talk about how you might be sorrier. I'm an attorney, in partnership with my husband. We employ over thirty people, and we're very energetic. It would take us half an hour to prepare an injunction for, let's say, unequal treatment of minorities. That's always good for trouble. That might upset your famous parents, those heads of corporations. Especially after election day. Think of the headlines, 'JEWISH WOMAN JUDGE'S CHILD EXPELLED.'"

To her astonishment, Connor smiled boyishly. "Mrs. Cantor, is that really what *you* want? A woman in an important position? Gossip? Notoriety? We're discreet. Nobody needs to know why Rachel is leaving, except you. Is it worth all the fuss? She's very young. This isn't the only school in New York."

"It's the one my daughter is in. It was a lot of fuss getting her in. You chose her over a lot of others, after a lot of testing. A twelve-year school, where she could stay till college. No, Dr. Connor. We'd better compromise."

"College. You don't listen any better than your daughter," Connor said angrily. "Rachel isn't going to college."

Rhea found herself on her feet, in courtroom stance, too angry to sit.

"Why the hell not? Why shouldn't she go to college?"

"Oh, maybe some community college, some Bible-beater." Connor was openly contemptuous. "Sorry. In my mind there's really only one sort of college. Yale. Princeton. Harvard. The sort this school is concerned with, Mrs. Cantor. Rachel hasn't got a prayer."

Through a red haze of rage, Rhea recalled Rachel as a fragile, tiny baby in a pink and ruffled bassinet.

"You're talking about a baby, a small child."

"No sweat," Dr. Connor said. "We can predict. Rachel will have trouble getting past eighth grade in any school, not just here. She'll fail in high school, except possibly in subjects she likes and applies herself to. Just because you and your husband made it by the sweat of your brows to the Ivy League doesn't mean Rachel is going to."

Rhea felt her hands curl into fists. How great to hit him, stop the sound of his voice.

"I see," she said. "Are you a Gypsy? Where do you keep your crystal ball?"

Connor sighed.

"Dear Mrs. Cantor. You may know the law, but we educators have a few trade secrets too. These things are documented. Rachel's behavior shows an unsettled attitude, a troubled personality. She needs a great deal of help. And I'm prepared to sit down with you, not this morning, alas, but another time, soon, and explore with you the best ways of getting it for her. We would even assist you in placing her. If you'd like to discuss Rachel's future, where she would best be served, I'll ring Miss Knowlton, who's right on top of things, and Rachel's head teacher, and set up a conference for you."

He beamed. "Not to worry. We'll manage the transition smoothly."

Rhea put her hands flat on the desk and leaned toward him, using her body for emphasis. She was long past waving her hands at witnesses like amateur intimidators. She knew how to use her eyes, expression, and height. And her voice, pitched low and gravelly with menace.

"I've got news for you, Dr. Connor. I came here to make you keep Rachel. And you know something? You've changed my mind. I don't like you, Dr. Connor, and I don't like what you're saying about my child. It shouldn't be hard to find a better school. But I need time. I need two years. So you're going to carry her for those two years. Most admissions are settled in May. That's what my contract with this school says, incidentally, May renewal. Renew once more. I'll do the rest. Leave the transition to me. And in return, I promise not to embarrass you in any way."

Not embarrass, she thought, but bury you with the board.

Ruin you. Wait till I tell this to Phil. He'll be wild. Half the kids in this school are his patients.

Connor's face was growing red.

"For a lawyer, you're not very quick. You don't seem to understand your daughter isn't normal, let alone bright. I can prove it. In a courtroom, if you like. I have her scores on file, ready to produce for anyone in authority who wants them. She's not as bad as that crazy Barclay kid, or the Fuller child, who's slow as molasses. But her prospects are decidedly dim."

Barclay. Fuller. The names wrote themselves on a yellow pad in Rhea's mind. The man was a Nazi. They'd persecuted school children, the dumb ones, the handicapped, the Jews. For openers.

Rhea put her face close to his, so close she could smell his cologne.

"Two years," she said.

"No. I need her place for a child who's moving to New York next year. A bright child."

Was he crazy? They could always add another child. The school wasn't that crowded.

"Doctor," she said. "I'll slap an injunction on you so fast you won't know what hit you. I'll give you gossip, a black eye, for twenty years, never mind two."

"There are schools for dummies in this city, plenty of them," Connor shouted, as if he'd enjoy putting all those dummies into boxcars and shipping them off to concentration camps. "That's their purpose, nursing dummies along, giving them what they can take. A good mother would go out and find one. But no, you're a big-deal lawyer who likes to make trouble. The kind who's ruined the public schools with demands. You'd rather yell and stir up trouble than look out for your own child."

Rhea kept silent, hearing the clock ticking off seconds, a car honking in the street, and Connor's heavy breathing.

It *was* important to listen. You could get ideas even from a fascist.

Yell and stir up trouble.

Heaven knew she was busy. But a busy person could always handle a little extra.

And she had help—the campaign organization. The volunteers could type a few more letters, make calls, set up meetings. What they couldn't handle, the firm certainly could.

"JUDICIAL CANDIDATE BATTLES FASCIST HEADMASTER." Now, *that* would be a headline.

Rhea felt as if she'd just been handed the case of her life. Connor was persecuting innocent children. Persecuting her Rachel. She would stop him.

And without realizing it, he'd even told her how to start. Miss Knowlton. One of those lesbians all the schools were full of, but a decent woman. She probably knew all his plans and would enjoy talking about them.

I don't have time for friends, never have, Rhea thought. My energy goes to fighting for strangers every day: women dumped by their husbands, families kicked out of their apartments. Last month that skinny black boy not much older than Rachel, facing a jail where he'd be raped the first hour.

Now I'll fight for Rachel.

She leaned over, picked up her pocketbook, and came up smiling. No sense telegraphing her punches.

"Dr. Connor, maybe we're both getting a little excited," she said agreeably. "I'd like time to think. Perhaps you'd think, too, about some less drastic action. But I won't waste time. I'll take your suggestion. I'll go up and see Miss Knowlton right now."

Rhea turned, feeling pleased with herself, satisfied she'd done her best, resolute.

She marched through the secretary's office, out into the corridor.

Then, astonished, she realized her face was wet, that for the first time in years, she was crying.

CORNELIA HEADED STRAIGHT for the elevators. She felt like an intruder in her beloved school, like some shopping-bag lady, ragged and lost, wandering in off the street.

And yet, the lobby was just the same as when she was small. Underfoot, the floor felt the same, black marble squares more worn than the white. Her heel slipped as she hurried, just as it had in her scuffed childhood oxfords. The lobby even smelled the way she remembered, a mustiness of woolen coats soaked in rain, a faint hint of sweat, cooking odors from the kitchen just below.

She moved quickly past the receptionist's glassed-in desk, suddenly wanting to turn around, hurry back out the door, run out into the street.

The receptionist lifted her head, but Cornelia didn't stop. She couldn't smile now. Anyway, the woman knew who she was. And probably knew why she was there. Everyone knew everything in the Boston School. There'd never been anything to hide.

As Cornelia reached the elevator the doors slowly parted, and she realized someone was inside.

A man. He walked straight at her, broad, burly, in a

dark overcoat that brushed softly against her face as he
passed.

Harvey Bache. How great, Harvey being here now. She'd
been thinking about him ever since the letter and had once
even picked up the office phone to call him, but an actress
had pushed open her door, talking. Now it was as if she'd
conjured him up, her own bulky genie.

"Harvey," she said breathlessly.

She longed to put her head against that beautiful coat.
If only he'd smile, say a few words and make her misery
go away, just as he had during her separation.

But Harvey looked annoyed at being stopped. Then he
focused, and the irritation faded from his square, heavy
face. Cornelia was so close she could see the black dots
of his beard under the skin.

"Well, Cornelia," he said. "In a hurry?"

"Oh, Harvey, it's so good to see you. That's an under-
statement. I've been thinking about you for days and days."

He looked wary. Just a flicker of his eyelids, but she
was close enough to catch it. Strange. Why?

"What's up?" he said. "Money tight? The big Broadway
star skipping his payments?"

"Worse," she said. "Much. I need to talk. Can I come
see you soon? It's *real* trouble."

The lines on his face seemed to iron themselves out,
leaving his expression blank, unreadable.

"Sure you're not exaggerating?"

His blandness worried her and made her feel she'd better
explain. He was leaning away from her, as if he expected
something trivial, something he wouldn't want to bother
with.

"It's trouble here. In school. You're still on the board,
aren't you?"

"Yes. Matter of fact, I've just been up with the new
accountant. Take a genius to straighten out the budgets
that old woman left behind. So now I'm running late," he
said, twisting his wrist to expose his handsome watch, more
like a reminder for her than for himself. "Big matrimonial
today, and a judge who hates to be kept waiting. Call me."

"Please. Harvey, I'm really out of my mind. They want
me to take my little girl out of the school."

His eyes snapped to hers.

"I see. Well, that's hard to handle. They have a right. It *is* a private school. On the other hand, it's hardly the only private school on the block."

"It is for me," Cornelia said. "The *only* school. Harvey, can't you help me?"

"Give me a day or two. Call."

In a flap of cashmere—or was it vicuña—he was past her, the click of his heels on the marble fading quickly.

Cornelia, feeling bereft, stood at the elevator, still smelling his cologne. Musky, heavy, it hung on the air, evoking the hours she'd spent in his office, the bank, at a conference table facing Tim, Tim's lawyer, battling.

The scent reminded her of something else, something she'd pushed aside and gratefully buried. She *was* grateful to Harvey for getting Tim out of the apartment, talking those bankers into giving her a mortgage, and letting her pay his bill in spurts.

But now, a memory began forcing its way into her mind of the evening she'd spent with him.

Shaking free of Tim had seemed a giant step. After the first feelings of relief, Cornelia had felt down, a failure, concerned for Livvie. Perhaps, she'd thought, having an uninterested father is better than none. But Harvey encouraged her, said she'd been right, and made time to talk, explore her feelings.

"What kind of guy is he, your actor husband?" he'd asked, leaning forward, eyes on hers. Cornelia told him how Tim had been playing character leads when she was an extra, seemed talented, brilliant, till she'd been around stages and studios and learned some things herself. How he'd welcomed her quitting the theater, scoffed at her work in casting, and resented her rush of love for a baby. "No, but what's he *like*?" Harvey had said. She'd considered, then said, "Well, when Tim gets out of our big bed on a hot summer morning, he turns the air conditioner off, pulls up the blind, opens the bedroom door, and walks out." Harvey nodded, then laughed, a great, expansive roar. And she relaxed, even in his imposing office, pleased he'd understood.

Through the months Harvey had done so much more than she expected. He had helped with her budget, dealt with her landlord, arranged for credit in her own name, and explained how to handle her income tax. And warned her about custody. He joked about it first, saying it was so important a bargaining point that nowadays he asked for it automatically, even when there were no kids. She couldn't just be a good mother, she had to *look* like one to the world. Which meant no dinners out with men, no taking a man back to her apartment at night, no weekends away with anyone, until the separation agreement had been signed.

Cornelia hadn't been concerned. Except for business people, clients, actors, agents, there wasn't a man in the world to have dinner with, much less bring home.

So when, at another meeting, Harvey suddenly asked her to come on out and have dinner, she was surprised and said the obvious—that he'd told her no dates. But Harvey laughed and said he was the exception, the one safe person.

She called Margaret Rose and asked her to stay with Livvie. Harvey, she knew, was married. She'd seen his little girls at school. But men seemed able to have dinner out without thinking twice. Women always had to call somebody.

The dinner was far more exhilarating than she'd expected.

It felt marvelous being with someone who wasn't always on, didn't just talk about himself, didn't criticize what she was wearing, ask her why she kept salt and pepper and Tabasco sauce in her handbag along with a million other useful things. Harvey made *her* feel like a rising star.

Right at the entrance to his office building, his shining car with its "BACHE 1" license appeared the instant he raised his hand. Harvey maneuvered the big car expertly through rush-hour traffic, and kept talking easily, telling about a sensational win he'd just had, a woman who'd come back from a business trip to find her ex-husband had taken possession of her apartment, changed the locks, fired her nursemaid, thrown out her clothes, and refused to let her see her own baby. Cornelia had thought, gratefully, how simple her own problems were in comparison. If Harvey could handle a bastard like that, he'd be able to take good care of her.

The restaurant was way downtown, Rector Street, un-

prepossessing outside, elegant inside. Sitting with him on
a soft little couch at a table covered with fresh flowers,
she kept thinking it was her first dinner in ten years with
someone who wasn't Tim.

The staff treated them with courtesy so elaborate it approached reverence. A bottle of champagne before dinner
was replaced by another during it. Cornelia leaned back,
enjoying Harvey's exuberance, and admired the elaborate
food he ordered, the pleasure with which he attacked it.
Tim had always been at his worst in restaurants, sitting
where his profile would be seen by the other diners and
going on and on about his latest rotten director, a costumer
who was crossing him up, suspiciously checking the bill.
Harvey obviously didn't care what anything cost.

Cornelia had thought she'd feel awkward, a first date
again, after being married so long. But Harvey made
everything simple. He asked about her clients, her problems. She told him about her day, the assignment to find
an elephant to wear socks in a commercial and the client
who asked, after hours of talk, if elephants were paid
residuals. Cornelia had said no problem, she'd found them
an unknown elephant and broke herself up over the joke,
then realized that no one else was amused. But Harvey
had laughed a big, appreciative chuckle that turned heads.
She relaxed, let the waiter keep filling her glass, and even
ate a rum dessert when Harvey insisted, saying she was
too thin. Over Armagnac and coffee she found herself
talking about things she'd never dared tell Tim, how much
she loved the country house, her hope of casting for one
of the great directors—Pakula, Nichols, Coppola. By the
time Harvey signed the check she was almost ready to tell
him her real dream, to *be* a great director.

She hadn't imagined the evening could change into
something she'd never want to remember.

In the car again she felt lazy, easy. But Harvey got her
talking again, asking if she'd ever cast for a porno film.
Cornelia told about the film producers who'd occupied the
office space next door for a few months, with people running in and out all day. She and Stella had marvelled at
the enormous amount of business they seemed to handle.
Then Cornelia talked to one of the guys at the elevator
and went on in to see his film reel. Every foot of it had

been hard-core porn, dogs leaping onto models, men with impossibly gigantic erections attacking little girls, beautiful boys writhing on satin sheets with other beautiful boys. Cornelia, trying to look cool, had made professional comments on lighting, makeup, special effects, anything to keep from talking about the content. When she finished telling Harvey, he put his arm around her and hugged, roaring.

Then she'd just sat, watching the city lights stream past, unknotted, almost happy, half-listening as Harvey talked about how much she'd enjoy being free again, how for an attractive woman like her the world was open. By the time they reached her building she felt light, dreamy.

He double-parked the car, handed her sleepy doorman a bill that seemed to shock him wide-awake.

Cornelia came awake too. Harvey was obviously coming up with her. And he couldn't. Livvie. And Margaret Rose, asleep on the couch, waiting for her.

Or was she imagining? Turning into the kind of woman who thought everyone was after her? After all, this was Harvey Bache, hardly the man to be overwhelmed by her charms.

But Harvey pressed close in the elevator, and Cornelia suddenly thought of a remark she'd once heard on the Fire Island ferry, riding home with Tim on a depressing, misty Monday morning. Two teenagers, sulky, sat glaring at each other, the boy saying crossly, "You had no fucking right to say no. You come to Fire Island, it's *expected*."

When you went to dinner with Harvey Bache, was it *expected*? Then why hadn't he taken her somewhere, a hotel, his office? Had he forgotten Livvie?

Evidently. She'd started to say good night at her door and his big hands had cupped her rear end, hard. "Dessert," he said suddenly. "Let's have a little, Cornelia." And then his mouth was on hers, his knee between her legs.

Hey, she tried to say. No.

But she couldn't, because his teeth were hurting her, his tongue rough inside her mouth. Bad as that was, something else was worse, Harvey's breathing. For all his struggling, it remained as calm and even as if he were still at dinner. With his fingers clutching her arms, the quiet, steady breathing seemed weird, terrifying.

Then the ache left her arms, and she realized he'd stopped, stepped back.

Cornelia felt enormously relieved, glad she hadn't said something virginal and silly. Maybe this was Harvey's idea of a good-night kiss. Perhaps he thought she'd want this, need it after months of being alone.

So she wasn't ready for the thrust of his hand under her dress, scratching her thigh, sliding up toward the join of her panty hose. Or for his thick finger probing at her, bursting through the fabric, stabbing into her, wriggling like some repulsive little animal.

She yelled, then hit out at him, and hearing sounds echoing in the uncarpeted hallway, realized they were the thud of her hand beating at his ear.

All in one swift move Harvey withdrew his finger, released her, and straightened up.

Then, without a heavy breath, in his usual calm voice he thanked her for a pleasant evening, said he'd see her at the office soon, and turned toward the elevator.

Stunned, Cornelia stared at his broad back until the doors opened, then found her key, and after one or two attempts to make it work, stumbled into the apartment. The whole thing had seemed so quick, so peculiar, that even while the ugly word "finger-fuck" formed in her head, she almost thought she'd imagined everything.

But a moment later, in the light, she saw her thighs with the marks of his fingers and her panty hose split at the join, run to the toe-tips. Head thick, stomach heaving, she went to the kitchen and kicked off her shoes, stripping away the tattered nylons, shaking them like some moldy leftover into the garbage can. She stood trembling until she could calm down enough to wake Margaret Rose and thank her for staying with Livvie.

Next morning, her head heavy from the champagne and brandy, she felt ridiculous. She owed Harvey, needed him. She was out of touch, that was all. Maybe everyone did that stuff now. Anyway, what was she supposed to do, find a new lawyer in the middle of everything? Didn't she have enough to worry about?

She'd been nervous about their next appointment. But

Harvey said nothing about their evening, never once looked as if they shared anything but business. And never again asked her out. In fact, he was so circumspect, Cornelia began feeling sure she'd dramatized the scene out of all proportion.

Still, he'd moved away from her fast enough this morning.

She made herself concentrate on the present. She'd put so much effort into this school visit. Last night she'd made Livvie read ahead in her book over and over till she'd understood the new vocabulary words. At breakfast she cautioned her about behaving in class.

Cornelia pushed the elevator button and went up to Nanny's floor, Livvie's floor.

The moment the doors opened she saw the new wall cutting off the far end of the hall. The new research room. It destroyed the proportions of the corridor, swallowing up two classrooms that had been in its place. One had been the children's music library.

Cornelia had loved that room, filled with pictures of Brahms, Mozart, Beethoven, with instruments the children could touch, explore, borrow.

Why couldn't they leave the school the hell alone?

Cornelia felt somehow ancient, the world changing around her.

She remembered Nanny talking about the new facility. Cornelia would learn a great deal, she'd said, watching Livvie without the child's knowing. The room had already been helpful to parents. And had those parents gotten letters too?

She looked up at the big clock on the wall. Still early. Nanny's little office looked tightly shut. Probably she'd taken over some class for a teacher who was late. Cornelia would have to wait, and somewhere Livvie wouldn't see her. Christ, how sneaky. She felt like a traitor. Only how else could she show the school they were wrong?

Cornelia didn't want to go all the way back downstairs. She went through the fire door onto the concrete stairs, sat on the top step, hugging her knees. Five minutes. Then Nanny would surely be there.

Looking up, she saw a little plush bear on the steps above her. One of the nursery children must have dropped it coming down from the roof playground. The bear had a mournful expression. It looked forlorn, abandoned. Cornelia picked up the soft toy, rubbed its worn fur, wondering if she looked that way too.

Was Harvey going to abandon her now? Had her wrestle with him that night turned him off her forever?

But for months now he'd helped her and gotten her through all the shouting with Tim. He could have given her short shrift, pressed her for money. And he hadn't. Only a few weeks ago, at the last parents' meeting, he'd said a perfectly pleasant hello.

She went back to the hall and knocked on Nanny's door. The cultivated voice asked her in.

Cornelia had seen Nanny often enough since Livvie had started school, but always busy at something, clipboard in hand, bending down to talk to a small child. Now she looked straight at the older woman and studied her with a casting director's eye.

Nanny Knowlton had grown handsome since she was a girl. Back straight, shoulders squared, her short hair in thick, wonderful waves. She had a good smile, white, even teeth. She was so like her teachers of long ago that Cornelia almost curtsied. Nanny was a long way from the gawky girl who'd been the curtain-puller for school plays, elected to the student-government offices nobody wanted.

"Somebody's lost a friend," Cornelia said, handing over the little bear.

Nanny reached for the toy, wishing she could reach for Cornelia. She let her fingertips graze the back of Cornelia's hand, felt her heartbeat quicken.

Cornelia Ames. How long had it been?

Nanny had been home from college for Christmas and gone to school one evening to watch the dance group perform. She had hardly expected to enjoy it. Simply something to do. Except for a few deb parties, invitations from her friends' mothers, there had been dull, empty evenings.

For her, watching dancers was always bittersweet. The lithe bodies onstage made her feel awkward, gawky, aware of her knees pressing against the seat in front of her, the girdle digging into her waist. She always envied the dancers their rounded arms and legs, wistfully comparing them to her own.

And then Cornelia.

Lightly, swiftly, she had floated and spun. Her pale face seemed moonlit, her hair gleaming. Her black leotard had outlined all the young curves of her slight body.

Nanny had been mesmerized. She had sat straight, yearning, thinking how heavenly to cup those tiny breasts, to cradle that slim waist in her own strong arms.

When the curtain fell, she had felt a dampness in her palms, in the warm place between her legs.

Next afternoon, she'd returned to school to watch for Cornelia and ask cautious questions. A scholarship girl, professor's daughter, an absentee mother. But with lots of friends, at the center of every play and performance, the darling of the acting and dance teachers. Nanny had sat chatting to the receptionist, waiting for the upper-school girls to come down, and had seen Cornelia in the middle of a crowd, laughing, setting down an enormous schoolbag to roll her skirt at the waist, up, way past the regulation knee-length. Then she'd raced off on long, skinny legs, waving at the receptionist, who'd shaken her head, smiling.

Nanny had almost forgotten until years later, when Cornelia appeared one September day with her own little girl by the hand. Still lithe, with the look of a dancer but no longer ethereal, a chaste ballerina. Cornelia now was angular, striking, with a mass of heavy hair, like the girls on the covers of the fashion magazines Nanny saw at newsstands. Later Nanny had heard Cornelia was separating from her handsome husband. Her heart had stirred. Could Cornelia possibly be turning away from men? Was she one of the beauties for whom men were too easy?

Now Nanny tried to listen, but her thoughts kept wandering. Here was Cornelia, vulnerable. And there were so many avenues to her heart. Teacher to parent. Schoolmate to schoolmate. Friend to friend. One lonely, unhappy woman to another.

Could she reach out? Could she make Cornelia realize what most women know deep down, even if they refuse to acknowledge it? That men and women have opposing desires, must battle, act out their differences. That women share a wealth of memories, emotions, experiences. That no man can ever be as close, as true for a woman as another woman.

If I comfort her now, explain what must be done for the child, Nanny thought, perhaps Cornelia will turn to me. And then I can begin to help her.

Nanny put her hand on Cornelia's arm.

"Oh, Nanny," Cornelia said. "That letter. How could they? I came here when I was three. So did Livvie."

"I'm so sorry," Nanny said. "I really love Livvie. And I know it's hard for you to think of her in a different school."

"Not hard," Cornelia said. "Impossible. My God, Nanny, I hoped Livvie's *daughter* would come here."

"Now, Cornelia," Nanny said. "Don't be like those fathers who went to Harvard and Princeton, so their sons had to, no matter what."

"Is that what you think? It's not so," Cornelia said. "I want it for *her,* not me. I can't explain that to outsiders. But you should certainly understand. I mean, if she can't learn *here,* how is any school going to help her?"

Dear Lord, Nanny thought, if only I had my Saturday school, *I* could help. We wouldn't be forced into this drastic move, expelling these children.

"Dear Cornelia," she said. "With things as they are, Livvie can't manage here. Surely you've seen her frustration, her anger?"

"No. I haven't," Cornelia said. "And I pay a *lot* of attention. I'm with Livvie most evenings and weekends. We *talk.* I wake her to see the sunrise, take her almost everywhere, even the plays and stuff I have to see. The only person I ever leave her with is my nurse, who's much more than a nurse. She's a friend, and she's wonderful with Livvie."

"Still," Nanny said carefully, "you do work full-time. You're not often in school. Many of the class mothers volunteer, you know, for the library, trips, those things. They *know* how their girls get on in school."

Color was coming up in Cornelia's pale face.

"Cornelia, Livvie seems so angry, so unhappy. Perhaps it's your home situation, your separation. I'm not as quick to recommend therapy for small children as many of the younger teachers here. But divorce is *so* difficult for children, especially sensitive ones. Then again, perhaps it's the pressure for achievement now. It's different from when

we were girls. It's not enough to be a lady, interested in
the arts, music. Now we expect babies to read, count. Now
the parents demand pushing. That's why the board chose
Dr. Connor. He's trying to make us far and away the best
school in the city."

"Fine," Cornelia said stubbornly. "Just so Livvie's a part
of it."

She loves that child, Nanny thought. But she doesn't
see that Livvie's blocked by her emotions, that her reading
scores are hopeless. In a public school, she'd be lower-
middle. Here, with so many bright children, it's worse.
And lately she's seemed so closed in.

She looked at her watch.

"It's time for Livvie's class," she said gently. "Let's go
along and have a look."

Perhaps, this morning, Cornelia would see it. Nanny
almost hoped something would upset the child in class.
Then there would be reason to keep in touch. Better still,
she might tutor Livvie a bit on her own. Only a stopgap
measure, of course, but it would mean reporting to Cornelia, seeing her.

Cornelia felt as if a door were closing. She'd counted
on Nanny. And she'd only criticized.

At least she could defend her child against one of the
ugly things Nanny'd said.

"Livvie's *not* angry and unhappy," Cornelia told her,
feeling angry and unhappy herself. "She's sweet and nice
and good. At least, she is at home."

Immediately, into her mind shot the memory of Livvie
yelling "Fuck" and throwing the book. Jesus. Could Nanny
be right?

But Livvie had been pressured when she'd done that.
*Usually*, she was gentle, agreeable. Did she ever refuse to
come in mornings and read? Wasn't she a lamb with Margaret Rose?

As they walked across the hall, Cornelia's throat began
aching, and she had trouble swallowing.

Nanny unlocked a door with her key, and led her into
darkness.

Out of nowhere came the memory of a terrible audition
in a dark theater, when Cornelia had sung for a director
everybody knew was a bastard. Frightened, she suddenly

couldn't project, couldn't make her voice reach him in the fourth row. Halfway through the lyrics, she'd seen the man get up and disappear. Then she'd begun hearing giggles, whispers, out in the darkness. Sensing something, she'd looked around to find him behind her, mimicking her gestures, mouthing words without making a sound. Cornelia had wanted to step into the trapdoor, fall, die.

The airless room seemed oppressive, a hot cave of darkness.

And Nanny seemed suddenly very close.

Cornelia pulled gently away, slipped into a seat.

"In the classroom, that glass looks like a mirror," Nanny said, her voice shaking just a little. "The children don't know its use. They behave naturally. It's far better than being right in the room, observing."

Cornelia forgot about Nanny and began concentrating on the classroom spread before her like a stage. Sunny and attractive, it was lined with bookshelves to the ceiling, with ladders on rails so the children could climb to the top shelves. Window seats with bright cushions. Gleaming tile floor. Small tables and chairs back against the bookshelves, so the children had plenty of room to play.

They were playing now. Cornelia's eyes zoomed instantly to Livvie. She was near the window, sun gilding her hair, dappling her jumper, bathing her in light.

Cornelia beamed her a message. Remember everything. Be wonderful today. I'm praying for you. Please, please be like the other little girls.

Nanny was whispering. They mustn't speak loudly and must be careful of the lights. The glare of the lamp, a flare from a match, would show through the one-way glass. The classroom was soundproof. When she turned the switch, they would hear the children through microphones.

Suddenly Cornelia heard noise, the children, their voices echoing strangely.

Oh God, she thought. This is so hole-and-corner, so overblown. Like something for the CIA. We're spying on little children.

She kept her eyes on Livvie, happy in a group busy with a sturdy dollhouse. Cornelia recognized Susie, Cricket. The girls were playing nicely. They made a pleasant picture through the dark glass, like a well-shot television commercial.

Livvie and Cricket had on the same brand of sneakers. Cornelia knew how important it was to wear the right things, what everyone else wore. She'd learned the hard way, never having had them. Her father hadn't understood at all.

Now the children were putting away their toys and getting ready for a work session. Work and play periods alternated, even in second grade.

Nanny was whispering that relaxation was necessary for children so young. Apologizing? Did she think Cornelia expected them to work, study every minute?

Cornelia leaned forward again. Now the children were breaking up into small groups, going to the shelves for notebooks and pencils. They were pushing the small chairs into a semicircle around Miss Montgomery. The noise of the scraping chairs echoed through the microphones, hurting Cornelia's ears.

There was confusion for a moment, the children pushing their chairs about. Then the group got slowly into shape, each little girl in a chair. In the press, Livvie had been pushed to the back. She stood now with her chair in both hands, looking for a place to put it down.

And then, her breath catching, Cornelia saw what was going to happen.

The children had packed their seats tightly together in a circle. They'd formed a little wall, leaving no space for Livvie. Cricket was out in front, her chair jammed smack against the shelves.

But they're making a barrier, Cornelia thought. Against Livvie. Like cowboys and Indians. And Livvie's an Indian.

Frightened, she turned to Nanny, remembering to whisper. "Why doesn't Miss Montgomery tell them to move, make room?"

She saw Nanny put a finger to her lips, looked back at the glass. Now the little girls were sitting demurely, feet on the floor, books in their laps. All the navy-blue jumpers seemed to make a solid dark wall. Only Livvie was apart, away from the circle. Cornelia could see her knuckles whitening on the back of the chair and could almost feel the turmoil in Livvie's mind. Her heart began to swell, pressing painfully against her rib cage.

Miss Montgomery was writing on the blackboard, her back to the children.

"Nanny," Cornelia said softly, keeping her eyes forward, on the glass. "For God's sake. What's wrong with Miss Montgomery?"

No answer. Chest aching, Cornelia saw Livvie try to push again between two of the children. Again, no help.

Cornelia stood up then, stumbled forward in the dark toward the glass. Her heart seemed pressed now against her lungs, making it hard to breathe.

Closer to the glass, she saw one little girl with her head down, shoulders shaking.

She was laughing.

Cornelia felt Nanny's hand on her arm. She had come forward too.

"Cornelia, you *must* be quiet," she said.

But Cornelia's hands were on the cold glass, pushing at it, as she watched Livvie moving around the outside of the circle, trying to get a corner of her chair into a crack between two seats while the children shoved with their little bottoms to keep the circle closed.

She saw Livvie put both elbows back, push her chair across the floor, hard. It skidded, the way her reading book had at home, crashed into the broad window seat, and overturned with a thud.

Then, at last, Miss Montgomery looked up, pointed to a place between two of the girls, told Livvie please to pick up the chair and sit down.

"High time," Cornelia said into the glass.

But when Miss Montgomery turned back to the blackboard, no one moved. Livvie still stood helplessly with the chair, her face pink, her eyes glinting tears.

Cornelia felt her heart explode. She began shaking in the darkness, hearing the children's laughter horribly distorted by the microphones.

"Stop them," she hissed at Nanny. "Go in there and make them behave."

She wouldn't watch this horror show another second. She'd crash through that glass, get to Livvie, hold her, take her away from the jeering, horrible children, kiss and comfort her.

"You see," Nanny was saying quietly.

Find the door, Cornelia thought, feeling desperate. Get in there, protect Livvie, yes, and shake that idiot teacher, make her see what's going on.

But she froze then. Because Livvie was picking up her chair and holding it high.

Taking a step toward the half-circle of children, she crashed the legs of the chair down on the shoulder of the girl nearest her. Then she became a little whirlwind, arms flailing, sneakers kicking, hair tossing. Through the speaker came the high, piercing sound of her screams.

For Cornelia, the screaming was a match held against her flesh, burning, sending her into action.

"No," she shouted, slapping at Nanny's restraining hand, dashing for the door. She *had* to get out, get to Livvie.

Through the glass she saw Miss Montgomery finally tuning in, kneeling, taking Livvie in her arms.

Hot, seething, Cornelia saw that Livvie was crying, bent over with her face in her hands. She seemed to be pulling herself in, closing herself up.

Cornelia could feel herself curving into the same bent misery. She was consumed with terrible fear, for Livvie's sanity, for her future. Her mind filled with black terror, dark as the shadowy room.

Something was wrong with Livvie. She'd looked like a little savage, howling, kicking, punching those children. And they knew, and banded together against her.

Something was wrong with Livvie. Cornelia saw pictures in her mind. Livvie in a bare white hospital room. Livvie slumped in a chair, staring at the floor. Livvie with dull eyes, her brightness, her lively expression gone forever.

The pictures came faster then, Livvie in a straitjacket, in a large room full of people with hollow eyes.

Burning, Cornelia hardly felt Nanny's arm on her shoulder, Nanny's cool cheek pressed against hers.

Livvie lay on the bed in the nurse's office.

She felt empty, torn, all used up, like a popped balloon. Miss Bevin had said to rest. She'd turned off the lights, taken off Livvie's shoes, put her under the scratchy blanket, and tiptoed out.

But still Livvie felt cold.

How long before she could go home? Would she have to stay till the end of the day? Susie and Cricket, it was all their fault. Scumbags. If only she'd bashed them with the chair, made them hurt and cry, the same way she'd hurt.

Only she shouldn't have done that. Getting so mad was no good. And hitting could mean bad trouble. When Miss Knowlton told her, Mommy would be sad. And Margaret Rose would be good and mad too.

Livvie felt a tear run out of the side of her eye and roll down into her ear.

Oh. The door was clicking open.

A slice of light was sliding in from the hall and going away again. The floor was crackling. Miss Bevin, Livvie thought.

The nurse was nice. Old, crinkled, and very small. But she smelled good, like cherry cough medicine. And she smiled when she looked down your throat in the morning before school started.

Livvie turned her head to the door.

And there he was. She felt herself get icy cold. She squeezed her eyes shut and froze.

But it didn't help. Now she was seeing him inside her head.

In the bathroom, leaning on his mop and watching her pee. And then at home, coming out of her closet late at night and standing by her bed, like a ghost.

Now she could really hear him. He was coming closer. She could *feel* his eyes making holes in her. Her legs were starting to shake under the blanket, her fingers curling tight.

He was next to the bed. She could smell his garbage smell.

Then he *could* see her anywhere in school. Even with the door closed, in the nurse's office. So he didn't tell lies. He would do what he said. To Mommy.

If anything happened to Mommy, Livvie would die. She'd make herself die.

Something was happening now. He was putting his smelly hand on her head.

Livvie knew she was choking. She felt a noise come into her mouth. But it wouldn't come out. And no, she better not *let* it out. Miss Bevin might.hear. And he could say that was the same as telling.

Oh, Mommy, Livvie thought. You're nicer than anybody. You like me even when I'm mad, even when I'm dumb. You take me in bed, even into your bubble bath. And you're funny, making my dolls talk, singing so many songs. Only a horrible creature from outer space could think of hurting you.

The man's hand felt all crawly like the lice that time she'd had them in her hair, itching all around on her head. Livvie hurt inside her chest, like an ache from being punched, as if she'd been running too hard.

"What's the matter, little beauty?" the bad man sort of whispered.

Now Livvie's mouth tasted like vomit. She tried to answer, but no words came.

She swallowed, and tried again.

"Nothing, thank you," she said.

"Wet again? Let me see," he said.

No. *No.* Red and green exploded into her shut-tight eyes. Her ear buzzed now, like the time the big dragonfly had flown right in, and she'd screamed so hard she'd thought she would burst. Stop, she wanted to yell. Mommy. Somebody help.

She felt her forehead bang into the cold, hard wall.

"Let's see," he said. "Let's just see."

Oh please, don't. Don't touch me, please.

But his hand was coming under the blanket, touching her leg, turning it into fire.

He wouldn't stop. He'd do what he always did, and then she'd feel sick and smelly and dirty, so dirty she could stay in a bubble bath all night, scrub with Mommy's scratchy bath mitten and spray herself with perfume and *still* not feel clean.

He was starting now, pushing her skirt up.

Her hands flew over her eyes. She bit right down on her tongue to stay quiet.

"Poor little beauty," he was whispering. "Don't you

worry. Johnny's going to make you better. Much, much better."

Now she could feel his other hand coming under the blanket too, reaching for the elastic of her pants, stretching it.

He was pulling her pants down, sliding them over her knees, then her socks, taking them away. She could feel cold air on her skin.

Livvie screwed her eyes even tighter shut and put her hands over her mouth. She knew what came next, but she wanted not to know. She tried to make her brains dead.

Fingers. Big, thick fingers. Poking, scratching a little, tickling, pushing into her. Hurting.

She bit her lip and felt more tears coming out of her eyes.

Oh. Now she could tell his hand was gone.

Slowly she peeked. Maybe he was going away now.

She started to yell, but stopped herself just in time.

His dark face was right there, filling her eyes. He was bending. Putting his mouth *down there.* She felt it, muddy, wet, horrible.

She couldn't hold still anymore. She just couldn't. She even let a scared sound come out of her mouth.

Suddenly the bad man jumped his face away.

She heard steps in the hall.

Lots of tears were falling out of her eyes now, wetting her whole face, the blanket. And sounds were choking her throat.

"You don't tell, right?" he whispered. "You remember what happens if you tell?"

"I won't tell," she said.

"That's right," he said. "You don't want your mama cut."

Light flashed on and off from the door. He was gone. Magic, like a genie, his feet not even stepping on the floor.

Now Livvie felt the dark pressing down all around her, making her dizzy, making it hard to breathe.

She needed to go to the bathroom, too.

She put her hands under the blanket and pulled her skirt down as far as it would go. Then she pulled the blanket high up around her.

It didn't matter about her underpants.

Last time, she'd told Margaret Rose she wet them and left them in the school bathroom. She'd just say that again. Margaret Rose had been mad. But what else was there to do?

She *couldn't* tell. He *would* hurt her mother. And she wasn't just an ordinary mother, like other girls had. She was beautiful and soft, and she loved Livvie more than anyone in the world. Even a tiny cut hurt a lot, made blood. If people had enough blood gone, they died. And a big knife could hurt much, much more, make enough blood go so her mother could die.

That's why she could never, never tell anyone.

At least now she could cry out loud.

She sobbed and breathed in and sobbed, while all the tears came out of her eyes.

She didn't even try to wipe them away. She just closed herself all up and kept still, let them melt into the pillow.

Mrs. Arthur F. Barclay
165 East 96th St.
New York, N.Y. 10128

Dear Mrs. Barclay:

This confirms the appointment for your daughter with Dr. Snyder on November 3rd, at 10:00 A.M.

Please make sure Tucker has had a good night's sleep and a sound breakfast before your arrival. The tests are lengthy, and it is important that the child not be hungry or tired.

The charge for the session is five hundred dollars. We would appreciate your paying at the office, in order to facilitate our billing procedure.

Very truly yours,

*Margaret C. Marion*

Margaret C. Marion
Secretary to Dr. Snyder

Yale Child Study Center
230 South Frontage Road
New Haven, Conn. 06510

BIBB TOOK THE chocolate-pudding bowls into the kitchen, hoping the children would excuse themselves from the table quickly and get to their homework. The boys, she knew, had mountains of it, Latin, math, *Macbeth*. And Tucker had promised to play by herself with her dolls and not call Mummy till bedtime.

The moment she heard their chairs clatter she left the dishes in the sink and hurried out.

The dining room was empty. Where was Arthur? The living room? Empty too.

In the bedroom? Odd. Only a minute ago he'd been telling the children one of his amusing stories about the Navy. She wouldn't have hurried him for the world. But she *did* want to talk to him.

She went down the long, narrow hall to the back of the apartment, past the boys' hockey sticks, school bags, and the pile of library books she'd better return soon.

Through the open bedroom door she saw Arthur. Good. But, dear God, in a fresh T-shirt? And lacing up a shoe?

"You're *not* going out," Bibb said, feeling downcast.

Arthur looked up and smiled. "Rehearsal," he said, balancing on one foot while he laced the other shoe. "I told you."

Had he?

Yes, probably. Why hadn't she listened more carefully? Ah, but she'd been trying to stay calm, to keep her temper.

Poor Arthur. He looked tired, a bit grim.

She remembered when he'd first joined the Blue Hill Troupe. Not nearly so many rehearsals then. But the director was new this year, with a reputation to make. (And *Yeomen of the Guard* was more complex than most Gilbert and Sullivan any amateur group could produce, even the best and oldest.)

But maybe it was good he was going out. Perhaps he'd say yes right off, to settle things quickly.

"Darling," she said. "There's that appointment about Tucker tomorrow. I made it early, nine, so it wouldn't interfere with your day."

Arthur stopped smoothing his socks, turned toward her.

"I thought you'd given that up," he said.

Bibb felt herself stiffen.

"Oh, Arthur. You *promised* to think about it. I need you with me. It'll make *all* the difference."

Alone, she thought, I'll be just another complaining mother. But with a father, a senior bank officer, taking time away from business? That's a whole other thing.

She sat down on the bed, watched Arthur straighten up, fold his arms. Such muscular arms. In T-shirt and shorts he looked magnificent, ready to hoist a sail, smash a tennis ball. She hadn't any brothers. She hadn't seen a man undressed all the way until Arthur, and hadn't dared look, *really* admire male bodies, till she had the boys to bathe and diaper.

"Bibb, we've been through this. Going back to Rosenzweig is ridiculous. What good can it do?"

"It'll do *me* good. Honestly, Arthur. For six years I've taken Tucker around to doctors. Every one of them predicted disaster. Said she was hopeless. And everyone was wrong. Why *wouldn't* I go back and tell them they were fools?"

Oh God, he was turning toward the closet.

"It's uncalled-for. Rosenzweig's not a bad fellow. He's taken care of the children competently for years."

Rage pricked her sharply, as if she'd run a darning needle into her finger.

"Competently? Last week you agreed he'd been pretty damn casual about Tucker. If he's the same with other mothers, botching things for their children, it's time *someone* told him."

"Bibb," Arthur's muffled voice came from behind the closet door, "you know I try to back you up. I know you love a fight for a good cause. But this is just stirring up trouble. Can't you *ever* let something go?"

And where would Tucker be now, Bibb thought, if I'd let things go?

"Maybe this is a bad time to talk," she said, straining to keep her voice cheerful. "Of course, you could just say yes. End of discussion."

Arthur came from behind the door, wearing gray slacks, holding his blazer. The new one.

Its crested gold buttons distracted Bibb. She'd have thought khakis, loafers, an old sweater. Why dress up for a rehearsal?

"Bibb. I hate seeing you all worked up. And for nothing. No matter what we tell him, Rosenzweig isn't going to change."

"Worked up," he'd said. That phrase suddenly made Bibb realize what a sight she must be—sandy hair straggling out of its pageboy, glasses smudged, chocolate blotch on her shirt front, scuffed loafers, threads dangling from her old tweed skirt.

Looking down at the floor, she could see how shabby the room had grown, too. Her mother's Tabriz was too threadbare to last much longer. And the beautiful lowboys badly needed refinishing.

"Arthur, darling," she said wearily. "Men listen to other men. Doctors listen to fathers. So do teachers, in case you hadn't noticed. And lawyers, bankers, ministers. But especially doctors."

She saw him frown, but she couldn't stop herself.

"Please," she said. "You didn't take Tucker to his office, month after month. *I* did. *I* listened to his joshing. His stupid old saws. When Tucker was so late starting to walk, he said not to worry, she'd be walking long enough. He used to pat my shoulder, say she'd grow out of her trouble. In first grade, when she was screaming every day in school, he was *still* saying it."

Arthur shrugged into his blazer and reached into his bureau drawer for a handkerchief. Then he came and sat down, putting his arm around her. His sleeve felt soft, comfortably fuzzy against her cheek. He smelled fresh, soapy. Had he found time for a shower?

"Bibb, I know you. You want to fix the world. But now you're not being fair. Rosenzweig isn't a magician. Nobody was as close to Tucker as you. And how many years did it take *you* to find out what was wrong. Remember how many doctors you saw?"

Bibb felt her anger threaten to erupt. Explode.

My God, did he think she needed *reminding?* The man at New York Hospital saying Tucker was retarded, waving a computer printout as if that proved it. The Park Avenue neurologist who pontificated for a whole hour about the irreversibility of brain damage.

"Arthur"—she struggled to keep her voice low—"Rosenzweig was no outside consultant. He *knew* her. He saw her the same day she was born."

And signed her birth certificate. Tabitha Ann.

Bibb remembered how proud, how thrilled she felt. A daughter at last. And such a beauty, long lashes, tiny mouth, impossibly small hands.

If they'd let me, she thought, I'd have held her all day, kept her in bed with me at night. The nurses had to keep chasing me away from the nursery glass.

"After all," Arthur was saying, "you hardly left Tucker

a minute that first year. And even *you* didn't know she was in trouble, not for months."

Yes. I was so busy wishing things for her, praying that she'd grow up like you, attractive, self-confident, accomplished. Not plain, gawky, high-strung, and emotional, like me.

But Tucker *was* emotional. And Rosenzweig had said she'd change.

"He wasted years," she said, feeling stony-hearted. "He made me feel clutchy, silly. All those patronizing doctor jokes. I tried so hard to believe him. After all, the best pediatrician in New York, everyone said so. We'd leave his office and get on the bus and someone would have a loud radio and Tucker would turn purple and scream."

Even now I dream about those bus rides, heads turning, people winking at each other, scowling at me. I always wanted to shout at them, staring at poor Tucker, so small, so frightened. They were so *cruel*. Lady, something's very wrong with that kid. Why don't you shut her up? Give her a good smack?

Though her eyes were wet, she could see Arthur's mouth tightening.

Then she felt ashamed of herself. It was bad enough to harangue Arthur, worse to cry. He *never* burdened her with his worries. She sensed them, of course, knowing him so thoroughly, seeing past his beautiful manners, his diffidence. She knew, when Arthur saw William's C's in math, that he fretted about the entrance exams for St. Mark's. And when Harlan's backhand was weak, she sensed his impatience. She was well aware that he worried about moving up at the bank, with all those minority people they were pushing now.

Dear Arthur. Brought up, of course, never to complain. But he didn't understand. Rosenzweig wouldn't upset her. She'd feel wonderful speaking out on behalf of all the little helpless children in doctors' offices. Shivering, poor lambs, on cold examining tables in their tiny underpants. Seeing scary instruments. Hearing nurses call them abnormal, watching their mothers cry. Someone *must* speak for them.

Arthur was patting her shoulder.

"Rosenzweig was trying to boost your confidence. I'd

have done the same, I *did* the same. Nine out of ten times it's the best approach."

"But Tucker was the tenth," she said, feeling desperate. "Don't you remember? How she'd panic when the door-bell rang, when Tigger barked suddenly. Get stiff as a little board and howl. Good Lord, Arthur, I spent *hours* holding her, showing her where the sounds came from. The vac-uum has a worn spot where I used to pat it so she'd know it was harmless. And Rosenzweig would say be glad she had two good ears."

Wrenching her head away, Bibb caught a look at herself in the mirror, flushed, eyes shining.

Like a cross child, she thought. She almost expected to hear her mother's voice saying, "Elizabeth, if you're going to lose your temper, please go into the bathroom, and stay till you can control yourself."

"Those doctors were so awful," she said. "Remember that neurologist who said Tucker had an attention-deficit disorder? The whole time he was talking, the poor child was getting pink in the face, focusing on what he was saying."

Arthur stood up abruptly.

"Bibb, I can't keep them waiting," he said. "If you like, we'll talk when I get back. Or in the morning, if I'm late."

"You're always late these days," she burst out, not car-ing if she sounded like a shrew. "If it isn't the bank, it's a rehearsal, a seminar, a meeting. Tucker is your child too."

She watched lines etch themselves on his forehead, gray come up on his cheeks.

"That's not called for," he said quietly. "Of course she's my child. But there's something you don't seem to under-stand. Tucker's troubles are over. You've found the an-swer."

"That's *exactly* why I want to go back to that bastard and tell him," Bibb shouted.

"No."

He stepped closer, frowning.

"You simply can't stop. You're so used to fighting for Tucker, you've made it a career. Seeing Rosenzweig, that's just another way of holding on to Tucker's problems. Can't you let go? Can't you see how lucky we are?"

Bibb felt a flash of pure fury.

*Lucky?*

After she'd sat with Tucker night after dreary night cajoling, bribing her into doing lessons a day ahead? My God, it had been terrible, Tucker so balky, Bibb so despairing.

And after she'd worn herself out having children over almost every day after school, every Saturday, thinking up the best birthday parties, so Tucker would have friends.

And the PTA. What hadn't she volunteered for? Typing envelopes, dusting library books, sewing costumes. Raising money, patrolling crossings, collecting dues. So the teachers would feel grateful, make allowances for Tucker. How else could Bibb have been invited to join the teachers in their lunchroom, pick up so quickly on all the gossip and sense danger for Tucker? So when some secretary made a mistake and sent a letter about Tucker leaving the school, Bibb could go straight to Miss Knowlton, get her to straighten things out.

Was *that* luck? Ridiculous.

Suddenly she realized tears were trickling onto her shirtfront.

"Wait for me," she choked out, making for the bathroom. "Just please wait one damn minute."

In the bathroom she banged the door, turned on the tap, and sat on the edge of the tub.

Why did her rage always erupt in tears? She never cried when she was miserable.

And there'd been so much misery. She grew dry-eyed, remembering.

The teacher saying at the end of first grade that Tucker must have a learning disability. Frightening, of course. But still, better than Rosenzweig's insistence that nothing was wrong. Bibb had thought: a problem with a name. Now I can start to solve it.

She had spent hours at the Forty-second Street Library, looking up every listing about learning disabilities in the endless catalog, deciphering monographs and learned papers, searching for a case, a description of symptoms that might match Tucker's.

Learning disabilities, Bibb soon grasped, were neurological breakdowns, a sort of tangled wiring in the brain.

They produced peculiar handicaps. Either they prevented children from getting information into their heads, or kept it from sticking there for them to retrieve when they needed it. Some children couldn't fit letters with sounds. Others saw letters and numbers in a jumble, couldn't perceive them in the right order. Some could manage complicated geometry, but not arithmetic. Others remembered a zillion baseball statistics, but couldn't add six and five.

The children were often intelligent. But they were blocked in some odd way. A disability, the books all stated, was not an inability. Many of them gave accounts of famous people who'd overcome learning disabilities—Woodrow Wilson, Patton, Churchill, Kennedy. And of others, like Lee Harvey Oswald, who'd never been helped, whose frustrations grew year by year.

And Tucker's were growing. She was hitting children, smashing toys, having tantrums.

Then the visits to doctors began. Bibb noted the names in the articles and made appointments with neurologists, psychologists, child psychiatrists. At first, she'd thought she could go by herself and not put Tucker through so much trouble. But the specialists needed to see Tucker. And all of them cost the earth.

Putting so many bills on Arthur's desk, Bibb felt guilty, as if she'd been squandering their capital. But he'd been wonderful, encouraging her each time a new doctor drew a blank. And hadn't Arthur backed her on the Boston School, instead of Nightingale, where his sisters had gone? Even after his mother said it was an undisciplined school filled with the rude children of nobodies?

Bibb thought of the winter afternoon when two enormous bills came in the mail and, feeling desperate, she had forced herself to take her grandmother's rose diamond bracelet out of its rubbed-velvet case, guiltily wrap it in a hankie, and stuff it in the zipper pocket of her handbag. She showed it from booth to booth at the Diamond Center, finally handing it to the pale, bearded dealer who bid highest. Then she'd taken the money straight to a bank on the same street and hidden the bankbook in a beaded evening bag, feeling like a thief each time she took it out for a withdrawal.

And it was after that she began waking at night, losing

weight, watching her hair turn, day by day, into straw matting. She started working harder than ever with Tucker, with the PTA, staying longer at the library, past the popular books now and into the medical journals.

Then one afternoon, when the library seemed unbearably stuffy, when trees were blossoming outside the window and she knew she'd soon have to pack the children up for the summer in Wainscott, Bibb found an article called "Anatomical Approaches to Developmental Dyslexia." It described new diagnostic approaches being used at the Yale Child Study Center.

By now, Tucker was balking at all tests, blood, urine, eye, ear, as well as psychological ones, and having to tell what she saw or imagined in pictures and ink blots, playing with dolls that were supposed to be families, solving puzzles. On her seventh birthday Bibb had bought her a two-story Victorian dollhouse with the most cunning gingerbread trim, filled it with tiny oil lamps and knickknack shelves, copper pots and pans, needlepoint rugs, and velvet draperies. She'd spent hours and nights arranging it perfectly, making it neat and spotless, the way her own apartment had looked a year or two ago. And Tucker had examined it gravely, tentatively put out a hand, and then asked what kind of a test it was, what was she supposed to do with it. Bibb had felt such pain she'd wanted to stamp on the beautiful toy, smash it into fragments.

But after the summer, Bibb had to try again. She'd promised Tucker that Yale would be different. An outing, a trip on a train, orange drink from a vendor.

And the Center *was* different.

From the moment they went through the door, everyone, doctors, nurses, technicians, treated Tucker like a guest, a princess. She responded by behaving like one.

They let Bibb stay with her through the day, moving from one examing room to the next. None of the staff ever got cross or impatient, even when Tucker grew tired and began fidgeting.

By midafternoon, when a woman in a starched white coat asked if Tucker would wait in the playroom while her mother came away for a talk, Bibb too was drained.

But she braced herself, shook hands with the chief neurologist and accepted a cup of tea.

An unusual problem, the woman gently explained. Tucker's ears were actually too good. She heard different sounds all at the same intensity, absorbed them into her brain all at the same time.

Bibb felt depression settling over her like foul tobacco smoke, making her eyes tear, her throat thick.

She forced herself to listen while the woman went on. To a tiny infant, all sounds are the same, just noises. But a baby soon learns the difference between a car honking in the street and his mother's voice. His brain picks out important sounds, amplifies them, at the same time it screens out peripheral ones.

Tucker's brain wasn't working that way. The slightest whisper in a classroom seemed as important to her as the teacher's voice. Commands got lost in a babble of sounds. Sudden noises struck her with terrifying impact.

The neurologist gave Bibb earphones and let her listen to a replaying of one of Tucker's tests. Bibb felt lost, miserable as she heard the simple sentences, spoken simultaneously. In her left ear, the cat is in the tree. In her right, the fish is in the bowl. Left, French people live in France. Right, German people live in Germany.

And then, Tucker's answers, making no sense at all. The cat is in the bowl, she'd said. French people live in Germany.

The last drop of hope bled from Bibb's heart. Nothing would help. No point encouraging Tucker, working with her, battling for her. Bibb couldn't change Tucker's ears. She couldn't hear *for* Tucker.

Then the doctor, smiling, taking two little objects from her desk drawer. A hearing device. And a tiny microphone. One for Tucker. The other for her teacher. With these, the teacher's voice could reach her without background sound, confusion. At home, simple earplugs would keep noise out while she studied.

"I'll give you the name of a New York therapist," the doctor told Bibb. "She'll do the measurements, get the amplification right. And later on, she will show Tucker how to face people and watch their mouths, separate the different levels of sound, focusing on just one at a time."

Bibb felt uncertain. Was *she* hearing properly? This doctor sounded as if everything was going to be all right. Was it possible? Did she dare start to hope again?

"She's a wonderful little girl. So very pretty. And obviously quite intelligent, having gotten so far in school without this help. You see, she's like children who need glasses. They don't realize how clearly most people see. They think everyone sees blurs, just the way they do, and that they're the *only* ones who can't catch the ball, read the book, whatever. Tucker's never understood that her ears don't work the way other children's do. She'll be much happier when sounds make sense."

Bibb had felt a rush of joy flooding her heart, expanding it, pumping out into her veins. She'd wanted to hug this woman, give her all her worldly goods, laugh, weep, kneel and thank God, all at the same time.

There *was* a problem, and it could be solved. Now Tucker's life could start over, as if she'd just been born.

But she'd only been able to sit trembling, dazed by thoughts of all she must do: telephone Arthur, rush to school, meet the therapist, find a taxi, speed the Amtrak train home. She would never complain of anything again, never ask God to do anything more for Tucker or for herself, ever again.

Arthur paced the bedroom. Why the devil hadn't he gone out right after dinner? Why had he taken the time to change?

Poor Bibb.

There she'd been, excited, ecstatic for a week or two.

And then slowly she'd realized that she was out of a job. That Tucker didn't need her night-and-day devotion, not at school, not over homework, not among her friends.

He knew Bibb's evenings were empty. Last week he'd watched her turn out a perfectly clean closet, vacuum, brush, wash, rearrange everything in it. When he'd poured her a drink and asked if she wouldn't rather play cribbage, she'd burst into tears.

Who'd have guessed she'd find something new to worry about so fast? Good Lord, a crusade against doctors, starting with Rosenzweig?

True, Bibb always had been a crusader.

He remembered at the deb dance in Boston, rescuing a

tall, gangling girl from the little gold chair she'd sat on all evening. Even then she'd had a cause. He'd seen her grow pink with excitement about it, some march on University Hall to unearth files that would prove Harvard was a slumlord, leasing rat-infested apartments to the poor to pay for teaching that simply wasn't relevant to today's problems, she'd told him earnestly. Naive, of course. Well-meaning, like her Cambridge lady ancestors, fighting for women's rights, classes with Harvard men, hot lunches for poor Irish kids. But still, she was lively and amusing, not diffident, cool, like so many Cliffies. Bibb made him feel wise and important, not just another harried third-year law student. And it had tickled him to listen to radical rubbish from a girl wearing roses, waltzing demurely in a long white dress.

And then, when they'd married, she'd begun crusading here in New York, lobbying for remedial-reading programs for black kids, collecting money for the public library, standing on corners with petitions to move animals out of the overcrowded Central Park Zoo, God knew what all. He'd supported it, thought it good for her, precisely what a wife of his should be doing. Bibb was a born Junior Leaguer. He enjoyed her seeking his counsel and admiring his suggestions. She'd never be content just playing bridge, shopping, lunching at the Cos Club. And her work had had its effect. Those kids got their reading program. The zoo was being improved. Though she hadn't time for lady friends, Bibb had masses of acquaintances to keep her busy.

Only when Tucker became her cause had she changed and become different, stopped turning to him, and grown earnest, humorless, even grim.

She had demanded the principal of the small trust her grandfather had left, making an embarrassing fuss at the bank. Old Simmons had called him in a rage. He'd had to sit Bibb down and explain that trustees were bound by law. But Bibb had kept on so, telephoning day after day, insisting. Finally he'd helped work out riskier securities, so there'd be dividends high enough to cover the bills for Tucker's therapy. Two hundred and forty dollars a week. For a seven-year-old.

Arthur got up, kicked at a chair leg.

God. Who *wouldn't* have begun looking for a little peace and companionship?

He'd only meant to while away a few hours while Bibb was preoccupied. And at first, dallying a bit with one of the girls in the chorus at Blue Hill actually made him kinder, more patient at home. He even began bringing Bibb flowers from the man at the Lexington Avenue subway exit.

And the next girl, who always wanted him to bring her presents, helped him appreciate Bibb still more. Bibb was too busy giving to demand, too New England to want frills and trimmings. She was his sort, through and through.

But everywhere he went these days, even the Harvard Club, there were girls, lively, reaching out, welcoming. They all seemed to be going to law schools, taking advanced degrees in financial management, or were in the training programs of the big banks. They asked about his work, all the things he really knew, and listened to every word, using the most astonishing language he'd ever heard from women. At first, their flatteries surprised him. After all, he was no prize—middle-aged, conservative, too mannerly to be much fun. And then one of them had taken him to her apartment, the smallest he'd ever been in, one room, filled with cats, cushions, music, marijuana. A box bed had taken up most of it.

That bed. What an education. A little pleasure garden.

And no harm to Bibb. After all, most nights she was absorbed in Tucker. And he was discreet as hell, especially in bed, never slipping up on her name, her particular wishes. Bibb, to be fair, had brought all her bubbling enthusiasm to bed in the early years. But now she talked half the night, or else collapsed into sleep, exhausted.

After all, he'd soon be fifty. For God's sake, hadn't his father died of a stroke at fifty-four? And didn't he weigh exactly the same as he had at Harvard, still wear the same size tennis shorts?

Besides, those girls had nothing to do with his real life. He'd forgotten them the moment he opened his front door, heard the boys' voices or saw the table set for family dinner.

Until now. Until Rosa.

Rosa stuck. She was in his mind while he was handing

the kids their cones at Häagen-Dazs, waiting for the boys to spring the next play in their park football games, or even singing a hymn at Brick Church. The lovely curve of her cheek was somehow etched on the printouts at the bank. Her fragrance, exotic and flowery, seemed to fill his nostrils quite suddenly, out of nowhere. And lately he'd found himself comparing: Bibb's scrubbed hands with Rosa's, tipped with long crimson nails that clacked so excitingly on the computer keyboard; Bibb's loafers with Rosa's tiny shoes, all towering heels and enticing delicate straps that showed her toes peeping out; Bibb's faded bob with Rosa's waist-length hair, black as his patent-leather evening shoes.

He went to the window and seemed to see her face in the dark glass, oval, honey-skinned, more beautiful than any woman he'd imagined since the Wyeth and Rackham illustrations in his childhood books—Tehani bare-breasted on a tropical beach, Maid Marian beneath an oak tree in Sherwood Forest, Morgan le Fay with clouds of dark hair.

Soon he'd have to tell Rosa he couldn't keep on getting out night after night. Last week he'd even cleared his throat and tried. But she was suddenly kneeling at his feet, kissing him where he'd never in his life expected to feel a woman's mouth, tongue, making him feel so huge, so powerful, he wanted to keep plunging into her forever, clutching that glorious hair, letting the world go to blazes.

She was waiting now, just four blocks uptown, in the little room filled with its spicy cooking odors and the warm fragrance of her body.

Jesus, he was getting hard.

Dammit, where was Bibb? He'd better just agree, give in, go with her tomorrow. What the hell difference did it make?

Here she came at last, woebegone, eyes red, skin blotched.

He shivered, seeing Rosa's face, dark, creamy, beautiful. Young.

Bibb watched Arthur turn away as she came out of the bathroom and knew he was upset. Dear man, he cared about her so much. She wanted to go close to him, hold him, rub the back of his neck. It was a long time since she'd done that.

"I'm sorry," she said with a sniffle. "But I can't help it. Please say you're coming with me."

Holding her breath, feeling horribly strung-out, she saw him walk toward the door, then turn.

"Bibb, listen. I've never steered you wrong. But now I think you're headed for rough water."

Oh no, Bibb thought. He still isn't with me.

"Isn't it time you got involved in something else, something besides Tucker? Hear me out, now. There's a PTA at St. Bernard's, too. The boys might like seeing you there once in a while. Better still, what about spending some time on yourself? Your hair, clothes, some new, pretty things."

Hair.

Clothes.

Each of the words hurt, like the bites of the mosquitoes on the beach at night. She wanted to slap them away, rub at the hurt places they left behind.

Bibb looked at her handsome husband, at the neat blue blazer, the pressed slacks.

And then she noticed the watchband.

She'd first seen it last week, cloth, striped, tan with crimson and blue markings. Arthur must have bought it to replace the heavy leather strap he always wore. It had bothered her somehow, each time he checked his watch.

Why would he wear something like that?

Bibb felt a little pain in the pit of her stomach.

Clothes, he'd said. Hair.

Who was at that rehearsal? Some deb in a tight sweater who fluttered at him? Who smiled and talked about causes the way *she* used to? Arthur always had been beguiled by spunky, chatty girls.

"Relax, Bibb," he was going on. "Do some of the things *you* like, galleries, lunch with your sister, bridge, even. How long since you played tennis? Went shopping? How long since you went anywhere but the library, that damned school?"

Again, a little stab of pain in her middle.

The cigarette stub.

Last time she'd taken the car it had been in the ashtray, burned to the tip, smeared with dark lipstick. She'd thrown it away, thinking the garage men probably sat in the cars with girls at night.

Could Arthur have been with someone who wore dark lipstick?

Bibb tried to wave at the invisible insects that seemed to swarm around her. She was being silly. Arthur was her husband, a good husband. He'd always helped her, comforted her, loved her. This was a loving, concerned conversation.

The phone rang. Arthur jumped for it.

Why? Was he expecting a call? Whose?

"Just a minute," he said, looking relieved. "Mrs. Barclay's right here."

"Wait," she said, wanting to finish this out. "I don't know how we got into all this. I only asked you to spend an hour with me tomorrow morning."

Arthur was looking at his watch. The wristband seemed more peculiar than ever.

"Bibb, for God's sake. If it means that much. There's a meeting at ten. But I'll go to Rosenzweig at nine with you if you're going to make such a thing of it. And now I'm really late."

One turn, quick footsteps, front door slamming. He was gone.

Bibb stood holding the phone.

She'd won. Yet somehow she wanted to cry.

He'd been dead against it. Why had he given in so suddenly?

*Was* she neglecting the boys? Could he have meant she was neglecting *him*?

She heard sounds from the receiver in her hand, put it to her ear.

"My name is Rhea Cantor," a voice said.

"I'm sorry?"

"Rachel's mother. From school."

What had she expected? A schoolgirl voice asking for Arthur?

This would be about the PTA. She'd be patient. And then think. Arthur *had* leaped for the phone. Had he been waiting for someone?

Perhaps she ought to ask if something was wrong. Or find out on her own. Call Linky Harnett, whose husband was at the bank with Arthur, who'd know about anything brewing down there. And she could look around a bit at home, Arthur's pockets, bureau drawers, his desk.

With that thought, shame flooded over her. How could she even *think* of doing such a thing?

"Mrs. Cantor," Bibb said. "I wonder if I might call you back. I'm in the middle of something."

Well, why not? Arthur was her husband. She cared for him more than anyone in the world, even, in an odd way, more than Tucker. Tucker needed her. But she needed Arthur, the way she needed her arms and legs. Without him, she'd be helpless. She needed his presence in the big chair in the living room, at the head of her table, most of all, by her side in bed. She needed his hand heavy on her bosom, touching her tentatively between her legs. He was the center of her life.

"It's important," Mrs. Cantor was saying. "I just need a few minutes."

The insistent voice made Bibb remember Mrs. Cantor.

It was at a meeting in a classroom at school, a year ago, two. Grown-ups were folded into tiny chairs pushed into a circle, each set of parents introducing themselves while the rest listened and smiled.

Then Bibb noticed a woman who was not just listening. Head down, pad in one hand, pencil in the other, she was, of all things, taking notes. Jewish. Big. Obviously older than most of the mothers.

Later, while Arthur was speaking, Bibb noticed the woman suddenly stop writing, use her pencil to tap her husband's knee. Why? The parents had droned on, one mother using her turn to wonder aloud how to get her child to bed on time, another demanding a book list so she could coordinate her own book-buying program with the school's. Then the woman's turn came, and Bibb understood. They shared something. Both the Cantors had gone to Harvard, like Bibb and Arthur. And the men had graduated from the Law School.

How nice, Bibb thought.

Later, over punch and cookies, she'd approached Mrs. Cantor and asked, smiling, where she'd lived at college. Mrs. Cantor told her Briggs, and then smiled. "I guess my Rachel will be competing with your Tucker," she'd said ruefully. "Later, for Harvard. Not many places from a school this size."

Bibb couldn't believe it. The children were in first grade. She'd murmured something, and gotten away.

"Look," Mrs. Cantor was saying now. "It would save time if we could talk, now we've connected. I'm sorry to break in on you like this, but I'm pressured myself. I'm campaigning for a judgeship. Ask your husband. Believe me, he'll know what kind of pressure I'm under."

Yes, Bibb had heard at school that somebody's mother was running for office, but she'd never connected the talk with this woman.

And she'd heard something else. Only a few days ago, in the teachers' lunchroom.

Mrs. Cantor was making trouble. Calling parents. She'd had a letter from the headmaster too, about her little girl. But hers had not been a mistake. And she was broadcasting the news, telling everyone.

And now me, Bibb thought. Poor woman. She's angry. Who wouldn't be? But she's doing the worst possible thing.

"Look," Bibb said, "I'd be happy to talk. Tomorrow morning?"

"Mrs. Barclay," Mrs. Cantor's voice kept on, as if Bibb hadn't spoken. "Did it come as a surprise that Dr. Connor wants to kick out your child?"

Bibb suddenly found herself focusing on the voice as if she'd put on Tucker's hearing device, as if it were the only sound in the world.

Yes. No. Don't mix me up. He doesn't. How *dare* you say that?

"Mrs. Cantor," she said, "I can't imagine what you've heard. Let me set you straight. Tucker has a disability, a rare one. It baffled us for ages. And it's only just been diagnosed. But it's quite simple to handle. She's quite fit to stay in school. I'm aware of Dr. Connor's letter. And it *was* shocking. I understand how upset you must be. But you see, my situation is different. Miss Knowlton assured me. Everything is fine."

"Mrs. Barclay," she heard. "You may think everything's fine. But it's not. It's all wrong. Your kid's in a mess, just like mine. And a bunch of others."

"Oh, no." Bibb forced herself to speak calmly, firmly.

"I've been at the best clinic in the East. My child is *not* in a mess. In fact, she has an exceptionally high IQ."

"Connor couldn't care less," Mrs. Cantor came right back. "Rachel's IQ is above average too. But the school's case is that she doesn't concentrate, focus, like everybody else."

Then she's got a learning disability, Bibb thought. She *is* like Tucker.

"Oh, but there's so much you can do," she began.

"You bet," Mrs. Cantor interrupted. "Mrs. Barclay, I want us to get together, fast."

No, no. The more time you spend like this, the less you'll have for your own little girl.

"They're not getting rid of me without a fight," Mrs. Cantor went on. "Connor is ruining a good school. But if we make enough noise, we'll stop him. Twelve, fifteen families are involved in this. That's plenty."

Bibb began feeling frightened, the way she had at Yale with the earphones clamped on her head.

"I know I'm hitting you fast," Mrs. Cantor drove on. "But Connor is bad news. Would you believe he asked Miss Knowlton for a list of her difficult kids? So he could dump them? Like Hitler."

Hitler! The French people live in Germany, Bibb thought. Of course, who could blame Jewish people for seeing persecution everywhere. But the Boston School was different. Everyone was equal. That was one of the reasons Bibb liked the school. Anyway, the Cantors were hardly the only Jewish family there.

"Well," Bibb said carefully, "Miss Knowlton isn't happy about those letters. In fact, she was quite upset."

"Miss Knowlton," said Mrs. Cantor firmly, "knows from nothing. In a courtroom she'd tell a cross-examiner anything he wanted to hear, anything to save her precious school. She certainly had no idea what she was telling me. Connor's said, in so many words, he's getting rid of the mistakes."

"Mistakes?"

"Yes. Kids who slipped through the screening process at the beginning."

Bibb remembered that process. The First Judgment, the Sandbox Scramble. Discussed by mothers on park benches with awe and fascination, the way they'd whispered about sex when they were girls. Everyone with questions, no one with answers. Was the newest article in *New York Magazine* right? Wasn't the *Times* more authoritative? Which *were* the feeder nurseries for the best schools? How would your child do in the independent testing? Did he know colors, coins, synonyms, antonyms? Should you investigate the groups that coached preschoolers for entrance tests? If a four-year-old could read, would they think you'd pushed? If he shook hands politely, would they say you'd repressed him? And how on earth should parents act? Was it better to say a calm good-bye and leave, or ask to stay at an interview? Put your toddler daughter in overalls or a dress? Your son in jeans or Christopher Robin pants? The applications all left spaces for the name of the child's psychiatrist. A trap? Better to have one or not? And should mothers look chic or dowdy? Did it help or hinder to arrive in a limousine?

Bibb had felt blessed. Good family, good manners, welcome everywhere. Better still, Miss Knowlton had met Tucker in a quiet room and watched her play all alone, building a tall house with blocks, then putting the blocks neatly in their bins. Easy. Still, when the trouble began at school, the first-grade teacher had acted as if Bibb had squeezed the child in under false pretenses. And later still, the second-grade teacher had blamed the first-grade teacher for not doing her job.

"Look," Mrs. Cantor kept on. "Connor wants to trade in our kids for bright ones. By the way, *rich* bright ones."

Stop it, Bibb thought. This is the Boston School. People know what it stands for. There's a board, full of able, distinguished people. They wouldn't *allow* anything terrible to happen.

"So we should get busy. Organized."

Hush. Please. I really can't bear the sound of your voice.

"I don't think I can help," Bibb said breathlessly. "Especially now with my own little girl to worry about. But I hope things work out for your child. You mustn't let anyone make you give up hope, doctors, experts, *anyone*."

Good-bye. I've got problems of my own. Arthur. I *must* find out what's going on, help him through it.

"Mrs. Barclay," she heard, "let me tell you something you don't know. About the Thanksgiving Festival."

"The Thanksgiving Festival," Bibb repeated, distracted. What was there to tell? It was always the same. Lovely. The children brought food to school and marched to music onto the big stage where they piled up a huge heap of turkeys, hams, canned vegetables and fruits, nuts, meats, cheeses, candies, America's abundance. They applauded each offering, jumped up to cheer when the stage was filled, and later watched the food go off in vans to be given to poor, hungry people, homeless people. Tucker had already begun talking about whether a big pumpkin or several cans of stewed tomatoes, her favorite, would be better.

"Did you know your child won't be at the Thanksgiving Festival?"

Bibb suddenly felt dangerously full, as if she'd just finished Thanksgiving dinner, had eaten far too much, mixed too many tastes—buttery sweet potatoes, rich dark turkey meat, sugary cranberries, sticky chocolate candies.

"Sorry?"

"Tucker won't be there. Neither will Rachel. Or the Fuller child. Or any of the children they want to dump."

My God, was she going to be sick?

"Are you listening, Mrs. Barclay? Our kids won't bring food. Won't march. Won't even be in the theater. I got that straight from Miss Knowlton. This year, the Festival is extra-important. Publicity. Good for the school. *New York Magazine* is covering it, sending a reporter, a photographer. So they can't risk interruptions or upsets. *Our* children get crazy. They're unreliable, hard to control. One might cause a disturbance. She obviously felt awful, but that's what she said."

Reporters? At the Boston School?

"But *everyone* is in the Thanksgiving Festival," Bibb said, stomach aching. "I mean, that's the point. *All* the children give thanks for their blessings."

"Are you listening or what?" Mrs. Cantor said. "This year, some aren't blessed. I couldn't believe it either. I told Miss Knowlton she should be ashamed, keeping a few kids out of something all the rest are doing. She apologized, said she felt dreadful. And that she'd plan a trip for the special children that day, something like that."

Bibb felt a greasy taste on her tongue, a disgusting need to belch.

"But they would *know*," she said, making an effort to control herself. "Tucker would know. It's a tradition. For everyone. Seniors. First-graders. Everyone."

"Used to be," said Mrs. Cantor.

"But why?"

"To show they mean business. Make it clear these kids aren't wanted. Show us we'd better move, that it's going to be tough for our children. You see? We have to go to work. You. Me. Mrs. Fuller."

Bibb swallowed.

Fuller. The child who was having such trouble reading. Bibb had heard the teachers talking in the lunchroom.

Did they talk about Tucker in the lunchroom?

I'll call Miss Knowlton.

*But what if it's true?*

And my God, Rosenzweig.

Never mind, I'll do it all. If this woman's right, I will fight for her. Nobody's putting Tucker out of school.

And I'll fight for Arthur too. Fix my hair, buy new clothes, if that's what he wants. I'll even go to those boring rehearsals. No Junior Leaguer is going to distract Arthur's attention. He's my husband.

"Mrs. Cantor," she said, pronouncing the words carefully. "Give me your number. Let me see what I can find out. I'll call you tomorrow."

She reached for the pad on Arthur's desk, a pencil, wrote with slippery fingers, said good night.

Then she put down the phone and stood up, walked across the room to Arthur's bureau.

She saw herself in his mirror, frowning, tearstained, hair awry, collar rumpled. A plain girl grown into a plainer middle-aged woman.

Well, she wasn't stupid. She could change the way she looked. Arthur had even told her how.

Somehow her hands, all on their own, were reaching out and pulling open Arthur's top drawer.

Handkerchiefs in the proper place, stud box, watches, scarves. A relief. Her churning stomach began settling.

But was there something under the oilcloth lining of the drawer?

Yes. Flat, smooth, a little notebook. A bankbook. My goodness, like her own. In a little plastic folder.

She slipped it out of the folder, opened to the first page.

In the name of Arthur Fremont Barclay.

Just like the bankbook she'd hidden away for Tucker.

Why was Arthur hiding a bankbook?

Bibb clung to the drawer as she felt her stomach lurch uncontrollably, her throat fill, the clammy sweat break out on her forehead.

## Thanksgiving Hymn

*We gather together to ask the Lord's blessing,*
*He hastens and chastens his will to make known.*
*The wicked oppressing, now cease from distressing,*
*Sing praises to his name, he forgets not his own.*

CORNELIA KNEW IT must be warm in Dr. Nilssen's office because she could see steam on the windows and hear heat hiss from the radiators. But she felt so cold, she might have been alone, shivering on a park bench.

Even now, hours after she'd left school, she still saw Livvie exploding. Her mind kept playing and replaying the scene, like a videotape she had to study over and over.

"It was the worst," she said, shivering. "One minute she was fine. The next, berserk."

Silence.

Please say something, she thought. I've told you all of it. You seemed glad to see me again. And I just walked in, didn't even call. But now? Not a word?

Cornelia made herself look straight at him.

For an instant she wondered if she'd gone color blind. Gray all around, no color anywhere. Just Dr. Nilssen's pale face, silver hair, dark jacket against the white wall, the black desktop. And around him, only the slate color of the couch and chairs, the drawn blinds, the gunmetal lamp.

Then she noticed his eyes.

Color there, yes. Brilliant blue-white, like sky seen from a plane window, high above clouds. Looking into those eyes shocked her into realizing she did have more to tell. Jesus, the worst thing of all.

"I felt so trapped by that glass wall between us. I'm her mother. I only want to protect her, make life wonderful for her. And I couldn't do anything, *anything*."

Cornelia wrapped her arms around her body, trying to get warm.

She did feel a touch of heat, like a tiny flame. How could he stay so silent?

"So there it is," she said.

He bent his head, those marvelous eyes still on hers.

Come *on*, Dr. Nilssen, she thought, anger kindling, making her cold fingers tingle.

"Please. What do I *do*?"

Dr. Nilssen leaned back in his chair, stretched his long arms, closed his eyes. His lashes were silver, like his hair.

"You might like to know this isn't the worst story I've ever heard. Not even right here in this office."

Slap. She felt heat come up on her neck, her face.

"Oh, right," she shot out. "Livvie could have killed one of those children. Definitely worse."

The videotape began again in her mind, this time with a new scene cut in, Livvie swinging a chair, thudding it against the red curls of the little girl closest to her.

Dr. Nilssen nodded.

"You said it, I didn't. But think. Haven't you learned something? Didn't you see for yourself? Now you know it's not the school inventing a story, misjudging Livvie."

"But it's *worse*, much worse. Something has to be terribly wrong with her."

"Really? According to you, she was quite happy until the others ganged up on her. Then she reacted. Got angry. Fought back."

"Angry? *Raging*. Swinging a *chair*. She could have crippled someone."

"It's possible. A lot of things are. She could have stood rooted to the spot, helpless. Gone into a fit. And how would you feel if she'd just kept smiling? Never even noticed what was happening? It seems to me she related to a bad situation with relevant, decisive action."

"All right," Cornelia snapped, heat boiling up inside her. "It could have been worse. But it was horrible enough, for me, for her. And I came here, stupidly probably, hoping you'd tell me what to do."

"I'd like to. But all we know is that the children she's with make her angry, and the school can't or won't deal with it. I'd say we need more information."

Cornelia felt like leaping up, grabbing her chair, and swinging it, just like Livvie.

"When I talked to Dr. Rosenzweig," Dr. Nilssen went on, "he said there was nothing to worry about physically. Now, wouldn't it be helpful for Livvie to be tested by a psychologist? I can probably get her school tests, her private scores. But I'd like an opinion from someone independent, no theories to prove, no position to justify."

But that'll take days, Cornelia thought. What do I do *tonight*? Tell Livvie I was there, or what? Sympathize? Scold? Ignore it all?

"I'll get the best person I know. And fast."

Yes. Please, fast. So I'll know the worst.

"But there's something you should do right away, too. Help her feel good at home. Don't give her anything new to worry about, like telling her you were there today. If she brings it up, comfort her, help her think of other things she might have done—just sat down outside the circle, asked the teacher which chair was hers, things like that. Forget homework. Don't read with her. You've seen how tough things are for her at school. Make her time with you wonderful, no matter how miserable you feel."

Could she? Cornelia wondered.

"You wanted to be an actress," Dr. Nilssen said. "Act."

She imagined walking into the apartment, hugging Livvie, asking if she'd had a nice day, suggesting a game of checkers.

Suddenly she realized the videotape in her head had stopped.

She wasn't seeing Livvie pummeling the children anymore.

Startled, she stared at Dane Nilssen.

Maybe he *did* know what he was doing.

Why, his jacket wasn't gray, but blue tweed with saddle leather buttons. And he was not Olivier's Hamlet, all black and silver, the way she'd thought when she first saw him. More like one of those tall, grave men in Bergman pictures, a crusader, a knight.

His long fingers were turning the pages of his desk calendar.

"Next week's the holiday," he said without looking up. "But I'll be here on Friday. Suppose you come back then. If I get an appointment for Livvie tomorrow, the day after,

I'll have the report by Wednesday, go through it over the weekend."

Weekend? Thank God. He *did* want to help.

Cornelia suddenly saw color everywhere—vermilion pen, olive book binding, a huge rough lump of brilliant turquoise on his desk. How had she missed it before?

"By Friday I should have some idea what we're up against. And then I think we'll see some direction and have some real suggestions for you."

How could she have missed seeing that he was decent, kind? Missing out on his holiday to help her.

Then she remembered, and the room went gray again.

Thanksgiving. Her family was coming for dinner in the country. The first time without Tim. They'd sit around the turkey, her brother, sister-in-law, nephews, looking uncomfortable with Cornelia at the head of the table, faking holiday cheer.

Thursday night, thank God, they'd go. Friday she could drive into the city early and go straight back afterward.

Still, it would be a rotten ride in, worrying about what he'd tell her.

And worse going back, alone, knowing what the psychologist had discovered about Livvie.

Even now she felt frozen just thinking of leaving this room, this man, being alone.

Dr. Nilssen was pushing back his chair and standing.

He *was* tall. And straight, relaxed, as if problems didn't burden him at all. His face went into nice crinkles when he smiled.

Dr. Rosenzweig's words about him came back. Terrific guy. Good doctor. Had a lot of trouble. Lost his wife. Lonely.

"Listen," she heard herself saying. "That Friday. My family's coming for Thanksgiving, but they go, they don't stay overnight. And my nurse will be there with her two little girls. Could you possibly come out? It's only Phillipsburg, in New Jersey, not far. You could see Livvie yourself. Have a day in the country. Maybe stay the weekend, if you like. It's a different world, peaceful, beautiful. And I've got six bedrooms."

No sound. No change in his expression.

"It's a *good* idea," she kept on, fighting a rush of embarrassment, knowing she was overstepping, somehow not caring. "Good for you. Certainly good for me. My holiday's going to be grim. My brother will try to make it all Norman Rockwell, fill gaps, talk too much. He's an obstetrician, he's used to bossing women. He'll say I'm too thin, too pale, that Livvie isn't looking as well as his children, the house is too much for me, there's enough dust in the parlor to give us all silicosis."

Oh. He was smiling.

"I'd feel so different if you were coming, so much better. And think how it would amuse Phil Rosenzweig."

Silence. Only a siren shrieking outside, the desk clock ticking, thumps from the radiators.

Cornelia began feeling as if she were in a hot bath. Why? She'd only asked him to visit. Not anything really out of bounds like, say, asking him into bed.

Jesus, why was she thinking about bed? He *was* attractive, of course. She *was* lonely, if she let herself think about it. He listened so well, seemed able to hear words she hadn't said. Still, now? Was she losing he mind? Somehow, his eyes were making her dizzy.

"Well," she said, hefting her big handbag, tucking in the new batch of photographs of Livvie, the bunch of theater programs that had burst its rubber band. "Then thanks. I'll get Livvie wherever you say for the tests. And plan to see you that Friday."

Dane was clearing his throat. He'd make an excuse, of course. She'd heard *his* unspoken words this time, perfectly clearly.

"How do you get to Phillipsburg?" he said slowly. "One of the tunnels or the bridge?"

The words seemed to float toward her like rainbow-bright bubbles and burst cool and fresh on her skin as they reached her. She wanted to take both those long hands and lean her head against the blue jacket.

"Lincoln Tunnel," she said, as if the name were an endearment.

She reached for his pen to scribble directions on a piece of paper, then walked, head high, into the cold night.

On Friday morning, through the small panes of the parlor window, Cornelia saw the sky ominous with snow.

Ragged leaves whirled everywhere, bare trees thrashed in the high wind. The farm looked unkempt against the brown hills, cornfields bristling with stubble, metal silo dull, barn door askew on its hinges.

If only, she thought, he could see it for the first time green and soft with spring, or glittering white at Christmas.

First time? Why do I think there'll *be* more times?

Because he *is* coming. Because he made me think about bed. Because if he weren't responding a little, he wouldn't be coming at all.

Feeling lighthearted, she went to work, sweeping the rag rug free of walnut shells, pieces of games, and shreds of tobacco from her brother's pipe. Yesterday the children had played with all Grandmother's treasures. The clasps were open on the album of family tintypes, doors ajar on the corner cupboard that held the collection of glass prisms. Cornelia picked one up, admired its elegance and sparkle, lifted it to the faded curtains and started little lights dancing on the rose print wallpaper, the worn plum velvet chairs, the scarred front of the old Estey pump organ.

She could hear the little girls chattering out on the porch, Livvie giggling, Samantha echoing her mother's crisp accent, Lucy slurring her words, grown now into a New York child.

If Dane couldn't see the place at its most beautiful, at least he could feel its peace, its beautiful silence.

"Hey," Cornelia called. "Why don't you get your coats and boots and walk up to the barn. There could be kittens."

Margaret Rose came to the door, frowning.

"It will be safe?"

"Of course," Cornelia said, impatient now. "Remember, I had the floor fixed? And the ladders? It cost a fortune. But it was that or tear it down. And I love the barn."

So many things she loved, though, weren't fixed. Slates broken on the roof. Stones loose in the old walls, the mortar crumbling. Shutters missing their slats. The front hedge overgrown and uneven. There was no end. God knew, everyone had warned her.

She heard the children scurrying for heavy clothes and boots, banging the porch door.

Then, silence. Cornelia began feeling as if she were about to go onstage, with a curtain slowly rising.

She skimmed up the narrow stairs to look in the mirror over Grandmother's pine bureau and saw the reflection of the old four-poster bed—vast, graceful, high—and long enough even for a tall, lanky man. And wide enough for two people to stretch luxuriously and then turn, reach, come together. A haven, soft, dark, warm, inside the curtains.

She shook her head, as if she could shake out her thoughts. What did she know about him? Was she having visions because a man seemed perceptive, quick, intelligent? Because his rugged face was more appealing than Tim's handsome one?

In her mind, suddenly, she was touching his cheek, his long arms, thighs. Wrapping her arms around his body. She shivered, imagining his warm hand on her back, his tongue on her neck.

Then she heard a car grinding up the dirt road.

Curtain up. Drumroll. She ran downstairs, through the kitchen to the porch, around to the front of the house.

The children heard too. They burst from the barn and pelted down the hill. But when they saw Dane they stopped short and huddled shyly, the two dark heads bracketing Livvie's pale one.

Cornelia, heart jumping oddly, walked toward him.

Next to the tiny car Dane looked taller than ever. And different, in a wrinkled raincoat and heavy shoes.

They drank hot mulled cider on the porch. Dane produced three brightly wrapped packages. A basketball, a football, a soccer ball. The little girls were amazed and delighted, Cornelia astonished. She watched them thank him and run off with their treasures to the barn.

"You never told me Livvie was so beautiful," he said. "And so fair. Like a Danish child."

Cornelia's heart expanded. Praise. So long since anyone had praised Livvie. She wanted to fling her arms around him and hug him.

Then, her back stiffening, she remembered.

"Dane, tell me about the tests. Please."

He crossed the porch and poured more cider. Mug full, he sat down and smiled.

"It's a wonderful house," he said.

She felt confused. Hadn't he heard? Was he putting her off? Because Margaret Rose was walking in and out, fussing, collecting mugs, one by one?

"Cornelia, will you show me the place? I'd love a walk around, after that ride."

But Margaret Rose would hear. Whatever he was going to say, she'd tell Margaret Rose later on. She was a friend, someone to lean on, someone who loved Livvie too.

Only Dane was already going down the steps, following the flagstone path to the front. Cornelia reached for her old sheepskin coat and went after him.

She headed him uphill over the meadow toward the highest point on her land, the gentle beginning of the shadowy row of mountains that backed her fields. From here the house looked like a photograph in an architectural magazine, a patchwork of stone, two graceful chimneys, shuttered windows in a neat row, front door broad and welcoming.

Now. What more comforting place to hear bad news? And what better person to tell her?

"Whatever you're going to say, you can say around Margaret Rose," Cornelia said, to get him started. "I'll tell her anyway. She'll care. Start, please, before I explode."

"Nothing to explode about. Livvie tests within all the normal bounds. The countryside is perfection, Cornelia. How old is the house?"

My God. Didn't he know she couldn't wait anymore?

"Don't look like that," Dane said. "Livvie's going to be fine. One note in some of the tests puzzles me, and I need to explore it some more. I promise you, I'll be quick."

Livvie was *going* to be fine? What was wrong *now*?

"Jesus Christ. I've been frantic for days. I'm no good at waiting."

"Then change," Dane said calmly.

"Just like that, *change*? How?"

"Right now, do what I asked, tell me about this place. It's so familiar, somehow. You know, most Danes are only a generation or two away from the farm. This is like home when I was a child."

Cornelia felt the soothing effect of his words take hold, as they had in his office.

"All right," she said, somehow feeling lighter, more at one with the beauty of the country around her.

She led him down the far side of the hill, past the bare fruit trees, along the wintry meadow toward the pasture with its slanting wood fences. Her nearest neighbor kept his horses there in return for watching over the place. Two of them trotted toward them, brown, swaybacked farm horses, with huge, gentle eyes.

Leaning on a rough, splintery board, Cornelia felt at peace, grateful. A different world from New York, from a closed-in apartment, a crowded office. Her refuge. And so far she'd kept it safe.

"I always feel happy here," she said into the wind. "Even though everyone says I'm crazy to keep it."

Crazy. The word jolted her.

Her mother. The visit. She'd meant to tell him right away.

"Listen," she said, letting the wind take her hair back. "Dane, yesterday I saw my mother in the hospital."

"Tell me," he said.

She shivered and began walking along the fence, faster as the words came.

Cornelia drove over to the hospital most country weekends when she could leave Livvie with a neighbor. Always, she steeled herself to the place, to the slumped figure sitting silently in a chair, so different from the mother she remembered. That mother had been slender, straight, dressed in velvets and satins and soft lawns, scented with springlike fragrance from one of the bottles on her dressing table, set among rabbit's feet, colored pencils, little pots of red and blue creams. The makeup was left from her acting days, in summer Chatauqua tents, giving dramatic readings of Juliet, Prunella, Little Orphan Annie, Ophelia. Mother had talked wistfully about those days, and of how she'd had to leave the theater when she married the brilliant Harvard instructor who'd become Cornelia's father. Still, she'd never stopped playacting at home, doing monologues, sketches, poems with dramatic gestures for Cornelia and Quint.

All through Cornelia's childhood, when her mother was well, life was starred with surprises. Mother would wake her and Quint to watch a sunrise, appear without warning at school to rush them off to plays, concerts, ballets, impromptu picnics in the park. Then, after a few months, she would sleep all morning, sit listlessly in a chair all afternoon, turning her head when the children came near. And finally Father would pack a bag, take her away, and the world would grow ordinary again.

It was Cornelia's grandmother who'd found this country hospital near her farm and left almost all the money she had to take care of everything. But the responsibility was Cornelia's now. Quint came up so seldom.

And when he did, Cornelia felt an extra wrench of misery, seeing Mother through his eyes as well as her own.

They'd driven to the sanitarium, peaceful and pretty with cottages, flowers, and trees to hide the fact that all the windows were barred.

Quint signed them in, identifying himself to the nurse with keys clanking at her waist, and they walked together through the halls decorated by patients with childish pictures, pumpkins, turkeys, autumn leaves. Quint wrinkled his nose, and Cornelia grew sharply aware of the heavy smells—carbolic soap, urine, pine disinfectant.

Yesterday, the doorkeeper at her mother's ward had been an old woman, faded hair tucked behind her ears, wearing a washed-out dress and sneakers. Cornelia, walking toward the blare of a television set, saw fifteen or twenty women sitting around, curled into themselves, heads down, arms folded, legs crossed. Nobody was watching the screen. One woman held a torn magazine on her lap, another knitted, stabbing at a length of wool dotted with dropped stitches.

Cornelia felt her heart shrivel as she smiled and looked for her mother, and saw her before Quint. She was prettier, straighter than the rest, sitting quietly, hands folded in her lap, her hair a dark mass like Cornelia's, her eyes violet like Livvie's.

"Well, Mother," Quint said in the hearty, encouraging voice he used to women giving birth. Cornelia almost expected him to tell their mother to push, hard.

She leaned down and touched her mother's shoulder, sharp, thin. "Hi," she said softly. "Mother, it's us. Cornelia. Quint."

The eyes turned toward her. They weren't really like Livvie's. Livvie's shone. These eyes were empty.

"Cornelia," came the deep, marvelous voice she remembered. "Quint."

"We've come to see you. To bring you something. Here." She laid a candy box on her mother's lap.

No response. Cornelia hadn't expected one. Still, unreasonably, she felt a pang of disappointment.

Quint fussed, moving chairs, setting them nearer. The television program ended, its music rising to a deafening climax.

"Let me open it for you," Cornelia said. Quickly she tore the pretty paper, lifted the lid.

"Candy," her mother said with a brilliant smile. "From an admirer."

Slowly, clutching the box, her mother rose, steadying herself against the back of the chair.

"Oh God," Quint said. "Here we go."

Their mother, swaying a little, was walking slowly around the room offering candy to everyone in turn. "Christ," Quint said. "Every time. Theatricals. Playing the great lady. Giving it all away. Never eating a single piece. See her drag that leg? That's the Mellaril, keeps her off balance. Wonder if the doctor's around."

"Why don't you go see," Cornelia said, feeling sorry for him. Seeing Mother so seldom, each visit was a shock. And while Cornelia had adored her mother's quicksilver changes, Quint, orderly and even-tempered, had always been embarrassed and disturbed by them. "I'll stay. Just come back and get me, all right?"

She watched her mother pass the candy as she'd have done in her living room. But here, one woman glared, another grabbed. After a while her mother came back and sat down, holding the empty box on her lap. Cornelia reached for her hand. It felt dry, boneless.

"Mother," she said, suddenly longing to get through somehow. "It's Cornelia."

"Cornelia," her mother said politely.

"That's right. How are you? Did you have Thanksgiving dinner today?"

"Turkey," her mother said. "On Thanksgiving, we have turkey."

Cornelia felt herself sink into misery, remembering the songs, the exciting stories her mother used to tell, the lilt of her rich voice. Misery rose up over her like water, making it impossible to breathe, as if she were submerged, until she closed her mouth tightly and sat silently.

Quint came back. "I think that does it," he said into her ear. "No change. Good physical health, I can see that myself. The doctor's new, a Pakistani. He knows to call me if anything changes. Let's go, Nellie."

Cornelia found her breath coming more easily. The visit was over. She leaned to kiss her mother good-bye, and felt a sudden, stunning blow on her cheek.

"Don't start," she heard, in a voice strong enough for the top balcony. "Don't touch me. I won't be touched by anybody."

Dazed, horror-struck, Cornelia put a hand to her stinging cheek. What was happening? Her mother had never slapped her, not once, not ever.

Nurses came running. One, hefty and strong, twisted her mother's arm back and held it.

"Okay, Emily," she said. "We're not hitting anybody. We're just staying right in our chair."

Cornelia watched her mother make fists, eyes gleaming now, almost fluorescent.

And instantly she saw Livvie, kicking, slapping out at the other children.

My God. Had her mother once been a child who screamed and hit? Would Livvie end behind barred windows, with nurses holding her down?

Now Cornelia realized she was clutching Dane, curling her fingers into his arm.

She looked up and saw him shake his head no.

"It's hard not to compare," he said. "But don't. You needn't."

Why is he so sure? Livvie is her granddaughter.

"Nobody knows if schizophrenia is passed on. Most of us now believe it comes from a chemical imbalance, something missing in the body. It doesn't seem due to outside pressures. Almost every society has about the same percentage of schizophrenics, industrial Swedes, tropical islanders. Someone like your mother, ill so long, who's had shock treatment, insulin, hydrotherapy, every fool thing that came along, probably has brain damage by now. But that's not Livvie."

Cornelia, watching his breath make little puffs of white frost, felt comforted. His voice calmed her, even though she scarcely absorbed the words.

What would happen if she stood on tiptoe and kissed him? Would the frosty breaths stop? Would she be enfolded in a soft white warm cloud?

"I read twenty tests yesterday. Not one shows the slightest mental disorder. Not one, Cornelia."

Cornelia willed herself to believe him. Livvie was *not* sick like her mother.

Then she remembered there was something else important to tell him.

"You know, the school is making trouble for other children too. A mother called. She got a letter just like mine. And so did some others. This Mrs. Barclay, her child's been tested up, down, and backwards. When I told her about Livvie's reading, she said it sounded like a learning disability. Dyslexia."

She felt Dane urging her forward gently, walking again, his arm around her. She had to move fast to match his stride. Frosty earth crackled beneath their feet.

"Cornelia," he said. "There are lots of reasons why reading can be a problem."

Cornelia, disappointed, shook herself free. "Listen. I was glad to learn I'm not the only one."

"Didn't anyone ever tell you not to borrow other people's troubles? You have only so much energy. Aren't you better off putting it into helping Livvie?"

"Yes, but Mrs. Barclay knows a lot," Cornelia said. "She doesn't work. She spends time at school, knows what's going on."

Dane put his hands in his pockets and looked at her.

"Cornelia, listen. Your daughter isn't like anyone else, alive or dead. Your mother. Your husband. You. Or any other child, even at the same school. Her problems are her own, just like her pretty hair, her eyes and hands. I'm almost certain she's not schizophrenic. And I don't think she's learning-disabled, either."

Christ. If he knew what *wasn't* wrong, why didn't he tell her what was?

Then she felt the snow on her forehead and her nose—big furry flakes whirling up all around them. The air instantly seemed to thicken, turn gauzy white.

"You got here just in time," she said, feeling softened, somehow, by the snow, cooled, more ready now to postpone difficult talk, do what he wanted. "Let's go back, get the kids and start a fire."

Dane took his hands from his pockets and gravely applauded her.

She found it easier, after that, to smile.

In the kitchen, stamping ice from his boots, shaking off his snowy jacket, Dane suddenly stopped and stood staring at the back wall.

"Odd," he said after a moment. "This kitchen looks like mine, in my house. I told you, I grew up a few paces from Hans Christian Andersen's house? In a house that was timber and plaster, like a Tudor building. With a stone hearth."

"Well," Cornelia said. "If you call a brick fireplace a stone hearth."

"That's just it. Last time I saw the cottage, long after the war, wealthy people from Copenhagen had modernized it. Bricked in the fireplace. And then it looked like this one."

Cornelia was holding a lighted match. She waited for him to get out of the way, so she could use it. When it began burning her fingers, she dropped it, reached for another.

"Did anyone ever really examine this fireplace?" he said urgently.

Examine? We put wood in it and light fires. What else?

Now Dane seemed somehow to quicken, turn eager, hot, as if he were after something exciting. He was leaning into the opening in the wall, probing, stretching, using the poker to tap the brick.

"What is it?"

"I think there's a much bigger hearth behind this brick," he said urgently. He began tapping with the poker to show her. "Listen. It's hollow. All around here. And here. And on top, I think there's a beam all the way across."

Why not? The house was more than two hundred years old.

"Can we see?" he asked.

He looked like a small boy now, hair rumpled, wisps in his eyes. Cornelia wanted to reach out, touch him, push the strands back in place.

"What do we do?"

But Dane was doing it, banging at the mortar with the poker, hammering the brick. The children came from the barn. Livvie ran for the toolbox, brought hammers, wrenches.

Cornelia watched Dane look eagerly at the tools, then shrug.

"Any more and you'll have chaos," he said, dropping his hands to his sides.

Cornelia's thoughts whirled. My beloved house. Isn't there enough to fix already without making more trouble? Isn't there enough chaos in my life already? It's a gamble. And suppose he's wrong? Suppose the whole kitchen collapses into dust?

She looked at Dane's muscular arms, his strong shoulders.

If I'd run scared, I'd still be married to Tim. I'd have sold this house. Anyway, suppose Dane's right? He can't unearth a fireplace in one weekend. He'll want to come back, work on it. Wonderful.

She picked up a hammer, turned, and smashed at a brick. The children squealed with destructive joy, grabbing at tools, banging and smashing. In minutes, everyone was covered with ashes and greasy soot, hitting, crunching at the bricks.

The noise brought Margaret Rose running. Cornelia glanced at her face, grim with disapproval. But Dane's feelings were for once on his face too, making him look utterly relaxed, sure and happy.

One brick crumbled. Dane reached for it and used the claw of the hammer to loosen the bricks around it. Slowly, at the corner, he dug out a small hole, then a larger one. He stopped and leaned his hand way inside. Cornelia ducked her head alongside his waist, to see. Her body brushed his. She felt tingling all through her and jumped a little, as if she might catch fire.

"I can't tell," he said, intent on the fireplace. "I'm positive it's a big one. Livvie, Lucy, stand back a minute. Way back."

He touched Cornelia's shoulder. "You most of all," he said. The words seemed to send warmth all through her.

He swung the heavy hammer, widening the hole, shattering the bricks. The noise was terrifying, almost painful. The air filled with dust, white as the snow outside, smelling of damp and smoke. Dust stung Cornelia's eyes, made her sneeze.

But behind the bricks, an arm's length, she now began to see a few inches of stone, like the walls of the house. More plaster flew as Dane exposed it. The children watched, awestruck, Cornelia pulling them back from flying chips and stone splinters.

Slowly, magically, through the late afternoon, a dark cavern emerged under Dane's hands.

When crumbles of mortar and plaster in chunks lay at her feet, Cornelia could see one side of the old hearth. It was four times the size of the modern one, probably, almost the width of the kitchen. Opened up, it would be a prize, a place where for centuries people had found food and warmth.

Finally Dane stopped and leaned on the poker, sweaty, filthy, exultant. His face was almost as black as Margaret Rose's.

"Like my house," he said. "I knew it. That brick, just like the junk they put in my house to make it modern. I wanted to pull *that* down too, with my own hands. Look, Cornelia. A niche for a candle. And probably a bread oven on the other side. That's how they are in Europe, anyway."

He looked around, and stopped smiling. "My God. Your kitchen."

He was seeing cupboards flaked with soot, walls filthy, rubble thick on the floor. And Margaret Rose's face, filled with contained fury.

"You've found buried treasure," Cornelia said. "I always wanted to be a director. I wish I'd filmed the whole sequence."

She looked down at his hands, crisscrossed with tiny cuts, black and gritty, and thought how exciting to put her mouth to each little wound, sucking it clean. Face burning, she turned to the sink, reaching for soap, warm water.

The children peered into the dark opening, their feet slipping on chips and brick dust.

"Even my grandmother didn't know," Cornelia said, turning back to him, not trusting herself to deal with the cuts just yet. "It must be the original fireplace."

Dane lifted each of the little girls in turn, so they could see the enormous cavern. Then he took them all into the parlor, where Cornelia could hear him telling them about Odense, Andersen, the Snow Queen. Margaret Rose shrugged her shoulders and began sweeping away the worst of the mess, while Cornelia moved to put the leftover turkey casserole in the oven, brush soot from the countertops, and rinse plates, listening to the lilt of Dane's voice.

Suddenly she heard a choked scream. Livvie appeared in the doorway, white and stricken, Dane behind her.

Margaret Rose was moving quickly forward.

"Stop that noise," she was saying. "How can you behave so? When everyone is sitting nicely, hearing the story?"

Cornelia, watching, feeling frozen with shock, saw Livvie burst into tears as the other little girls came into the doorway, staring.

Dane pulled out a kitchen chair and took Livvie onto his lap.

"My fault," he said. "We got to a bad part, that's all. She's a beautifully behaved child, Margaret Rose, anyone can see that. All your girls are."

Margaret Rose relaxed, mollified.

Cornelia watched them all, feeling lost, frightened.

She watched Dane rock Livvie gently, patiently, until the sobbing subsided.

"Tell me, Livvie," he said finally. "Is it the story? You were listening before. Is it this part you don't like?"

Livvie nodded gravely, eyes wide, mouth pressed tight.

Dane kept rocking Livvie.

"It *is* a bad part," he said. "Lots of people get frightened. The little robber girl teasing the reindeer with a big sharp knife."

Cornelia saw Livvie wince, saw Dane's arms settle more tightly around the child's shoulders.

"I'm sorry to scare you," he said quietly. "But sometimes when you're scared it's good to hold on, wait a little.

You'll see, it turns out fine. It's fine that she had the knife to cut the reindeer's halter. To set it free. Listen to the rest, and then if you want, we'll take a walk, just you and me, up to the barn."

Cornelia relaxed a little, watching him, listening to him finishing the story for all the children.

When it was over, Dane found Livvie's coat and boots, put them on himself, and swept her out into the snow, while Margaret Rose, looking cross again, whisked her girls upstairs.

Cornelia concentrated on her work till they stamped back in the door and Dane waved Livvie upstairs with the others.

"Leave that," he said, looking around. "Let me take you somewhere. Is there an inn? A good one? Good enough for the way I feel right now?"

He was following Livvie up the stairs before the words were out.

Cornelia stood still, imagining what was in his mind, candlelight, beautiful china, country food, privacy.

Wait, she thought, till he sees the restaurant in town, checkered tablecloths, overcooked spaghetti, soggy lasagna, vinegary wine, farmers banging big fists on the bar.

Still, better than staying in this dust, crunching grit everywhere on the floor, powdery plaster rising like smoke from the cushions when she touched them.

And she'd love being out with Dane, sharing a bottle of Chianti—not as his patient or Livvie's mother but just as a woman holding a glass of wine, sitting close to a man who could swing a hammer, lull a frightened child and keep patiently on till he reached the happy end of a story.

Hearing his footsteps on the stairs, she poured a beer for him and took it into the parlor.

He emptied the glass in one great tilt.

She turned to fetch another bottle and suddenly felt herself caught in his arms, pulled close to him. His body against hers seemed to burn where they touched, sending waves of heat through her whole body, and she felt like crushing herself against him harder still.

He tilted her head up, bent, his mouth meeting hers full-on, his tongue touching hers, releasing something deep inside her. His warmth seemed to flow into her, like heat from a hearth where bread was baking. She basked in it, wanting more, clinging to him with all her strength.

So different from Tim, she thought suddenly.

Tim was so cool, so studied. Dane is hot, burning. Tim's hands were smooth. Dane's are rough. Tim kissed like a movie star. Dane's tongue is everywhere, lips, ears, neck.

She was breathing hard now, knowing her nipples were hardening, heat coming up inside her body. She felt Dane burning as no one ever had in her arms, reaching for her with a hand more certain than anyone's had been.

He was tugging now at buttons, urgently trying to get closer.

Cold air touched her skin deliciously, but only for a moment, before he was covering her again with his body. And now he was taking her hand, as if he wanted her to guide him, as if he wouldn't enter her without invitation.

She gave herself up to him, melted into mindlessness, all eager mouth, clutching fingers, tingling breasts, burning core.

Suddenly, shocking her, he let go.

Feeling bereft, opening her eyes wide, she watched him stride toward the parlor door, reach for the old iron bolt.

He's remembered where we are, she realized. But, darling Dane, that lock is old and rusty, and you look like a boy, impatient, furious at being thwarted. My explorer, my Thor, my swinger of hammers. How sweet you are now. Your hands, all thumbs, can't even send a bolt home.

She began moving to help.

Out of his arms, though, away from his warmth, the cold air rushed at her.

Chilling thoughts blew into her head.

Margaret Rose. The children. We can't stay here. Upstairs? My beautiful bed, those sheets, washed a thousand times so they feel like silk. But there's not even a rusty lock on the bedroom door. The barn, maybe? The hayloft?

But she could see the windows layered over with snow, hear the wind gusting in the chimney.

We'd freeze, she thought, feeling desolate. Anyway, it's corny, a hayloft. Hay's supposed to be soft, but it's prickly, full of dust and sneezes. And the place is all smells— leather, cow pats, cats.

And what if he thinks I asked him here just for this?

That I wander out to that barn with someone different every weekend?

Dane was giving up on the bolt now, striding back to her, reaching for her as roughly, urgently, as before.

She found herself taking a step back.

"Dane," she said slowly. "We can't. Margaret Rose, the children. The weather out there. It's just not for now. You see, don't you?"

But even as she said the words, Cornelia ached for him. She felt as if she were spurning the most wonderful present anyone had ever offered her.

He stood quiet for a moment, looking at her. Then he smiled.

"But soon," he said.

He took her cold hands in his hot ones, held them gently. She felt his warmth flow into her and knew suddenly that the present was here for the opening, a gift worth the waiting.

The U.S. Office of Education:

Children with special learning disabilities exhibit a disorder in one or more of the basic psychological processes involved in understanding or in using spoken or written language. These may be manifested in disorders of listening, thinking, talking, reading, writing, spelling, or arithmetic. They include conditions which have been referred to as perceptual handicap, brain injury, minimal brain dysfunction, dyslexia, developmental aphasia, etc. They do not include learning problems which are due primarily to visual, hearing, or motor handicaps, to mental retardation, emotional disturbance, or to environmental disadvantage.

Public Law 94–142
The Education for All Handicapped Children Act of 1975

OPENING THE DOOR to the second-grade classroom, Nanny was pleased to see it looking neat as a photograph in the school catalog, chairs set squarely under tables, blackboards washed pale gray, books straight on their low shelves.

She took Livvie's hand, led the child to the window seat, sat down, and snuggled her close, pleased when the warm little body curled acceptingly into hers. Tutoring always reminded her of her student teaching days in public school. Once her supervisor had come in to find her working with one child while the others read their books. The man had waved cheerfully at her and said, "Never mind, I'll come back when you're teaching."

A few weeks ago, she remembered, Livvie wasn't snuggling back so trustingly. At their first tutoring session she'd sat stiff as a pencil and screwed her eyes shut at the sight of the big green arithmetic workbook.

And now see, Nanny congratulated herself. Nestling at my side like a little kitten. I *am* a superb teacher.

She reached for her big carpetbag, and one by one, set out her teaching aids, placing them on the table as if they were presents. A roll of toilet tissue, the cheapest kind with exactly a thousand sheets. A small and shiny brass scale, a set of little weights. A box of poker chips in jolly colors.

"Now, Livvie," she said brightly. "I'm going to make two piles of these pretty chips. Then you think hard and tell me which pile is bigger."

She heard Livvie breathe a little faster, saw her lean forward.

There, Nanny thought. I've got her started. My simple, inexpensive teaching aids always work wonders for these poor, sweet, learning-disabled children.

Livvie *was* a problem. At the beginning of the year only her reading scores had been worrisome, below par. Now, at the start of December, she'd slipped to the bottom in almost everything. And when Nanny had begun working with her, she'd been so stubborn, so emotional.

Just like her mother.

Ah, but yesterday, when Livvie had torn the toilet paper, sheet by sheet, counting perfectly to a thousand, she'd smiled to herself, then turned suddenly and thrown her arms around Nanny.

Lovely, that warm hug. It told Nanny once again what she had held as an article of faith, that *this* was what the Boston School meant, somehow finding the key for each child, unlocking a door to happiness. Besides, children often knew more than they thought. She remembered Junie Ansorge saying she'd never learn to read, when the child had *been* reading all the storybooks in the classroom. When Nanny pointed out that she was already reading quite nicely, Junie said, "Oh. You mean *that's* reading?" Sometimes the parents anticipated trouble and the poor children obligingly gave it to them.

Parents, Nanny thought. Two or three more sessions like this and I'll be able to call Cornelia, reassure her a bit, tell her how nicely Livvie is doing. She's bound to be pleased about that.

And right now, how pleasant to sit here, to enjoy the quiet, to feel the sun's warmth on her back, admire the play of light on Livvie's beautiful hair.

So different from the turmoil in the school lately. Like last week's upheaval. The new business managers, imagine, three of them, snooping into everything, as if the school were some business whose stock had been falling. Troubleshooters, Dr. Connor called them. Troublemakers was more like it, Nanny thought. She would never forget the brash young man who'd been so clumsy, knocking over something on her desk every time he turned around. He'd been in her office for three whole days, looking at files, asking endless questions about schedules, budgets, expenses. As if she were supposed to keep tabs on every second passing, every penny spent.

Thank goodness he'd finally packed his briefcase, gone off to bother someone else, and left her to do her real job. Teaching—especially the kind she liked best, one child at a time in a quiet room.

Crash. The door abruptly flew open, banging hard against the wall.

Startled, Nanny tensed in her seat. Her knee hit the table, scattering the chips. A number of them rolled off, clicking on the polished floor.

Dr. Connor.

For a moment her heart seemed to clatter too, her thoughts roll in all directions at once.

An emergency, perhaps? A fire? Had she been so relaxed she'd missed hearing the alarm?

But that new fire bell made enough racket to reach every corner of the school.

Besides, Dr. Connor didn't look cross or hurried. He was simply standing there, not saying a word.

Nanny's thoughts stopped spinning, settled down. She began feeling calmer.

"Good afternoon, Dr. Connor," Nanny said, at her most gracious. "This is a surprise."

As she said it, "surprise," a thought jolted her. Could he have *meant* to surprise her? Heard some remark, some nasty whisper? Come in suddenly, hoping to catch her at something?

She'd had nightmares about surprises like that. A tall, frightening figure bursting in while she was holding someone close.

Nanny took her arm away from Livvie, then realized she was being silly. After all, a small child.

At any rate, if Dr. Connor *had* heard something, now

he'd see there was nothing to it. She was simply doing her job. Better. Giving a child extra attention. And on her own time, too.

A rare teacher. He'd said that himself.

Remembering how thrilling those words had been, Nanny smiled up at him. She gave Livvie a gentle push to remind her to stand for a grown-up.

"I think you know Olivia Fuller," she said. "She's called Livvie."

But Dr. Connor didn't speak. Or smile back. He just went on staring. Nanny found his gaze disconcerting. Evidently it alarmed Livvie too. She was stiffening at Nanny's side.

Finally Dr. Connor moved his head, slowly looked down at the things on the table.

"Miss Knowlton," he said flatly. "What's happening here?"

Of course, he's astonished, Nanny thought. He can't imagine what we're doing. Toilet paper, a scale. They must look odd to him.

"They're arithmetic helps, Dr. Connor. Remember, I wrote them up in my proposal about the Saturday school? We're having a special lesson. Livvie's been a bit mixed up. But we're setting everything quite straight."

"Somebody's a bit mixed up," Dr. Connor said.

What did he mean? Was he saying *she* was mixed up?

Then she *had* skipped a meeting?

Oh dear, she'd probably misplaced some notice, what with that bossy young man crowding her out of her own office. Well, she'd just apologize. And tell Dr. Connor how nicely Livvie was doing. At least he'd know she'd slipped up in a good cause.

"We're coming along very well," Nanny said quickly. "Today we're doing concepts. Less than, greater than, equal to. That's what the little piles of chips are for. We'll decide which is bigger. Greater than. And then, which is smaller. Less than. Last of all, we'll take some chips away, make the piles exactly the same. They'll be equal to. Of course, Livvie's going to do the same thing with numbers, on paper, a little later."

Goodness, wasn't she babbling! Somehow Dr. Connor always made her talk too much.

"Wrong," Dr. Connor said. "I'm afraid Livvie won't be doing the same thing later on. She's going straight down to the lobby right now. Where she belongs."

Nanny felt shocked, as if he'd suddenly clapped a hand over her mouth.

Why? What was the matter? He'd always been so polite, so courtly. How *could* he contradict her in front of a child?

"Go downstairs, Livvie," Dr. Connor said impatiently. "Wait for your mother, or whoever picks you up. School is over."

Nanny felt Livvie tremble. Dr. Connor was upsetting her. How thoughtless. How damaging, after her own hard work.

Besides, how could the child go down alone? There'd be nobody there for her. Her nurse wasn't coming till half-past five.

Should she tell him?

Did she dare?

Nanny felt bewildered. Perhaps her first thought had been right. Danger. A fire. And Dr. Connor up here, like a good captain, shooing out anyone left in the building. Brusque, because he was startled to find her. At this hour, the place was usually empty.

Still, he was hardly setting an example of the proper way to behave in an emergency.

"Livvie's a brave girl," Nanny said, setting one herself, and not just for Livvie. "She knows what to do. We can all go down together, Dr. Connor."

But Livvie was already up, bumping more chips off the table, scurrying to the door. Nanny could hear her running down the long hall toward the elevators.

She looked at her watch. Just five. The janitor would be running the elevator himself, now the operators had gone. Dr. Connor might even have told him to wait.

She reached down for her bag, got to her feet.

But Dr. Connor wasn't turning to go. In fact, he seemed rooted to the spot, head bent, staring down at the floor.

"Poker chips," he said. "Miss Knowlton, are you out of your tree?"

Nanny's mind began whirling again. Words and excuses bubbled up in her mouth. "Dr. Connor, I'm sorry. I simply never thought. If something from a gambling game bothers you, I'll find something else."

Feeling choked, anxious, she watched his face, hoping it would soften and show he'd accepted her apology.

But his expression remained severe.

"Come on, Miss Knowlton," Dr. Connor said. "Don't you play games. You're the one who's gambling."

Nanny's mouth went dry. Why was he speaking to her like this? And with such nastiness in his tone?

"I really don't understand," she stammered. "They're for my tutoring."

To her shock, Dr. Connor suddenly smiled widely and clapped his hands, as if at last she'd produced the one word he wanted to hear.

"Tutoring," he said triumphantly.

."Yes," Nanny said, utterly lost. "To help the slow ones. When they're having trouble."

She watched Dr. Connor walk slowly across the room and sit on the edge of her table, fold his arms, and cross his legs.

"You thought you'd get away with it," Dr. Connor said accusingly.

Strangely, Nanny remembered her father bursting out at her when she was little and saying exactly the same thing when he caught her with a handful of chocolates. And then snapping that she'd get fat. Nanny hadn't known that chocolates made people fat. How hurt she'd felt, how misjudged. How *could* he think she'd do something wrong on purpose?

And how could Dr. Connor think she'd deliberately do something that was bad for the school, bad for her children?

Because it was Livvie? Who'd be leaving school at the end of the year?

"But I don't just tutor Livvie, you know," Nanny said quickly. "I try to get round to *all* the children who've fallen behind."

The foot tapped faster.

"Come off it, Miss Knowlton," Dr. Connor said furiously.

"Please," Nanny said, feeling helpless.

"You've got no business tutoring *anybody*," he thundered. "It's a conflict of interest. Definitely, a conflict of interest."

With a wave of his arm, Dr. Connor swept the last chips off the table. They spun, fell, and chinked against the polished floor.

"You're a head teacher. You make more than most. Far more than the young ones."

Dear Lord, what did he mean? That she was old? Was this more talk about dead wood on the faculty?

But she mustn't think about that now.

"You're paid to teach here, Miss Knowlton. Not to help yourself to any kid you like, make a little extra money on the side. Arithmetic, indeed. You've been doing some adding, all right. To your own bank account."

Money. The word clanged in Nanny's mind like the fire bell.

It jangled her badly. But it also alerted her. Dr. Connor thought she was *paid* for tutoring.

How could he? She really did feel a shock of anger at the idea of being so unjustly accused.

"Dr. Connor," Nanny said, sitting perfectly straight, using the voice she knew could quell unruly children. "I'm sorry, but you're most dreadfully wrong. There's no money involved. None at all. I wouldn't *dream* of it."

Why, she could easily prove she'd never asked for money to tutor a child in the school. He could ask the mothers. Besides, she didn't *need* money. She was earning almost the top of the school scale. Her mother had left her the apartment, and the maintenance was positively prewar. And a trust fund. Not large, of course. But she spent so little.

Opening her mouth to speak, Nanny realized Dr. Connor was staring at her again.

"You're telling me you do this tutoring for nothing?"

"Of course," she answered quickly, feeling enormously relieved, happy to be able to put his fears at rest.

And now Dr. Connor's face was turning red. The man was embarrassed, of course. Perhaps even ashamed of himself. He *had* jumped to a conclusion. And such a *wrong* conclusion.

"Then you're out of your mind," Dr. Connor said viciously. "If it's not even for money, how *dare* you mess things up. If I can't trust my head teachers, who can I?"

Nanny felt herself shrivel. My God, he was looming over her, and she was a child again, hardly daring to look up at her furious father, heart pounding, hand stained and sticky with chocolate.

"There's an evaluation program going on here, Miss Knowlton. You know it. Everybody knows it. Our new psychologist is setting up an integrated testing *system*. You knew. I explained it myself."

When? What was he talking about? Nanny, desperate, tried to follow, remember. But what? She could think of nothing. The man was raving. Like a drunk, a lunatic.

Wait, yes, she did recall someone. Dr. Something, a faceless little woman, the new psychologist. She had been introduced for two seconds at a faculty meeting, then whisked out of sight into an office on the administrative floor. And yes, Dr. Connor had mentioned that she'd be testing. Psychologists. Nanny remembered one years ago, who'd asked a child to draw a house and been horrified because the result was far too perfect. Then Nanny had to explain that the father was an architect, so the child wasn't anxious, only especially competent. Still, *this* woman had only dealt with the upper school. Nanny had hardly seen her. So how in the world could she have interfered?

"I took Dr. Krakauer from a high-powered job in private industry. Her first charge is evaluations. On every modern measure—IQ, achievement, psychological disposition, potential, the whole shooting match."

He's mad, Nanny thought. And I have to get hold of myself. Not panic.

"There were reasons for that, Miss Knowlton. Admissions standards. Demographics. Performance estimates. Efficient grouping. Method, Miss Knowlton. Of which I've seen damned little in this school."

Humor him, Nanny thought. If he goes on long enough, perhaps you'll understand what he's driving at. After all, he's the headmaster.

Nanny suddenly saw Miss Creighton, as if in a formal photograph in the yearbook, small, straight, her dress hanging to her ankles, teaching her special Greek class, just a few of the older girls. Once, observers had come from Teacher's College. Miss Creighton was explaining the subjunctive, telling the girls they would never again say "If I was king" when they meant "If I were king." She'd asked the visitors if they didn't agree. And a solemn professor had said that none of them knew a thing about Greek, it was her *method* they'd come to study. Miss Creighton had let her eyeglasses drop to her flat bosom on their little black cord, stared coldly at them. "Method?" she'd said. "I explain until they understand. That's my method."

The headmaster was still shouting.

"How dare you mix in? Suppose Dr. Krakauer put that kid in a slow group? The right group for her capabilities, her level of understanding?"

Nanny hated talk about levels of understanding. The new librarian was all for them. Children's books that used only the words a child already knew. Dreadful, no strange words to stretch their minds, beguile them with language and make them think.

"And suppose your meddling muddied the waters, blurred the lines?"

Lines? I explain until they understand, Nanny thought. That's my method. That's teaching.

"Miss Knowlton. This school is coming out of the Dark Ages. You better come out too. Because I tell you, if you can't hack it, you won't be here."

Nanny snapped to attention, as if he'd smacked her. He'd get rid of her? The way he was chopping away the teachers who were dead wood, the children who held the others back?

And then, face flushing, rage making her heart pound, she wanted to shout at him. Who do you think you are? What fools chose you? This is *my* school, not yours. You don't know anything about teaching. You don't know *anything* about children.

Now hot tears were spilling over her cheeks. Dear God, when she knew so much. When she'd spent her life in this building. Why, except for college and vacations, she'd been here every day of her life since she was a child.

Nanny lifted her eyes. This man should see how strongly she felt, should know what anguish he was causing one of his best teachers, someone who cared about his school.

Good heavens! The man was *smiling*!

"Word to the wise," Dr. Connor said calmly, as if he hadn't ever raised his voice. "You just let Livvie there manage on her own. Let all of them manage. It's a cold world. If they need propping up in first grade, what will they need in fourth? Eighth? You talk about a Saturday school, Miss Knowlton, for the dummies. Saturday school, yes. Dummies, no. Plan for the gifted ones—astronomy, theater arts, creative writing, languages, that sort of thing. That's what Saturdays are for. And sports. Even girls' parents are sports-oriented these days. Forget the tutoring. Save yourself for better things, Miss Knowlton."

Nanny felt dizzy, as if she'd been spinning wildly in the children's wooden roundabout on the rooftop playground.

"Now. I came up today to consult you about a little problem. With the Barclay child."

The room seemed to rock all around her. How could she just forget all he'd said and talk calmly about something else? How could he expect it?

And to think, only this week she'd defended him against some of the other teachers at lunch. Waging a war on drugs in the school, threatening to expel any girl he even suspected. Good, Nanny had said. Drugs, in our school? Dreadful. And his new plan about unemployment insurance. Dr. Connor wanted the part-time teachers and athletic staff dismissed at the end of the school year, to collect unemployment-insurance payments all summer, then be rehired in the fall. The amounts they got from the state would be deducted from the school budget. And nobody would lose a penny. Nanny wasn't a fool. She knew it took more than inspired teaching to run a school. She was even pleased that Dr. Connor was taking such zealous interest in school finances. That was his job. Hers was teaching.

And in return, this.

Head whirling, Nanny realized how wrong she'd been. Now she'd seen him plainly. A bully, a dictator. Not an educator at all. And he could do anything. Even make her leave the school.

Feeling faint and queasy, Nanny tried to collect her wits.

The Barclay child, he'd said. Did he want a report on Tucker's progress with her new earphones? Was he wor-

ried that too much time was being spent on her? Had he
come this afternoon to chide her about that? Disgusting.

"Now, this trip the kids go on, to the farm," Dr. Connor
said. "Neat idea, by the way, Miss Knowlton."

She *would* faint. Again, a whole new subject.

Through dizzying rage, Nanny tried to focus on the third-
grade trip, a school tradition. Every year, the eight-year-
olds made a week's visit to a working farm in Connecticut.
Cows to milk, pigs to feed, horses to ride, barns to explore.
Country life. Valuable experience in a school where for
so many children the country meant a Gwathmey house
on a private beach, an English cottage pictured in *Architectural Digest*, a mountain retreat filled with precious antiques.

"I wanted an unofficial rap with you, Miss Knowlton.
Out of my office. I want the Barclay child kept back."

"Kept back," Nanny repeated, mystified.

"Right. Without any fuss from Mrs. Barclay. I want her
told at the last minute, when it's too late for her to do a
big number. She's made enough noise already. Just because she's in the *Social Register* doesn't mean she runs
things here. We don't need her calling more parents and
teachers and disturbing our work."

The thought of that little book, always near her own
telephone at home, comforted Nanny for a moment. People *were* envious of those listed in it. Was Dr. Connor
envious?

And Bibb Barclay had *succeeded* when she'd called her
friends in that little book. She'd managed to get Dr. Connor to revoke his decision about the Thanksgiving Festival,
and ever since, Nanny had heard the whispers. Mrs. Barclay had been telling people all over town that Dr. Connor
was wrong for the school.

Still, Mrs. Barclay had acted like a lady, especially compared to Mrs. Cantor. Someone in the lunchroom had said
that Mrs. Cantor actually threatened to sue the school.

Nanny tried not to listen to gossip like that. After all,
with an active group of parents, there were always complaints and differences of opinion. Most of them, thank
goodness, died quickly.

But evidently Dr. Connor *did* keep an ear out for gossip.

"You're not surprised, Miss Knowlton? Makes perfect

sense. A child with earphones? On a farm, day and night, for a whole week? It's not fair to the rest. To the group. It's not even fair to Tucker. Suppose a bull gets loose, and she can't hear a warning? Or she wanders off and doesn't realize people are calling her? No, we can't be responsible for a thing like that."

Only this morning, Nanny realized, she'd have taken him at his word.

Now she knew better.

Vindictive, that was the only word. Hurt the child because he was angry at the mother. Or Machiavellian, getting Bibb Barclay so upset she'd take Tucker out of school on her own.

Anyway, how could I? Nanny thought, feeling anguished. We've always taken everyone. Martha Cross, with her leg braces. Susie Schaftel, asthmatic, allergic to hay and grass. Even, a few years ago, the Jensen child, a diabetic who needed an insulin injection every single morning. And he was telling her to leave Tucker out. Worse, he wanted *her* to break the news. Why, the whole school would think *she'd* made the decision.

"Oh, but I can't," Nanny stated firmly, trying to ignore the hammering of her heart. "It's been a tradition for years and years, one the children look forward to just as soon as they understand about it. And then look back on it the rest of their schooldays, Dr. Connor. Why, there's never been a yearbook without pictures of the farm."

Dr. Connor shook his head.

"And I'm sending some of my best teachers," Nanny kept on. "Six of them. For just thirty-two children."

"Thirty-one, this year, I'm afraid, Miss Knowlton. Teachers aren't magicians. Can't be everywhere at once. Think how you'd feel if something happened. Don't take too much on yourself."

He stood up, looming over her.

"Like the tutoring," he said emphatically.

Nanny felt herself dwindle down to child size. How could she battle this man? She was powerless. Dead wood. He'd simply chop her off.

"Just handle it with Mrs. Barclay," Dr. Connor said calmly. "And we'll forget about that."

Shaking, Nanny understood. A bargain. Punish Mrs. Barclay for making trouble. And become a favorite again.

But how on earth could she *do* it? Mrs. Barclay was probably packing Tucker's things this very minute.

Well, she could say she was just doing what Dr. Connor asked. That was her job. She'd never shirked her job.

But she'd *never* deliberately made a child unhappy.

Nanny imagined the scene. She couldn't stop herself. The yellow bus at the curb. The little girls squealing happily, out of their uniforms for this special occasion, in blue jeans and jackets, lining up, climbing the steps, driving away singing.

All except Tucker.

Poor child, she'd think she hadn't heard properly, hadn't understood what to do. She'd stare, confused, at the others, her eyes would fill with tears.

"Well then," Dr. Connor said. He made an elegant little bow. Then he turned, walked swiftly to the door, and was gone.

Nanny sank back on the window seat. The room now was almost dark, she realized. She felt cold air seeping through the windowpanes. Why, her blouse was damp with perspiration, like awakening, with nightgown clinging, out of a terrifying dream.

But this was no dream.

Shuddering, she fumbled for the handkerchief in her pocket, dried her face, hands, neck.

Home, she thought. Get hold of yourself. Put this out of your mind for a while, till you've rested. Take a big glass of brandy. Pick up *The Eustace Diamonds* and plunge in. Trollope makes everything come out all right, villains get punished. Then, later, you can think what to do.

Nanny went quickly through the dark corridor to her office, tossed her carpetbag into the cupboard, and picked up her coat and purse.

In the elevator she nodded politely to Johnny when he clashed open the gates with his muscular arm. She felt relieved that no curiosity about why she was so late seemed to show on his blank, dark face.

The lobby was empty, cold as a stone church.

No. A child was curled on a bench near the door. Livvie?

But it was so late. Hadn't anyone come to collect her?

Nanny felt as if she couldn't bear any more. Would this horrible day never end?

Now the receptionist, Miss Carraway, was coming to the door of her cubicle, waiting to pounce. She couldn't leave for the day with a child still in the lobby.

"Really, Miss Knowlton," she said crossly. "You'll *have* to speak to Mrs. Fuller."

Another person came out of the cubicle too, someone who'd been standing at the receptionist's desk.

Nanny saw a young girl, small, plump, her hair a mop of frizz. Wearing a short leather jacket and patched blue jeans. She strode toward Nanny.

"Thank God someone's here," the girl said, her voice deep, sure. "Can *you* solve this? I came for Livvie Fuller."

Nanny looked at the square-set little body, the face clean of makeup.

A jolt went through her, interest, intrigue.

Miss Carraway, elaborate hairdo almost bristling, turned to Nanny.

"I don't know this person, Miss Knowlton," she said. "And worse yet, she has no written permission. You know we need a note. I can't let a child go off with just anybody."

The girl smiled at Nanny, her expression friendly, trusting as a child's.

"I've *tried* to explain," she said. "I was late. Mrs. Fuller asked me to pick up Livvie. She had to go to the doctor. And straight on from there to a meeting. Who remembered a note? Look, Livvie knows me, if someone would just ask her. Incidentally, she says she walked all the way down the stairs herself. How come?"

Strange, Nanny thought. Johnny just brought me down. He'd have brought Livvie. Why would she choose all those stairs?

"I can't have people I don't know talking to the children," Miss Carraway broke in crossly. "Coming late. Way past closing time."

"I'm Miss Knowlton, in charge of Livvie's part of the school," she said, at her most authoritative. "And you?"

"I'm Stella Waldman," the girl said. "I work for Mrs. Fuller. In her office, that is."

Nanny looked closely. Those clothes. Those gestures.

The girl looked . . . well, like a young boy. And she worked for Cornelia. Could it mean anything?

"Cornelia got stuck late. She couldn't make her meeting and fetch Livvie too. I'm supposed to bring her to her mom at someone's house."

Nanny heard Miss Carraway sniff, as if she didn't believe a word. The woman was ridiculous. Anyone would think she was guarding Buckingham Palace.

"Look," the blue-jean girl was saying. "I have the address here."

She dug in her pocket, straining the seams of her tight pants, and produced a scribbled note.

"If we called, they'd tell you Mrs. Fuller was expected. I don't have the phone number, but you probably do. It's someone from this school."

The girl squinted at the note in the dim light. "Mrs. Arthur Barclay," she said. "Up on Ninety-sixth Street."

The name struck Nanny's ears with the impact of cymbals crashing in a lower-school concert. She felt her skin tingle and goose bumps break out along her arms.

If Cornelia were at a meeting at Bibb Barclay's, it *had* to be about the school. About Dr. Connor. What else did they have in common?

Nanny shivered, excitement welling up in her as if she were going into play in a field-hockey game.

How ironic that Dr. Connor himself, keeping her late, had led her to this discovery.

Nanny stood straight, trying to keep her eagerness under control.

"Come along, Livvie," she called.

Then she turned to face the receptionist.

"I'm going toward Mrs. Barclay's myself. I'll just walk along with Miss Waldman, see Livvie safely to Mrs. Barclay's. That settles it, I think. You've been absolutely correct, Miss Carraway."

The receptionist looked from Nanny to Stella Waldman, back again. She sniffed.

"Well, I hope you'll tell Mrs. Fuller when you see her," she said. "It's quite irregular. Anyone could come in off the street, pick one of the children up, walk right out. And I'd be blamed."

Her excitement rising, Nanny took Livvie's hand and

walked into the night, Stella Waldman at her shoulder. With every step she felt more keyed-up.

She'd walk right into Bibb Barclay's apartment. Find out what was going on. At the least, she could break the news about Tucker's trip gently, make sure they knew it wasn't her doing. And at best? Well, perhaps she could help them. Didn't she know more about the school than they possibly could?

Stella Waldman's voice broke into her thoughts.

"The minute I saw you, I knew you'd understand," she said. "That dip wasn't about to let me take Livvie till she'd reached Cornelia. And I knew she wasn't *going* to reach Cornelia."

Nanny was distracted by a new feeling, a little glow of pleasure.

Miss Carraway *was* a silly woman. How nice that this girl didn't think *she* was a dip too. Nothing silly about Stella Waldman. She radiated energy, purpose. Her hair bristled, her little rump strained the seams of her jeans as she strode along the street. She worked for Cornelia. Was that all? Were they special friends?

"So you assist Mrs. Fuller," Nanny said.

"Yes. Since college. I love it. And her. She *cares* about casting, getting the person who'll make a scene really go down. About people, too. Tonight she got caught with this old actress who's been sending her a card every week for five whole years, asking for work. Cornelia coaxed an agency producer into adding an extra, just for her. But it took doing. And she's rushed off her feet with work, home, and a kid. That's why I help with Livvie when she's really pushed."

"I've known Mrs. Fuller a very long time," Nanny said. "We were girls at school together. Though of course I'm older."

"You went to Boston too?"

"Oh yes," Nanny said. "All my life. And then Smith."

"Smith," Stella Waldman said. "I had a couple of friends there."

The girl slowed, stopped, turned. Then she looked directly into Nanny's eyes.

"One of them was president of the gay group. Like I

was at Bennington. Which was a lot better college before they took the men, they tell me."

Shocked, stunned, Nanny felt as if all the cars on the street had suddenly veered straight at her, blowing their horns wildly. Everything vanished from her mind except this girl at her side.

The girl was sending a signal. A clear signal. And to *her*. But how could she be so sure Nanny wouldn't mind? Be embarrassed? Even disgusted? Good heavens, Nanny wondered, had she *invited* a signal? She began moving again, her insides all stirred up, shaken. Could this girl really feel sure of herself, speaking out like that? Wasn't it risky? Or was it? Suppose Nanny *had* been shocked. Why would the girl care? She wasn't hiding anything.

Nanny blushed, feeling a hot wave of envy, a yearning to be able to speak out, feel unfettered. Did Stella Waldman announce herself to everyone?

And what did Cornelia think? She'd hired Stella. Did that mean anything?

But now, she realized, shivering with excitement, they were almost at Mrs. Barclay's.

Nanny looked up at the building facing Ninety-sixth Street, but with its entrance on Park Avenue. Old, run-down, fire escapes, graffiti, garbage outside. But inside, surely, spacious, high-ceilinged apartments. It was rent-controlled, she knew. Several Boston School families lived in it, paying next to nothing each month, enjoying a good address. A borderline building. Everywhere to the south, stately buildings lined the broad avenue. But a few steps to the north, Harlem began, full of danger.

As she crossed the street, Nanny's nervous excitement grew. She was leaving safety now, walking into danger too. Until this moment a loyal faculty member of the Boston School. Once upstairs, she'd be suspect. If Dr. Connor ever found out, she might lose everything

Her breath coming faster, heart knocking against her ribs, Nanny tried to postpone thinking about Stella Waldman, to concentrate.

"I'll take Livvie upstairs," she said. "You go along. I'll be sure to tell Mrs. Fuller all the trouble you took."

"Okay," Stella said, smiling.

Nanny watched her squat down on her plump little haunches to hug Livvie.

"So long, Livvie baby. Wow. You're cold. Your mom's probably wondering why you're late. See you, Miss Knowlton."

She was gone, heading toward Lexington Avenue.

Nanny took Livvie's hand. Such a strange, terrible day—and far from finished.

But she felt so alive, exhilarated, better than in months, as if something exciting were about to happen. As if she could actually *make* it happen.

Pulse faster than ever, breath coming in little bursts, she searched the list of names on the doorway and pressed the proper button.

The President and the Board of Directors
of the Matrimonial Bar Association
of the City of New York
request the honour of your presence
at a
Dinner Dance

The Plaza Hotel
Grand Ballroom
December 18th
eight o'clock to midnight


Tickets $100
Black Tie
RSVP


GETTING OUT OF the cab in front of Dane's office, Cornelia almost bumped into a Santa Claus ringing an enormous bell and jingling coins.

She smiled at him, reached deep into the bottom of her bag for loose change, and spilled it into his coin box without waiting for thanks.

Coming to Dane, I *feel* like Christmas, she decided. As if I'm a bell clanging jolly sounds, as if I'm dressed in warm red, holding a pack full of presents to make the whole world happy.

She rang the outer bell. The buzzer seemed to send a shivery thrill through her whole body. And send memories shooting like Christmas stars through her head.

Dane on the past weekends, sweating to uncover the hidden glory of her country kitchen. Dane sitting by her mother's chair in the hospital, touching her arm, saying, "Why, you're pretty, Emily. So pretty." Dane in the silent country nights, stretched in front of the parlor fire, his silvery head in her lap. Dane showing Livvie how the tools worked, talking softly, pausing at the sound of her small, clear voice. Dane striding into her city apartment the first time, blinking once at the clutter, then laughing, throwing back his head.

Her spirits kindled like a thousand Christmas candles as she walked swiftly down the hall and saw his door swing wide.

She still wasn't used to his height, still forgot to tilt her head back enough to meet his eyes.

But oh, she was growing used to his grip on her arms, his clean tweedy smell, his hot mouth on her own.

Longing to dance, she walked with him into his office, watching his hair glint silver in the light of the desk lamp as he sat down.

Then, curling into a chair, she saw his desktop, and remembered why she'd come here today.

Livvie's tests. So many for such a little girl.

She began feeling worried. He'd put off talking about them so long she'd almost relaxed. Now?

She could read some of the headings upside down. Gray Oral Reading. Wechsler Intelligence Scale. Wide-Range Achievement. Psycholinguistic Abilities. Draw-A-Person. TAT. IOTA Word List. Visual Motor Gestalt Test.

Feeling dismayed, she looked up, saw his eyes.

"Cornelia," Dane said quickly. "Don't panic. There's nothing frightening here. It looks like a library because I went over everything carefully, and got second reports on some. Knowing you, I wanted to think hard before we talked. But it's tests, not gospel. You know the most important things. There's no evidence of serious psychological disturbance."

She nodded, trying to relax.

"There *is* something I don't understand," he went on. "Something she won't give about. But in the main, Livvie's easy to test, an open, articulate child."

"Then what? Why all the trouble at school?"

"Cornelia. Livvie's got to get out of there."

She leaned back, feeling a dreary, day-after-Christmas grayness saddening her.

"Why? What's in those papers?"

"Some of them can be misleading, especially for a small child. But others deal with intelligence."

"Well?"

"Cornelia, Livvie's scores are low."

The words seemed suddenly amplified, like a radio just turned up.

"Low. How low?"

"They put her IQ under a hundred."

His voice was hurting her ears, giving her a headache.

"You mean she's dumb? I don't believe you."

"I mean her intelligence is average."

"Average? What's wrong with average?"

"Nothing at all, for an ordinary school in an ordinary town," Dane said quietly. "But in a New York pressure cooker of a school, a lot."

"But she's bright everywhere except there. I mean, she can do a million things, dress herself, set the table, memorize the whole week's television schedule."

"Cornelia, we're talking about a school full of super-achievers. I hate labels like *gifted*. It's like Gilbert and Sullivan saying 'When everybody's somebody, then no one's anybody.' But the average IQ in yours is almost certainly much higher. Nothing's wrong with Livvie. But she *is* slower than the children she's with."

Slower. Pain pulsing through her head, Cornelia imagined Livvie blank-faced, slack-mouthed, hobbling after other, faster children.

"But that's horrible."

"No," Dane said, getting up, coming around the desk. "Unless you've decided she has to be an academic whiz. School isn't the world. IQ isn't everything. There's emotional stability. Talent. Motivation. Character. A sense of humor."

She felt his hand on her shoulder.

"Cornelia, she's the best little girl. She says wonderful things, she's got imagination and sense, even wit. And you're her sun and moon. She'd do *anything* for you, and she knows you want her to like your school. But sometimes her eyes get wide when she talks about the place and she looks almost frightened. I think she's got to be somewhere less pressured, a special school."

His hand seemed threatening now, and she stiffened.

"That's the premise you started with. All these tests haven't changed it. What kind of special school? Like for a retarded child?"

"No. Retarded children have IQ's far lower than Livvie's. And at that, plenty of them learn, with the right
teaching. Livvie only needs a gentler, perhaps a smaller
school. So she won't quit trying."

Cornelia's headache smashed at her, pounded down now
into her neck, her shoulders.

Another school. But her greatest hope for Livvie was
this one. Changing would mean visits, interviews, tests,
dragging Livvie around. How could *that* be good? Hadn't
she had enough change, Tim leaving? Shouldn't her school,
at least, stay constant? Anyway, who'd want her once she'd
been tossed out of the Boston School?

Worse still, suppose Dane was wrong? Suppose she de-
prived Livvie of all she'd had herself as a child and then
was sorry? There'd be no going back, once out of a school
so sought-after, so famous.

Anyway, how could Dane, whom she'd trusted and loved,
want her to give up so easily? Suppose Livvie were *his*
child, would he be so calm, so sure?

"Wait a minute. We're talking about a great school. Why
the hell can't *they* help her? Once we explain that she's
having a harder time than the others?"

"Cornelia. They have these same scores. Schools have
safes full of confidential files on their children, the families,
everyone's reports. They may misjudge psychological tests.
But reading scores are different. Livvie's are almost certainly why you got the letter."

"But she gets reports. They never said a word about
being slow."

"Come on." Dane was shaking his head. "You weren't
listening for that news. And if a teacher, even that head
teacher, had told you, you'd have been furious. You can
hardly bear hearing it from me, even now, knowing I care
about her, about you."

If you *care*, how can you say it? Besides, you've only
known Livvie a few weeks. You've only known *me* a few
weeks.

"That teacher said Livvie had emotional problems, that
if she felt better about herself she could learn."

"I think the opposite. Once she learns, then she'll feel
better about herself. Kids know where they stand. Even
when teachers group them, Bluebirds and Daffodils, they

know which is supposed to be the smart bunch, the dumb one."

"Well then, Margaret Rose. She knows Livvie better than anyone but me, and she's *always* said Livvie could do better if she'd just try."

"Dead wrong," Dane said firmly. "She *would* do better if she could. Do you think she *wants* to be slow? She's trying so hard she explodes!"

Cornelia felt as if *she'd* explode. "For God's sake, couldn't *you* be wrong? Or your psychologist? That mother who called me saw twenty, maybe thirty doctors. And they *all* missed her child's learning disability."

Dane shook his head.

"We talk about learning disabilities when a child's intelligence is held back by something. That's not Livvie. She's doing damned well with what she's got. Anyway, didn't you say that woman got a letter too? That they still want to get rid of her child?"

"But she's not letting them," Cornelia answered. "She's fighting back."

"Cornelia. You're Livvie's only full time parent. You work. Your fighting can only make it tougher for her in school. She's a gentle, fragile child. You have eyes. You *saw* what the other children do to her."

"I have damned good eyes," she said, feeling her stomach twist with pain. "I work. So I'll be a whole person, an earner, fit to take care of Livvie. The rest of the time I give her my entire heart, not like all those mothers with causes and charities, or the ones who live in Bloomingdale's. Can't you see Livvie's more than a batch of tests?"

"I told you, they're only guides. If we get Livvie trying, she'll be able to do almost anything. And her scores aren't anyone's fault, yours or hers. They're the way she *is*. School isn't a race. There's no time limit on learning, we all have a lifetime."

Cornelia's head was throbbing.

"What if I send her to a child psychiatrist? And things change?"

She watched Dane turn away to the window.

"I'd like her to have a few sessions with someone good," he said. "There *are* indications that she's keeping something way in. But I don't think Livvie needs a lot of time with a therapist. Or more discipline. She's not a cause, a war for you to fight. She's just a very small girl, bewildered and scared. You've got to show her you want her the way she is. That you'll love her even if she *never* learns to read."

Cornelia felt the pulsebeats of her headache come so fast they fused into one unbearable pain.

"She *knows* fucking well I love her," she said.

Dane lifted his head.

"Don't count on it," he said, his voice accented, thick, foreign. "A child doesn't know that automatically. Right now, Livvie thinks she's dumb. Not the smart girl her mother wants. Or the good girl Margaret Rose wants. And not what her daddy wants, obviously, since he left her."

Cornelia felt as if her head would shatter.

"Please," she said. "Don't hurt. You're not supposed to hurt."

"Dearest love," Dane said. "I'm sorry it hurts. But I'm trying with all my strength to make you listen to sense. If you *keep* pushing, it's going to hurt more."

She looked at him through blurring eyes.

Now his face seemed changed, stern, cold.

He bent his head and moved to gather the papers. The gesture reminded Cornelia that he was a doctor, giving an opinion, she a patient, diagnosed, done with. As if he'd told her she had a lump in her breast, that while there were choices, chemotherapy, lumpectomy, he recommended radical surgery, not that it would make any difference in the end.

"It *couldn't* hurt more," she said, feeling as if he'd swung at her, battered her with pickaxes and hammers, destroyed every dream she'd had of loving him, of his loving back.

Rising, holding her heavy handbag, she seemed to be standing numb in a room destroyed, whirling with plaster dust and mortar, crumbling into nothing.

She's even more forceful, now she's won her election, Cornelia thought.

Later, sitting cross-legged on Bibb's rug, Cornelia tried to pay attention to Rhea.

And maybe if I concentrate on all the wise things she's saying, I'll stop feeling so empty, so betrayed. Why did I imagine he could fix everything? Why was I so certain he was good for me, for Livvie? But he *seemed* so good. He'd settled what most middle-aged men are in turmoil about, he *knew* so much. Somehow, he made me glad to be strong, thrilled to be yielding, he cherished me, let me cherish him. Only I must have invented him. Because the man I thought was there doesn't exist anymore.

Restless, she got up and settled in a straight chair. Now she could see Bibb's grandfather clock, its minute hand well past seven. A new fear struck her. Where *was* Livvie? Had Stella missed her? Lost this address? Had an accident?

Then the doorbell buzzed. The sound seemed to zap through her body like an electric shock.

Instantly she was up, feeling some relief, sensing the rush of runner's high, pounding heart, quick breathing, that always came seeing Livvie after hours apart.

Reaching the door, she pulled it wide.

Christ. Nanny.

Cornelia froze.

"It's all right, my dear," Nanny said quickly. "Here's Livvie. All's well."

Then why *you*, Cornelia thought, feeling shock waves. Where's Stella?

"I didn't mean to startle you," Nanny said. "I happened to be a bit late tonight. So I was at the door when your assistant was dealing with Miss Carraway. No note, you see. I was coming uptown anyway. So I brought Livvie along."

I *am* a rotten mother, Cornelia thought. I can't even remember school rules.

Bibb was in the hall now, saying hello. Feeling all her misery come flooding back, Cornelia bent to kiss Livvie, unbutton her coat.

The child's cheek was burning cold. Her eyes looked heavy, as if she were starting a fever.

Cornelia suddenly longed to sweep her up, warm her, rush her away home, and lock the door against everybody else in the world.

How dare Dane say Livvie was less than perfect?

Oh God, she thought, I'm going to think about him every two minutes. I'm going to ache, missing him.

"Go eat, baby," she told Livvie. "Mrs. Barclay's got

good stuff for you and Tucker. Hamburgers. Chocolate pudding. And then the second you're done, we'll go home, put you to bed."

She watched Livvie go off with Bibb and straightened her back, steeling herself to think only of the present, to look at Nanny, thank her.

But Nanny's attention was somewhere else.

She was staring into Bibb's living room, eyebrows going up, eyes opening wide.

Aha, Cornelia thought, the sight distracting her, helping her forget her dull misery. She's getting a look at Rhea, sitting at Bibb's own desk, scribbling away on a yellow pad. Even Nanny's got to know we're up to something.

Bibb, coming back from the kitchen, saw Nanny's face.

She blushed, looking guilty, like a woman caught with someone else's husband.

Poor Bibb, Cornelia thought. Mrs. PTA. Seen with subversives right in her own living room. She knows Nanny will run straight back to Connor and tell.

"Oh," Nanny said finally, "I didn't realize. Good evening, Mrs. Cantor. Judge."

Cornelia watched Rhea put down her pencil, lift her head, and smile across the room.

"Why, Miss Knowlton," she said, "What a surprise. Now you're here, come on in."

Forget it, Rhea, Cornelia wanted to say. She's already figured us out. Don't give away any more.

"I'm sure you can guess why we're here," Rhea said. "Join us. Maybe you ought to know what we're thinking. You could do us a favor, go back and tell Dr. Connor everybody isn't thrilled with him."

Cornelia watched Nanny's hands fly up. Press tightly together.

"I won't tell him *anything*," she said, her voice strained, high. "Truly. I'm *glad* you've found each other. I've been so worried about your children, about Rachel, Tucker, darling Livvie."

Come on, Rhea, Cornelia thought. Don't listen. I used to trust Nanny, I always believed she truly cared about the children, but now, who knows?

"So don't stand in the hall," Rhea was saying. "I'm sure

Bibb's got more coffee. You know, Miss Knowlton, you're not exactly alone, worrying about the children."

Cornelia, feeling helpless, watched Nanny take a step toward the living room.

"I do know," Nanny said. "All these changes. The teachers are upset too."

Bibb turned, fled into the kitchen.

Cornelia wanted to follow her. But Rhea might not understand about Nanny, know that while she was sympathetic to the children, she'd be worrying about the school's reputation too.

She made herself sit where she could face Rhea and beam warning messages.

"He's certainly making changes," Rhea was saying agreeably, as if Nanny were already one of them, a volunteer too. "This must be hard on you, after all, running the whole lower school. Managing those young teachers."

"They *are* young, so many of them," Nanny said, sounding more like herself. "Full of education courses and theories, but so little experience. Not like the old days, is it, Cornelia? Those forceful women who taught us, years ago?"

"Oh, they're gone," Rhea said. "I've been visiting schools for Rachel. Seeing things you wouldn't believe. At Calhoun the other day, I watched a teacher make two spelling mistakes on the blackboard."

"Well, Calhoun," Nanny said. "Though it's true all over. Teachers now are half the age they used to be. Dr. Connor mentioned that recently. And so many of them are just marking time, on their way to careers that pay better."

How can you *listen*, Rhea? Cornelia wanted to shout. Why let her quote that bastard?

"But everything's so different now," Nanny was saying. "Teachers used to lead. People looked up to them."

See, Rhea? Cornelia wanted to say. Not her fault. That's what she's trying to tell you.

"And they used to have backing," Rhea said pleasantly. "Strong people at the top."

"Well," Nanny said. "We *do* have someone strong. Dr. Connor is very sure of his ideas."

"You can say that again," Rhea said. "Only some of them are a little hard to take."

"Oh, Judge Cantor," Nanny said, her hands flying together. "You don't know. Today he and I spoke. Actually, we had a sort of confrontation. He was terribly angry, almost out of control. And he's made a dreadful decision about Tucker."

Cornelia saw her glance nervously toward the kitchen, then turn toward her again.

"Actually, Cornelia, I have some news for you too. I shouldn't be telling you, of course, but it might help Livvie. We're about to change the way we score reading tests."

Bibb came bustling back, with a silver tray, coffeepot, fresh cups.

"It's quite wrong," Nanny went on, sounding earnest. "In the spring, we'll score on a new set of numbers. But they'll be compared with the present ones. Do you see? It's going to look as if *all* the reading scores have shot up this year. Even Livvie's. Still, it *will* help her record for a new school."

*Even* Livvie's, Cornelia repeated to herself, seeing Dane's face in spite of her resolve to blank it from her mind. Nanny thinks she's hopeless too.

"I don't get it," Rhea broke in. "I mean, he can only do that once. He can't change the scoring system *every* year."

Nanny took a deep breath.

"Here's the thing," she said. "Dr. Connor plans to *lower* the scores next fall, blame the losses on something he calls a summer slump. Say that children lose ground during vacations. And it's not true. Often they gain. But of course, you must never say I told you."

Cornelia forgot Dane again and blinked, dazzled, as if all the lamps in Bibb's living room had suddenly gone on.

My God, she thought, Nanny's giving away a secret. Why? Why would she trust us?

"Miss Knowlton," Rhea said in a different tone, quiet, sad. "Let me ask you something. Aren't you disturbed? Scared? This man is bad news. Everyone who sticks with him is going to be in trouble."

"Of *course* I'm disturbed," Nanny said. "That's just what I'm telling you. But you see my position. He's the headmaster. I only have an annual contract, that's all. Even with all the years I've been at school, he can give me notice, Judge Cantor. He can do *anything*."

"You needn't remind *us*, Miss Knowlton," Bibb said gently. "He's given our children notice."

"I know," Nanny said. "And I'm ashamed for the school. It's *good* you've found each other. Perhaps together you can do something. And perhaps I can help. Only no one must know, you can see that."

"Oh, Miss Knowlton," Bibb said. "I knew you'd see. You've always been understanding about Tucker. I could *never* believe you'd support that dreadful man."

Cornelia felt her head start to ache. She got up and walked away from them toward the window.

*What if Nanny's telling the truth? She knows things we don't. She could help us. Maybe Rhea's right.*

"Cornelia," Rhea said. "I know you want to get Livvie home. But it's a comfort, isn't it, knowing Miss Knowlton's on our side?"

Now they were all watching her, waiting.

Cornelia looked at Rhea, at Bibb.

She could almost hear them praying she wouldn't blow it, scare Nanny away.

Suddenly, in spite of everything being so awful, perhaps *because* everything was so awful, she found herself fighting a strong desire to laugh.

*Ladies,* she longed to say, *don't worry. I won't screw you up. I'm no lawyer, no debutante. But I am an actress. I can be nice to Nanny too, though I think we're wasting our time, she's too afraid to speak up for us, ever. Dear Rhea, what would you do if Nanny moved in on you? Draw yourself up like a plump pigeon, squawk, sentence her to hard labor? Bibb? Scream for your Arthur?*

The fantasy restored her, carried her through their stares, their good-byes, till she made it into a taxi, Livvie asleep by her side.

But in the dark cab, tossing about as the driver blitzed through the traffic, reality came back, bringing depression with it.

She was different from Rhea and Bibb.

She had no power. And no one to scream for.

Coming out of her elevator, carrying Livvie, Cornelia knew immediately that something was wrong in her apartment.

Strips of light outlined her door. Footsteps thudded beyond it.

She felt her body snap taut, like a marionette on a string jerked stiff. She shifted Livvie's weight and slipped her key cautiously into the lock.

Lights blazed in the empty living room. And someone banged in the kitchen.

Clutching Livvie, she tiptoed across the hall to look.

Tim, for God's sake. Almost too handsome, as always, blond hair glinting in the light, busy clinking ice cubes into a glass.

Cornelia went slack.

"My God. I thought you were burglars."

As he turned, she saw the bottle of Scotch on the counter.

"Where *were* you?" Tim said crossly. "Do you know the time? Is this how you treat Liv, hauling her around in the middle of the night?"

Wanting to shout, but reminding herself Tim wasn't worth shouting at, Cornelia turned away and went to put Livvie on her bed, spread a blanket.

"Some doctor called you," Tim said from the doorway. "Sounded surprised when I answered."

Dane, she thought, feeling her heart pump up. What rotten luck, Tim answering. Still, what was the difference?

"Never mind," Tim was saying. "I have to talk to you."

"Why not?" The words snapped out faster than she'd intended, because it *did* make a difference what Dane thought. "It's only nine-thirty. I have no more plans tonight."

Tim looked unkempt. A button was gone from his collar. It left a little lopsided wing at his neck.

Don't you dare feel sorry for him, she cautioned herself. There are laundries, plenty of little actresses to sew on his buttons. Anyway, how did he get in here? My God, does he still have keys?

"Sometimes I wonder if you ever plan," Tim said. "Nell. Margaret Rose called again today. She told me about Livvie."

Cornelia sat down, shocked, numb. She felt as if Margaret Rose had stolen up behind her, and thrown a strangling cord around her neck.

"What about Livvie?"

"That she's been kicked out of school."

"Damn Margaret Rose," Cornelia couldn't help saying.

"She was one hundred percent right to call."

"Livvie's *my* responsibility. Remember?"

"Not if you can't handle it," Tim said.

This new betrayal was choking her, making tears come to her eyes. She'd considered Margaret Rose a *friend*.

"How could she *do* a thing like that?"

"She says that school is ruining Livvie. And that she needs a father."

Cornelia's throat burned. Her mouth felt dry as blotting paper.

"Did Margaret Rose tell you the rest? That I took Livvie to a psychiatrist? Who says she's got a low IQ?"

"A psychiatrist? For God's sake, she's seven."

Cornelia sat down, feeling shaken up, limp, as if an attacker's hands really had been around her neck.

"Look," she said. "I'm sorry you heard it from Margaret Rose. I'd have told you, once I'd figured out how to handle it. But it's more than just Livvie, it's a vendetta at school. There's a new headmaster. He wants to build records fast, wants to get rid of children who're hard to teach. He doesn't understand the school."

Tim put his drink on the table so hard it splashed.

"There's a lot not to understand. No grades. No desks. Running around every five minutes on trips, garbage plants, farms, the blood bank. Livvie should be in public school."

"Oh, Tim, we've been all through that. It's this *man* who should be out. I'm working on it."

"And *you're* going to get rid of him? With some other mother hens? What's Livvie supposed to do in the meantime?"

Cornelia seemed to hear Dane's voice, echoing Tim. Oh, if only she had *him* on her side, she wouldn't care what anyone said.

"Listen, that's what mother hens do, fight for their chicks. Besides, I think I've got Harvey Bache. He runs that school board."

"For God's sake," Tim snapped. "He probably picked this man. Look. Margaret Rose is right. Livvie needs me. So do you. This arrangement is ridiculous. Maybe I should make a move, bring you to your senses."

"Like what?"

"How'd you like to change our custody agreement?" Tim said.

Like a fire alarm suddenly going off in a theater, the words alerted her, pulled every muscle tight.

"If you can't take care of Livvie, she'll be better with me," Tim said, his voice pompous, heavy with importance.

"Is *that* how you think you can move back in here?" Cornelia said, anger shaking her. "Try another scene. Better still, just go. Discuss your ideas with Harvey."

"Harvey. You sure pick professional men, Nell. A high-priced shrink for babies. A shyster lawyer."

"He did just fine against that society friend you made coaching those amateurs in Blue Hill. Just start *anything* about custody, I'll ask him to hire someone to kill you."

"I'm sure he could handle that," Tim said hotly.

He stood up, reached for her suddenly, and Cornelia squeezed her eyes shut, almost expecting a blow.

But Tim's hands were on her shoulders, pulling her close, his arms going around her. She could feel the scratch of his tweed jacket on her cheek, the tickle of the little point loose on his collar.

"Cornelia, you're mixed up, making a mess. And it's all unnecessary, I'm here. It's time to forget this separation business. Nothing's gone right since we split, doesn't that tell you something?"

For an instant she thought perhaps he was right. After all, wasn't she doing everything wrong, making a mess for all of them? Couldn't Tim make Livvie, at least, happier than she seemed now?

Then pictures shot into her mind: Tim picking up Livvie's dollhouse and slinging it into her room, getting it out of his way; Tim shouting at Livvie for banging pots and pans in the kitchen when he was memorizing a part; Tim shaking nickels and dimes out of Livvie's beehive bank.

Furious at herself for even a moment's weakness, she pushed, hard.

Tim stepped back.

"You're too far gone, I suppose," he said. "Margaret Rose told me that, too. She says someone's interested in you."

Dane, Cornelia thought, feeling a wave of longing for

him, almost seeing him swinging at the fireplace, sweating, flushed, working for her. And then seeing him pale, mouth tight, tapping Livvie's test papers together.

"Well, she's wrong," Cornelia said shakily.

She turned, picked up Tim's coat from its chair, walked to the front door. Wrenching it open, she threw the coat hard, watching it skid along the floor, hearing the buttons scratching on the tile till it reached the wall, crumpled in a heap.

Cleansed, emptied, she could look at Tim again.

"There's no talking to you," he said. "Lawyers. That's all."

Cornelia slammed the door behind him, enjoying the heavy thud, starting to feel she had *some* power after all, her own, that she could still fight.

And she'd thought of someone to scream to.

Harvey.

All she had to do was make him listen.

Next morning, head aching, heart heavy, she left Livvie at school and went straight to the corner drugstore where she changed five dollars into quarters and installed herself in a phone booth.

Two secretaries, five quarters, and half an hour later, Harvey came on.

"Harvey," Cornelia said, putting all the heartthrob she could summon up into her voice. "You've *got* to help me. Tim came over last night."

"And?" Harvey said.

"And he wants to take Livvie away from me. He knows she's in trouble at school. And Tim claims it's my fault."

"Naturally. What the hell, getting divorced gives kids trouble. So does *not* getting divorced, if people can't stand each other. Kids straighten out when things settle down. *If* they settle down. I'm telling you, forget it. Tim's broke. Let him think about court costs, lawyer's fees."

Cornelia lowered her voice to a despairing whisper.

"But if Livvie *is* thrown out of her school? Harvey, you've *got* to help me. She mustn't leave now. Not with the way Tim's acting. Besides, she thinks she's why Tim left."

"They all think that. Listen. I see more kids with divorcing parents than the shrinks. If your kid has problems, they come from Tim Fuller's side of the family."

He paused.

"Dumbest bastard I ever met, treating you like shit," he said clearly.

"Harvey," Cornelia said softly. "I'll do anything you tell me. But shouldn't I maybe have dinner with him, talk to him?"

"Not on your life. Ever hear of condonation? That's when you get back in bed with a snake and he uses it against you. You want to talk to Tim, call. Better yet, write, and show me the letter before you mail it."

"So no dinner? Just wait? Till Tim does something?"

"Listen, you're so hungry, have dinner with me."

The recorded voice of the operator interrupted, asking for more money.

Another quarter for Harvey? A bargain, Cornelia thought.

His voice came back.

"Where the hell are you?"

"Phone booth," she said. "I just *had* to get you first thing."

"I haven't a second today. What about tonight? I've got a banquet, the Plaza. Join me and we'll show, get out, go someplace and talk."

Cornelia's wrist ached. She realized she was gripping the phone, hard.

Not tonight, she wanted to say. Too soon. I'm not ready.

But it was stupid to feel squeamish. She knew plenty of actresses who did this kind of thing every night of the week. Besides, she was doing it for Livvie.

"I'd *love* to," she said firmly.

"Right. It's formal. Hundred bucks a plate. Better than you'll ever get from Tim Fuller."

I hope I'm up for this, she thought, feeling as if she were sailing toward a new hemisphere, nearing the equator, nervously awaiting a rowdy ceremony, a dunking, laughs at her expense.

She took a deep breath of the stale air in the booth.

If it helped Livvie, what was the difference? Whatever she had to do, it couldn't really touch her. She only had to play a role, *act*.

"What time?" she asked.

"Eight," Harvey said. "Upstairs, the ballroom."

"Right," Cornelia said.

She hung up, feeling excited and pleased with herself, armed against Tim, against Dane too, because now she was in command again, running her own show.

Stepping out of the huge white-and-gold elevator, Cornelia felt keyed-up, set to play an enchantress.

She'd dazzle Harvey from the start, floating across the room, hair flying, eyes shining.

But where was he?

Masses of people were rushing away from her, waving to each other, lining up to check their coats, crowding toward the ballroom doors. Some of her certainty ebbed away.

Maybe I'd better run while I still can, she thought.

Half an hour ago at home, wriggling into the most seductive dress she'd ever owned, she'd felt so sure. She remembered finding it one rainy Saturday with Livvie in a Third Avenue thrift shop, a flapper's dress all silver beads, backless, nearly frontless, with a flirting handkerchief hem. And then Margaret Rose taking it home, spending days sewing beads back, mending, patching.

Poor Margaret Rose, who'd wept when Cornelia reproached her for calling Tim, saying she'd never do such a thing again, especially since Mr. Fuller hadn't done a thing, just reported back to Cornelia. Cornelia had told her nursemaid she was finally getting the message about Tim and given her a forgiving hug.

She and Margaret Rose were both menders, Cornelia thought. Still, if Harvey made a move like last time, this dress would go to pieces. *She'd* go to pieces. My God, was she starting to shake?

Don't be dumb, she told herself. You're a grown woman. And grown women fuck.

She lifted her head and sailed to the ballroom entrance, where officials were handing out seating assignments.

Waiting her turn, she looked at the other women. Good, everyone dressed to the nines. Only a few in short dresses, suits, tailored pants. Lawyers, she decided, probably straight from the office.

Reaching the table with the seating lists, she learned
that Mr. Bache had gone in and left a ticket for her, and
said that if she missed him in the cocktail crowd it was
table three for dinner.

No one to scream to, she thought. But I'll find him. And
I'll *make* him keep Livvie in school, whatever it takes.

She lifted her chin, moved toward the doors, and went
down the steps into the crowd.

It was like walking into a bear pit, noisy and steamy,
with men looking as if they'd put their dinner jackets on
hastily in their offices, shaved quickly a second time with
electric razors. They shouted at each other, as if they were
still in their courtrooms. And every one of them was with
some woman, guarding her, helping her through the crowd.

Do-it-yourself time, Cornelia thought, trying not to mind,
struggling through the crowd at the bar, capturing a dripping glass, drinking quickly to tune out the clamor and
turn the men in dinner jackets into plump penguins, the
women into fluttering birds, to make herself feel less alone.

She found a tiny chair against the wall and sank into it,
keeping an eye out for Harvey.

If only I were waiting for Dane, she thought. If only I
had *him* to make me laugh at this bunch, had his arm
around me. I bet he looks marvelous in dinner clothes.
And I'll never know. Forget Dane. Anyway, remember
Bibb saying shrinks make everything worse, telling about
that three-year-old she knew, in therapy a *year* till someone
discovered the child was deaf.

She took another drink from a perspiring waiter with a
tray, wondering what Bibb would say, watching her now.

Maybe she'd applaud. Both Bibb and Rhea had surprised her these past weeks. They'd helped her out, taken
care of Livvie, called to see how she was getting on. They'd
asked all about her work, laughed about the cast calls for
forty midgets, for children who rode sidesaddle, for someone who looked like Eleanor Roosevelt at twenty. They'd
marveled at her endless supply of theater tickets, preview
and showcase invitations, at the numbers of actors who
wanted to take her out, buy her presents, do *anything* for
her. Rhea had been thrilled when Cornelia found out that
Connor was listing the school as a movie and TV location
for a fat fee, and offering the use of the school's name for

an even fatter one. She'd added that to her file of mis-
cellaneous damning information, along with Connor using
the school car and driver on weekends and moving the
best of the school's antiques to his apartment.

But would they understand now, those two paired-off,
protected women? Back her no matter what? If she *could*
turn Harvey against Connor, would they rejoice? Or would
religious Rhea shudder, preppy Bibb wrinkle her tiny nose?

Wanting to stop thinking, Cornelia looked around.

People were still crushing in, joining the battle for hors
d'oeuvres at the buffet, for drinks at the bar. But now the
lights were flickering, signaling dinner.

She moved toward the ballroom with her head high,
every bead on her dress shimmering.

Table three was at the far end, directly opposite, and
practically underneath the dais.

And there was Harvey, back to her, gesturing, talking
to some man.

Damn him, Cornelia thought, irritated. This huge crowd,
and he can't even watch for me? When I've come up with
the best dress in the place, the right face for it, all this
liquid white and beaded mascara, this beestung mouth?

But Harvey was turning, smiling now, eyes sweeping her
from rouge circles to satin slippers.

"Hey," he said. "Fantastic."

He stood, put an arm around her waist, and helped her
with her chair.

"We'll have a few drinks, that's all," he said into her
ear. "You look too good to share with a bunch of lawyers."

The orchestra began, blasting out sound, making so much
noise she didn't have to answer. Teams of waiters began
bustling, shoving trays between her and Harvey, pouring
champagne as if it were soda pop.

She drank, letting the bubbles pop in her head, the liquid
sting her tongue, gulping.

Someone was handing her a program. She glanced through
it, pages of names, all Esqs. and Honorables. More waiters
came, perspiring, rushing around the table. Soup splashed
from big ladles into bowls. Slabs of roast beef dealt like
playing cards from enormous trays. The music crashed
through her head too, making Harvey seem like a televi-

sion announcer who'd lost his audio, mouth moving sound-lessly.

Cornelia pushed away her plate, drank her champagne, accepted more, and began feeling pleasantly light, buzzy. She realized her foot was tapping, her fingers drumming to the beat of the music. A drumming disco sound now, amps up, synthesizer wailing.

Suddenly people were leaving their tables for the center of the room, a tiny space between all the tables.

Cornelia felt her heart twang like the electric guitar.

Waste, she thought. Those fat people. Trying so hard, looking so stupid. God, I do love dancing.

Harvey was pointing to her plate.

"Leave it," he shouted through the din. "Later we'll get something. Come on. Let's dance."

No, Cornelia thought, horrified. With *these* people? With you? I'm a *real* dancer. I don't want a partner who stumbles and clutches.

Rising, she realized how fuzzy her head felt, how un-steady her step.

She followed Harvey past people who were fox-trotting, oblivious of the music, and waited a partner's beat for him, determined to go where he went, follow anything he did.

In another moment, amazed, she realized.

Harvey could dance. For a big, heavy man, he was ter-rific. No natural, she could tell. But obviously he'd had a thousand expensive lessons. Best of all, he *thought* he was good, took chances, made big moves. Arms high, head back, he'd have made an ordinary partner look good. And Cornelia knew she wasn't ordinary. Ever since she'd gath-ered crowds doing the twist in the school gym, she'd been her absolute best, her happiest, most wonderful self, danc-ing.

Excited, mindless, she let herself soar, dip, fly. Beads jangling and flashing, she tossed her hair recklessly, flung her arms wide, smiled at Harvey.

Warm, dizzy, she could sense they were clearing space, pulling an audience together. The orchestra was shifting too, the leader catching sight of her dress, switching into a booming Charleston. And Harvey was going into it, arms flailing, legs kicking out.

She followed him, feeling light, beautiful, thoughts coming like syncopated trumpet bursts.

*Years* since I danced with anyone so good. Tim? He always had to be the star. Dane? Who knows? He probably likes Danish folk dances. But oh, I felt like this with him in the night, in the country. Forget him. Charleston. Head back. Kick high.

When the music lo-di-o-doed to a stop, she was blazing with warmth, laughing, letting Harvey hug her hard. She even responded, enjoying the feel of his rough chin on her cheek, the sharp smell of his cologne mixed with sweat.

Dancer's smell, she thought. Maybe this won't be so bad.

Now Harvey was pulling at his pocket and handing a bill to a waiter, pushing him toward the musicians. In a moment they began again, this time a waltz, gentle, lilting.

"This time," she heard him say, "travel. Follow me."

Her heart skipped as he edged her, swirling, swooping, toward the doors.

Not now, she though dreamily. Can't leave now. Not with *this* music, best of all, romantic, slow.

She came face to face with herself in the mirrored door of the ballroom, flushed, smiling, and remembered she hadn't come tonight to dance.

But the dancing had been wonderful. Even in the cold air, inside a taxi speeding somewhere, she still felt relaxed, light with champagne and music.

"You're something else," Harvey said, squeezing her hand. "You're some girl, Cornelia."

They stopped on a dark block. Cornelia stepped out onto a gutter full of papers, broken curbing. Before she could wonder why, Harvey was pressing her toward a doorway with a flashing neon sign.

Restaurant, of course, she thought. He said we'd eat, talk. I'd better get myself together.

They entered a big, plain room with wooden booths, a long counter, and a pump near the door with water spilling from it, paper towels.

"Barbecue," Harvey said. "Best in town. Ribs. Biscuits. Key lime pie, pecan. Raise your blood-sugar level. Get your energy back."

She tried to shake the dizziness from her head while

Harvey steered her toward a booth and left her to get the food. Soon he came back with piled plates.

"Sweetheart," he said. "Eat. Drink your coffee. You're still on that dance floor."

She thought he sounded nice, concerned. And she ate, amazed how good everything tasted—ribs crisp as bacon beneath sweet, glossy sauce, biscuits melting into doughy sweetness on her tongue, corn slippery with butter.

He's not so bad, she thought. He can dance. He's no snob, he knows where good food is, even in funny places like this. He's no fool. He'll help me.

Then Harvey reached for her plate, put it on top of his own, and finished off what she'd left.

The rough move shocked her awake.

My God, will he be hungry like that in bed? she wondered uneasily. Will he grab like that?

When every scrap was gone, Harvey straightened up.

"What's up?"

Cornelia realized she felt terribly full, queasy.

"I need you," she told him. "I want my little girl to stay in school, Harvey."

He smiled, and her stomach began settling.

"I might swing something," he said.

"I'd give anything. Because it's unfair. She's so little. They can't know yet whether she's bright or not. They used to give everyone as much as they could. Now Dr. Connor's changing everything. Livvie isn't the only one, you know, you're on the board."

Harvey gulped coffee, his eyes never leaving hers.

"I'm sure you know Judge Cantor," Cornelia went on. "She's got a group of parents going. We've heard horror stories about Connor, Harvey. He's a disaster."

"How, a disaster?"

"A dictator, making the place over his own way. A bully, pushing people around."

"Cornelia," Harvey said. "Don't get in over your head. We hired him because he took over a lousy California school, no morale, drugs in the halls, all kinds of violence. When he finished, kids were buying their own uniforms, learning their stuff, and beating up the pushers. He weeded out bad apples and laid down the law."

"Livvie's not a bad apple," Cornelia said, feeling sick.

"She's only seven. The Barclay child is eight, Rachel Cantor not much older. Who knows if they're smart? Since when is our school just for smart kids, anyway?"

"Come on," Harvey said. "Since the public schools went into the toilet. Since we got bussing, equal opportunity, pushers, switchblade knives. You and I know that if they abolished private schools, made the high-class people use public schools, they'd improve overnight. As it is, of course everybody wants private schools. They're beating the doors down—sixty, eighty applications for every place, glad to pay anything. The private schools have their pick. That makes it tough on middle-level kids, ordinary ones."

"But it's wrong," Cornelia said, bursting to say that Livvie wasn't ordinary, that she was beautiful, special.

"It's how things are," Harvey said. "I've got to tell you, we think Connor's doing a job. He took over a mess, Cornelia. And he's starting to straighten it out."

She began feeling lost. He'd never listen about Connor.

"Now, special people with ordinary kids, that's something else," Harvey was going on, laying out his case. "Let me tell you something, Cornelia. I thought you were special the day you walked into my office. You've got spirit. Jazz. Forget those broads. Take care of your own. I do."

She felt her heart quicken with hope and throb with misery at the same time.

What would Rhea do? Would she dump me for Rachel? And Bibb? She'd kill for Tucker.

Cornelia bent her head and sipped her coffee, feeling Harvey watching her.

And with the bracing heat of the coffee she felt sense come back.

Bad enough to go to bed with Harvey. I'll mind less if it's for everybody, if he helps us all.

"Cornelia, I do for clients. That mortgage on your house, nobody else could have fixed it. That husband of yours wouldn't even talk to a lawyer at first, and I got you an agreement. I told you right off, you've got no worries. You've just met the best attorney in New York."

"Harvey," she said. "Don't you think I'm grateful?"

"What I did so far, that was for a client. This would be for a friend. Maybe better."

Well there it is, she thought. All out front. I can't act
surprised *this* time. I have to keep seeing Livvie, that's all.

"Finish your coffee," Harvey said.

Settling into a taxi again, she thought he'd close right
in. But unpredictable as ever, he sat back, gave an address
to the driver, and added, "Move it."

Sensing a man after his own heart, the driver swooped
around corners, shot through the park.

When they stopped, she looked for a street sign. Second
Avenue, Seventy-sixth Street. Not far from home.

Only she wasn't going home.

"Come on," Harvey said, leading her into the building,
past a television monitor, a doorman drinking something
from a cardboard cup, through a beige lobby. He steered
her toward the elevator, pushed a button, and held onto
her till the door opened on a long, narrow hallway.

"Where's this?" Cornelia asked.

"Pied-á-terre. My firm keeps it. Not too bad."

It wasn't, she saw. The firm evidently kept a decorator
too. She had a quick impression of the latest of everything,
curved walls, face-powder colors, pine armoire, slivers of
mirror, lights gleaming out of nowhere. Harvey propelled
her past a little stainless-steel bar, a tiny kitchen. Cool,
impersonal, designed for business, like the one they were
about to engage in.

The bedroom was almost as small as the kitchen.

My God, it's all bed, and I'd better have another drink.

But before she could ask, he was all over her, like some
enormous bear. She could feel his hot, heavy hands moving
everywhere, cupping her rear end, stroking her thighs.

Jesus, she thought, a little frightened. He's like someone
in an empty subway, ready to smash if you resist.

"Zipper?" Harvey said, his hands searching.

"Wait," she answered, reaching for the long row of hooks,
standing back and letting the dress fall with a chink of
beads. Not much under it. She pulled off her panty hose,
feeling like a stripper on some sleazy stage.

Harvey was tearing off his dinner jacket, pulling at shirt
studs, kicking out of trousers, shorts. She saw muscled
shoulders and dark hair on his chest before he tugged her
onto the bed, yanking at the gray flannel spread.

"Look at me," he said urgently. "Keep your eyes open."

And kissed her so she could feel his teeth, jamming his tongue into her mouth, chewing her the way he chewed food. His hands were rubbing her breasts, groping between her legs.

Pinned beneath him, half-smothered by his mouth, Cornelia tried to keep from panicking, from pushing him away.

Then he stopped kissing.

And began to talk.

Mutterings. Indistinct sounds.

Slowly she caught them.

Holy Christ, she thought, stunned. He's telling me what he's doing. *Describing*. As if he's dictating a memo.

"Now I'm rolling your breast in my hands. Nice. Small, but nice. Now I'm getting hard. Big and hard. My prick is growing. Ever feel such a big one? Such a big hard prick?"

He's out of his mind, Cornelia thought, dismayed.

"Now I'm putting my prick in your cunt," Harvey was saying evenly, calmly. "Now I'm rubbing it up and down."

It's worse than that, she was realizing now.

Because Harvey was only talking. He wasn't actually doing anything.

Except for groping and grabbing, nothing at all was happening.

He took one of her hands then, pulled it down toward his crotch.

Sure, she thought, if it helps, just let's go, finish, let me get up, out of here.

She touched something so soft, so limp, it could have been a warm moist sponge.

After all the talk, that scene at my door last year, hustling me like Don Juan. He's nowhere. We'll be all night.

She gently pushed him away so she could reach for his limp penis with both hands, then touched, stroked, careful to use her fingertips lightly.

Nothing. He stayed a limp, spongy nothing.

Then he was pulling at her hair, yanking her head downward, hard.

She bent with him, willing to do anything to hasten things, opening her mouth. Face hot, neck hurting, she began kissing the lifeless thing she'd been holding.

She ran her tongue along the sensitive underside, sucked

the tip, moved her mouth with all the skill she'd ever amassed.

But it wasn't enough.

Cornelia felt her head start to swim.

Who'd believe this? she wondered. Mr. Macho, king of the world, and he can't get it up. So *I'll* never get up, out, home. Poor man. Of all the people this shouldn't happen to, not tonight, not with me. When I get home, if that ever happens, a steaming bath, scrubbing soap, a big rough towel. Two baths. And a long shower, hot and then icy.

She raised her head, rested it against his side.

Maybe if I get him talking again, let him pour his heart out, cry, tell me he drank too much, or he's all used up from screwing his secretary this afternoon, anything, and I'll pretend to believe it, then maybe he'll stop.

"Harvey," she said gently. "Maybe this is the wrong night. Too much champagne. Dancing. Shouldn't we give it a rest? Wait till next time?"

His hand went to the back of her neck again, but she shook free, leaned on an elbow.

"Truly," she said. "Maybe just as well, our first time. I loved being with you, especially dancing. I never dreamed you were so good. Maybe that's the trouble, all that rush."

She moved to the edge of the bed, sat up.

Harvey stood, towering.

His face, she saw, had gone dark red.

"You broads," he said. "You cunts."

"Hey. Wait," Cornelia began.

"Never," Harvey said, louder. "Never before. This is the first time. Only with you."

Don't explain, she thought. It's all right, I understand.

"There's broads all over this city who can't get enough. They call *me*. In every law office. Half the Women's Bar. Never except with you."

Somehow, she felt shaken. Could that be possible?

"Harvey," she said. "It's *nothing*. Don't be upset. It was a terrific night, we shouldn't have pushed it."

Suddenly she felt a sharp pain at her temple.

He hit me, she thought, astonished. *Hit*.

She was so shocked, stunned, for a second she couldn't move.

And then she was terrified, the way she always felt with

a drunk actor, a druggie, without a clue to what the next move would be.

"Get out," Harvey said in a matter-of-fact voice. "And get your file out of my office, find yourself another lawyer. You're just a dumb cunt. No wonder your kid is dumb."

The words came at her like bullets.

She stared at him, lost, wondering how she'd arrived here, wretched, in this strange room, discovering an enemy.

But she'd done it to herself. Ignored warnings, buried them deep, the way Dane said was so dangerous. She'd been false to herself, to her friends, and worst, to Livvie.

Somehow, she almost wished Harvey would hit her again.


Livvie sat on the kitchen stool watching Mommy work on the big cake.

She swooped the last smudge of white frosting out of the bowl with her finger and licked it. Then, feeling full, sleepy, she put her elbows on the table and rested her chin in her hands.

It's so safe here, she thought. All the dark is outside the window. In here it's shiny and warm, and the cake smells like toast and candy.

Nobody made cakes like Mommy. Even in cake stores, nothing like this.

A patchwork cake. For Stella's birthday. Little squares of icing all over, each a different color, from the little bottles Mommy let her mix with water. And on each square a picture or a word, telling something about Stella's year, a theater ticket, a T.V., a tattoo like the tiny one on Stella's arm.

The best cakes were the ones Mommy made for her. But Livvie only saw those all finished, with candles to blow. Last birthday, Margaret Rose said the cake should be in a magazine.

Livvie felt proud, helping, seeing the pictures grow. And she knew the cake would taste wonderful tomorrow, when Mommy took it to the office and surprised Stella.

"Livvie," Mommy said all of a sudden. "You know it's past ten o'clock? Better scoot to bed."

Bed? Livvie bit her lip, feeling cross. It wasn't fair. The

cake wasn't finished. A lot of the little patches were still plain white.

"I'm not tired," she said, touching a chocolate place gently with her little finger.

"Hey. *Now*," Mommy said, standing back, staring at the empty patches. Livvie knew she wasn't thinking about bed. She was thinking what she'd draw next with the shiny tip of the frosting bag.

"Soon," Livvie said. "Why don't you make a funny picture of me? I'm Stella's friend."

She saw Mommy stop working, look straight at her.

"Good idea. I'll do it and you'll see it in the morning. Now, get going. I'll come tuck you in."

"No," Livvie said.

Then she reached for one of the frosting bags, squeezed it, made a red blob on the kitchen table.

Surprise. She felt herself swinging up in the air, heard air swoosh by, saw the kitchen tilting on its side.

Mommy was *carrying* her, straight to her room. And putting her on the bed so she bounced a little.

She felt Mommy's hands reaching to pull off her school shoes.

Livvie began feeling angry, cheated, as if Mommy had turned off the television before the show was over.

"I *said*," she heard, and looking up, saw Mommy making a fierce, funny face.

Then Livvie just had to laugh, throw her arms up, hug hard.

She felt good again, touching Mommy's soft hair. It smelled like flowers and soap.

She hugged harder, and her fingers touched Mommy's ear.

Suddenly she could almost see the bad man standing there, right behind Mommy, holding up his shiny knife.

Livvie tightened her arms around Mommy's neck.

She felt everything inside her swell up, grow very big, get ready to burst out.

"Mom," she whispered into the ear. "Listen. I have to tell you. A secret."

"A secret?" Mommy said, hugging back. "All right. My lips are sealed."

Livvie clutched Mommy hard, opening her eyes wide, thinking how to begin.

"There's this man at school," she said finally.

Out in the hall the phone rang.

The noise made Mommy jump.

"Hold on, baby," she said, pulling away, slipping off the bed. "I'll be right back."

Looking after her, Livvie almost yelled.

There, right inside her black closet, she was almost sure she could see the man's hand. With the knife shining like a million suns.

Livvie squeezed her eyes tight, yanked up the blanket, scrunched way under the covers.

She could feel her heart slapping this way and that inside her chest.

She felt her mouth closing tight, her lips sticking together. As if someone had put Krazy Glue all over them, so she couldn't possibly tell a secret to anyone, ever.

To Parents and Alumnae:

Happy New Year! The Boston School is proud of last year's response to the major Development Fund drive. The number and amount of pledges received is truly gratifying.

However, in this new year, we have identified a special need: updating our science laboratories. An efficiency study shows that space and materials are totally outdated. We need state-of-the-art equipment so students can compete and excel in today's world.

*Science Leadership* donations of $5000 will be recorded on plaques in each laboratory. *Science Associate* donations of $1000 will be posted. All donations will be reported in our publications.

We know we can count on you.

Dr. Billy Connor,
Headmaster

RHEA COULDN'T SLEEP. She kept turning, back to stomach to side, uncomfortable in every position.

Saul was breathing softly, and she knew she'd feel guilty if he woke. But she couldn't lie still. The night seemed filled with the rumble of heavy trucks, the shriek of sirens. And even with her eyes closed, she could almost see the green light of the digital clock on the bedside table.

Worse, she couldn't stop going over her plan for tomorrow's meeting. She kept imagining herself in Bibb's living room greeting the parents who'd agreed to come, persuading them of her facts, cajoling them into joining the fight. A small group. But if she were effective, certainly enough to start a petition to the board, to make waves.

Turning over again, thinking of all the parents who'd ignored their calls and the others who'd said they *liked* the strict attitude of the new headmaster, Rhea realized she was starving.

Cocoa, she thought. With a marshmallow, maybe, beaten up nice and frothy. Just this once. So I can sleep, face tomorrow evening with my head straight.

She edged out from under the quilt, reached for robe and slippers, and padded out to the kitchen.

Then, opening the icebox, she felt guilt well up inside her. Hadn't she dieted away six whole pounds since her induction? Kept away from chocolate as if it were treyf?

Sighing, she lit the gas under the kettle and reached for a tea bag, a packet of Equal.

The tea tasted like boiled syrup, horrible, cloying. She splashed it into the sink.

Looking at the row of copper pots on the wall, she had an inspiration.

Borscht. She'd make borscht. All that scrubbing, peeling, chopping, stirring, would wear her out so she could sleep. And in the morning there'd be a big pot of the crimson soup Saul loved.

She began moving quickly, ducking into a bibbed apron, reaching for beets, onion, celery, tomatoes, green pepper, grateful that Dahlia kept the cupboards so full food practically fell off the shelves.

Some people, she thought, would open a can, use a blender. What do they know? I'll never forget my grandma, may she rest in peace, hardly taller than her kitchen table, banging greens off the tops of beets with a big knife.

Smiling, she began slicing, feeling more relaxed with every movement. By the time she'd swept onions in a pan, added a chunk of butter and started them sizzling, peeled celery and tomatoes, Rhea could feel her shoulders easing, her head clearing.

Humming now, she curved her arm to sweep the vegetables into the hot pan.

Then, far back in the apartment, she heard a door opening.

All her tension came back.

You woke Saul, she berated herself. The man hasn't got enough, now you don't even let him sleep?

She stood still, remembering Saul comforting her through Rachel's visits to the ear specialist, the fittings for her tiny hearing aid. Holding Rhea when she wept at night, that her baby should need such a thing. Saying, sweetheart, if it were glasses, would you carry on? It's the same, nothing.

Here he came, walking barefoot on the cold vinyl floor. His face looked so lined, his body so thin under the faded bathrobe.

I'm wearing him out, Rhea thought.

Then Saul smiled. The lines on his face all suddenly turned up.

"I understand you're worked up about tomorrow," Saul said gently. "The apron I don't understand."

Rhea picked up the strainer and began pressing peeled tomatoes through it into the pan.

"You know me. I'm hungry. I could eat or I could cook. Cooking is better. Go back to bed, Saul."

He pulled the robe closer and sat down.

"You, cooking," he said. "This is not something I see every day. Dr. Johnson admired a woman who could translate Epictetus *and* bake a pudding. Think what he'd have written about a judge making borscht."

Rhea felt tears behind her eyes. Dear Saul.

"Some judge," she said. "I misjudged how much work this school business would be. So many people duck trouble, don't want to believe bad news. It *is* like Hitler Germany, their saying he'll settle down, sure he's doing some bad things but it'll blow over. I got hopeful when Miss Knowlton turned up, but she's running too scared to be any use. Tomorrow's going to be tough."

"I don't know about that," Saul said. "Let's see."

He cleared his throat, frowned, and barked, "Judge Cantor, this Dr. Connor hasn't been in the school for long. Why not give the man a chance? See how his ideas work out, give him some room to operate, before we start trouble?"

Rhea had to smile. Saul looked so funny playing the critical parent, especially in that old maroon robe, frayed at the sleeves, one pocket badly torn. She bought him gorgeous robes, silk, Viyella, and this he clung to. But he wasn't dumb. Tomorrow, if anyone actually said that, she'd be ready.

"Come on," Saul said. "Tell me."

"You want to know, I'll tell you," she said, feeling her emotions simmer and bubble in her mind like the soup in the pot. "It took Dr. Connor three weeks to start moving the school's best antiques into his own apartment. A month to start kicking out upper-school girls for being suspected—only *suspected*—of smoking pot in school. About ten minutes to start bullying teachers who didn't suit his style, great teachers. Do you want to wait till the whole school's in turmoil? Or start now questioning his arbitrary rules, his vendettas, his personal ambitions?"

"So what are you sleepless about?" Saul said. "You've got the answers."

"Oh, Saul," she said. "Don't I wish it."

"You'll be fine," he told her. "Believe me, some of the things you'll say will stick. Next time he tries something, they'll remember you. And they'll tell their friends, it'll catch fire. Shouldn't you add the water?"

Rhea turned, measured water from the tap into a pitcher, poured, enjoying the hiss of steam, the rich smells, adding diced green pepper, sprinkling salt, pepper, a bay leaf.

"Just watch it with Sharon Pransky. She's a lawyer's wife, smart, thrilled her girls are at the school. Her husband tells me every time we meet in a courthouse corridor."

Rhea looked at Saul, saw his shoulder bones standing out under the flannel robe, the gray that had come into his hair these last months.

Dear Saul. He thought of every little thing.

Crossing the kitchen, she stood behind him, put her arms around his neck, kissed the top of his head.

Then, to *do* something for him, she reached for the milk carton and a pan, found the honey jar and began beating the sticky stuff in with a fork.

At least it's not cocoa, she thought a few moments later, pouring it, foaming, into two mugs.

She felt bursting with love, seeing Saul warming his hands on the mug, swallowing the hot, sweet milk in one gulp.

"Now can we go to bed?" he asked.

And I complain, she reproached herself. When he's always there, when there's nothing he wouldn't do for Rachel and me.

"I could turn the borscht off," she said. "Finish tomorrow."

"Rhea," Saul said, reaching for her hand. "Don't agonize so. Years ago, you worried over every exam, and you always came out on top. You threw yourself into every case, and you had a terrific percentage of wins. You made yourself sick over Rachel, and look, a tiny hearing loss. She's perfect."

That's not what the Boston School says, Rhea thought, feeling as if the milk were turning sour in her stomach.

"Tomorrow you'll be Portia. Esther. Forget the soup, Rhea. Come to bed."

Yes, she thought, reaching to untie the apron strings. I'll love you, Saul. And after, so you, at least, won't worry anymore, I'll *pretend* to sleep.

Almost an hour into the meeting, Rhea *was* feeling like Portia.

She stood next to Bibb's piano looking down at the little circle of parents, some on chairs, a few lithe fathers cross-legged on the floor.

Voice steady, presenting her case point by point, Rhea still could make mental notes, things to tell Saul. Things like one couple calling at the last minute to say they couldn't come, had remembered another engagement; how people looked coming in, stiff, even furtive; how their nervousness seemed to spread, making Bibb seem edgy and downcast, though she dutifully served coffee, made introductions, and commented on everyone's daughter by name. And oddest of all, the mysterious absence of Cornelia, who simply hadn't showed up.

Now, thank the Lord, someone was waving a hand, taking the floor.

Mrs. Pransky, Rhea saw, feeling a pinprick of worry, drawing up her forces.

"I suppose nobody's noticed what's happening to the school newspaper?" Mrs. Pransky said. "Suddenly it's full of articles about all the famous parents. They're using that paper like an advertisement for the school. And *we* know it's supposed to be for the benefit of the children."

Rhea got ready to congratulate Mrs. Pransky on her contribution, but now a father, a Wall Street type, was on his feet.

"I responded to your invitation tonight," he said, as if anyone had asked him, "because I've been asked to help with some new fund-raising material. It's come to my attention that the headmaster had a Discretionary Fund of over a hundred thousand dollars. In a school with tremendous deficits, I don't like to see anyone playing around with a fund like that."

Aha, Rhea exulted, as everyone began waving and talking at once.

"Why is Dr. Connor hiring professional songwriters for the school musical? What about encouraging the talents of the children?" one mother contributed in a timid voice.

"Never mind that," the Wall Street father returned. "Ask why the offices are being redecorated when the school's so impoverished."

"To please all those yuppie parents," one older woman called out. "Haven't you heard the latest Boston joke? That kidnapping last year, that fabulously rich diet doctor's child? How it upset the other parents, since after all, *they* were just as rich as the victim, why hadn't *their* kids been kidnapped too?"

Where *is* Cornelia? Rhea thought. She promised to take notes. Did she forget?

While the talk rose around her, she thought about Cornelia, so young, so racked about Livvie, about her poor mother, no husband, no money.

The sudden sound of the doorbell brought her to attention while the talk still swirled around her.

She saw Bibb get up to answer it.

Thank the Lord, Cornelia, Rhea thought.

But a moment later she saw, feeling surprised, that it wasn't Cornelia.

Bibb was leading a middle-aged woman, plain, dowdy in a severe suit, laced shoes.

Why, that's Mrs. Irving, Rhea thought, her spirits plumping up, as if a surprise witness had arrived to save her day. I didn't know Bibb had dared ask her. Good. We've snagged a board member.

Quickly Rhea held up a hand for silence.

"We're fortunate tonight," she said, "to have Alison Irving, one of our most concerned parents, at this gathering. Welcome, Mrs. Irving. There's been a lot of discussion here that should interest your board."

She watched Mrs. Irving acknowledge the greeting with a polite nod, take one of Bibb's chairs and move it a little apart from the group.

"Good evening, Judge Cantor, parents," Mrs. Irving said. "I'm always interested in anything that concerns our beloved school."

Her voice, her elegant manner, immediately irritated Rhea.

Mrs. Irving's not exactly Eleanor Roosevelt, even if she talks like her, she thought. She's probably as rich, certainly as badly dressed. But the woman's Jewish, though only another Jew would know.

As Rhea launched energetically into the reasons for the meeting, reviewing for Mrs. Irving alone what parents had complained about, her mind was going over what she knew about the woman she faced.

*Fortune* magazine had known about Mrs. Irving. Last year, in an article on foundations, they'd noted that Mrs. Irving's great-great-grandfather was a peddler, selling needles, pots, fabric, from a pack on his back, then starting a shop that grew into a huge chain of department stores. Rhea had curled her lip, reading how the Irvings were now staunch Unitarians, how they downplayed the money, employing au pair girls, not nannies, driving around in battered station wagons, and keeping dogs as if they were the royal family.

Rhea remembered the last time she'd seen Mrs. Irving so close. At a big PTA meeting, a fuss about the school magazine, a story by an upper-school girl with a lot of four-letter words. Mrs. Irving had sounded off in a speech about artistic freedom and aesthetic values. And then, she insisted on reading aloud words she'd been *proud* to see in the magazine—fuck, shit, cunt, clit—while half the parent body froze with embarrassment, and the rest sat bored.

"So you see," Rhea said, finishing neatly, "we have good reasons for getting together. Reasons you may wish to report to the board."

"Thank you for explaining, Judge Cantor," Mrs. Irving said, sitting straight, hands politely folded in her tweed lap. "Now. Aren't there reasons for this meeting you have *not* mentioned?"

"I beg your pardon?"

"Isn't it true that you've had a personal encounter with Dr. Connor? Because he's asked you to take your child out of school?"

Rhea felt her throat suddenly close. Like the time she'd almost choked on a chicken bone that wouldn't go down, couldn't be coughed up.

"I don't bring this up frivolously, Judge Cantor. It must be a painful subject."

When she'd choked, Rhea remembered, someone had come up behind her and done that Heimlich maneuver, squeezing her middle till it hurt. Then she'd had pain in her throat *and* in her ribs, her belly. And now it felt the same.

Was Mrs. Irving bringing out such a heavy gun to prevent even a small rebellion? My God, ten parents in the room. Was the board so afraid of ten parents that they'd send this woman to clobber the opposition?

Mrs. Irving, Rhea saw, was starting to drum her short unpolished fingernails on her handbag. God, even Saul hadn't figured anyone would bring up Rachel. Make a public issue out of a child's problems. And it *would* be public now. Mrs. Pransky was looking all excited, alert for good gossip. Tomorrow every lawyer in town would know Saul and Rhea Cantor's daughter had been kicked out of school. Mrs. Irving might as well have put an ad in the *Law Journal.*

Misery began settling over Rhea like foul cigar smoke, making her eyes water, her throat feel scratchy.

"Judge Cantor," Mrs. Irving said. "You must see it's a fair question. You're trying to enlist these people in your personal attack on Dr. Connor. Perhaps a natural reaction. But is it fair to make your child a cause?"

Rhea was watching the studied tilt of Mrs. Irving's head, the sour-lemon tightness of her mouth as she used her cultivated voice.

My God, she thought, I'm taking it from one of my own who's decided she's a debutante. She doesn't attack Bibb, because Bibb's her hostess, the genuine article, the faded WASP she's pretending to be. Me, an Eastern European Jew, she goes after. Well, I'm a better person than she is. A better mother. My Rachel knows who she is, she's proud to be a Jew.

She realized that everyone was silent, frozen, watching Mrs. Irving.

"I mean to say, if your daughter needs special help, shouldn't you concentrate on taking care of her? You're a judge, a terribly busy woman. One has only so much time to give."

Rhea was thinking rapidly, her mind sifting possible responses.

Sidestep? Say it's a subject I can't discuss? No, she's made it an issue, *the* issue.

Deny it? The big lie, like Nixon, eye this whole crowd and say it's not true? I can't. These aren't stupid people.

Wait, isn't that the clue? These parents have noticed what's going on in the school. Why can't they be made to see what Mrs. Irving's doing, fighting a personal war and enjoying it. Is she the kind of board member they want deciding the future of their children?

"Mrs. Irving," Rhea said pleasantly, "I fight battles where I find them. That's made trouble for me, of course. But the trouble usually comes from people on the wrong side of an issue, people with their own axes to grind."

Good. Her voice, deliberately tough and strong, was bringing every head up, all the eyes turning toward her.

"I went to public school, Mrs. Irving. And a city college. But we all want our children to have more than we had. Of course I worked to get my child in the best school in the city. I was thrilled by that school, and the opportunities it provided for its children. And then something happened. One man started changing it."

They were tuned in, one hundred percent. She could almost *feel* them absorbing what she was saying.

"I've seen institutions change. So did my grandparents in Europe. I know the signs. I see them at the Boston School early, maybe before most people would. Parent get-togethers like this are important. Talk is helpful. We're bringing up questions that had better be asked now, before there's real trouble."

Rhea watched heads swivel back toward Mrs. Irving.

Probably the first time anyone's crossed you since the Flood, she thought.

"Surely you don't imagine," Mrs. Irving said, "that our board is not fully aware of everything Dr. Connor is doing? Or that we don't approve? No, Judge, I think you should take heed. Not stir up all these good people who come out on a cold night. And perhaps consider if you shouldn't be spending your time more constructively, finding a school where your daughter will fit in."

Rhea watched Mrs. Irving rise quickly, nod at Bibb, turn and go.

When her own eyes found Bibb's, she was sure she could see shame in them, fear and despair.

Half an hour later, while Bibb was saying the last goodnights, and welcoming Cornelia, who'd finally walked in, Rhea retreated to the bathroom, hoping to get herself together.

She saw a plump face framed in the bureau mirror, haggard, worried-looking.

I can't even go home yet, she thought. There's still work. I've got to get who said what straight, compare notes with Bibb, *make* notes, now that Cornelia's here. The big PTA meeting with Connor's state-of-the-school speech is only a month away. And all I feel like doing is walking out, going home and telling Saul what I brought on Rachel. Better I should have taken her out of the school, picked up and left, the way my family left Europe.

She ran a comb through her thick hair and patted her suit jacket.

At least, she thought, we'll sit down, have a cup of coffee together, dish, the three of us. At least I'm finally among friends. Funny, having a Jewish enemy and two gentile friends. Good old Bibb, with her world handed to her on monogrammed silver, rising tonight to the occasion, being so polite to Mrs. Irving in spite of her nastiness. And Cornelia looking like a flower, managing so much without anyone to help her.

Rhea closed her bag, tiny, compared to the enormous thing Cornelia had lugged in tonight, and smiled, remembering how at their last get-together Cornelia had taken out of that pocketbook a pair of Livvie's blue jeans, a

strange tool, and a bunch of bags filled with brilliant sequins. And proceeded, all through their meeting, to stud
the little pants with a design of sequins, a peacock with a
hugh tail positioned where Livvie's tiny rear end would
be.

Feeling livelier, she walked briskly back into the living
room.

And then stopped.

Bibb and Cornelia were *embracing*.

Stunned, Rhea blinked. What now, mitn drinnen?

Bibb's arms were wrapped around Cornelia's waist, her
head buried in Cornelia's shirt. And she was *crying*, big,
unladylike sobs, shoulders heaving.

Was Bibb *that* affected by Mrs. Irving? The woman hadn't
even mentioned Tucker, only picked on Rhea. Was *that*
troubling Bibb?

"Rhea," Cornelia said, looking up, her face white,
strained. "Do something."

"What *is* it?" Rhea asked, coming closer.

Seeing Cornelia's face closely, she felt another shock.
Lopsided, swollen. With a bruise marking one of her high
cheekbones, an ugly blot on her paper-white skin.

"What *happened* to you?"

"Nothing good," Cornelia said, reaching up to touch
her cheek cautiously.

Rhea sank wearily onto the couch, her mind charging
ahead. Someone had hit Cornelia. A crazy actor? That
awful ex-husband? But then why was Cornelia calm and
*Bibb* crying? Rhea took a breath. A good lawyer, she
began at the beginning.

"You look like something from a matrimonial case,"
she said. "Was that a sock in the eye, maybe?"

"I walked into a door," Cornelia said, smoothing Bibb's
hair. "Tell you about it later."

"I see," Rhea said, feeling miffed for a moment, then
realizing quickly that Cornelia was right, that they'd both
better concentrate on Bibb right now.

"We've got to help Bibb," Cornelia said.

Looks like a job for a doctor, not a lawyer, Rhea thought.

"Come on, Bibb. Stop," she said, making her voice
peremptory, like a slap in the face. "Tell us what's wrong."

Bibb raised her head and Rhea saw how woebegone she

looked, how frightened. Then she suddenly felt like hugging Bibb too, as if this were Rachel, scared, miserable, needing comfort badly.

"I can't possibly tell you," Bibb said, choking.

"Come on," Rhea murmured encouragingly, just the way she'd talk to Rachel. "We'll help. Whatever it is. Only stop crying. You can't think when you're crying."

"Oh yes I can," Bibb said, as if she *were* Rachel. "I've been thinking all day. I may never *stop* thinking about it."

"Tell us," Rhea said, reaching for Bibb's hand. "You'll feel better."

Probably something about Tucker, she thought. The other kids poking fun at her earphones.

"What *is* it?" Rhea asked Cornelia. "She hasn't told you *anything*?"

"No," Cornelia said quietly, "just that she's got to quit."

The word seemed to pierce Rhea's skin like a bee sting. "*Quit*?"

"Yes. She says she can't fight the school anymore."

Oh my God, Rhea thought, as if the sting were poisonous, making her weak, helpless.

"Why? What happened? Did somebody say something to her?"

Or, she thought then, did someone promise her something? Someone like Alison Irving realizing that Bibb's a crusader, worth ten parents all by herself with her connections, her energy, her *niceness*?

Immediately Rhea reproached herself. Bibb *was* nice. She'd never fall for Alison Irving.

"She won't tell me," Cornelia said. "I thought maybe *you* could find out."

Rhea watched while Bibb scrabbled in her skirt pocket for a handkerchief. When her hand came up empty, she simply picked up the corner of her skirt and wiped her nose.

Rhea couldn't believe it.

"I didn't want to tell Cornelia," Bibb said to Rhea, as if Cornelia had vanished. "I feel so guilty. Because she's already alone. Divorced. I feel stupid, perfectly dreadful making such a fuss."

Then Rhea began to comprehend. In her heart and bones, as if she'd heard Bibb on the stand in a matrimonial case, she knew what was coming. Arthur was asking out. And Bibb, nice Bibb, had never dreamed such a thing could possibly happen to her.

"Bibb," Cornelia was saying, "what are you talking about?"

"Arthur. He's in love with somebody."

Rhea thought: Oh, if it were Saul, what would I do? All those women out there with teeth and claws, waiting to pounce, preying on dumb middle-aged husbands. Can't they find someone who doesn't have children, belong in a family?

"I feel so *stupid*. As if this only happened to other people. Couldn't possibly happen to me. It's my own fault. I was so involved with Tucker, he got involved with someone else."

Trust Bibb to blame herself, Rhea thought. She can't even give herself the satisfaction of hating him.

"I'm sorry to be doing this, here, now. But there's never been anyone *but* Arthur. And now there won't be anyone at all."

Rhea looked at Cornelia, who was wide-eyed and flushed. Maybe feeling guilty, having pushed her own husband out.

"How do you know?" Rhea asked Bibb, as if Bibb *were* a case, someone asking for legal help, counting on the law to get her balance back. "Did he tell you? Or did you find out?"

She saw Bibb flinch.

"Found out," she said. "The worst way. I knew something was up, little hints, here and there. Mostly I ignored them. I've been so *stupid*. After everything I've read, everything I've heard from friends."

She wrapped her arms around her knees and hugged them tightly. Rhea thought: That's how she must have looked at Radcliffe, earnest, telling her classmates the horrors she'd discovered in the Boston slums.

"Vaginal problem," Bibb said, syllable by syllable, as if she were steeling herself to get out the words.

Now Rhea found herself flinching. Good Lord, how poor, protected Bibb must hate it, finding out that way. No wonder she's gone to pieces. And now, with all this AIDS business. Thank God, it's just one of those old loathsome diseases we learned about in law school. If it were Saul, I'd kill. Him. Her, whoever she was.

Glancing over at Cornelia, she could tell from her troubled look that she knew what was coming too. Actresses, after all, didn't live in cocoons.

"My gynecologist asked what I'd been *doing*. I didn't know what he was talking about. Then he got all red in the face, said he'd call Arthur himself. Gave me antibiotics. Made me promise to come back. Can you believe it, it wasn't till he said not to go to bed with Arthur that I actually understood."

Rhea saw Cornelia turn, walk toward the window.

"I felt so *unclean*. Of course, I couldn't wait to ask Arthur what was going on, did *he* know he had a problem? He could hardly talk about it, but I pressed, because these things don't come from nowhere, from toilet seats, the way my mother used to say. He stamped out of this room, and then came back, looking ridiculous. Only then he told me about it, a girl in the bank. Puerto Rican. I couldn't *believe* it. I'd understand better if it were one of my friends. Arthur. He changes shirts twice a day, takes endless showers. And picks a girl with a horrible disease. I feel disgusting. Do you know, I actually went downtown this morning to try to get a look at her."

Rhea felt a sting of surprise. *That* didn't sound like something Bibb would do.

"And?" she said.

"She was a sight, greasy hair, chipped nail polish, plastic shoes. I'd never *dream* he'd touch someone like that. Much less bring her infections home to me."

Rhea felt wretched, seeing Bibb start to weep again.

"He's like someone in a play, a bad play. Says he *loves* her. A baby, a *virgin* when they went to bed, imagine. Can't stop loving her. He's ashamed, sorry, never meant it to happen, and by the way, he loves me too. But he's never had any fun in life, nothing but work and duty, so he's owed this, entitled. He *cried*, if you can believe it. Arthur."

Rhea could believe it. She'd heard it before, and often. Men losing their minds. Women surprised, realizing how many signs they'd missed. Maybe even she herself, knowing all she did, would act like Bibb, if the time ever came.

Cornelia walked back across the room.

"Bibb," she said gently. "Nothing hurts like somebody you love and trust betraying you. It's demoralizing. Devastating. You just never forget. I know. There were a couple of actresses, backstage girls in Tim's life too. But Rhea and I are friends. Whatever can help, we'll do. I know school seems unimportant right now. But give yourself a chance. You don't have to decide now, tonight."

My Lord, Rhea thought. Cornelia's taking charge. Doing what *I* should be doing, keeping this team alive.

"I don't *want* to abandon you," Bibb said through tears. "But what can I do? I sound like a soap opera, but if I'm not Mrs. Arthur Fremont Barclay, who *will* I be? You've both got careers, you're interesting women. Honestly, if there weren't Tucker, the boys, I could see myself swallowing pills."

"But there *is* Tucker," Cornelia said. "Just the way there's Livvie and Rachel. And the other kids we're trying to help."

Rhea watched Cornelia straighten up. Somehow, she seemed to be growing taller.

"Anyway," she went on, "if you really feel like nothing without him, maybe it's *you* who should change. Could be Arthur's too used to you. Too comfortable. Better shake things up."

She seemed to glide into the center of the room.

"Starting now. This room. While we're here let's push your things around. You've got all that stuff covering the windows, the damask *and* the lace. There's no light. And this sofa's just where everyone would put it, on the longest wall, your chairs all in pairs. No surprises. No fun. Come on, Bibb. Let's break it up. Now."

While Bibb stared, Cornelia went into action, hauling the long sofa back, yanking at a Queen Anne chair.

Rhea felt a warm rush of admiration. Smart, *doing* something, distracting Bibb. At least she might get tired enough to calm down. And stop thinking about pills.

"Help, Rhea," Cornelia commanded.

All right, I haven't had enough today, now I'll move furniture.

Obediently she got up, helped drag the sofa from its place. She'd never paid any real attention to the room, seeing it merely as the right background for Bibb, subdued, conventional, shabby. But Cornelia must have studied it, thought. She certainly seemed to know what she wanted.

By the time they'd taken down the heavy draperies and fluffed out the lace curtains, made a cozy corner of two unmatched chairs and a heavy round table with an elaborately carved base, Rhea began to forget she was tired. And even Bibb was looking interested.

"That Chinese screen is the best thing here," Cornelia said firmly. "You keep it in the darkest corner, where no one can see it. Come on. Help me spread it right out against the wall."

We're crazy, Rhea thought, obeying Cornelia, pulling at the screen, wincing as it creaked across the floor, then unfolding it, extending the vermilion panels with their exotic birds, dragons, pagodas.

"Rhea," Cornelia said. "Go through that cabinet, take out all the ivory things, thimbles and animals and boxes, just those. Put them on that Belter table, together. The rest, Bibb can put away somewhere."

Rhea began separating the ivory chatchkas, while the others labored in a corner. Silly things, she thought. But they look nice put together like this.

She looked up, and saw Cornelia waiting, her expression determined.

"Now," she said. "The piano. It doesn't *have* to be flat against the wall. And God knows, it doesn't need that Spanish shawl covering up such beautiful ebony. You should *wear* that shawl, Bibb. To bed, as a matter of fact, with that terrific fringe. Now, push hard, both of you. It's got casters, even if they haven't moved in a thousand years. Swing the front end out of that corner, get it facing into the room."

And Rhea, pushing till her calf muscles hurt, watched Bibb bracing herself, digging her toes into the carpet, stretching her arms.

Stretching her brains, let's hope, Rhea thought. Finding out that sometimes anything different is better. Remembering how much she's got. Belter. I better look that up tomorrow. Maybe when Arthur comes home tonight from his hooker, he'll trip over something we moved and break his silly neck.

Twenty minutes later Rhea was sweating, breathless, hands gray, clothes ready for the cleaners. But the room looked gorgeous. Every beautiful old piece of Bibb's was showing to its best advantage, chairs inviting, screen blazing color out into the front hall.

Bibb was actually smiling, her face smudged, her dirty hands clasped together.

"You two," she said. "It's heaven. Cornelia, you're a director. A genius."

"Nothing like changing furniture around," Cornelia told her. "Whatever's the matter, you always feel better. When I'm alone in a hotel room, even, I do it." And then, suddenly serious, "Oh, Bibb, can't you stick with us? Keep going a little longer? Till we win, till it's over? We'll help you. After all, Rhea's a judge. She knows divorce laws. And I'll think of things, Bibb. I'll find you a job. Go shopping with you, the hairdresser, all that. A new life. Listen to us."

Listen to her, Rhea prayed silently. Cornelia's offering you the best help there is. Friends.

"Bibb, if you want," she said, "I could tell Arthur a few things. Loss of custody. Equitable distribution. Today he'd be giving up maybe half his capital, his income. Maybe all your friends. She won't exactly fit in at his clubs, Bibb. And what's he going to talk about with a bank teller? If she's been around enough for a serious venereal disease, he may not be so exciting for her in bed, either. Young girls like that get cross when a man can't keep up. Besides, half the divorced women in New York marry again and do better the second time. If Arthur's dumb enough to pick up a thing like that, of *course* you can do better."

Bibb sat down.

"You're both so good," she said. "Listen. A drink?"

Rhea relaxed, glowing, feeling almost as good as if she'd scared Mrs. Irving silly.

Bibb was staring at the place where the liquor cabinet had always been, remembering where it was now. Reaching for a bottle, she clutched it, turned to them both.

"I know you're trying to help. And you're darlings. But I need Arthur. I know what I've done wrong. Now I have to do things differently. Rearrange my life, Cornelia, not just my living room. When Arthur told me, it was like a plea, a cry for help. I think he's halfway home. But he just can't dream I'd forgive him, or that he'd forgive himself."

No, Rhea wanted to shout at her. When a marriage cracks, it's finished. How could you ever trust him again?

Cornelia was shaking her head too. "Listen, Bibb," she said. "You felt idiotic telling us, right? But you hoped we'd understand. Well, now I'm going to confess something, and hope *you* understand. You think you're dumb, listen to this."

Now comes the story about the black eye, Rhea thought, feeling uneasy.

"Last night I went out with Harvey Bache. Kind of in cold blood. To get him interested in me, make him help us. Whatever it took."

My God, did *he* hit her? That ox, with his big hands? This girl, maybe a hundred and five pounds?

"I didn't make out very well," Cornelia went on. "And I'm ashamed. I didn't want to tell you. Anyway, I ended up making things worse, turning him into a real enemy."

"Because you wouldn't do what he wanted?" Rhea had to ask. "I could have told you. He's got some reputation."

"I don't doubt it," Cornelia said. "But there it is. I was playing Mata Hari. I spent all day thinking about quitting this, because he's on that bloody board, and now I'd be holding you back. So look, Bibb. I've made a mess. You too. Now, why don't we just dust ourselves off and keep going?"

Cornelia smiled.

Amazing, Rhea thought, she smiles and looks sixteen, glowing, black eye or no black eye.

Rhea took a step to hug Cornelia tightly. She felt wonderful when Cornelia hugged back.

Like a present, she thought, exulting. I never *had* women friends. The smartest girl in the class doesn't have friends.

She felt, somehow, that she was closer to these two than to her mother, to Saul, even. With him, she wanted to look smart, good. With these two, she didn't have to care *how* she looked.

Bibb's elegant voice caught her attention.

"I can't," she was saying. "I can't do both things at once. Arthur comes first."

She sounded absolutely certain, case dismissed, no appeal.

In the quiet that followed, Rhea began slowly to realize that her back ached, her feet hurt, that she was hot and dirty and exhausted.

She sat down, feeling bereft, despairing, as if someone had held out a gift, maybe one of the Chagall oils she'd yearned for as long as she could remember, and then laughed at her and snatched it away.

*One by one we praise our school*
*singing to the skies*
*one by one we learn and grow*
*reaching for the prize:*
*from little child to woman grown*
*separate yet ne'er alone*
*each one precious, each a jewel*
*daughters of the Boston School.*

—"The Boston School Song"
(words and music by Anna Martins Grace, 1924)

WEAK LIGHT FILTERED into the corridor of the school basement from barred windows high in the walls. A steady hum came from the boiler room, echoing from the concrete walls, underlying the gurgle of water running through the pipes.

Nanny felt the damp through her shoes as she led the first-graders toward the superintendent's office.

I always forget the *cold* down here, she thought, shivering. Good thing I reminded the children to wear their sweaters. It won't do for them to have sniffles after the very first trip.

A quick look back at the little girls made her feel warmer, cheerier. They looked so sweet, walking two by two, holding hands, with Miss Kittredge so tall behind them. All their dark blue uniforms and knee socks seemed to blend, making them seem like a long dragon with many heads, some curled, some frizzy, some with neat braids.

Lucky girls, Nanny thought. First they'll see all of this fascinating basement. Then the busy telephone room, the kitchen, with those huge dishwashers and stoves, the offices, typewriters, Xerox machines, that new word processor. They'll be so filled with new things to talk about, to put into their stories and paintings.

She smiled, remembering how she'd felt as a child, scurrying after Miss Creighton. The headmistress had insisted that the children learn about their building, top to bottom, and had made sure they met all the people who made their school run—superintendent, handymen, office workers, cooks, maids.

Crochety Miss Creighton might have been, but then she always found ways, even if some were outlandish, to interest children, make them *want* to learn. Dr. Connor just cares about what other schools are doing, about what impresses the important parents.

Hearing the high-pitched giggles behind her, Nanny paused at the door to the janitor's office.

"Come along, girls," she said, enjoying their excitement, knowing the superintendent would be waiting for them, ready with his usual little speech of welcome and to show them the boilers, furnaces and laundry machines, the storerooms crammed with costumes and scenery, hockey sticks, nets, Easter and Christmas decorations, battered chairs and tables.

In fact, Nanny told herself as she tapped at the heavy door, she must remember to point out that three girls in this class, Justine, Martha, Bryn, had mothers who'd made this same trip when *they* were small, perhaps even played with some of the things in the storage bins.

But no one, Nanny realized, was answering her knock.

She tried again, eager to begin, expecting to see Johnny, looking like a soldier in his crisp khaki, his wide belt hung with small tools and keys.

Johnny Mescalero did hold the girls spellbound. An Indian, after all, with a limp that thrilled the children. And so did the story of how he'd gotten it, doing skyscraper construction work, taking a bad fall, working as a handyman in Miss Creighton's apartment building until one day she'd hired him for her school.

So like Miss Creighton to do that, Nanny thought. She considered Johnny *educational*, the symbol of a downtrodden race. A strange man, though. So impassive, almost without expression. And so silent, turning up everywhere without his feet making a single sound. Still, how could we manage without him? Only last Monday he had unstuck Peg Brompton's head from the stairway uprights without frightening her, and then gone straight off to fix the toilet after Jiffy Baines flushed her arithmetic text down it.

Nanny realized her knuckles were hurting from so much knocking.

Where *is* the man? she wondered, starting to feel disturbed. He can't have forgotten we were coming. He never forgets anything.

She could sense the children moving restlessly behind her, letting go each other's hands, starting to push forward.

She put out a hand and turned the knob, feeling a pinprick of surprise when the door swung in smoothly.

The office was black dark. Certainly no Johnny here. Perhaps he'd had some emergency, a leak, an unscheduled delivery, a cupboard that wouldn't open? Perhaps there was a note somewhere, to say when he'd be back.

"Go ahead, Miss Kittredge," Nanny called. "Take the class into the boiler room, look at the storerooms. Go right along, girls. I'll catch up in one shake of a lamb's tail."

Silently she blessed Laura Kittredge, young, pretty, just out of Wellesley but experienced with children as the oldest in a big family, and bright, flexible, imaginative. What she didn't know about boilers, she'd have the girls look up and discuss later on. If only there were more young teachers like her.

As the children moved off, Nanny pushed the door wider and stepped into the room groping for the light switch.

She tried the dank wall to the right, then the left, but found nothing.

Finally, stepping cautiously into the darkness, she flapped a hand over her head, hoping for a chain that might work a ceiling fixture.

Almost immediately she caught hold of a string and pulled it, finding herself in a ring of blazing light.

It had been sensible, Nanny could see, not to bring the children.

The room, without Johnny, seemed so bare, so gloomy. Clean, of course. But somehow forbidding, with its dented metal lockers and battered desk, the ancient television set, the single tipsy armchair.

She looked at the desk, its top half-hidden under Johnny's big tool chest and a pile of old newspapers.

But she saw no note, no scribbled message.

A calendar was taped to the wall. Nanny looked at the square for today's date. Blank.

Feeling disappointed, she thought, He's failed me. And the children.

The top half of the calendar held a big picture of a smiling baby and Nanny had an inspiration.

The baby nursery. She'd take the children up there, to visit the only people smaller, younger than they in the Boston School.

Pleased with herself, she clapped her hands together, her disappointment gone now.

A *real* nursery, another of Miss Creighton's ideas, started ages ago so upper-school girls could learn to be good mothers. She'd hired a trained nurse, set aside rooms, filled them with pretty cribs, tubs, a kitchenette, ultraviolet sunlamps, and a library of books on infant care. And then invited a few of the poor Irish families in the neighborhood to send their babies, free, all day every day.

Nanny, as a girl, had worked in the nursery and loved the warm weight of a baby in her lap, loved watching the tiny mouth pull so hard on the rubber nipple of the bottle she'd sterilized herself, loved soaping the baby's tiny body, pinning on fresh diapers and touching the incredible silky skin.

For years now she'd longed to show the nursery to her first-graders. But the nurse these days was a gorgon, ferociously on guard against colds and infectious diseases, never letting Nanny's children get any closer than the glass observation window.

Perhaps today, if I troop the lot of them up there, she'll relent and let us in, Nanny thought, reaching up for the light-pull.

Then she paused.

Suppose, she thought, Johnny misunderstood? Got the time wrong and hurries back from wherever he's gone and doesn't find us? Shouldn't I write a note saying we were here, were sorry to miss him?

She looked around for paper and pencil. Seeing neither, she pulled out the narrow middle drawer of the scarred desk. There was only a jumble, chisels, screwdrivers, scissors, a prickly mess of nails and screws. Johnny ought to *lock* this desk, she thought. These things could be dangerous. A child might stray in here.

Feeling annoyed, still searching for a pencil, Nanny opened one of the big square drawers down the side of the desk.

It seemed crammed full of rags, small pieces of clean soft cloth.

Frustrated, she started to push it closed.

But these rags somehow didn't look right. They reminded her of something, as if she'd seen them before.

But it's *underwear*, she realized, amazed.

She stared down at the soft little pieces of fabric, white, pale pink, yellow, blue, showing bits of lace edging, inked markings and nametapes, elastic banding, all crumpled together.

Breathing faster, she picked up a handful of the stuff. One piece slipped from her fingers and dropped to the concrete floor.

She look down at it, lying under the strong light, next to her shoe. Flat, no longer crumpled, unfolded, it clearly was a pair of panties. Tiny. Not even as big as her foot.

Nanny felt sick, as if the floor were dropping away beneath her, like an elevator sinking much too fast.

She longed to scoop up the little garment, bundle it back into the drawer, shut it away and get out of this shadowy, shabby room.

But she couldn't stop staring into the drawer.

Dear God. It was *filled* with panties.

Nanny felt a fierce tug at her heart, as if someone were trying to claw it right out of her breast.

Dear Lord, could he have taken them from the children? Here? In this office? Did he frighten them? Force them to undress?

Holding her hands to the pain in her chest, Nanny wondered if she were having a heart attack. Now her ears were ringing too.

No, she commanded herself. Stop it. You're jumping to conclusions. You're a head teacher, you're supposed to stay calm. You're hallucinating, sick, because you're overworked, worried, pressured.

But the floor still seemed to be sinking, and the bare bulb swinging overhead sent frightening shadows creeping

along the walls. Looking around wildly, catching sight of
a pile of old newspapers, Nanny saw imaginary headlines,
large, black, before her eyes.

SEXUAL ABUSE. SCHOOL FOR SCANDAL. INDIAN MOLESTS
POOR LITTLE RICH GIRLS.

Struggling for breath, Nanny screwed her eyes shut and
leaned against the desk.

I *must* take hold, she told herself. I've got to. I *know*
how to handle emergencies. There are procedures, meth-
ods.

But the pain was still hammering at her chest, keeping
her from thinking straight.

I *can't* manage this, she thought. I oughtn't even to try.
I should go straight to Dr. Connor. But he'll be furious.
And he lashes out so when he's in a rage. Besides, will he
believe me? He thinks I'm dead wood. Now he'll think
I'm imagining things, going mad.

All right, then, she'd *take* the evidence with her. For
proof. So if he bullied her, she'd just be able to put the
nasty things right down on his desk.

But she'd better move, get out of here. Any moment,
Johnny might come back.

Frightened, she scooped up underwear from the drawer,
turned, almost ran from the room.

Far down the corridor she could hear the children's voices
and saw Miss Kittredge leading the group back.

Carefully Nanny squeezed the bunch of cloth together
and pressed it deep into her smock pocket.

"Miss Kittredge," she called, astounded at herself for
being able to speak so calmly. "Would you mind taking
the children straight upstairs, please?"

Even in the gloomy light, she could see the surprise on
the younger woman's face, eyebrows going up, mouth
opening. "Why, we've only just come down," Miss Kittredge called, moving closer. "And, Miss Knowlton, you've
dropped your hankie."

She bent quickly, then went rigid with surprise. Finally
she picked up the little underpants and looked up at Nanny,
at the bulge in Nanny's pocket.

"Please," Nanny said. "It's nothing. You mustn't say a
word. I know you don't gossip. Forget all about this. Girls.
You're all to follow Miss Kittredge now."

Hearing their little flutter of protest, like birds cheeping, she felt sorry for them.

"Miss Knowlton, is something wrong?" Miss Kittredge said, staring at her. "Can't I help?"

"Yes, dear," Nanny said. "Just get the children where they belong. There's something I must do."

She turned away, anxious to go first, be ahead of the children before they began clambering up the stairs.

Hurrying up to the lobby floor, she began feeling sick with dread all over again. Just getting past Dr. Connor's secretary would be a trial. And when she did, *anything* could happen in his office.

Why, dear God, hadn't she sometimes *sent* children to Johnny, for supplies, for emergency help? What if Dr. Connor leapt on that? What if he actually blamed her for this terrible thing?

She stopped on the top step, her breath catching painfully in her throat.

Do I dare face him with this? Knowing I'm partly to blame, that he can attack me too?

Dear Lord, he'll be terrible. Ferocious. Far worse than the other day. He'll terminate my contract now, this minute, for cause.

And then, there I'll be—dead wood. Facing all the days of my life with nothing at all. I can't imagine how I'll bear it.

But I *must* face him. The children come first. Over everything. This horror must be stopped, no matter what Dr. Connor does to me.

Hands pressing into her pockets, heart smashing against her breast, Nanny walked toward the headmaster's office.

Billy Connor heard something. A soft knocking at his door.

He slumped back in his chair, exasperated.

For God's sake, he'd told the woman no interruptions. Couldn't she head anyone off? Couldn't he get ten minutes to himself?

He slammed his hand on the blueprints spread across his desk, then smoothed them as if they might steady him, give him back his patience. His eyes went straight to the lettering in the lower-right-hand corner.

The Irving Communications Wing.

Somehow now he *did* feel calmer, soothed by the smooth touch, the faintly acrid smell of the paper.

Yesterday, he remembered, when the architects had first spread out the drawings, he'd felt awed, almost in a state of grace. He hadn't felt such peace since he'd been a skinny boy in a white suit, making his First Communion.

Smoothing the blueprints, he could almost *see* the spacious rooms, spotless, soundproofed, filled with ranks of computer keyboards and screens, with little cubicles for taped language study, with laboratories for film and videotape, with banks of ingenious storage space. No school, city or country, would have better. And Alvo Altschuler, a world-famous graphic designer and a school parent, would be executing a new logo for the school, with the Irving Wing incorporated as a symbol. Christ, in a few more years he'd have fifty applications for every place. He'd get invitations to speak at educational conferences, probably be elected president of the Independent Schools Admissions Association of Greater New York, start getting national, perhaps international publicity.

Now Connnor felt a rush of air at the back of his head and heard the squeak of a hinge.

He looked around, feeling more at peace again, prepared to speak softly, deal courteously with his secretary.

When he saw Miss Knowlton, looking timid and pathetic as usual, he felt anger strike up inside him like a match set alight.

"Dr. Connor," he heard her say in her Back Bay intonation. "I must speak to you."

How *dare* she, he thought. This relic, this kindergarten teacher. Does she think doors don't mean anything, that she can blunder in like a cow in a parlor?

He jammed his feet into the rug, shoved back his chair, strode to the door.

Closer to her, despite the heat of his anger, he saw that something was really wrong. Miss Knowlton's skin was the color of the chalky lines on his blueprints. She was clinging so hard to the door that her fingertips were blood-red.

"Dr. Connor," he heard. "Trouble. In the basement."

The words seemed to enter into him somehow, like little puffs of smoke, irritating his eyes, making his nostrils smart.

"What *is* it?" he asked, feeling his throat thicken up. After all, she wasn't a complete fool, wouldn't come through his closed door without some reason.

"In Johnny's office. His desk drawer."

Connor now found he could cough, clear his throat. Then it wasn't some catastrophe, fire, burst pipes, an explosion.

Still, something was frightening her, something in a desk drawer.

Of course, Connor thought, wanting to smile. She's probably found grass, pipes, papers, bottles of cough syrup, glue. Or maybe glassine envelopes with white powder. Enough to knock her socks off. But not mine. What school *doesn't* have a drug problem now? Especially in nutsville Manhattan? In the best of them, kids are walking into walls, zonked in class, rolling their sleeves down to hide track marks.

At the last interschool conference he recalled a principal talking about salad-bowl parties, for the love of God, kids collecting a lot of pills, tossing them all together into a bowl, then actually taking turns swallowing a handful.

Connor fixed his face into a stern expression. "Just what did you find, Miss Knowlton?" he asked.

He watched her take a timid step into the room, turn, close the door softly behind her.

"I was with the first grade," she said, looking earnestly at him again. "On their trip."

Jesus, Mary, and Joseph, Connor thought. It's going to be "Once upon a time," from the beginning. Can't she just get it out? Why the hell trek kids through the basement anyway? They should all be in class, learning to read, raising those rotten scores.

"All right," he said. "Just tell me what upset you so."

"These," she said.

He watched her reach into her big pockets and fish out a bunch of scruffy cloth which she heaped on his desk on top of the blueprints.

Connor couldn't believe what he was seeing. Was this her idea of a joke, her revenge for his being angry the other day?

He watched Miss Knowlton lick her dry lips, open her mouth again.

"Dr. Connor, don't you see? It's *underwear*. I found it in Johnny Mescalero's desk."

Connor looked down for an instant, then closed his eyes.

He felt so angry he was rattling. He itched to slap Miss Knowlton silly and throw her out the door, or better still, out the window.

For Christ's sweet sake! he almost shouted. Johnny. The one man I felt sure about around here. I even drank with him. Take this stuff away. Take yourself away, you're nothing but trouble. How dare you bring me chickenshit like this?

But through his fury he seemed to hear buzzing in his ears, like the little alarm on his watch, warning him it was time to cool down, be careful.

Miss Knowlton, he realized, was speaking.

"You see, I was looking for a pencil, paper. To leave him a note."

Mustering up all his control, Connor said, "Sit down, Miss Knowlton. I can see you've had a shock."

He made himself take her elbow, guide her into the visitor's chair. Then he walked slowly around and sat down.

It was time to concentrate on those rags, face up to all they could bring—hysterical mothers, angry fathers, smirking reporters, maybe even the police.

But somehow he could only focus on Miss Knowlton's face, all pursed mouth and downcast eyes, like a pathetic throwback to the nineteenth century.

Wouldn't it be her, he thought, to carry in the dynamite that can blow me to smithereens? And she'll clack to everyone. Christ, I could even get sued. Indicted.

He spun his chair around to the window, away from her.

At least *I* didn't hire that pervert. They can't lay that on me. What rotten luck this didn't break while Miss Creighton was still here.

Turning back, he saw Miss Knowlton sitting silent, her hands clasped in her lap.

All right now, boyo, Connor told himself. You didn't go through all those years of slaving, kissing ass, to get knocked out by a bunch of panties. And besides, this isn't a public day-care center, some crazy religious institution. If you walk softly, handle this carefully, the way the Jebbies do, you'll be all right.

The first step over the stile, he decided, was to settle this biddy down.

"Miss Knowlton," he said. "I know how shaken you must feel. In fact, I'm going to insist you take a little drink. It's terrible, really, that this discovery fell to you."

And that's the truth, he thought, going to his cabinet, reaching for a stemmed glass, and pouring it full of sherry. Pity it wasn't me. I'd have tossed that filth right into the furnace.

"Just drink it up, and then we'll put our heads together. For my part, I'm grateful it *was* you. I don't know where we'd be if it had been someone less experienced, a young teacher overreacting, getting frightened, gossiping."

Miss Knowlton, he was pleased to see, jumped a bit at his words, then settled back in her chair.

He leaned forward, fixed her with his eyes.

"Now we have to consider together what's best to do. Tell me, Miss Knowlton. Have you ever had an inkling of anything like this? The slightest hint something was going on in the basement?"

Miss Knowlton shook her head, looking terrified.

"Think carefully, now. Not a word from any child? Any parent? Nobody *ever* complained about Johnny?"

"Oh, no," she said breathlessly. "The girls adore him."

The moment the words were out of her mouth she blushed, an ugly brick red that rose from the collar of her smock up into the gray hair at her temples.

"Now, Miss Knowlton, you needn't choose your words with me. We're partners in this, responsible for the safety, the honor of our school. Johnny might have some sort of police record. That's why you must try to remember. Could *anyone* say they'd warned us about him? That we'd failed in our duty? Didn't *one* mother ever report that her child had come home without her underwear?"

He watched Miss Knowlton shake her head decisively, from side to side.

Glory be to God for that, at least, Connor thought.

"Now," he said. "What about this man? You've known him for years, isn't that so? Has he ever caused trouble? Been familiar with the girls, anything like that?"

"Oh, never," Miss Knowlton said. "Miss Creighton was

fond of him, you know. So were we all. He did his job. I
suppose we took him for granted, never really watched."

"I see. And he was able to go everywhere in the school,
open any door, talk to any girl in passing, right?"

"I suppose so," she said, her mouth tightening.

"Now, these things, these garments. Have you looked
them over?"

He saw her shudder.

"No," she said. "I really didn't know what to do, Dr.
Connor, I was so shocked. I simply took them and brought
them here."

Connor dropped his eyes, looked down at his desk.

"I see that some of these have nametapes. There, you
can see them, the ones just on top. Rosen. Fuller. Spaight."

Saying that last name, he felt a burning stab of fear.

If that fire inspector finds out, he'll come after me with
a hatchet, taking his girl away from the holy sisters and
getting her into *this*.

He saw Miss Knowlton put out a shaking hand, touch
some of the little panties, turn them over.

She peered at nametapes, her face now the color of rare
roast beef, her lids down, nearly covering her eyes.

"I can't look at these," she said. "I *know* these children,
these lambs."

Ah, there she's right, Connor agreed. Lambs, God's
innocents. Scared to death, probably. He should be punished, that chemical castration they talk about, a jail, that's
what he needs. But that'll never happen. There'd be some
civil-rights group jumping up to defend him, a prize, a
genuine American Indian, for the love of God. No help
to those poor little girls.

No, saving this whole flock was up to him, and him
alone. And first came Miss Knowlton. He'd have to push
her safely into the fold to silence her bleating and keep
her from hurting the school, losing all the ground he'd
gained. Especially now, with such glorious vistas ahead.

"Now," he said. "Let's share our knowledge of this sort
of thing. Mine's fairly comprehensive, sad to say. I've been
in seminars, read quite a few articles. Usually this type of
behavior involves someone in a trusted spot, a scoutmas-
ter, a counselor, even a policeman. Mescalero fits the profile perfectly. An Indian, on the fringe of society, poor,

almost illiterate. Works in a rich girls' school. Bitter, hates the world. So he induces a child to come where she could get in trouble, where she'll be blamed for being. Maybe he gives her a present, maybe he bullies her. Why, in that one California case, a first-grader testified that a man actually cut the ears off his pet rabbit, threatened to do the same to the child's mother, if he told. Anyway, he meddles with one of our girls. And keeps her underwear for a trophy, or to hold over her, frighten her with, if she dares to say anything. And she doesn't. So soon he finds another victim."

Now Miss Knowlton's glass, he saw, was shaking. Connor, feeling pleased with himself, watched her set it down and clasp her hands in her lap.

"The fact that nobody's complained is standard, too. Children seldom do. Usually this kind of abuse comes with threats. They'll get killed, blamed, punished in some terrible way, if they tell. The psychotics who do this know who they're picking on."

"Yes," Miss Knowlton said softly.

She cleared her throat. "Since he kept these things here, doesn't that show he felt safe, certain that no one would ever look?"

"It *shows* he's psychotic," Connor said, "Only a psychotic keeps other people's underwear in a desk drawer."

Seeing Nanny's skin turn gray, her eyelids flutter, he felt deeply satisfied.

"Now, if you'd found these things in some public area like the theater or the back stairs, well, we might have a real problem. But in the man's *desk*, well. That's clear. We know what we've got, isn't that so?"

"Yes," Miss Knowlton said.

"Now, this is most important, Miss Knowlton. You know children far better than most people, even most teachers. You know, I'm sure, that it's not what happens to a child, it's the perception, how the child *sees* an event that makes the difference. We know about battered children who love their parents, put up a terrible fuss against being taken away to safety. In sexual episodes like this, it's *not* the initial act. Children don't focus on that. To them, it may appear to be just some new adult demand. After all, doctors remove their clothes, nurses, camp counselors. No, what we know, you and I, is that it's the *aftermath*, the questions, the hysteria, the tears, that do the real damage, that they *never* forget. Think of the children in those newspaper cases, on witness stands in courtrooms, being subjected to cross-examining lawyers, intimidating judges, court psychiatrists, reporters. That's what burns the experience in so indelibly, so children are devastated, damaged beyond repair. And that's not, I think, what we want for *our* children."

"No," Miss Knowlton said.

"Or frankly, Miss Knowlton, for ourselves. I'm sure *you* wouldn't be comfortable testifying in a public courtroom, answering hostile questions that would disgrace us and might or might not send Johnny to jail."

Miss Knowlton shook her head and tightened her grip still more.

"Well, then, I think we agree. It's something for us to handle. For me. And this is what I propose to do. First, I'll have a talk with Johnny Mescalero, put the fear of God into him. Then I'll get him out of here so fast he won't have time to collect things that *do* belong to him. I'll remind him that child molesters have a tough time even in prison, with other inmates. When I'm finished, I promise you, he'll never come near this school again."

"I couldn't bear to look at him," Miss Knowlton said slowly.

"Of course not," Connor said. "And we don't want our children looking at him again, either, in a courtroom, a police station, anywhere. This way, they'll put it behind them, forget. And come through this just fine, especially with you to look out for them. And you and I will know that nothing like this can happen here again. When Johnny goes, it's *finished*."

"Dr. Connor," Miss Knowlton said timidly. "These panties. Do you think there's anything wrong with them?"

He stared at her, wondering what the devil she could mean. Was anything wrong? *Everything* was wrong.

"You see, it's so horrible. The idea of anyone touching those children. They're so tiny, such babies, all of them. All the mothers in the school would be beside themselves."

Well, you've got that right, he thought. Especially those

cunts who hate my guts. With this piece of news, Judge Cantor would have my balls for a necklace.

"Suppose," Nanny went on "he goes somewhere else, some other school?"

Connor felt an anxious twinge. Miss Knowlton had been so quiet, subservient, he hadn't expected questions.

"I won't allow it," he said gravely. "Because, don't misunderstand me, *I* don't intend to forget. I don't for a moment mean to forgo a thorough search, an investigation. But I want it done with care, discretion, consideration for the innocent. I won't have the police in here, frightening the children, making trouble for all of us. No, what we need here are private detectives. Trained, tactful men who'll proceed without hurting anyone here."

"Oh," Miss Knowlton said, nodding.

"That's why, with your approval, Miss Knowlton, I'm going to share this secret with just one other person. Mr. Bache. I feel he's exactly the man to help. He's bound to know the best investigative agency, experts who won't upset our children or trouble our school more than is absolutely necessary. He'll help keep this from our insurance people. Of course, I hardly need to caution *you*, Miss Knowlton, that nothing can be said about this. To anyone."

He saw her mouth open, then close again.

"But of course, you're too sensible, too loyal. And too far-seeing. You can imagine how dreadful the talk would be, how much harm it could do. Innocent people could suffer—you, other teachers. Even our children would be suspect. Why, it could be the end, Miss Knowlton. The doors of the Boston School could close forever."

He leaned back and passed his hand over his forehead. His skin was cool, dry. He felt calm, pleased with himself.

"Now, I think you should get some rest, Miss Knowlton. And I'd like to send you home in the school car. You've done enough for us today to merit a little coddling. I can't begin to thank you or tell you how grateful I am. And how encouraged I feel about working with you on our future projects."

Miss Knowlton, seeming to hear the note of dismissal he'd put in his voice, pushed back her chair obediently and got to her feet.

One last warning, Connor thought.

"Remember now, I'm trusting you," he said. "Any gossip about this around school, Miss Knowlton, I'll look to you."

He waggled a finger at her, making it a playful gesture.

"But of course, that's not like you. I think you should just put the whole thing out of your mind, pretend it never happened. Tell my girl outside to call the car for you, tell her it's with my permission. And then, get a good night's rest. Tomorrow, just go right on doing your own wonderful work."

He got to his feet, reached for her hand, feeling repelled when it seemed like a hot-water bottle, moist, slippery.

"Do I understand you correctly?" Miss Knowlton said faintly. "You're not reporting this to the police?"

Connor suddenly realized the whole room felt steamy, that he was overheated, his collar tight, sodden.

"Now, Miss Knowlton," he said. "We've been all over that."

"Well," she said slowly, "I suppose it's good that I came to you. That I was helpful to you."

"Oh, my dear Miss Knowlton," Connor said. "Had it been anyone else, any of the others, well . . ."

"Yes," Miss Knowlton said. "That would have been different, wouldn't it? I mean, I'm such an old-time Boston School person. With the welfare of the school my greatest concern. It's not everyone who feels that way, is it, Dr. Connor?"

Connor felt as if his skin were sizzling.

"No. At least, not many. And of course, I shan't forget. I'm sure we'll discuss our good handling of this terrible situation for a long while to come."

"Will we?" Miss Knowlton said. "Our good handling. Yes, well."

She turned and walked to the door, paused.

"If you're sure that's the case, Dr. Connor, that you'll take my faithfulness and loyalty to you into account, if we should have another little disagreement, ever."

"Why, Miss Knowlton," Connor said. "We've never had a real disagreement. Discussions, yes, but disagreement?"

"I see," she said. "Yes. And now I believe I *will* go home."

She went, closing the door behind her with a soft thud.

Why, that menopausal old hag, Connor thought. She's threatening to hold this over me.

The sound of the closing door hit him like a gale-force wind.

Breathing hard, he sat down, resting his elbows on the precious blueprints.

A drop of sweat rolled from his damp forehead, falling onto the paper.

He watched it staining the color, spoiling the pristine look of the sky-blue page.

Livvie, seeing that Miss Montgomery was busy handing out the recess cookies and milk, tiptoed to the stairs.

Feeling happy, she skipped down the steps, one floor, two floors.

Then she pushed in the big door slowly and ran down the hall to the baby nursery. Her heart felt as if it was growing inside her chest as she got closer to the big window and could see the pink, beautiful babies.

They lay all in a row in their little boxes, like the dolls at FAO Schwarz, but much more exciting.

Just looking at them curling their tiny fingers and turning their little heads made Livvie want to stretch up on her toes and dance.

When I'm big, she thought, I'll be allowed in. And I'll have my own baby to wash and feed and rock.

She leaned her forehead against the cold glass to see where they'd put *her* baby today.

Then her heart bounced.

Most of the babies were sleeping, but *her* baby's eyes were wide open. It was almost waving its hands.

Livvie felt so happy she waved too.

Leaning against the glass, she remembered the day Miss Knowlton had brought her class here. This baby had been crying then, its mouth a circle, its face a big tomato. Nobody came to help, not the scary nurse or any of the big girls. So Livvie tapped on the glass and made little faces. And the baby *heard* her. *Saw* her. And smiled!

That's why I picked you, Livvie whispered through the glass. It's *you* I come to see.

She remembered, too, how the next time she'd come,

she realized there were cards on each of the boxes, with
letters on them.

Hard to read, most of them. But *her* baby's weren't hard.
She just sounded out the letters.

Kitten.

A wonderful name. Better, prettier than stupid Livvie,
Olivia. Better than *any* name, ever.

Right then, Livvie felt a cold little breeze blowing her
hair.

When she saw the man at the end of the hall, she felt
as if the breeze was making all of her icy cold.

He was carrying a mop and a pail, and coming straight
to her on his quiet shoes.

Livvie shivered. Her hands felt cold too.

She burned down there, in the place where he always
touched her.

Coming right up close, he opened his mouth.

"You like the baby?" he said.

Livvie could feel her tummy drop right out of her.

"No," she said.

"You tell, I cut off that baby's fingers and toes," he
said, smiling his horrible smile. "I cut, they come right
off."

Livvie froze. She could *see* him do it, see his red knife,
hear the click of the blade, see the tiny fingers and toes,
the blood on the clean white crib. And hear the baby
screaming.

"I *hate* the baby," she managed to say, making herself
look right up at him.

The man laughed in a terrible way that didn't make any
sounds.

Then he turned around, walked away down the hall, and
went through the stairway door.

Livvie, her legs feeling like melting ice cream, slid her
back down the wall and sat on the floor.

And now her head felt dizzy, hot, as if she had a temperature.

He could come back anytime. And if he wanted, he
could go right inside the nursery. No one would stop him.
No one could.

And it would be her fault. She'd stood there. He'd seen

her. And that was how he knew she loved the baby so much.

Feeling sick to her stomach, as if any second she might throw up, Livvie got to her feet.

Those tiny little fingers, she thought, swallowing, trying hard as she could to keep her throat locked tight, her stomach still. And the darling toes. There'd be dark, sticky blood. The baby could even *die*.

She just had to save it. But how? She felt so scared.

Well, she'd just better do what Mommy said, try to make believe she wasn't scared when she was.

Livvie closed her eyes and pushed in the nursery door.

Then, her heart jumping as if she were skipping double-Dutch, she opened them and looked around.

She could see the big girls in a room far back, sitting in a circle. And the nurse, standing up and talking, writing on a big blackboard.

Livvie turned to the window and slipped quickly through the cribs to the front.

She looked out the glass. No one was in the hall.

She reached into the little box with both hands and picked Kitten up.

So warm, she thought, feeling surprised, excited. She smells milky and powdery, and she makes herself fit right in my arms. So *different* from a doll.

"He won't hurt you," she said softly to the baby. "I won't let him."

Now her stomach seemed better. She reached back for Kitten's blanket and tiptoed out the door, holding her breath and starting to feel funny. Then she ran along the hall, through the big door, up the stairs. The whole time, she kept repeating to herself, "Now I lay me down to sleep," because it was a prayer, and she didn't know any other one.

The prayer was working, she could see, because her hall was still empty.

Livvie slid her hand into her locker for her coat, making sure not to bang the door. Then, holding Kitten close to her side, she ran back to the stairs. Down and down she went, *all* the way down, right into the awful basement.

If he sees me now, she decided, I'll yell and yell, even if he does kill me.

Holding her breath, shivering, she hurried up the basement steps into the street. She ran all the way to the corner
before she realized it was snowing. And that the baby was
getting heavier.

"Don't worry," Livvie told her. "I'm taking care of you."

She tucked Kitten under her coat and walked on, trying
to go as fast as she could.

Being out in the street alone, without a grown-up, made
her skin feel prickly. But that was silly, she told herself,
because she knew the way to walk home.

Suddenly a pain came into her side.

I *can't* go home, she thought, feeling tears behind her
eyes. Margaret Rose isn't there. She's home with Lucy and
the measles.

Tears began spilling out of Livvie's eyes. She could feel
them, hot, on her cold face.

Oh, Margaret Rose, she thought. Why aren't you at my
house? This time I'd tell you about the man, I'd have to.
But you'd try to help me keep this baby safe. Even if you
were mad at me for leaving school alone, you'd help. I
want Mommy. But she's the one I can't tell. So where are
you, Margaret Rose?

Crying, she still remembered to wait carefully for the
traffic light to change. The red seemed runny, like blood,
through her wet eyes.

Then it turned to green, looking much nicer, somehow
giving her an idea.

She'd *find* Margaret Rose. She knew the address by
heart. Hadn't she heard Margaret Rose say it into the
phone a million times? Everyone knew you couldn't get
lost if you knew your address. And she knew Margaret
Rose's just as well as her own.

Two-ten East One Twenty-six Street.

Livvie felt her tears slowing down. She began feeling
bigger, and her skin wasn't prickly anymore.

She peeked into her coat at Kitten.

Asleep now. Smiling, blowing a tiny bubble. Not a bit
of snow on the blanket, either.

Pulling her coat close again, Livvie walked.

She knew the numbers were high up on the street corners. Even grown-ups had to look up to read them.

Oh. *Read,* she thought then, feeling a gross, disgusting pain in her middle.

*How could she find Two-ten East One Twenty-six Street if she couldn't read?*

If she asked anyone, they'd look hard at her and want to know why she was out all alone, and with a baby. They'd take her straight back to school, and then the man would kill them both.

Pressing the warm baby against her hurting stomach, Livvie looked up through the snow at the next corner.

Eight-one. That was Eighty-one. She could sound out numbers because they didn't come in such big bunches as letters.

But the *other* side of the sign had letters, one short word with no hard places. Park. Was that right? She wasn't anywhere near the park.

Hugging the baby, Livvie stared hard at the other word. Av something. Avenue, she figured out, feeling a glow of heat in her chest. Park Avenue.

Wow. I'm reading, Livvie told herself.

She felt dry, hot, as if the snow couldn't touch her anymore, as if the sun had come bursting out of the sky.

I can *read,* she thought. And I can find Margaret Rose. She'll help me. She might even call a policeman and make him help, too. I don't care at all if I get measles.

Feeling bigger, stronger, Livvie walked faster, left, right, left, right. She kept as far as she could from the other people on the street. They were all hurrying with their heads down. But in case they looked at her, she was making believe she was taking her doll home to her mother.

She tried hard, too, not to mind that Kitten felt heavier and heavier, or that snow was coming in her eyes, and her hair was dripping. Her hands were freezing, and there was no way to put them in her pockets because she was holding the baby.

Now the sign at the corner said Nine-Two. Ninety-two. She read it without even trying.

"I can *read,*" Livvie said, right out loud.

She felt so terrific, even her hands stopped hurting.

She could see now that Margaret Rose had told the truth, after all. She *was* seven and she *could* read.

Mommy will dance all over the house, Livvie thought.

And Miss Knowlton will smile. Even Cricket and Susie might be nice now.

She wasn't scared now. The grown-ups walking by were all acting as if she were just another grown-up. And someday she would be.

Now she seemed to hear music from somewhere.

The music got louder as she walked, and soon she knew why. It came from a radio, a big one. She saw it, in a doorway, with a bunch of boys, big ones, standing around it.

One of them was looking up. At her.

Livvie got cold again. Way deep inside.

He was moving now. Walking toward her. His face was black like Margaret Rose's, but not nice like hers. Mean. Up close, he smelled awful, like a whole lot of smoke.

"What *you* got, honey?" he said.

His voice was scary too, deep, like the bad man's.

She pulled away, but his hand came on her shoulder, heavy, his fingers tight.

"Something nice in there?" he said. "Groceries? For your mama? Some change, maybe?"

Livvie felt him pull at her coat, felt his big ugly hand touch the baby. The baby jerked, began to squawk.

Before she even thought, Livvie was kicking out with the toe of her oxford, once, twice, a hundred times.

Then she was running in the snow, holding the screaming baby as carefully as she could.

The buildings turned into a gray blur, she was running so fast.

But she couldn't keep going. Her legs hurt. Her chest felt stuffed up.

Livvie let herself run down, look back. He wasn't there. Just a lot of snow and an empty street.

Then she looked into her coat at Kitten. Quiet again.

But she hadn't come all that far, Livvie knew. He could still get her if he wanted.

Now she saw she was standing near a low iron gate, with steps behind it going down.

Her own house had a gate, steps, exactly like those. They went to a basement. With a boiler like the one at school, good and warm.

I'll go there awhile, Livvie decided. The boy won't be

able to find me. I'll get warm, dry. There's no hurry. I can *always* find Margaret Rose's house because I can read.

Feeling grown-up, proud of herself, she went down the slippery steps, pushed hard against the big basement door. It moved easily, letting her inside the warm darkness.

The school cannot be responsible for releasing a lower- or middle-school student in the company of anyone but parents, or an adult known to the receptionist. Written permission, signed by a parent, must be held by anyone sent to pick up a child.

ELBOWING HER WAY up the subway stairs, Cornelia saw dirty white sky ahead, realized the rain had turned to snow.

Snow, in April.

How much more do they expect me to handle? Cornelia asked herself. Bad enough not to have Margaret Rose for a whole week. Now it's getting Livvie home in this mess without even an umbrella. No taxis, of course. The buses will be impossible. And tomorrow, rounding up her boots, scarf, mittens from God knows where. All we need is for *her* to catch cold. Then I won't be able to go to work. And she'll get even farther behind in school.

Cornelia yanked her hood over her head, started for school, trying to dodge the spray from passing cars. One, turning right in front of her, splashed icy water on her boots, her coat.

Safely back on the sidewalk, walking, the touch of snow on her cheek reminded her of the country, of Dane. Soft, lovely, for an instant, then sharp, stinging.

When had he finally stopped calling? Two weeks ago? Three? And why was she counting? Why couldn't she forget?

"I think about you," he'd said. "Every damned day, you, Livvie. I won't call, if you say so. But I'll think."

What was the point? They were so far apart about Livvie. But she thought about him every damned hour, and had longed to call him after the revolting night with Harvey. She'd forced herself not to, knowing it was hopeless. Dane was going to Arizona, thousands of miles away.

Dreadful, when images of him filled her mind so. Dane swinging that hammer, possessed, happy. Dane swooping up Livvie and cradling her in his long arms. Dane turning out Danish apple pancakes from a skillet with a flourish.

Keep going, she told herself. Don't give yourself time to think, to see pictures like that.

Rounding the school corner, she wondered if a limousine or two might be waiting, perhaps holding someone she could ask for a lift home.

Not a single car was in front of the school.

Oh Lord, she thought. I'm probably the last mother again.

Suddenly cross, she kicked at a puddle, sending a big splash into the air. The childish gesture made her feel looser, better. Maybe after she collected Livvie, she'd do something equally impulsive and satisfying. If they had to walk in the snow, they'd stop at the Indian restaurant where the owners fussed so over Livvie, gobble spicy curry and puffy bread, sticky baklava for dessert. So what if it wasn't a balanced meal? So what if she couldn't afford it?

A motor whined behind her, and lights slowly swept the snow at her feet. Cornelia turned, saw a car with bright paint, a roof light, and drew herself up tight with hope.

Taxi? She waved, shouted.

Then she realized that the paint was blue and white, the roof light red.

A police car.

She felt her heart expand, as if it were a balloon inside her chest.

The car swung over to the curb, headlights fading, motor cutting off. It looked like a large dark animal crouched at the school door.

Don't be dumb, she chided herself, putting her hand back in her pocket. Just a police car. Probably here for a burst pipe, a window blown out in the storm. Nothing to do with you, with Livvie.

Still, she moved faster, pushing through the doors, watching out for slippery places on the marble floor.

Lifting her head, she saw the lobby was almost dark, entirely empty. Her heart ballooned again, making her breathless, a little dizzy.

But it's hardly past six, she thought. They can't *all* have gone home.

She heard a door click and saw Miss Carraway coming out of her little cubicle, galoshes flapping, plastic rain hood over her curls.

Turning, seeing Cornelia, Miss Carraway put a hand to her breast like an actress in a bad soap opera.

She looked so ridiculous, so prim, Cornelia's heart somehow shrank back to its normal size.

"Rotten night," Cornelia said. "What's wrong, Miss Carraway? Where is everybody?"

"Mrs. Fuller. You *startled* me."

"Sorry. I didn't mean to. Where's Livvie? And everybody else? Why the police car?"

She watched Miss Carraway's mouth tighten into a thin, straight line.

"We had a snow warning," she said, looking away, fussing with her coat. "Dr. Connor closed the school early. I had to make dozens of phone calls. Almost everyone was gone from here by four o'clock."

"No one called me," Cornelia said, and then wondered if that sounded like an excuse, as if she'd shrugged off a message because she was busy.

"I wasn't responsible for calling the lower-school people," Miss Carraway said. "But I'm sure someone tried."

Then Cornelia remembered, and felt ashamed. No one *could* have reached her. She'd been on a closed set all afternoon, casting for a toy commercial. Little girls, but more like midgets in disguise. She remembered one, not much over four, telling her tearfully she *needed* this commercial because her daddy was out of work. Cornelia had felt wretched rejecting the children her client didn't want. She'd taken time to promise each of them another call, soon. And then, eager to get to Livvie, she hadn't stopped to ask for messages.

"Anyway, where's Livvie?" she said. "There's nobody but me to pick her up. She'd *have* to wait here."

Miss Carraway pursed her lips, making Cornelia feel she'd just admitted to something shameful, as if she should have a staff of backup servants to fetch Livvie, like every other family in the school.

"Perhaps she left with a friend. We *were* trying to clear the building."

Cornelia wanted to stamp again, this time square on Miss Carraway's foot.

"Perhaps? Don't you keep lists? Don't you *know* who they go home with?"

Miss Carraway frowned.

"Perhaps Mrs. Barclay took her. Or Judge Cantor's nursemaid."

Cornelia felt her heart swell again, hurting her ribs.

Was Miss Carraway hinting she'd heard the gossip about the three of them? Were they being discussed in whispers around school?

Silly to worry about it, she thought. Finding Livvie's what's important right now. I'll have to call *both* Bibb and Rhea.

"Can I use your phone?" she said, heading into Miss Carraway's cubicle.

"I *was* going along," Miss Carraway said.

Cornelia felt the balloon in her chest grow dangerously large.

She turned slowly, let the last air in her lungs carry her words.

"Don't worry, Miss Carraway. Your pencils and paper clips are safe with me."

She sat down firmly in Miss Carraway's chair, knowing her coat was sopping, bound to drip water all over the leather seat.

Bibb's line was busy.

Oh God, Cornelia jittered. Is she making phone calls to parents tonight? I'll *never* get through.

Behind her, Miss Carraway coughed.

"We've had a terrible day, Mrs. Fuller," she said nervously. "It's a job, you know, calling so many people. And the lower-school teachers were upset to begin with. Miss Knowlton went home ill this morning and left the class lists locked in her office."

And you can't wait, Cornelia thought, to let her know that she left you with a lot of extra work.

She tried again.

*Still* busy.

The pressure in her chest felt more intense, bringing pain with every breath.

Rhea, she decided. And if her line's busy too, I'll ask the operator to break in, say it's an emergency.

But at Rhea's the telephone was picked up immediately.

"Dahlia? It's Mrs. Fuller. Is Livvie with you?"

"Evening, Mrs. Fuller," Dahlia said, so cheerfully that

Cornelia suddenly felt a pang of envy, an overwhelming
longing for a nursemaid who was pleasant and dependable.
"You want to talk to the judge?"

In a moment Rhea came on.

"Hi," Cornelia said. "I'm at school. Listen, there's nobody here. They closed early."

"You bet," Rhea said, her voice urgent, heavy. "Wait
till you hear. They've got real trouble. We've got to talk."

Her energy seemed to crackle out of the phone, making
Cornelia feel exhausted.

I can't, she thought. Not tonight. Put Livvie on Rachel's
guest bed again, wake her to go home, have her pale and
listless one more morning.

"Rhea, it's terrible out," she said. "And Livvie's had
it. If Dahlia could just get her things on and bring her
down to the doorman in about fifteen minutes? I'll pick
her up and get her home."

A short silence.

"Cornelia. Livvie's not with me," Rhea said.

Thank God, Cornelia thought. Then I won't have to get
to the West Side, back again. I can just walk up to Bibb's,
it'll be much faster.

"What made you think she was?" Rhea said.

"Miss Carraway. She said one of you took her. I'll keep
trying Bibb."

A longer silence.

"Cornelia," Rhea said slowly. "Bibb is *here*."

The balloon in Cornelia's chest blew way up suddenly,
hurting her ribs, cutting off her breath.

"Where could she be?" Rhea asked.

Cornelia fought to breathe.

"Now look," Rhea said. "That nudnik is supposed to
*know* who takes a kid home. It's her job. Make her think.
Have her show you the list."

Cornelia inhaled as hard as she could, her body aching.

"Cornelia? Are you listening?"

"Yes," she whispered.

"Don't fall apart. I'm sure it's all right. Livvie could
have gone back to her classroom when you didn't show
up. She could be there now. Or perhaps her father picked
her up."

"He's out of town," Cornelia said, remembering Tim

in Philadelphia, doing an industrial show she'd gotten for him. Then her mind seemed to become a VCR, with tape spinning. She saw pictures, Livvie asleep on a hard bench upstairs, waking in a pitch-black room, frightened, calling out for her.

"Cornelia? Could she possibly have left by herself? Just walked out and gone home alone?"

Cornelia immediately saw a different scene. Livvie, alone, making her way along the icy street, hair blowing across her face. A quick cut, and she saw a car rounding the corner, with a frosted windshield, striking Livvie, sending her falling in the wet street. Another cut, and a man was getting out of the car, looking around furtively, picking Livvie up, putting her inside, driving off.

She felt weak, dizzy.

"Cornelia," she heard Rhea say. "Now look. I'll put Bibb on my other phone, get her calling all the class mothers. One of them *had* to take Livvie home. I'll keep this line clear. Call home right away. If Livvie doesn't answer, go look around upstairs. Call me back, say, in ten minutes, *whatever*. By then you'll know where she is, or we will, okay?"

"Miss Carraway seems to want to shut the school now," she said.

"Well, she can't. Put her on the phone. I'll tell her so she gets it. When she hangs up, you call home."

Unable to speak, she held the phone out to the receptionist. A new tape had begun in her mind. The apartment, cold, Livvie sitting in wet clothes, waiting for her, wondering where she was, crying.

Slowly she grew aware that Miss Carraway was spluttering.

"Judge Cantor, of *course* we're all upset. The school was chaos. It's the worst thing that ever happened here."

Why then, Miss Carraway *knows*, Cornelia thought, bending to ease the pressure in her chest.

"Well, if you've heard that, Judge Cantor, then you can imagine how frantic we were. I was told to clear the school quickly. I couldn't do that all alone, of course, so several people made the calls, not just me."

She's afraid to tell me, Cornelia thought. Probably thinks I'll blame her.

"I just don't know," Miss Carraway was saying. "The police are upstairs right now with Dr. Connor."

Police, Cornelia remembered, suddenly feeling air in her lungs. She'd seen their car. What on earth was going on? If they knew Livvie was missing, why hadn't Miss Carraway said so in the first place?

"Yes," she heard. "I'll stay. And I'll make sure Mrs. Fuller calls you back."

Miss Carraway hung up.

Then, as Cornelia watched, her face seemed to crumple. Lines creased into the pink-and-white skin around her eyes, her mouth. A mist came over her glasses.

Why, she's crying, Cornelia thought. This ice pick of a woman is actually crying.

"How could *anyone* keep a list?" Miss Carraway was sobbing. "With such news. Such pandemonium."

She took off the glasses, waving them helplessly.

Shall I say I won't blame her for losing Livvie? That all I want is for her to run in right now? That I *ache* for her, this minute, so I can touch her, so I can breathe? Well, Miss Carraway can't help. There's only me.

She picked up the phone and dialed home.

Let Livvie just pick it up, she prayed to herself. Let her please say hello, *be* there.

It rang four, six, eight times.

"All day," Miss Carraway was gabbling behind her. "Everything going wrong. The fuel delivery, imagine, that huge truck blocking the entrance and Johnny nowhere to be found. I *had* to leave my desk, go searching for one of the handymen. I *can't* be everywhere at once. And just then Miss Knowlton needed the driver, and he's always off somewhere smoking. So then I had to go looking again, leave the door another time."

Can't she keep still? Cornelia wondered. I'll have to go find those policemen.

"I know I'm not supposed to talk about it, but I'm nearly out of my mind, Mrs. Fuller. And Judge Cantor *knows*, heaven knows how, so it's bound to be all over the place."

No, Cornelia thought. There's still Miss Montgomery. Rhea said to call her.

"A baby," Miss Carraway wailed. "Nobody can *imagine* how. One minute in her crib sleeping. Then vanished. We *announced* snow, so people would take their children, wouldn't stand around here making a fuss. But now *everyone's* going to make a fuss."

"Look," Cornelia said, because Miss Carraway's noise was distracting her, "I'm sorry you're upset. But I can't listen now. I have to find Livvie. She's only seven. She's waiting somewhere, probably scared because I haven't come. So please stop talking while I try to find her."

Miss Carraway's eyes grew wide.

"Mrs. Fuller. Aren't you listening? I'm trying to tell you a *baby* is missing from school."

Not just Livvie, Cornelia thought. A baby. What's wrong with these people? Can't they keep track of anyone?

"From the *nursery*. Right out of her crib. She's not even old enough to walk, Mrs. Fuller. Someone must have come in while I was looking for Johnny or the driver. And I'll never get over it, I'll never be the same."

Through Miss Carraway's gushing words Cornelia heard a familiar sound. The elevator door crashing open. Then voices, footsteps. People were coming toward the front door.

Her eyes went first to Dr. Connor. His head was bent, so she couldn't see his face. He was talking to the man next to him, a square, solid man with his coat over his arm, a hat in his hand. Other men, a little younger, were trailing behind. And a good-looking, very young man, in sweater and blue jeans, with his arm around a girl. The girl was leaning on him, hiding her face on his shoulder.

"There," Miss Carraway said, now whispering. "You see. The police. Dr. Connor. That poor baby's mother and father. They told me to go home. I shouldn't be here talking to you. Talk to *them*, get them to help you."

Cornelia got up and walked out of the little cubicle.

She watched Dr. Connor focus on her, saw his eyes widen for just an instant. Then his face smoothed out, became still.

"Just a minute," she heard him say to the man at his side.

He was walking quickly toward her.

"Mrs. Fuller," he said, blocking the door of the cubicle. "What are you doing here?"

Cornelia tilted her head back to look at him.

"I'm waiting for Livvie."

"Livvie? Didn't someone call you? The children are all gone. The school is closed."

"Then where is she?"

"I assume at home, like everyone else."

"Then you assume wrong," Cornelia said, struggling to keep from shouting.

She saw Dr. Connor frown, turn his head to look at the group near the front door. When he turned back, the frown rippled away, leaving his expression blank.

"Mrs. Fuller, we had snow warnings. We alerted all the parents. Everyone else understood. Everyone else responded. The school's empty."

"Don't tell me about everyone else. Livvie's not here. She's not home. So where is she?"

"I'd guess," Dr. Connor said, "someone took responsibility for her when you didn't show."

Cornelia felt the balloon inside her chest expand past its limits, hurting her unbearably.

"Don't talk about responsibility. Until a minute ago you didn't even know she was missing. You're the headmaster, you're supposed to run this place."

"Now, let's keep cool," Dr. Connor said, taking a step forward, crowding her back into the little room.

She felt the balloon stretch, burst, releasing her cramped ribs, filling her lungs with a rush of pent-up air.

God, how she hated this man.

Why, he was the snake in the garden, *her* garden. He'd ordered Livvie out. He'd made her miserable, allowed teachers to persecute her, children to shut her out.

And now he'd *lost* her.

Cornelia suddenly felt strong, capable of picking up her chair and swinging it, like Livvie, of screaming and clawing like her mother, when two nurses couldn't hold her.

"You're the *worst* excuse for a headmaster I ever heard of," she said. "You don't care about the kids. You're just making a nest for yourself. Everybody knows you only care about the rich parents, the famous ones. You're a real starfucker, majoring in Mrs. Irving. You shouldn't be responsible for children. You shouldn't be *near* children. You only like the smart ones, the ones who'll make you look good. They're all scores to you. You don't know they're each different, special, marvelous, even if they can't read or don't listen or won't behave."

Dr. Connor stepped back a little, his face blank.

His expression reminded Cornelia of the glass room, when she'd shouted and no one paid attention.

"That's bad when parents do it, when they only want successful kids, perfect kids, when they push," she said, shouting now, to try to shatter the glass, reach him. "But you're supposed to be an educator. You've got degrees. You're the head of a school that sets standards for others. You're supposed to give *each* of them a chance, teach them all. But you don't try. And you don't give a shit when one of them gets lost in the shuffle."

Dr. Connor put out a hand. "This isn't quite the time," he said.

"Never mind time," Cornelia shouted. "It's time to find Livvie. If those are **poli**cemen, get them over here, let them go find her. She's a little girl and it's snowing. And I don't care if she never learns to read. Just the way she is, she's the best thing that ever happened to me. And if anything's happened to *her*, you'd better watch yourself."

Her face was wet, somehow, her eyes liquid, so she saw him, and the men clustering close behind him, blurred and distorted in the dim light.

Dane, sorting papers, heard the wind banging at his bedroom window. Snow, he saw, was mounding in the corners of the panes, on the sill.

He turned back to the small pile next to the bottle of beer on the desk, kicking the large cardboard carton at his feet.

He reached for a red bankbook, the cover riddled with holes, canceled. Opening it, he saw dates, 1969, 1970.

Enough, he thought, feeling impatient. Forget the bottom drawer. You haven't opened it for years, maybe. Why the hell would you miss anything in it? And what if you do?

He yanked it out, tipped its contents into the carton, shook it clean of pencil stubs, bits of paper, black grit. Tomorrow, heading for the office, he'd shove the whole carton outside the back door.

After all, it wasn't the first time he'd sorted out his past and dumped most of it. His boyhood scrapbooks, soccer ball, fishing rods left in Odense, the books and furniture of his student days sold in Copenhagen for a few kroner when he'd come to New York.

In the kitchen, he reached for another beer.

When Grete died, he reminded himself, he'd thrown out everything. Gone through her orderly closets and bureau drawers, taking up dresses and shoes, watercolors and drawing pads, a half-finished embroidered tablecloth, and thrown them all into cartons, calling a thrift shop.

Instantly he remembered Cornelia's hall closet, crammed with coats, an old television set, piles of theater programs, evening gowns. A jeweled cardboard crown glittered on the shelf.

He shut his eyes, then opened them, and saw that only one more beer was left in the six-pack he'd carried home this evening.

Too bad you can't sort memories, he thought. Dump most, and move on with just the good ones—the thick, sweet-smelling thatched roof of his childhood home, a stork nesting in its chimney; Grete glowing in the firelight, knitting a flowered sweater, almost without looking at the needles; Cornelia warm against him in her firelit parlor.

He opened the Carlsberg, swallowed half the bottle in one thirsty gulp.

Knock it off, he told himself. Forget her. You thought you could help her see herself, see Livvie, the whole world even, through your eyes. But you were wrong. Playing God, the analyst's disease. Be glad you're going, leaving this city. Turn on the news, watch the stalled cars, people falling on icy streets, homeless men freezing to death. Think about Arizona, big sun, dry air, the way memories will wither and blow away in that heat.

He reached for the little television set on the shelf, next to the pile of newspapers he hadn't bothered to read.

A picture slowly bloomed on the screen.

As Dane watched it form an image, his heart started to flutter and smack against his ribs as if he'd just run twice his usual distance in the park.

Livvie Fuller.

Hold on, he warned himself, feeling an ice splinter in his heart, the Snow Queen's touch. You're projecting.

You're only seeing that because you keep thinking about Cornelia.

Now a word was coming onto the screen.

*MISSING.*

You see? Only it's not Livvie who's missing from your life. It's Cornelia.

He wrenched the knob to turn up the sound, and heard the words blaring.

"Recent picture. The little girl is seven years old, blond, with blue eyes."

No, Dane thought. Flaxen hair. Violet eyes. Too big for her face, like her mother's.

"Last seen wearing a navy-blue coat, a navy school uniform."

School uniforms, to make the children look alike, think alike.

The picture cut away to another, black and white, fuzzier.

A round-faced baby in a bonnet.

"The baby, Kitten Carlson, is four months old. Both children were last seen on East End Avenue in Manhattan."

East End Avenue. The Boston School.

You're drunk, Dane told himself. You haven't eaten. You're holding your fifth beer.

"A thorough search of the school building revealed no trace of either child. Police suspect that Olivia Fuller, the older child, carried the baby out earlier today when snow warnings closed the school. We have a special hotline number if you see either of these children, or have any information. 555-1000. We repeat, 555-1000. Keep an eye out, folks. Tough night to be out in the cold."

A special number. Then Livvie had been missing for some time, enough to organize, set up systems.

What could have happened to her?

And, sweet Christ, what was happening to Cornelia?

Dane knew, as if she were here in this room. She'd be worse than when she'd first come to him, frozen, almost catatonic.

If Livvie were lost, she'd be lost too.

Dane seemed to hear hospital intercoms announcing ER blue code, STAT, blue code STAT, urgently, relentlessly.

He reached for the phone, dialed.

It'll be busy, he told himself, feeling panic. Or she'll hang up when she hears your voice. Or tell *you* to get lost.

The line *was* busy.

Dane said a loud "Skit," followed it with a rush of Danish he hadn't used in years: balls, piss, fuck.

Slamming down the phone, he dashed to his closet and grabbed the first coat he touched. Out in the hall he buzzed for his elevator, thinking about the idiot television newscasters, reciting a whole stream of gutter Danish—sheepfuckers, ball-suckers, assholes—until the doors opened.

Running in the street, he began feeling better, looser, even slipping now and again on treacherous ice patches, even with stinging snow in his eyes.

He was running to Cornelia. He would hold her, comfort her. He would stand between her and disaster. It was what he was trained for, ached to do.

The streets were empty. Even the snowplows weren't out yet.

But Livvie's out, he thought. In this cold. Maybe wet, numb, freezing.

He picked up his pace, heart pounding, breath white in the icy air.

At the front door of Cornelia's building he nearly crashed into a man scattering salt on the ground. He kept on, panting, ran for the elevator, breathing hard as it swallowed him and lifted him to her floor.

A moment later, pressing her doorbell, he saw a peephole slide back.

The door swung open. Excitement shook him.

But it wasn't Cornelia.

A man, large, heavy, blocking his way.

Startled, he realized it was Phil Rosenzweig.

Dane stared, feeling his breathing settle, snow and sweat trickling from his forehead.

"Holy cow," Phil said. "The doorman thought you were the cops, the way you belted in here. Or the robbers. He just called to say barricade the doors."

Dane tried to get his breath so he could demand Cornelia.

But then, behind Phil, he saw her, walking toward him from the living room.

A peculiar peace seemed to settle over him. Some silent inner voice was telling him he could take it easy now, wind down. He'd crossed the finish line.

Cornelia seemed different. There were lines around her eyes, enlarging them, making them enormous in her white face. Her hair looked different, too, flat, stringy. Her rough sweater hung on her loosely, as if it were sizes too big.

How beautiful she is, Dane thought, his arms tensing to hold her. More beautiful even than I remembered. The most beautiful woman I ever saw.

He reached for her, took her cold hands.

The most beautiful woman I ever touched, he thought.

"I wanted you," Cornelia said.

Her voice was the same. Lovely, just as he remembered, low, resonant. Somehow the sound of it cleared his head, restored him, like a splash of cold water at the end of a race.

"I saw the news," he said. "And I ran."

She needs rest, he told himself. Sleep, sun, air. Rich milk, cream, butter from Friesland cows. Meadows full of sweet grass, golden mustard seed, quiet. And when we've found the child, I'll see to it, I'll take care of her.

"What's going to happen?" Cornelia said, looking up at him as if she were a child and he would surely know.

"Whatever it is," Dane said, wrapping his arms all around her, "I'm here. *Altid*. Always."

"Jesus H. Christ, you didn't even want to meet her," he heard Phil, behind him. "I had to cook up a consultation. Now it's always. You Swedes work fast."

Dane looked around, saw Phil's grin, strained, full of effort.

Behind Phil, he realized, stood other people. A woman, who looked oddly like Phil's double—same big build, same pleasant, lined face. And a pair of women, standing together, one tall, spare, gray-haired, frowning, the other short, round, young.

"Dane," Phil said. "You look lousy. Rhea, believe it or not, this lunatic is a well-known psychiatrist. Don't hold that against him. Dane Nilssen. My sister, Rhea. And this is Miss Knowlton, from the Boston School, and Cornelia's chief helper at the office . . . Stella? Is that right?"

Dane nodded, keeping hold of Cornelia.

"Now you've made your entrance, go sit down. Cornelia too. We were just getting coffee. And maybe you ladies should run along. No sense your hanging around here all night."

Phil took his arm. Dane, though, wasn't letting go of Cornelia, so they all became a chain, linked, standing in the hall. Dane finally realized he was supposed to shake Phil's hand, nod at the others.

Then, to take off his sodden coat, he had to let Cornelia go.

"Listen," he heard the younger woman say in a deep, emphatic voice. "Nanny's coming with me, to my place. She shouldn't go home in this snow, alone, worrying. We'll wait together, and if you hear anything, doctor, call me, okay? I'll write my number here, by the phone."

Dane, impatient for the little ceremony to end, watched the older woman nod, take the hand the girl offered her, let herself be led out the door.

While Phil let them out, he steered Cornelia toward the living room, pulled her to the couch, and curled her in the curve of his arm, taking her cold hands. He rocked her, stroking and smoothing her hair.

"How long, Cornelia? How long has she been gone?"

He felt her shrivel in his arms.

"Six or so."

Dane turned his wrist to see his watch. Almost midnight.

Six hours, he thought. In that cold. Or worse, she's been taken somewhere warm, somewhere terrible.

Cornelia, as if released from a vow of silence, started to talk, quickly, breathlessly.

"You can't imagine. The school's like a war zone. Police, reporters. Even some fire inspector. And Connor looks as if he could kill all of them. They knew the baby was missing. But can you believe, nobody knew Livvie was gone. Not till *I* got there, Dane."

"I know, sweetheart," Dane said, to make a comforting sound, to let her know he was there and would stay.

"I told him off. I almost hit him. But while I was shouting at him, I realized something, Dane. I want Livvie just the way she is. I wouldn't change anything about her, even if I could."

"I know, sweetheart, I know," he said.

Ridiculous, useless words. Dane seemed to feel the cold seeping into his bones.

But how *could* he help her? He couldn't muster an army, ride out on a white charger to find the child. He didn't have second sight, couldn't sense where Livvie had gone, run to her and carry her back.

*Jeg er traet*, he thought, the old hopelessness coming over him, nothing making any difference. *Jeg forstar*. I'm exhausted. But I must do something.

"Dane. Will they find her? Tell me."

He looked down, seeing the terrible, desperate appeal in her expression, feeling the fear flowing out of her thin, tense body.

He felt his backbone stiffen, his shoulders pull straight.

"Tell me about the baby," he said.

New lines seemed to spring into her face.

"That's the worst. From the nursery at school. Livvie *took* her, Dane. Just picked her up, stole her. I still can't believe it."

"Why, do you think?"

Dane saw Phil's sister coming back, holding two glasses. He gave one to Cornelia, noting the way her hand trembled. He set his down on the floor. Then, looking up to thank the woman, he found she'd gone away, to the kitchen probably.

"Cornelia, can you think why she'd do that just now? Did something trigger it? Was anything different?"

"I don't *think* so," Cornelia said slowly.

"That sounds as if you *do* think so. Tell me."

"Maybe Margaret Rose," Cornelia said.

Margaret Rose, Dane thought. Who thinks Livvie could do better if she would only try. Tough lady. He'd called the principal of her children's school once, after Cornelia asked him to, about Samantha's attacker. Mistake. The principal had been in a rush to get rid of him. Margaret Rose had wept about the whole incident all over again.

"What about Margaret Rose?"

"She's been gone a couple of days. One of her girls is sick. Livvie misses her. Me too."

Losses, Dane thought. Her father, her nurse. Her father didn't move back in. Does Livvie wonder if Margaret Rose is gone for good too? Christ, this takes so *long*. There's a child out in the snow.

"We'd just made it up about her calling Tim. I thought I'd never forgive her, but it's all right now."

Is it? Dane wondered.

"Cornelia, when you don't forgive people, it backfires, it's you that gets hurt."

She sat straighter, bumping his shoulder.

"I'm hurt now. I let Livvie get lost, Dane."

He hugged her tighter. "The school let her get lost. But for now, let's stay with Margaret Rose. Was Livvie showing she missed her nurse? Did she cry, ask questions?"

"No. She never said a word."

Not so good, Dane thought. Maybe afraid her mother might go too.

"I was wrong. Livvie must have been upset. It's the only reason I can imagine for taking the baby."

No, Dane thought. She might have felt wretched, powerless, and wanted to hold someone smaller, weaker than she. Or angry, wanting to hurt the baby, the way she felt she was being hurt.

"Unless," Cornelia said, "someone took them both. Grabbed up Livvie *and* the baby. So they're somewhere in a house, or driving away now in a car. People do, Dane. All the time."

Feeling stricken, he thought of a skinny two-year-old girl he'd seen once in an emergency room. Wailing, her arms and legs and back disfigured with round red cigarette burns.

"I haven't been any good," Cornelia said, anguish in her voice. "I didn't pay attention. You told me and I wouldn't listen. I wanted to make her different, better. And now it's too late, I won't have another chance."

The telephone rang. Cornelia seemed to turn to an ice statue under his hands.

The sound broke off. Dane realized that Phil would have jumped for it.

A moment later, Phil called from the kitchen.

"Don't get excited," he said. "Nothing. A blond child wandering around in an all-night supermarket. They found the mother right while we were talking."

Watching Cornelia's face crumple, Dane had a sudden

fierce desire to lift her up, swing her into his arms, take her into the bedroom, put her slowly, carefully on the bed, gently pull off that sweater and those rumpled slacks, stroke her breasts, kiss them and hold her tightly, so that for a little while, at least, she might even forget all this.

"If I do get her back," Cornelia said, startling him, "I'll never try to change her. I'll never make her stay one minute where she's not happy, or want her to be something she's not. I promise. I'll never use her to be what *I* want, Dane, never."

She stood up then, shaking him off, wrapping her arms tightly around her thin body, lifting her head as if she were no longer talking to him, but to the air, to everyone, to God maybe.

Margaret Rose woke suddenly. Banging, someone pounding on the door. Immediately her heart felt as if it were flying around inside her breast like a trapped bird.

Quickly she reached across to touch Samantha, then Lucy lying beyond her by the wall.

Both children felt warm, but not feverish, and were breathing softly, thank the Lord.

The banging sound came again then, louder, rattling the chain on the door.

She sat up, feeling cold and fearful, and reached for the lamp.

Everything looked as it should. But noise meant trouble. Fire? Or perhaps policemen looking through the building for someone?

Her heart fluttered a little as she thought of William. If only he were by her side, she wouldn't feel so frightened.

She moved, set her feet on the cold floor, hearing herself sighing.

Again the pounding.

But the police would shout, she thought. And the firemen, as well. A neighbor would call my name. So this must be a drunken man or a junkie, at the wrong door.

Thanking God for the steel bolt, the locks, the chain, she moved to the stove and took up the big frying pan. It felt solid, heavy in her hand.

Then she went close to the door.

The banging was coming from low down. She wondered if the man was lying on the floor outside.

"Get away," she shouted suddenly, to scare him. "Go make trouble for someone else."

The banging stopped.

Margaret Rose felt strong, pleased with herself.

Then she heard something else.

"Margaret Rose," someone said outside. "It's me."

Her heart gathered itself up and flew right out of her.

That was Livvie's voice.

But I'm asleep, Margaret Rose thought, feeling giddy. It cannot be Livvie.

Still, her feet were cold on the linoleum floor. And the frying pan was heavy in her hand.

"Livvie?" she said.

Then she heard crying sounds outside the door.

They seemed to make the roar of a high waterfall come into her ears.

Margaret Rose pulled the bolt, turned the locks, the doorknob. The chain stayed in its place, though, and she clutched her frying pan.

Looking out, then down, she saw Livvie's pale hair, stringy, dark with water, the way it looked when she washed the child's head.

She wrenched the chain away and pulled the door wide. Then she stood staring at the child, feeling as if the falls at Ocho Rios were spilling over her, knocking her off her feet.

But the child was drenched, filthy. And her coat was torn.

While Margaret Rose stared, Livvie struggled to take something from beneath her coat. A bundle, wet and dirty.

"Here," she said.

Margaret Rose saw a small white face inside the bundle.

Then she felt faint, as if the pounding water were drowning her, filling her throat so she couldn't say a word.

"I saved her," Livvie said slowly. "From the bad man. And I can read, Margaret Rose. I read the signs. So I could find you."

Shaking her head to try to get rid of the drowning feeling, Margaret Rose set down the frying pan. Then she took up the baby.

So small, she thought. So young.

She felt the tiny forehead, patted the arms and legs under the dirty blanket. Then she went to put the infant down on the big chair, as far from Lucy as she could, in case the measles were still catching.

Still feeling giddy, she turned again to Livvie.

The child stood stock-still by the door. Her face looked blue-white, like skim milk, and black circles seemed rubbed around her eyes.

Margaret Rose, her eyes filling with water, reached out and hugged Livvie close. As if she *had* been rescued from drowning, she felt blinded, choked.

Then she realized water *was* everywhere. Her nightgown was sopping. Livvie's coat was like a sponge.

Trying to keep her breathing even, to calm herself, she went to work, pulling off the wet coat, lifting the child's feet one, two, to strip off the wet shoes, the knee socks. Livvie stood like a stone as she unbuttoned the dripping jumper, blouse, undershirt.

Margaret Rose's thoughts swirled back to Samantha that day in school, crying, her drawers gone. Her little body had felt like this, naked, smooth, cold.

Shaking, she pulled a blanket from the bed and wrapped Livvie round and round.

Then she set the child on her hip, reached with one hand into the little icebox for milk, spilled some into a pot and turned on the gas.

In a moment she had it hot, and in a teacup.

Then she sat with Livvie on her lap, holding the milk to her mouth. All the while she felt herself trembling. The rage and helplessness of that day with Samantha seemed to come flooding back.

Beautiful child, princess child, how did you come to me? What terrible thing has happened to you?

She waited patiently for Livvie to finish the milk, then spoke as softly as she could.

"Why, Livvie? What happened? Tell Margaret Rose."

She looked into the child's eyes, like the color of the sea in sunlight, and not a tear in them.

"The bad man," Livvie said, frowning, solemn. "He said he'd hurt the baby."

Margaret Rose felt her heart go hot, her fingers itch.

"What man?"

She watched Livvie's mouth open, then shut tightly. Livvie was hiding something, she was positive. Perhaps she would tell her mother?

Margaret Rose quickly thought about Mrs. Fuller, no doubt at home sitting by the telephone, wide-eyed as Livvie, sick with panic.

She leaned over to look at her watch on the night table. Twelve-thirty.

She'll be a madwoman, Margaret Rose thought. And my God, the *baby*. Her mother too.

Somehow, thinking of those other mothers made her feel calmer, steadier.

You must manage this properly, she told herself. It is in your hands. They will be waiting, Mrs. Fuller, that other mother, the school people, even the policemen. You must get Livvie back. Then you can tell Mrs. Fuller what she hinted about a man.

Margaret Rose sat straight.

"Never mind now," she said to Livvie. "You are safe and warm. I will put you on my bed with the baby, with Lucy and Samantha. Sleep."

Feeling stronger, wiser every moment, she tucked the child in bed, hastened to the telephone by the door.

Quickly she dialed, suddenly remembering how undependable her telephone has been recently. Samantha's teacher had sent a note last week, saying she'd tried several times, without success, to call. She'd wanted to tell Margaret Rose that the child seemed quite happy again in school, none the worse for her fight in the playground. It had made Margaret Rose feel better, knowing that a teacher cared enough to do that.

Yes, something was wrong. She wasn't hearing a ring, even a busy signal. Just clicking sounds.

"Hotline," a man's voice said.

Margaret Rose hung up.

She tried again, and again got the same strange voice.

Something is wrong with Mrs. Fuller's telephone, she decided. I must dress. Rap next door, ask Mrs. Diaz to listen for the children. Take Livvie and the baby and go, put Livvie back into Mrs. Fuller's arms.

Hurrying now, longing to be there with Mrs. Fuller this

very second, Margaret Rose grabbed up shoes, stockings, skirt, shirtwaist.

Taxi, she thought. Outside the bar across the way there were taxis at night. The drivers stopped in and drank there. She would make one of them take her.

She tidied herself, checked the stove to be sure it was off.

Then, feeling wide-awake, strong, she cradled Livvie in one arm, reached with the other for the baby.


Dane, hearing the doorbell buzz, sudden and loud, felt Cornelia freeze again in his arms, saw her eyes go wide.

He heard Phil's heavy footsteps moving quickly in the hall, heard the door open, then a cry from the kitchen.

He leaned forward, trying to see into the hall.

All he could make out was Phil's back.

And then, beyond him, he saw a woman, small, dripping wet.

"Margaret Rose," he heard Phil's sister say loudly. "*Gott sei dank*. Livvie."

He felt Cornelia tremble.

Holding her, he still couldn't see what was happening out in the hall—just the broad backs of Phil and his sister, and glimpses of Margaret Rose. Her cheek, ebony black. Her scarf, wet as if dipped in water. A bundle in her arms.

Then he felt Cornelia leave him, shooting away, soaring across the room, her arms out.

Through the people crowding together, he saw a fall of wet pale hair lying across Margaret Rose's coat sleeve. And a child's slim legs in navy-blue knee socks, dangling against her hip.

Dane stopped breathing. But he willed himself to stay calm, summoning up all the strength he had left.

*Listen*, he told himself. Just listen. So you can help with whatever happens next. For Cornelia.

They were all still standing huddled at the door, silent, their backs to him.

Then abruptly they broke ranks, all moving at once.

Phil stepped toward the woman.

His sister stepped back, her hands over her face.

Cornelia took the bundle.

Tense, alert, Dane saw dark hair, fair hair, mingling, heard a child cry out.

"Do not frighten her, Mrs. Fuller," he heard a clipped British voice say, a voice that brought back Cornelia's farmhouse. "She is quite well."

He felt his muscles go limp for a moment.

"Who would believe it?" he heard Margaret Rose say. "The clever girl. Finding her way to my house."

Dane smiled to himself. See, Cornelia, he almost said out loud. Livvie got to Margaret Rose. She had to read signs, count blocks. She had to keep going through snow and cold. No little girl could do that without brains. Without love.

"We were fortunate," Margaret Rose was saying. "A police car. They took the baby. But I got my neighbor to stay in my house. I would not leave Livvie to them."

Margaret Rose's assertive voice was irritating him now, distracting him.

*Because* she acted, he realized quickly. While I sat here holding Cornelia. While I stand silent here, this minute.

He felt like a small boy again in a musty cellar, hearing his mother's voice, shrill, exalted.

*Is that all I can do, listen?*

He took a tentative step toward the hall, saw Cornelia clearly, her face gray, her body bent over Livvie.

And then he remembered why he was here.

To listen. To heal. Yourself and Cornelia. For all the time there is. Always. *Altid.*

He felt a surge of release then, as if he were deep inside her as she clung to the child, as if he were melting into her, and somehow the three of them were one.


Cornelia watched the morning light come through her bedroom window.

Gray, like so many mornings. Only now, magically soft, peaceful, beautiful.

Livvie was safe.

And Dane was safe with her.

It floated into her mind, his leading her to this bed, easing off her shoes, pulling her sweater inside out over her head as if she were a little girl, unhooking her bra as if she were the most desirable woman he'd ever touched.

And then curving his body around her like a bulwark, making her forget she'd ever been cold and alone.

She turned her head to watch him, asleep beside her.

So many men looked foolish when they slept. Not Dane, she decided. A good face. Worn and young at the same time. Strong and gentle at the same time.

She moved to touch his cheek, draw her fingertips gently over the silver stubble. There was a tiny white scar on his neck, just below his jawline.

Poor Dane. How had he gotten it? Had he been hurt?

Suddenly she longed to be with him always, protect him from hurts and scars, as he'd so miraculously come to protect her.

Oh, Dane, she thought, you tried so hard to help me and I wouldn't listen. Forgive me.

Dane's eyes were opening.

They were asking her something. What?

But she knew then, because he was asking her with his body too. She could feel him grow hard against her belly, feel heat kindling in his body.

And suddenly she wanted to be on top of him, push herself up so her long legs could straddle his belly, her knees tighten around him. She leaned on him, hands clutching, mouth thirsting, skin burning.

"Yes," she said. "Now."

But he was freeing his hand, using it to stroke her back, thighs.

She pressed down, to tell him to hurry for his own sake.

But he wasn't hurrying. His hands were moving, gently turning her, easing her to her back again. His mouth was at her breast now, licking, teasing, sucking gently.

I don't have to tell him anything, she thought, feeling astonished. He knows.

She slipped her arms around his back, held on as he plunged inside her, reaching, pounding, as if he were searching for something deep inside her, something precious no one had ever found.

And wanting to give it, she opened to him, wrapping arms and legs around him, until at last she heard him shout in triumph, heard herself making little animal sounds she'd never made before. She felt the two of them flowing into each other, becoming one.

Then, floating in warm, moist pleasure, she grew aware of the rough touch of his chin on her shoulder, the long muscle of his thigh against her side.

"*Det var dejligt*," he sighed.

"Yes," she said. "Whatever it means, yes."

"It means great. Unbelievable. It means I'll never let you go. I'll always love you."

Love. The word seemed to trigger a new sensation inside her, the kind of click flash of understanding she'd so wanted for Livvie, with reading.

I've been so busy battling, Cornelia thought. Fighting for Livvie and me. I didn't know that when you yield, lean, give, you get so much back. Now I've finally learned. And it'll be like reading: once you know how, you can't ever forget.

Then she stopped thinking altogether because Dane was cradling her, stroking her hair as if she were a child, a loving presence that would always keep her safe.

*This morning is the first of May*
*The finest of the year*
*So maidens all, both great and small*
*Come carol with great good cheer.*
*Come carol with right good cheer.*

CROWDED WITH ALL the other parents into the lower-school music room, Bibb sat on a tiny chair trying to get comfortable and not succeeding.

Even harder for poor Arthur, she thought. And the other tall daddies. Here Nanny schedules the May Fair first thing in the morning, so the men can come on their way to work. But why in heaven's name didn't she get some grown-up chairs brought in so they can really enjoy themselves?

Bibb reached over to pat Arthur's hand, smiling at him.

How wonderful he's here, she exulted. That he's with me, and soon we'll hear Tucker singing.

She shivered a little, remembering for the thousandth time the terrible day when she'd been so sure he'd pack, say good-bye to the children, and go off with that dreadful woman.

I was terrified to look in Arthur's closet, for fear it might be empty. And then, shaken when he came into the kitchen and told me he was finished, that it was me, us, he really wanted. I couldn't believe it. I am lucky, so very lucky. I could turn and hug him right here and now.

The doors of the music room were opening now. Bibb felt her heart swell as she saw the faces of the children, fresh, scrubbed, beautiful.

They came demurely, two by two, looking unbearably sweet in their strict little uniforms, topped today by wreaths of paper flowers. To Bibb, their skin seemed fine-grained as ivory. Their hair had a gloss no one past eighteen could ever achieve with any dye, any cosmetic. And each little girl, as she trooped in, held on to a strand of the long cloth daisy chain.

Immediately Bibb's eyes searched the group, looking for Tucker.

In the second row, of course, with the taller children.

Or can it be, Bibb wondered, feeling her heart lurch, she's been put in the back with the more awkward, un-attractive children?

The little girls were gathering into a semicircle, wrig-gling, turning their heads to eye each other sideways, each making sure she was in the right spot. Bibb felt as if she were onstage too, right along with Tucker. She thought back to school performances she'd been in herself, tall, awkward.

Dear heaven, Tucker's wreath is askew. If only I could get up, straighten it. Suppose it falls off? Or worse, sup-pose she loses the beat, sings out all alone in the wrong place? Tucker, darling, take care. You know the songs, you've been singing about buttercups and daisies for days at home. *I* know you're the fairest of them all, but I want everyone else to see too.

The children were nicely lined up now, next to the big striped cardboard maypole with its multicolored ribbons hanging loose.

That maypole, Bibb said to herself. They need a new one. This was battered *last* year. Nanny should see to it.

Nanny, at the door now, was silently pointing out the last of the empty chairs for the latecomers, hushing them. She looked the perfect teacher this morning, in command, grave, ladylike.

So different from the evening at my house, Bibb thought. She was distraught then, eager to help us. But she's done nothing. Too frightened, after all.

The plump little music teacher was moving to the piano stool now. Three older girls holding recorders moved to stand by her as she sat flexing her wrists for a long moment, then tinkled out an introductory chord.

Bibb remembered how, last year, she'd gone teary when the singing began. Tucker had kept her mouth closed through the whole performance.

She felt Arthur's hand squeeze hers.

The girls were facing the piano, smiling, ready.

Bibb heard the murmurs of the parents die away as the

children began singing. Their high, clear voices seemed to pierce the air with loveliness.

"May is here, the world rejoices, earth puts on her flowers to greet us, lovely May, blithesome May, winter's reign has passed away," they sang.

Bibb tried to relax. Perhaps winter's reign truly *had* passed away. Tucker seemed to be in time with all the others. And Arthur's been so good, coming home on time, taking me to play bridge, eat at the Colony. Still, I won't ever be so stupid again. And I'll go to Blue Hill rehearsals, plan our evenings, make things livelier at home. I'll get new underwear, nightgowns. Do something about my hair. Call him at the office more often.

The song slowed to a conclusion, and the little girls immediately sang another, about a tiny cowslip bell in the breezes ringing.

Nightingales, larks, cowslips, Bibb thought. I wonder if even English children still know what those are. Tucker's never set eyes on a cowslip. When Harlan began at St. Bernard's, they taught him to add in shillings and pence. The schools all act as if there *was* no American Revolution.

The music teacher was nodding now. The little girls broke ranks. A small group came forward toward the maypole. The rest, Tucker among them, massed at the back of the little stage to sing.

By now a number of the mothers had begun coughing, sniffing back tears.

It *is* affecting, Bibb had to agree. They're so dear, so cunning.

Here came Livvie, to take hold of a long pink ribbon. She waited for the others, then began gravely to dance, dipping gracefully under another child's arm, then holding her ribbon high for someone else to glide beneath.

A true beauty, Bibb acknowledged. That hair is like a spill of moonlight flowing down her back, even under that silly wreath. And she moves like a little sprite, her feet don't make a sound.

Bibb, wondering if Cornelia had come, turned slightly to look through the audience.

Yes, there, by the door. Standing next to a tall man, her arms wrapped tightly across her slender body.

She looks so torn, Bibb thought. As if she can't stand

being inside this building, and yet can't stand *not* seeing Livvie dance.

Now the man next to Cornelia was reaching for her hand, holding it.

Well, *who*? Bibb wondered. Still, how nice. Can it be that doctor? The one Rhea told me about? He must be awfully fond of Cornelia if he'll come here to a May Fair.

And Rhea? Had she managed to juggle her schedule and come this morning?

Bibb craned her neck, then spotted Rhea way in a corner, with her husband. She looked really uncomfortable on the little chair. But Saul Cantor seemed absorbed, his knee moving up and down, his foot tapping in time to the music.

She turned back to look for Rachel.

There, part of the group in the rear, standing way at the side, a big child, dark, unsmiling.

Seems unhappy, Bibb thought. I can't *bear* seeing a child look like that. Thank goodness Tucker only wears earphones, not a real hearing aid. And now I'm deserting Rachel and Livvie. It's going to be on my conscience for the rest of my days.

Feeling restless now, she tried to concentrate on watching the braid tighten around the pole as the children wove and spun. Then the dance ended, and all of them joined together once again, launched lustily into the last carol.

"We've brought you here a bunch of May, before your door it stands, all well set out and well set about by the work of our Lord's hands," sang the children.

Giggling now, eyeing each other, they all reached up to take off their wreaths at once, flung them into the crowd like bright Frisbees.

Then they stood flushed, squirming with pleasure, while all the mothers and fathers applauded. As the sound rose, one or two of the children dared to break ranks, wave, and one tiny girl put her hands to her mouth and shook with shy laughter.

But Miss Knowlton was up, at the ready, Bibb could see. She stepped quickly toward the children, whispered something.

Nanny, couldn't *you* take my place? Bibb asked her silently. Join Cornelia and Rhea to get rid of that horrible man? And where is he, by the way? Miss Creighton *always* came to the May Fair.

Under Nanny's eye, the children now settled down, stepped forward, and made neat curtsies to the audience.

Then, to a sprightly tune from the piano, they marched toward the door and exited, with only a few backward glances.

Immediately the room burst into noise as the parents gratefully got up from the little chairs, stretched, and gathered their things. Bibb saw a few of the daddies dashing out the door, making for the elevator.

"Bibb? Listen," she heard.

It was Rhea, calling out, struggling toward her through the crowd.

"Wasn't it wonderful?" Saul said, smiling. "The girls are beautiful, every one of them."

"We saw Tucker," Rhea said. "She was singing, really singing, Bibb. You must feel wonderful. Listen, now. Can you spare a little time? I've got a lot to tell you."

Bibb felt herself shrink, feeling as if she were coming out of a Sunday service at the Brick Church with Arthur, to face some shopping-bag lady who knew Bibb from her charity work. She wasn't at all sure how Arthur felt about the Cantors. And she wanted no upsets now.

She peeked at his face, but she saw no indication of distaste. Or of acceptance. Arthur simply looked blank.

"Cornelia's coming to meet us at the corner drugstore," Rhea said. "And her fellow too. He's all right, you'll see. He turned up this morning with the biggest bunch of spring flowers you ever saw, one for each girl in Livvie's class and one extra for the teacher, exactly the right number, imagine. Please join us. Saul and I will push ahead, grab a booth."

Rhea looked directly at Arthur.

"Good morning, Mr. Barclay," she said formally. "I think *you* should take time for this too. It could be important for your little girl."

Bibb grew cold, terrified. Suppose Arthur got angry? Suppose he really had to rush off, get to the bank? Worst of all, what if he thought she'd planned this, had used the May Fair to get him involved in still another crusade?

"I've a few minutes," Arthur was saying politely. "We'll be right along."

But that didn't mean anything, Bibb knew. Arthur had such beautiful manners. No one could *ever* tell when he was doing something he disliked. Even she was never positive.

They caught up with Cornelia at the elevator.

"Livvie was lovely," Bibb managed to say in spite of her nervousness. "She dances so beautifully, Cornelia."

"Thanks," Cornelia said without smiling. "I saw Tucker singing her heart out. You must be so pleased. Bibb, this is Dane Nilssen."

"Why hello," Bibb said. "Mr. Nilssen, this is my husband, Arthur."

"It's doctor," Cornelia said.

"It's Dane," the doctor said. "Let me get us on this elevator before we all get stampeded."

"I'm glad you're coming," Cornelia said softly, just for her. "It's good to be all together, even just this once. And I *did* want you to meet him, Bibb."

Bibb peeped again at Arthur. His expression had remained pleasant. She wished the elevator would hurry.

Finally they got downstairs, walked out to the street and down the block.

Rhea had commandeered her booth, even an extra chair for the end of the table so they wouldn't be so crowded. She began talking even before they all settled in.

"Listen," she said. "The announcements about the big parents' meeting have just gone out. And the rumors are flying."

A sloppy waitress in a stained green uniform slammed coffee and a plate of Danish pastry down in front of them. Bibb itched to take Arthur's cup, tip the saucer, put a paper napkin on it, so it wouldn't drip on his club tie. But she made herself keep still.

"Before Rhea gets going, I want you both to know how I enjoyed watching your children," Saul said. "Livvie is gorgeous, Cornelia. A real dancer. Takes after you, I guess. And Tucker sang right on key there, Mrs. Barclay. Now. You have to understand my wife. She never gives up on anything. She's spoiling for a fight with our headmaster."

Bibb felt startled. Though his tone was resigned, even

rueful, his smile, his tone, made it clear that he *approved* of Rhea's fighting.

If only Arthur would back me, she thought. Now I'm the only one left out, the quitter, sitting here foolishly toying with a coffee cup.

"Sounds like a man someone should fight with," the doctor said suddenly.

What a good voice he has, Bibb thought. And he seems nice. It was nice to bring flowers for Livvie. Whatever happens at school, I'd love to see Cornelia happy.

"Well," Rhea said. "I'm ready. I took our list last night and called every one of the folks who came to our meeting."

Bibb began feeling anxious again. Arthur wasn't touching his coffee.

"They're mostly pretty discouraged," Rhea went on. "Afraid Dr. Connor is too strong, in too solid, to take on. Mrs. Trager told me he'd handled the missing-baby business so efficiently she'd changed her mind about him. Mr. Powers, that investment man, said what the hell, it was just too tough getting his three girls into other schools, going through all those references and tests again. He's sticking to this one and watching the situation. And of all things, that Mrs. Pransky told me the new reading tests showed wonderful improvement. And we all know they're a complete cheat. I couldn't get the woman to hear a word against them. She was simply thrilled with what she called her daughter's progress."

"Livvie still isn't reading right," Cornelia said in a low voice. "I ran into her teacher just now, and she said she's convinced I'm reading to her too much, so she doesn't want to try on her own."

She looked so woebegone that Bibb's heart turned over.

"That's *ridiculous*," she said, shaking her head. "Anyway, she must have read the street signs to get to Margaret Rose's house. She must have read names on the doors in the building."

Cornelia didn't look comforted.

"The whole thing really shook up Margaret Rose," she said. "She's still feeling done in about her own little girl, and now she's afraid for Livvie. Anyway, she's talking about going to her husband in Scotland. The baby's parents gave her a reward, enough for plane tickets. I'm glad for her, but the thought of finding a new nurse makes me want to die."

Bibb saw the doctor lift his chin.

"I've been telling Cornelia I think it's good," he said. "Margaret Rose *should* be with her husband, she'd be happier. And all that anxiety, that wishful thinking, makes her the wrong person for Livvie right now. I'll try to help find someone who's right."

My, Bibb thought. He *will* be good for Cornelia. And he's absolutely right about Margaret Rose. She's far too strict for a gentle child like Livvie. Livvie needs someone jollier, like Rhea's Dahlia, someone who laughs, sings a lot.

Then she realized Rhea was talking again.

"Incidentally, Bibb, Mr. Barclay, that same idiot I talked to about the reading tests told me she was *pleased* that Dr. Connor kept Tucker away from the outing. She actually said Tucker took up too much attention, was a danger to the other children."

"That's nonsense," Arthur said after a moment. "Isn't that nonsense, Dr. Nilssen?"

"I wish you'd call me Dane," the doctor said. "Can we all use first names? Arthur? And it's Saul, isn't that right? I think, yes, it's nonsense. It must make you feel very angry."

Why, Arthur *is* angry, Bibb thought. He's getting red, puffing up.

"Arthur," she said quietly. "I've heard comments like that for years. I told you, darling, in the doctors' offices, from the nurses, other mothers. I don't pay the slightest attention. I simply act as if I don't hear. Otherwise I'd be angry all the time."

"Well, anyone could see, this morning, she's perfectly presentable, quite able to fit in," Arthur said crossly.

Why, he does feel the way I do, Bibb thought with a little burst of joy. He *does* care what people say about Tucker, and he's showing it.

"The woman's a moron," Rhea broke in. "Forget it. You haven't heard the worst yet. It seems my nemesis, Mrs. Irving, is giving the school a whole lot of money. Connor's going to announce it at the PTA meeting."

Bibb's head began aching. They all stared into their coffee cups.

"What a shame we never got any help from Miss Knowlton," Rhea said. "I keep having this feeling she could tell a lot, if she only would."

Saul coughed, shook his head.

"Rhea," he said. "You can't expect people to jeopardize their livelihood. Miss Knowlton isn't ordinary. There are still plenty of schools where they might not hire her. Here, she's a fixture. Why would she do anything to disturb being a fixture?"

"You have to know the man bullies all the teachers," Rhea went on. "None of them will say a word against him. They act petrified if you even mention Connor."

Bibb watched her reach for a second pastry, bite into it, and swallow.

"Well," Rhea said heavily. "It looks right now as if he's going be a cockamamie hero. That is, if we don't stop him."

Cornelia shifted, jogging Bibb's elbow.

"Rhea," Cornelia said. "How can we stop him? What can we *do*? He's got teachers smothered. Parents dazzled. That Irving woman ready to hand him a million dollars. That's all the board needs to hear, a million dollars. They'll give him tenure till the end of time."

"Oh, I don't know about that," Saul Cantor said. "I wouldn't go that far. He's not invulnerable. If he were a witness you wanted to break down, there'd be a way. Every human being is vulnerable, you know what I'm saying?"

"*Vulnerable*," Cornelia said, straightening her back. "For heaven's sake, Saul. He's a bully, a coward, a poseur. He writes letters when he should talk face to face. He's arrogant with weak people and a toady to important ones. He's got degrees in education and no feeling whatever for children. He talks about maximum capability theory and doesn't say good morning to the girls, doesn't know their names. My God, that first meeting, he announced that children mature at different *tempi*. I almost fell off my chair, it was so affected, so wrong for our school. And the worst is, you can't argue. He screams if he's opposed one little bit. Vulnerable. Where do you even start?"

There was silence.

"Well," Dane Nilssen said then. "You've offered a few clues. That's a long and healthy list."

Saul leaned as far forward as the Formica table would allow.

"Right," he said. "What about his degrees? Are they all up and up? Or his last job, and the ones before that? What about his finances—you can tell a lot from a bank account."

"Saul, there isn't time," Rhea said. "The meeting is practically here. What about trying to talk to Alison Irving? Telling her what we know, such as it is, the kind of man she's backing?"

"Sweetheart," Saul said, sounding weary. "You didn't have enough already with Alison Irving? Weren't you paying attention?"

Bibb began growing warm, feeling as if something inside her were simmering, bubbling.

Why, she could think of ideas. A petition from the teachers, if you guaranteed them anonymity. Or an all-out attack, the six of them marching into his office and demanding the reinstatement of their children. And demanding a decent remedial department so everyone could keep up, get extra help on a regular basis. She could think of *lots* of good ideas.

But she saw Arthur staring at his coffee cup as if he'd never seen one before. And she'd promised herself not to get involved, *promised*.

"Well," Dane said. "If he has a temper. And hates being crossed. Couldn't that be brought out in the open? Where all the parents can see?"

They all looked at him.

"There's a big meeting, isn't that so?" Dane said. "You'll all be there. What would happen if you took a hand? Spoke up from the audience?"

Bibb was startled at the idea, but then pictured it immediately, all of them standing up in the theater making cutting remarks, asking difficult questions.

"I mean, this headmaster seems to have counted on parents keeping quiet. He's dealt with you one by one, hoping you'd never want your children's problems discussed in public. There may be *more* unhappy parents. But if nobody speaks out, Connor can do anything he likes.

What if you shared your problems? Asked him to account for his actions at this meeting, even heckled him? That makes bigger people than Connor angry in public. It could be like baiting a bull, getting him to charge, so to speak."

Was Arthur acquiring a pinched look around his nostrils? Heckling was not his sort of thing.

"*If* it works," Rhea said. "He *is* a rat when he's cornered. I remember how he talked the day I barged into his office. And come to think of it, Miss Knowlton did say 'uncontrollable rage.' Those were her words. Saul?"

"It's an idea," Saul said. "But it has its drawbacks. We'd have to go all-out, be willing to look like rabble-rousers, troublemakers. Plenty of parents would think we were rude and vulgar, maybe not fit for their school after all."

*I* wouldn't care about that, Bibb thought. I've shouted my lungs out at rallies and political meetings. I could get up in that theater and make a wonderful fuss.

"Dane, you haven't met him," Cornelia said slowly. "He has a facade, a shell. I'm not sure we *could* make him lose his temper in public. Think, everyone. Remember what an actor he is. Remember how he sprawled on the stage steps, acting the new headmaster, at that other big meeting? For this one, he'll be taking command, leading the troops, wearing full-dress headmaster costume. He'll *never* lose his temper in public."

Bibb couldn't keep still one more second.

"But we'd *plan* it," she said. "Like a bullfight, as somebody said. With a pattern, a routine. You know, first the cape and then those little stinging barbs, then the horses with the big poles, that sort of thing. We'd *build* to it, make him so furious he couldn't stop himself."

As soon as she'd said the words, she was horrified.

She'd got into just the mess she'd been determined to avoid.

"Bibb is right," Rhea said. "We could. Like planning a cross-examination, step by step, building it. We'd all have to sit in different parts of the theater so we'd sound like a bigger group than we are. We might even get some of our backsliders to join in. I can go back over our lists, try one more time."

*I* could call, Bibb thought. I know so many of them. I could *appeal* to them. For the children's sake.

"You're all dreaming," Cornelia said. "This is Dr. Billy Connor we're talking about. He knows we want to make trouble. He'll be waiting for us."

"That's why you'd have to do it right," Dane said. "And nobody says it's going to work for certain. But think. At least, you'd have tried. You'd never have to feel you abandoned your kids."

Rhea broke in.

"But, you know? Saul has a point. Connor would answer back, *ad hominem*, no holds barred. It was certainly obvious that Mrs. Irving wanted to destroy me in public. Connor's probably willing to say anything about us, personal attacks, nastiness. We'd have to be ready to take it."

"We should only get that far," Saul said. "If we're willing, then it's fine. If he's attacking his audience, the headmaster, with a posture to maintain, *he'll* look bad, not us. What we should do is plot the whole meeting out on paper. Like a case. Anticipate him, coach each of you, as if it were for a courtroom. Decide on the method of the first interruption, zero in on the worst thing he's done, something the audience has to respond to. Plan who'll say what, in what order. I can *see* it, you know? Rhea in the balcony, she's got a good strong voice. You, Cornelia, smack in the middle of the audience, where you'll be seen when you stand up. And you, Mrs. Barclay, since you're quiet, in the front row, right under the man's nose."

For Bibb, a pit seemed to open, as if the table were sinking down and away, leaving only a dangerous hole at her feet.

She could almost hear her own heartbeat.

Now she had to tell them that Arthur would never join her in the front row. Sit still while she heckled anybody. He'd be contemptuous, just as he'd been when she wanted to confront Dr. Rosenzweig. Worse, he'd be furious, go back to that Puerto Rican creature and stay with her till the end of his days.

She tried to keep her hands from shaking.

Could she help plan what to do at the meeting, but not participate?

Oh, but how could she sit there listening to Cornelia and Rhea say what *she* should be saying?

Anyway, she'd already *decided* what was important to her, to Tucker. Pleasing Arthur, paying attention to him, not getting distracted by involvements, charities, causes. Was she so wishy-washy she couldn't even keep her word to herself?

"If we could stir up just enough fuss so Connor can't say he's got everyone with him," Rhea was saying, "then we could ask for a hearing at a board meeting, where we could present a case properly."

"There you go," Saul said, reaching up, patting her shoulder.

"You see," Rhea went on, "they think he's great now. But if we put things together, just the stuff we already have, it's a good case. You know, people really only worry about themselves. Get them worrying that their own kids might not measure up someday, that *they* might get a letter, I think we could start to convince them."

Of course we would, Bibb thought, looking down at her coffee cup. It was cracked, and the rim hadn't been properly cleaned.

Then she looked up and found they were all looking at her.

"It sounds feasible to me," she said carefully. "I should think you'd manage it. And with all of you, I don't imagine you'll be needing me. I mean, Rhea's all ready to sentence Dr. Connor to hard labor. Cornelia's a performer, she'll make everyone sit up and listen. I wouldn't be much good in a big scene like that."

There was silence.

Then she heard Arthur clear his throat.

"Why, Bibb," he said. "This doesn't sound like you."

She felt tears start, put her head down again, fixed her eyes on the dirty cup.

"You've never backed down before, old girl," Arthur said. "From the night we met, you've been organizing something or other. The remedial-reading program? You won that, Bibb. The zoo? That zoo ruined your tennis game, you were so exercised about the cramped cages in Central Park, you couldn't keep your eye on the ball."

The tears fell. Blinded, Bibb reached into her handbag for a handkerchief.

"Good Lord, Bibb," Arthur kept on. "Don't you want

to? Didn't we talk about your getting out more? You can't be frightened. Not at the Boston School. My God, you can stand up in their theater and say any damn thing you like. So can I. It's not St. Bernard's or Buckley, after all, where they know what they're doing because they've done it properly for years. Not even Collegiate or Trinity. I've seen that parent group, hippies, musicians, longhairs, rock stars. My God, who'd notice bad manners at the Boston School?"

Bibb began to laugh through her tears.

I really am stupid, she thought. I've guessed wrong about him again. I forgot that he used to listen, be interested.

The tears and laughter were getting all mixed up, making her snort in a dreadfully undignified way.

Arthur reached over, slapped her on the back roughly.

"I've never seen Bibb give up a battle," he said, looking around the table. "She's overwrought. But she'll come through. I can guarantee it. I'll stand by. Only I've really got to get to the bank now."

"Harvard women do come through," Rhea said without a smile.

"That's right," Arthur said, pausing, towering over their heads. "I forgot. You're a Cliffie too. Well. I guess that settles it."

Bibb watched him smile, nod, escape.

"Looks like you had it wrong," Rhea said to her.

"Very wrong," Cornelia chimed in. "Even a dropout Cliffie can see that."

Bibb looked across the table. Saul's face was blank. She turned to Dane, saw his puzzled frown. Then she realized that Arthur had left a ten-dollar bill under his saucer.

Somehow, the idea that he'd paid for the ghastly coffee sent her off again, into a fit of weepy laughter.

"Stop, now," Rhea said. "Get yourself together, Bibb."

"Right," Cornelia said. "We've got work. It's what's called putting on a show. And I guess Saul is going to produce and direct."

"So we'll get busy," Rhea said. "How's tonight? Our apartment?"

"Oh," Cornelia said suddenly. "We can't. Not tonight. Dane's taking us to a friend's house. He's been promising Livvie a real *smørrebröd* supper. And teaching her to say

'*Tak for mad, tak for iaften*.' You should hear her, she could be Danish. Can we do it tomorrow night?"

Dane leaned forward.

"Look," he said to Cornelia. "Don't put it off. I'll take Livvie to Ulla's, bring her home, and see she gets to bed. I'll wait for you."

Bibb saw, even through tears, the look Cornelia gave him, happy, loving.

She stopped feeling weepy, dabbed at her eyes, even took a sip of the lukewarm coffee.

Then she looked around at all of them: Rhea wise, motherly; Cornelia radiant; Saul frowning slightly; Dane serene.

Men are so *different*, she thought. The smartest lawyer in town. A good psychiatrist. Both bright, nice. But they're thinking their own thoughts, intent on the next step they plan to take. They haven't a clue to what's just happened here. Not that I don't like men. I do. And I adore Arthur. But Rhea took in everything that went on between Arthur and me, she knows how I feel *inside*. So did Cornelia, even with all the distractions she's got right now. It's just as if their own husbands had surprised them so happily, suddenly agreed to help them. They share, they *know*, just exactly as if they *were* me.

Bibb crumpled her damp handkerchief into a ball, thrust it deep into the bottom of her handbag.

"Now, what time shall Arthur and I be there?" she said.

invites you to attend the Annual Meeting on Wednesday, June 3rd, in the theater, at eight o'clock in the evening. A gala buffet will be served in the Teachers' Lunchroom right after the meeting.

CORNELIA WALKED TOWARD school feeling as if she were about to go on in a terrible play before an audience armed with tomatoes, eggs, stones.

She shivered, and then took tight hold of Dane's warm hand.

Stage fright, she told herself. That's why you're so queasy. Breathe. Blink. Swallow. You know what to do.

But she felt worse now than with any stage fright she could remember. She imagined trying to speak through catcalls and laughter, boos and hisses, people shouting for her to sit down, maybe even attacking Livvie.

"Easy," Dane said.

No, she told herself, he doesn't understand. I don't need to relax. I need to get revved up, feel strong.

With every step she wanted to lag behind, pull at Dane, turn and hurry home.

As they got close, even the familiar building seemed menacing in the dark, bricks gray, windows black, gates casting hideous shadows across the doors.

Once inside the lobby, she felt panicked, hardly able to move through the crush of people shouting, pushing, laughing, waving to friends, women in jeans, little furs, big jewelry, men looking strangely like soldiers in Burberrys, khakis, boots.

I don't belong here anymore, Cornelia thought. They're all members here, parents with children the school wants. And I'm an outsider.

She wanted to turn, get away, but someone was pushing her farther into the room.

The lobby looked different, too. The pale walls were covered now with splotches of garish color. The benches held an array of vases, bowls, strange little figures.

Cornelia, feeling oddly off balance, grasped that she was seeing an art show with the children's paintings, sculpture, and those spiky constructions they made in the workshops.

Pushed closer, she realized there were ribbons—blue, red, yellow—tucked into some of the glazed bowls and taped to a few of the pictures.

Suddenly furious, she couldn't breathe, felt she was choking in the smoky, perfumed air.

They've *judged* these things. How horrible.

She shut her eyes, almost able to see the lumpy red dish Livvie had carefully hugged home the other day, set on the living-room table proudly.

She wanted to wave her arms, shout at everyone. Are you all *crazy*? Don't you know nobody can judge children's paintings? They're all beautiful, made of love and dreams. And nobody can judge little children. They're *all* worth blue ribbons.

"That's better," she heard Dane say.

He *is* a mind reader, she thought, amazed, opening her eyes, reaching for his hand. It felt cooler than hers. Had her temperature gone up?

Unable to lift a hand to her forehead in the crush, Cornelia, pushing a silk coat, stepping on a polished boot, struggled toward the theater.

There, at least, she'd be in a place she loved, a place she'd danced so many times, surrounded by the beautiful, shabby cranberry seats, breathing in the marvelous smell of hot lights and dusty velvet.

But inside, she stopped short, with a sensation of shock.

This theater smelled of fresh paint, new leather. Its walls were white, the seats brilliant crimson. And where was the scarred piano that had given her Chopin and Delibes to follow? Now a huge gleaming curve of ebony stood beside the steps to the stage.

Can it be I just can't bear change? she wondered, walking slowly toward the front. Can it be I'm in love with the past, that there were always things that were wrong in this school I just didn't know about? Maybe it's better for children to be judged, the odd ones put away somewhere by themselves where they'll get special care.

Discouraged again, she let Dane go ahead of her, search for seats.

Though the theater seemed nearly empty, coats and shawls were draped everywhere, handbags propped to hold places.

"We can get closer if we sit on the side," Dane said.

"But you promised we'd be in the middle, right?"

It's not going to matter one way or the other, she thought, nodding listlessly, slipping into a row next to a woman doing needlepoint, working away as if she had a deadline to meet, jabbing scarlet wool into canvas on her lap.

Getting out of her jacket, and then facing the stage, Cornelia felt still another shock.

She'd expected to see chairs, all set in a semicircle for the board members, the head teachers, the headmaster.

But *screens*? So many of them, standing behind the chairs, white, sparkling, ten, twelve, more, large and small, some even on the steps.

Oh God, she thought, feeling sick. Connor's going to upstage us. It looks like one of those glitzy audiovisual experiences they use for selling desert land in Arizona. Who'll listen to us? This audience will be so busy, it'll be like shouting "Fire!" in a disco.

The doors were opening and closing now. People thumped down the aisles, bringing their commotion into the theater.

"Here we go," Dane said, touching her hand, motioning toward the balcony.

Cornelia tipped her head back and saw Rhea, high at the top of the theater, wearing her most imposing black linen suit, coming down the balcony steps toward the front. Saul was just behind her, his hand on her shoulder.

Cornelia watched them choose first-row seats, saw Rhea look at the stage and frown.

Dane pressed her hand again. She turned and saw Bibb and Arthur walking toward the front, to seats with coats on them.

Good for Bibb, Cornelia thought. She'd made sure she'd be in the right place. She's probably all keyed-up, ready to go. Not feeling empty and sick like me.

The board members were walking down the aisles now toward the stage.

As if they're at a graduation ceremony, Cornelia thought, as if they have every move planned tonight, choreographed.

One by one they climbed the steps, eleven people, most of the men in their fifties, neatly dressed, dignified, looking accustomed to stages and meetings, the women a bit more awkward, less sure in front of an audience.

How pleased they all look with themselves, Cornelia thought. One's a young girl, and even she looks smug. Must be the student member. And there goes fat Susie Solomon. She was just ahead of me at school, and she looks so *old*. Do *I* look that old?

Then she forgot Susie, because Harvey was bounding up the steps.

He looked enormous, as clean, moist, and pink as if he'd come straight from his expensive health club. His pin-striped suit lay on his shoulders as if it were painted on, his shoes caught the light when he sat down and crossed his legs. Cornelia watched him lean over toward Mrs. Irving, dowdy in tweeds and a big Scotch pin.

Just seeing him seemed to make her cheekbone ache, her face burn.

She turned her eyes away.

Then she discovered Dr. Connor.

He was standing by the huge concert grand, leaning in its curve, his arm resting lightly on the shining wood.

Cornelia felt a pang of fear and clutched Dane's arm, gesturing toward Connor so Dane would know *this* was the enemy.

Bastard, she thought. He's not up with all the others. He's all alone, a star. And look what he's *wearing*. That suit's so navy it's practically black. And, my God, a white waistcoat, to match that silly flower in his buttonhole.

"Cheer up," Dane said into her ear. "Anyone who looks *that* relaxed must be tense as hell."

Cornelia tried to smile, wishing *she* felt relaxed. But now Sarah Price, the PTA chairperson, was getting up. For a moment she stood staring down at her handbag, hesitating. Then she put the bag on her chair, walked to the front of the stage, and took tight hold of the lectern.

"Good evening, all you parents," she called out through the noise.

Sound rose, as the people who were still standing began scurrying for seats, whispering excuses as they climbed into rows, flapping coats, greeting neighbors.

Sarah released her grim hold on the lectern, reached in her suit pocket for her glasses. Waiting for the audience to settle down, she began twirling them nervously.

"Let's get started, everyone," she called out.

Start then, Cornelia thought, suddenly impatient with everyone's noise, bad manners.

"Welcome," Sarah said. "Welcome to our annual meeting. And an exciting one it's going to be, full of fascinating surprises. We've never had one like it. And there's a reason, parents. We've *never* had a leader as imaginative, as forward-thinking, as with-it as our new headmaster."

The hubbub rose again as people laughed, applauded, pointed at the screens.

Sarah waved her arms at the crowd.

Dane bent his head.

"Hyperkinetic," he whispered, squeezing her hand.

Thank God he's here, Cornelia thought. If I were alone listening to this shit, I don't know *what* I'd do.

"Important things are happening in our school," Sarah cried. "An ongoing excitement, a new and multidimensional viewpoint. And tonight we won't just *tell* you about it, we'll *show* you. So I'd like to dispense with the minutes of the last meeting. What do you say, parents?"

The buzz and hum rose again, as the crowd applauded. Nobody wanted to hear the minutes of the last meeting.

And nobody will want to hear us either, Cornelia told herself.

"And now I'll break still another precedent and dispense with introductions," Sarah said, tossing her head kittenishly. "You know our distinguished board, our beloved head teachers. But you don't yet know the force, the impetus our headmaster brings to this school. I'm proud to turn this meeting over to Dr. Billy Connor."

More applause, then, gradually, quiet, as people settled down, sank back in their seats, readying themselves for serious talk.

Dr. Connor kept right on leaning against the piano, languid, unmoving, waiting for silence.

Finally he lifted his head.

"Hi," he said.

Cornelia felt Dane's grip on her hand tighten.

Some act, isn't it, my love? Cornelia thought. Defies description. You really *have* to see it for yourself.

"Last year, a great lady stood here to report on your school. This year, I'm afraid, you'll have to make do with me."

Damn him, Cornelia thought, feeling her muscles tighten. He's making everyone remember that frail old woman, leaning on her cane, forcing them to compare.

"The screens you see are *not* left over from an upper-school production. They're here to give you a new vision of your school and its future."

He picked something up from the piano top.

"Naturally, I've been clued in on the traditional form of this meeting," Dr. Connor said. "And I don't want to break *all* precedents my first time at bat. So I'll start as Miss Creighton would have started. With the news I know you most want to hear. Beginnings. And endings. Applications from people who want to get into our school, colleges that want the students who are leaving *us*."

Cornelia heard a stir overheard, looked up.

Rhea, standing, looking ten feet tall among the people seated around her.

"Oh, Dane," Cornelia whispered, wanting to tell him she felt as if Livvie were standing up to dance, breathless, edgy, hopeful, all at once.

"Before you do that," Rhea called out, "I have a question."

Rhea heard the groans from the audience, saw the sea of people below her stir uneasily.

Good, she told herself. Let them listen. This is your moment. You've got him on the witness stand. Now pin him down, use every ounce of training you have, take him apart, piece by piece, for this audience. Do it for Rachel. Do it because he tried to blot her out, because he sneaked into a great school and used it for his own rotten ambitions, because he's cruel and evil, and absolutely unfit to be inside these doors. You're the chief counsel here, so do it right, win justice for Cornelia and Bibb and all the others, yes, and win for the school, so it stays great. Make Saul proud of you, reward him for all his teaching, his patience, his abiding love. Go.

"Why, Judge Cantor," Dr. Connor said calmly, looking up. "Glad you could join us this time. I'd be gladder, though, to hold questions, if you will, till the end of the program."

Quickly he raised his hand.

Rhea heard a little click, saw the theater go dark.

Her breath suddenly stopped, leaving her feeling choked, trembling.

Dear Lord, she thought, I'm overruled. He was ready for me. He's cutting me off, shutting everyone's ears. At the end no one will listen, they'll dash out to be first at the food, the drinks. If *I* can't get through, how can Bibb and Cornelia? I'm going to fail the others, we're all going to lose, just because I can't start, can't speak.

Feeling dizzy, she groped for her seat again, saw the screens burst into movement, making the stage a kaleidoscope of light and color.

Moving pictures were coming into focus on each of the screens, all playing at the same time. Pictures of little girls, a dozen of them, chubby-faced, cute, serious, all holding books, drawing pictures, piling up blocks, moving colored pegs about on tables. Rhea couldn't catch any one image clearly, because all the images kept fluttering, moving, changing, the little clicks from the instrument in Connor's hand sounding more frequently, hurting her ears.

Applause began, built, filled the theater.

Before it died, Dr. Connor spoke again.

"It's common knowledge," he began. People stopped clapping and talking, obediently quieted for him. "Common knowledge today that there's as much pressure getting into nursery school as into *law* school. Especially *our* nursery school."

He pointed at the screens. An arrow of glowing light flashed onto the screen, as if it came from his fingertip, and flickered here and there over the pictures of the children.

"You're looking at films of children, toddlers really, films taken through the one-way glass of our new research facility. You're watching them hard at work taking tests that may, or may not, allow them to come to this school. They're *our* tests, special, unique, developed and administered by our psychologist, Dr. Lillian Krakauer. She's been busy. This year, we had a record forty-three applications for each place next fall."

Through a burst of applause that assaulted Rhea's ears, the clicks now came faster, the pictures changing rapidly, some fading, some growing bigger, some zooming in on a small part of an image, a smile, an eye, a hand.

"I might remind you that these children, the ones who succeed in running this gauntlet, are candidates for our class of the year 2000," Dr. Connor said. "They'll be facing a world we can't even sketch. Their needs will be more complex, more diverse, more intense than at any time in history. They will strive to function in a post-chip, rather than a pre-chip world. Educating them for that fantastic world is our heavy responsibility, and our dazzling challenge."

The pictures froze.

Then, with a series of clicks, the screens flickered, changed, until just one picture, one giant image, stretched across the entire stage.

Feeling dizzy now, Rhea couldn't make out what it was—a mass of dark green, oddly textured.

"Well, hey," Dr. Connor said. "Now let's talk about endings."

She suddenly realized. Dear Lord, ivy. A close-up photograph of ivy clustered on a red brick wall.

"The Ivy League," Dr. Connor said, as if the words were an invocation. "The Seven Sister colleges."

To clicks, the screens began changing again, one by one. Now each picture was different, but all were black and white.

*Letterheads*, Rhea thought. My God, it's the colleges' stationery.

She saw Connor's arrow pointer flicker rapidly, picking out single words: Yale, Harvard, Brown, Princeton, Wellesley.

As he pointed, each picture quickly changed, became a scene: Widener Library, Nassau Hall, a banner that read "*Lux Et Veritas.*"

"Out of the forty successful young women we will graduate this year," Dr. Connor said through applause, laughter, "eleven will enter Harvard, Yale, Princeton, Brown, Cornell, Smith, Wellesley. Almost a third of the class."

The pictures seemed to ripple as they each became big close-ups of faces, young girls, all smiling widely.

Saul leaned close, patted her hand, spoke through the applause.

"Almost," he said. "Rhea, do they teach arithmetic here?"

Rhea knew he was trying to help her relax, turned to look at him. Then she turned back because a man's voice was calling out from somewhere below the balcony, at the back of the theater.

"Excuse me," the voice was saying. "Know I'm late, I apologize. But while you're on the subject of college, I've got a question."

Rhea tried to see who it was, but the balcony blocked her view. Most of the heads below her were turning away from the stage to see who was speaking.

Nobody we know, she thought. I've never heard that voice before.

"By the way, I'm Harris Stone, I should remind you, a parent here for the past nine years. My Debbie is one of your Ivy Leaguers, a sophomore at Harvard right now."

Glancing back at Dr. Connor, Rhea saw him standing straight at the piano.

Maybe he's been caught off guard too, she thought, feeling a touch of hope. Maybe he didn't expect a *man* to interrupt.

"I wouldn't want to hold things up here, this wonderful meeting," Harris Stone said, walking down the aisle below Rhea now, coming into view as a balding head. "And I know it's not the time for personal items. But this college business has me worried. Now, my Debbie had a college conference at the beginning of her senior year, there were choices, talks with those recruiters, and we sent out a lot of checks, applications, *you* know. But my *other* girl, Misty, who's graduating this year, well, there *wasn't* any college conference. I have to admit she's different from Debbie, not the same kind of student, but she came home and told us her adviser said junior college and that was that. No choice. Now, my wife got after me, I tried getting hold of someone here and couldn't get to first base. So I'm asking. What's going on? Different system this year?"

It dawned on Rhea that something wonderful was beginning to happen.

My God, she thought. Out of nowhere. Out of a dream. Like a surprise witness who walks into a courtroom and changes everything. Still, we hoped. We knew Connor was so terrible, other people had to be running into trouble with him. There was *bound* to be more opposition somewhere.

"It's a little different, Mr. Stone," Dr. Connor was saying affably. "This year we're easing the crush, sparing you parents and your girls that terrible college hysteria. You see, we know where they'll fit in and how to get them there. I work closely with college presidents, admissions officers, folks I've known from educational conventions and seminars through a lot of years. Yes, it's different now."

In the reflected light from the screens, Rhea saw him smile, snap the little clicker again.

No, she wanted to yell. Don't let that bastard cut you off too.

Suddenly her heart changed its rhythm, began beating slowly, steadily. Her breath, released, came evenly, and strength seemed to shoot all through her body. She was on her feet again, her voice rumbling up from her toes.

"Different," she burst out in an explosion of sound. "I'll tell you about different. Your kid can't get into college? Mine can't get into the fourth grade."

She seemed to hear a strange noise in the theater, almost a hiss, as if everyone had suddenly inhaled.

"Mr. Stone has a point," she kept on, feeling thrilled she had their attention at last. "What's happening to the rest of the class? Or don't they count? Why not turn the lights back on and talk about what's *really* different in this school now?"

She paused just the right length of time.

"Like *expulsions*," she said.

Rhea heard murmurs coming now from the audience, one or two hisses. On the stage, a ripple seemed to go through the board members as they sat dwarfed by the screens, some bending their heads, others straightening up. Harvey Bache showed no expression, tilting back his head, eyeing the balcony.

"There were *no* expulsions last year, or the year before," Rhea said, fast. "What is this, Ivy League or bust? Forget everyone who can't make it? If that's a policy, nobody ever announced it or asked what we think. Here sit the parents. Ask. How many children *have* you expelled, Dr. Connor? In particular, how many from the lower school?"

A hush came over the audience, a breathless pause, as if a stripper had come onstage and begun taking off her clothes.

"Hey, wait a minute," Harris Stone said, sounding indignant.

But the lights were coming up, and Dr. Connor was holding his hand in the air. Rhea saw him leaning back to look up at her, caught a glimpse now of Mr. Stone's flushed face turned up too.

"Precisely the number who need to leave, Judge," Dr. Connor said in a calm voice.

"Need to leave." Rhea pounced on the phrase as if he'd thrown it to her, thrilled to have him in a dialogue at last, ready to wrench his words into a weapon and hurl it back. "Now, why would they *need* to leave? Something wrong with those admissions tests we just heard about? They're *not* infallible? You mean, in spite of all that scientific method, the wrong children get in? Or are there other reasons they *need* to leave? Does something happen to them here? Anything the matter with our teachers? Can't they teach?"

"Oh, sit down," a man yelled from somewhere at the front.

His voice was followed by applause, and then another call for Rhea to stop interrupting.

"Now, Judge," Dr. Connor said, shrugging, looking around at the audience. "Surely you don't mean to malign our teachers. They're the most dedicated group of professionals you could find in *any* school. Don't we all agree on *that*?"

The audience responded with a burst of applause. Rhea felt Saul's hand on her back, pressing gently.

"I hoped this would be an upbeat meeting," Dr. Connor

said smoothly. "Everyone knows I'm receptive to parents' views, and my door, to coin a phrase, is always open."

He waved up at her.

"You come see me, Judge, when we can really get into it, when we don't take up other people's time, okay?"

More applause, a few catcalls.

"Come on, Dr. Connor," Rhea shot back. "Isn't it true you have not one, but *two* secretaries guarding that door? Isn't it true that you keep it closed, as Miss Creighton *never* did in all her years in this school?"

Go on, blow, she urged him silently. Please, get mad, lose your temper, oh, please show these people what you really are.

But Dr. Connor was relaxing against the piano, putting his hands in his pockets.

The pose made him look somehow frail, small boy taunted by a bully.

"Hey," he said mildly. "We got together to announce some sensational news. I don't want to upset the democratic process, especially in front of a distinguished judge, but shouldn't we consider the majority? You seem to be the only one who doesn't want to move along."

"Oh, that's not so," a voice called out, high-pitched, cultivated, the o's almost oohs.

Bibb, on her feet now, smack in the front of the stage, silhouetted against the screens.

Rhea's heartbeat began speeding, her blood pumping faster.

"That's not at *all* correct, Dr. Connor," Bibb was saying. "This audience is not united. There *are* parents who object to expelling children, who object to quite a number of your ideas."

Connor was turning to look directly at Bibb.

"Mrs. Barclay," he said slowly. "Not everything has to be discussed in public. I've insisted on quiet handling, privacy, for the problem children in this school. And I'd be surprised if *you* didn't agree with me."

Bibb felt the blow, felt her shoulders slump for a moment, as if Connor's words had actually struck her.

She hated being so close to the man, hated having so many people behind her. It was difficult not being able to see their faces, judge their reactions. Strangely, it made her remember her wedding so long ago, Arthur by her side, the two of them standing in that enormous church with their backs to everyone.

Reminding herself to be brave, she straightened up and stood the way she'd been taught in dancing class as a child, holding her head as high as she could.

I can do this, she told herself. Especially with Arthur at my side. I can do practically *anything*, now that he's with me again.

"You're trying to embarrass me," she said straight to Dr. Connor. "Letting this audience know *my* child is the victim of your policies. Why, yes, it's true. But it ought to embarrass you, not me. You wanted to expel her because she couldn't hear properly. And when her problem was solved, you *still* wanted her gone."

Feeling keyed up, on top of things, Bibb swung around to face the audience.

"Don't you see, everybody? You must listen. You ought to know what he's doing. After all, one of those children might be *yours*."

She felt better seeing all the faces, picking out the ones she knew here and there.

Better be careful, she cautioned herself. They're not all friends. Don't get maudlin. And don't break down.

"Before we get too impassioned here," Dr. Connor said, "I think we should do what we set out to do. Finish this program."

"Answer the question," Bibb heard Rhea's voice call from overhead. "Finish about the expulsions, finish now."

"Well, if we're getting down to cases here," Connor said. "It's tough. Without naming names, it's important to understand we have one child with a serious hearing impairment. A teacher could spend the whole day with her while the other children twiddle their thumbs. There are other problems as well. Look, I recognize that it's a big subject, but this isn't the forum for it. And I also recognize that you ladies speak from genuine emotion, and that your jobs as the mothers of these children haven't been easy. For that, you have the sympathy of everyone in this school."

There was a wild burst of clapping, followed by calls to move on, let the meeting continue.

Cornelia saw Bibb sway a little on her feet, saw her flush a deep crimson.

She heard Connor's little machine click again, saw the houselights begin to dim.

Darkness seemed to be covering her, plunging her into black despair. She felt as if Dane had left her side, as if the audience had vanished, leaving her all alone in the dark theater.

Rhea outmaneuvered. Bibb crunched. And what was she supposed to do, the youngest, the least confident member of the team? Not a pro. Not a society lady. Just a single mother trying her hardest to help her child.

Cornelia heard a voice calling out, realized it was *her* voice, that she was somehow on her feet, breathing up from her toes, projecting sound with every ounce of dramatic training she'd ever had.

"Forget sympathy. And forget those screens. This is a school meeting, not a sound-and-light show. Now, listen, everybody. I went to this school. I graduated. So did all my classmates, some smart, some not so smart. Some of us wrote terrific stories but couldn't hack math like Susie Solomon up there, or wrote music but couldn't learn Latin grammar. No matter. We were *all* somebody. Nobody *ever* gave up on a child. Miss Creighton would have fired any teacher who tried."

Dr. Connor, she grew slowly aware, was talking too.

"I suppose this is what you call parent involvement. No shortage of that tonight. Still, Mrs. Fuller, you might remember that a lot of people worked hard on this program. I've asked to hold discussion till the end. Actually, I'd like to *get* to the end. There *is* news, a magnificent gift I'm sure we'll all agree about."

"She's right," Cornelia heard Bibb call out in a shaky voice, as if Connor hadn't spoken. "If you want just brilliant children, that's a major change, it raises questions we should all deal with."

"A *million* questions," Rhea got back in, fast. "What's the measure, IQ? Will Dr. Connor expel everyone under 120, give *them* his sympathy too? Do you all know the disclaimers real educators have about standard IQ tests? Do you know that kids who're upset when they take those tests can score fifteen percent lower than usual? Anyway, if it's all just scores, well, fifty percent of the class has to be in the lower half, no way around that. If *your* child's in the lower half, does that mean she's dumb?"

Dr. Connor was moving away from the piano, up the steps. But he still looked relaxed, patient, like a teacher waiting for quiet in a roomful of disorderly children.

"We're getting rather far afield here," he said. "This is a small school. We have to make choices. If you know so much about modern education, you know scores are vital. In California, they want to allot more money to schools with good scores than the others. Severe learning disabilities are problems, alas, that we can't handle properly. Not the way they deserve to be handled. They're just beginning to be explored. They call for special educators, experts."

"That's rot," Cornelia said, buoyed up now. "I'm sick of that catchall. Half the time, if you can't interest a child, you say there's a learning disability. The teacher doesn't want to try, it's a learning disability. Even some of the *kids* talk that way if you let them. They learn to say it's not their fault they don't learn, they're dyslexic, they don't test well, they have a low attention span. As if God ordained that they couldn't learn. Good Christ, I thought a learning disability was a condition, not an excuse. There are blind children who learn, retarded children, badly handicapped kids who learn because someone cared, encouraged them, had patience. That's *teaching*."

"Mrs. Fuller," Dr. Connor said, shaking his head. "We're in a school here, not a psychiatric institution. Even the public schools drain off unsuccessful children, give them custodial care. The world needs smarts today, life's tough, the world is dumbing down all around us, getting tougher all the time. We choose to equip the best children for that struggle. If your daughter had a clubfoot, would you make her run a hundred-yard dash? Pressure her like that?"

Cornelia suddenly seemed to see Livvie with a twisted, hideous foot, stumbling, falling.

She felt dizzy, frightened, as if *she* were falling, as if her only hope now would be to sink back into her seat, reach for Dane again.

Then she felt his hand, warm, strong, gripping her elbow, shaking her arm, hard.

His touch seemed to cue her, like a voice from the

prompter's box, make her remember where she was, what she was supposed to be doing.

"No," she said, sending her voice through the theater clearly, forcefully. "I'd get her to a swimming pool. An archery field. We can't *all* be track stars. You talk as if the kids with clubfeet are failing you. I think you're failing them."

She reached back, down, groped for Dane's hand, feeling a rush of gratitude.

"He only *wants* track stars," Rhea was shouting. "Fast-track kids. Scores. You heard him, how many admissions, how many college placements."

"Fortunately or unfortunately, this *is* a school for achievers," Connor said to the audience, swiftly.

"Then it's no school," Cornelia heard Bibb call out. "Remember, all of you, what the word means, education. Latin, it means leading out, encouraging what's *in* people. Not stuffing them with information, judging them by how much they swallow. There should be room for ordinary children, nice ones, not just superachievers."

Dr. Connor shook his head, shrugged.

"You people have a lot of complaints, a strong viewpoint. But nobody makes you send your children here. If we do everything wrong, if you're not fond of this school, your course is clear."

"You mean we should go back where we came from?" Rhea declaimed in trumpet tones. "The world has heard *that* before."

Cornelia saw Dr. Connor take his hands out of his pockets, his eyes away from Rhea.

Now he was turning, staring directly into the center of the audience, at her, Cornelia.

"Before we get too dramatic," he said quietly, "let's get this audience straight on who *you* are, Mrs. Fuller."

Here it comes, Cornelia thought, hanging on to the back of the seat in front of her, trying to stay loose for the blow she knew would follow.

"You're the one whose child stole a baby from our nursery, right? Carried it all over the city half the night, isn't that so? Let me tell you, as an administrator, responsible for the children's physical welfare, I'm not very interested in keeping *your* child in this school."

Cornelia felt her knees go weak, heard the murmurs sweep through the crowd.

"I'm the one," she said, knowing she must come back at him instantly, or go under, "I'm the one whose kid was so sensitive to all the anger floating around this school, she *rescued* that little baby, took it straight to her nurse's house, the safest place she knew."

Her heart was banging like a great hammer now, each beat sending a rush of blood to her head.

"That's your opinion, Mrs. Fuller. Mine, I'm afraid, is that you're a neurotic woman with an equally neurotic child, or maybe worse."

Cornelia's face felt fiery. But she knew that something was happening now, that Connor was losing his temper, saying things he would never have said in front of an audience.

"Besides," Dr. Connor said, "the anger around here seems to be all yours. And there are laws, as I imagine your friend Judge Cantor could tell you, about libel, inciting people. This is not a stupid group. We can all see what you're doing. And only a sick, neurotic woman would do it."

Cornelia felt a stir at her side.

Dane was on his feet, towering at her side.

"Just a moment," he said in a pleasant voice. "That's simply not so. I didn't intend to take a hand in this gathering, but now you're getting into my field of expertise. I have to tell you that Mrs. Fuller isn't neurotic, isn't speaking wildly. I've observed the child. Something frightens her. I believe it's something here, in this school."

The theater suddenly seemed to grow even more silent, so that the smallest creak of a chair, the slightest cough, sounded amplified.

This isn't in the script, Cornelia thought, feeling shaken, thrilled, because incredibly, Dane was making her fight *his* fight, acting, not supporting her act, but taking over, doing something that meant more than all the love words, revealing her worth to him in front of these people the way he'd sweated to reveal her beautiful fireplace.

Now Harvey was coming to the front of the stage, pointing.

"Now, wait a minute," he said, frowning. "Just who are you?"

"Sorry," Dane said. "I'm Dr. Kurt Knud Nilssen. I'm a practicing psychiatrist."

"A psychiatrist," Harvey said. "Mrs. Fuller's psychiatrist? Or her daughter's? This is a Parent-Teacher Association meeting. You're not a parent, you're not a teacher. You have no right here."

"I don't know about that," Dane said, still sounding calm, pleasant. "I'm going to marry Mrs. Fuller, though she doesn't know it yet. And then, of course, I *will* be a parent here."

Noise rose to a louder pitch, as if everyone in the theater had turned to talk to his neighbor.

Dane, Cornelia thought, wanting to hug him hard. Who thought you were so dramatic? Who thought you were so funny? I adore you. You're better than even *I* imagined.

Somebody started to clap.

More applause came swiftly, and laughter, as people relaxed, welcomed the relief from tension.

"Will you?" Dane said to her through the noise. "Leave this? Come with me?"

But she couldn't answer, because now Harvey was at the front of the stage, waving his arms for silence.

"Okay, we've had the comic relief," he was saying. "Perhaps we can get back to business. Let's have some quiet, everyone."

Cornelia heard the noise fade, saw heads swing toward the stage.

"There's a lot on our plate tonight," Harvey was going on, his expression severe, his voice commanding. "News that will affect your children. Don't let this sideshow keep you from hearing it."

That's how he must sound in court, Cornelia thought, again feeling dismayed. Will they listen?

"As our headmaster observed, I think we're all well aware of what's going on here," Harvey said. "A few disgruntled parents came tonight to break up this meeting. To waste time and distract attention from the real progress Dr. Connor has brought to our school."

Cornelia saw heads nod, felt her stomach twist with pain.

The woman with the needlepoint stopped working, suddenly lifted her head.

"About time someone talked sense," she said.

"Are you going to let that happen?" Harvey was asking.

Cornelia swung her head and watched the audience settle down, sink back in their seats.

Somehow she was sinking into her seat too, feeling limp and exhausted.

"I thought not," Harvey went on. "Then, if you will, I'll propose an orderly course of action. The board welcomes parent interest—in the right place, that is. I move we create the right place, schedule a special meeting to hear about special problems. Things that don't affect most of us, that trouble only a few of you. We can hold it in this theater to make room for all the complainers. Assuming, that is, that there *are* more than four or five."

Somebody laughed.

Her energy was draining away, her eyes felt heavy, her head was beginning to ache.

Let's go home, Dane, she wanted to say. Harvey will box us off in some little meeting and finish us off. Who's going to hear us then? Who wants to? We've lost. Maybe we shouldn't have tried. Anyway, it's over now.

"Let's turn this session back to Dr. Connor," Harvey was saying in a brisk tone. "And get back to business."

Through blurring eyes, Cornelia saw Connor straighten up, take a step forward.

"Oh, *wait*," Cornelia heard a woman's voice call from somewhere at the front of the theater. "Wait, everyone. Please."

Why, that's Nanny, Cornelia thought, feeling a pinprick of surprise.

She rubbed her eyes.

Yes, Nanny, all done up in navy silk, with her hair waved.

Cornelia reached blindly for Dane's hand, felt her head starting to clear.

"Please," Nanny was saying. "You must listen. These people are right. Just ask the teachers."

Connor was turning on Nanny, scowling.

"That's enough, Miss Knowlton," he said fiercely. "We don't need a contribution from you."

Nanny felt as if she were growing taller. She could almost believe that all her years at the Boston School, as a child, as a teacher, had been meant to bring her to this moment.

She seemed to see the audience in a great mass, a mixture of colors and shadows and lights, of open mouths and glinting eyes. All the eyes were on her. Now she must tell them the truth, whatever it cost her—reputation, job, anything.

How many times, she wondered, have I stood in this theater to sing the school song? How many years have I believed in its words, made what they say a part of me? Isn't it time I started telling the truth about this, about everything, the way that little Stella tells it? If I can do this properly, won't I be able to announce who I am, what I am, to the whole world when I want? And won't it be wonderful to be free after so long, so very long?

"No, Dr. Connor," Nanny said, squaring her shoulders. "I'm tired of hiding things. You made me keep quiet, and I've been almost ill, worrying, and now I'm determined to speak."

Connor was moving quickly toward her now.

His face seemed terrifying, frowning, contorted.

"You made me keep still about Johnny Mescalero," Nanny said, taking a step back. "It was wrong. I *won't* keep it in another minute."

"She's upset," Nanny heard Dr. Connor announce in a firm voice.

Oh yes, Nanny thought. I'm upset. I'm frightened sick to be standing here. But I'd be *more* frightened to stop talking, to be false to my school. False to myself.

"Tell them, Dr. Connor," she said. "Tell what happened in that basement room, tell these parents what happened to their children."

Watching, Cornelia felt as if someone had started to wind her up, was turning and turning a screw that was pulling every muscle tight, making her sit forward, making her back straight and her head high.

What *was* Nanny saying? Dear God, had something actually happened to scare Livvie?

She felt Dane's arm come around her shoulders.

"You should all *know*," Nanny was saying. "I found evidence, real evidence. I didn't tell anyone except the headmaster. I kept still so he could handle it properly with the police and put that dreadful man away."

"What *is* it, Nanny?" Cornelia said softly, as if she could reach Nanny's ear through all the turmoil. "What happened to Livvie? What made her run away?"

"That's enough." Harvey was on his feet again. "There will be *no* more interruptions. I think it's high time for an announcement that affects *all* your children. High time for news about a great lady who's sat patiently and graciously through this nonsense. Alison Irving."

Cornelia had just time to see Mrs. Irving rise, walk to his side, when the theater went dark.

The screens came alive again, filled now with pictures of blueprints, bricks, derricks, cement mixers.

Then the pictures blended into one, a drawing.

Cornelia saw a building, modern, single, handsome.

On one of the screens a close-up appeared, a doorway, with carving over it. *The Irving Communications Wing*.

Quickly the other screens changed to pictures of men and women, the board members, standing around a table, pointing at a model, the building in the drawing. Mrs. Irving's picture, formal, smiling, appeared on the largest screen, froze there.

The lights came up, leaving Mrs. Irving standing beneath her own photograph.

Cornelia, feeling confused, frightened, thought it looked weird—the smiling close-up and the tense, nervous figure standing on the stage.

"Stop it," Rhea was screaming from the balcony. "Mrs. Irving, make them stop. We don't need a building. We need to clean up the rotten one we've got."

Mrs. Irving frowned.

"I think," she said, glancing at Connor, "perhaps it's time to stop this meeting. Wait for a quieter setting."

Billy Connor stood perfectly still, quelling his inner rage, realizing he'd almost nodded at Mrs. Irving, he was so used to bowing to her wishes.

What the hell was happening here?

Afraid now, wanting to explode in a fury, he remembered how it had been so long ago, the ring of tough bullies circling around him in his schoolyard, the desperate dashes he'd been forced to make to safety.

Damn these women joining hands against him, damn that bastard with his idiot college kid, damn that shrink who'd come here unasked, and above all, damn faint-hearted, traitorous old Miss Knowlton to hell and gone.

Was *this* where his endless, exhausting work was supposed to take him? Was *this* his triumphant meeting, the event that was to deliver him his tenure, his safety, his crowning success?

Ah, but he wasn't such a pushover, wasn't so easily counted out. With his mettle, he could turn things around, get them going his way again. Mrs. Irving could be settled down. Harvey could be enlisted. After all, he was the headmaster. He had the whole weight of the school behind him.

"I'm not stopping this meeting for three or four crazies," Connor said, pleased he could speak in such a mild tone, look so unconcerned, when inside he wanted to blast the lot of them.

"I move," Mrs. Irving said quietly, "that this meeting be adjourned."

"Please listen," Nanny was shouting. "He *never* told anyone. Afraid it would damage the school. Damage him. That dreadful man is probably in some other school, hurting other little girls."

Cornelia couldn't bear to hear any more, found herself half out of her seat, hurrying. She never told me, she protected me, that baby, she kept thinking. I've got to get home, hold Livvie, love her, make sure she's all right.

She realized that Dane was up too, holding her.

"Don't," he said. "She has us, Cornelia. We'll love her, heal her."

Straining away, Cornelia grew aware that something else was happening at the front of the theater.

A girl, slim, young, was hurrying up the steps toward Nanny.

"Stop!" she was shouting at Dr. Connor. "It's true. I saw. She found underwear, children's underwear, in the super's office. I was there. She went straight to you and that was the end of it. Nothing ever happened. Nobody knew."

"Get off this stage," Dr. Connor said in a calm, strong

voice. "Whoever you are, you have absolutely no business up here."

"Dammit, I'm one of your *teachers*," the girl said furiously. "And a lot of us think you've pushed us around long enough."

"Miss Kittredge is right," Nanny said through tears. "We do. And you parents should have been told. The parents of these poor children should have been told. Cornelia, I *know* you're out there somewhere, I wanted so to tell you. Mrs. Rosen, your Tammy. Mrs. Spaight, Mr. Spaight, you've only just *come* to the school. You should have been notified, had doctors, psychiatrists. And all Dr. Connor thought about was himself."

There was a flurry somewhere behind Cornelia.

Turning, she could see a large man elbowing his way out of one of the rows and hear the heavy thump of his feet as he headed for the stage.

"Why, you fucking asshole," the man's voice rang out, thundering through the theater. "You fucking mick asshole."

Heart pounding, she turned back to look at Connor.

Jesus, he was coming forward to the edge of the stage, eyes glittering, face dark with rage.

He was lifting his arm, making a fist, moving to strike Nanny where she stood.

He looked so menacing, so out of control, that Cornelia swayed on her feet.

She heard Dane's breath catch softly.

She saw the burly man stop walking, as if uncertain what to do next.

There was absolute stillness.

"Damn you, Miss Knowlton," Dr. Connor shouted. "Shut your big bull-dyke mouth."

As the words reverberated through the silent theater, Cornelia began feeling as if they'd touched off something inside her, heightened all her senses. As if a swallow of some magic drug had made her see more clearly, hear more acutely, and filled her with more power than she'd ever imagined.

Connor's blown up, she thought. Everyone's seen it. We've done it.

The audience seemed to be blowing up too, everyone

shouting, jumping up, making for the aisles. The board members were sitting frozen on the stage, all of them watching Mrs. Irving. And Mrs. Irving was starting to walk firmly and quickly down the steps.

Cornelia turned to hug Dane wildly, pressing her whole body against him, welcoming his warmth, the roughness of his chin against her cheek. She felt as if the piano had begun playing all by itself, as if all the spotlights in the theater had burst into flames and were sending bright sparks through the air.

Then she grew aware that everyone was up, talking, crowding the aisles, making for the doors.

Livvie, Cornelia thought. I've got to get to Livvie and make sure she's all right. There's Rhea, looking so pleased with herself, I want to get near and tell her she belongs in the U.S. Supreme Court. And over there, Arthur, holding on to Bibb as if he knows he'll *never* find anyone like her. I want to find that baby teacher. And Mr. Stone, whoever he is. And Nanny, who should have told me, who couldn't bear not telling me, finally turning out to be a true daughter of the Boston School.

But Dane was leading her firmly toward the front doors, then into the fresh, quiet night.

At the iron gates he stopped and held her.

He could feel her trembling inside the circle of his arms. Leaning back to look at her, he could see the sharp bones in her cheeks, the hollows beneath them.

And he had never, even in his office after Livvie's blowup, seen her skin so paper-white.

Then he wanted to wrap her inside his arms and tear away everything that kept his warm heart from touching hers. He wanted to put his hot mouth on her cold one, put his hands over her ears so that never, never would she hear anything to make her unhappy for the rest of her days.

Did she *hear* me, he wondered, in that crazy theater, with everyone shooting off like midnight fireworks over Tivoli? How much will she accept from me? Does she *see* now that her Livvie isn't an ugly duckling who's going to turn into a swan? That she's a dear, average child who'll have more love than most to make her wonderful? That *all* children grow to be swans, if people accept them, watch over them, love them? And how much will Cornelia give up for me? What about her work, her house? Can she take Livvie from Tim, to another state? Can all of it be worked out, can *any* of it be?

*Does she love me enough to try?*

"All right," he said finally. "You got your fight. And won. Connor will go. They can't possibly keep him on after this. Now, think about what I said. It came from my whole heart, Cornelia. Come with me."

Her eyes were on his, her beautiful wide eyes.

But she wasn't answering.

"Livvie will thrive there," he said slowly. "She'd be in a one-room school, probably. One of the brightest, for a change. That'll be good for her. The teachers will go slowly, patiently. The older kids will help her. She'll help the little ones. Later on, the Eastern colleges will be interested in her. How many girls apply to Radcliffe from Indian reservations? And for losing terrible memories, what could be better? She'll explore a new world. Touch the past. Find her own future. She'll get sun and air, and she'll bloom, Cornelia."

Cornelia put her head against his chest, closed her eyes.

Yes, she thought. No. Too fast. Marry. Arizona. Uproot Livvie. Just when we've won. It's insane. It's a million miles from here.

She felt her heart quicken, then skip.

Dear God, what about me? Would I bloom? What shall I do in Illyria? What shall I do in Arizona? I'm not eighteen, following my true love anywhere at all. I can't leave everyone, everything, just like that. My mother, who'd go to see her? And the house? It would sink into the ground. I can't abandon Rhea and Bibb now, when they're getting started at school, setting things straight. I can't just walk out on my work, on Stella. It's impossible.

"Phoenix is four hours away from here," Dane said, as if he could hear her thoughts. "Not the way places used to be, impossibly far, distant, the way Denmark seemed for me. You can come back any time to visit, come often, if you like. And there's so much for you there. You said you wanted to do a documentary. Well, no one's filmed those people the way they are, no one's even *seen* it yet, the disease, poverty, the tradition, the hope. Why couldn't you? Come, Cornelia. Rhea's got Saul, energy for six. Bibb lives for projects like school, and Arthur's with her. Even Miss Knowlton's beginning to find her world, herself, coming into the light, catching on. She'll find friends, lovers, a life. And Stella can step into your shoes at work. You're not walking out on the guy who owns the place or on her. You're coming toward something, and why shouldn't you? Isn't it *your* turn?"

She watched him look up at the school building, sigh.

"Cornelia. Isn't it *my* turn too? Look, who knows if *I'll* find what I want out there? My contract's not endless. If you're not happy, if it doesn't work for you, in a while, when Livvie's whole and well, we'll come back. She can even graduate from this school, if that's still what you want so much."

Cornelia closed her eyes, imagining a scene, a wide, bright sky, herself, Dane, wearing comfortable old clothes, walking together into the marvelous, peaceful desert, with a tall, slim Livvie, brown-skinned, silver-haired, just behind them.

"Your house will be here," Dane said slowly. "That house is forever. It'll be for summers, winters, whatever we want. Maybe when there's another child, our child, to put in it, *there's* an option. You make beautiful children, Cornelia. You battle. You're a terrific mother."

The words seemed to touch her like a blessing.

They sent her to her toes, flinging her arms around him, right there in front of the school building with people staring, crowding past them.

"Yes," she said, kissing him hard, feeling certain, somehow, that what she did on this spot, whatever she committed herself to do, must be right, good, because in the shadow of this school she had always been, would always be, a beloved child.

# *About the Author*

ANNE TOLSTOI WALLACH, former vice president and creative director of Grey Advertising, Inc., is the acclaimed author of *Women's Work*, a compelling novel of women on the move, which climbed to the top of the bestseller lists. She lives in New York City.